The Six

Catriona King

This is a work of fiction. Names, characters, places and incidents are used fictitiously and any resemblance to persons living or dead, business establishments, events, locations or areas, is entirely coincidental.

No part of this book may be used or reproduced in any manner without written permission of the author, except for brief quotations and segments used in reviews of for promotion.

ISBN: 978 1517174750

Copyright © 2015 by Catriona King
Photography: Goncharuk Maksim
Artwork: Jonathan Temples:
creative@jonathantemples.co.uk
Editors: Andrew Angel and Maureen Vincent-Northam
Formatting: Rebecca Emin
All rights reserved

Hamilton-Crean Publishing Ltd. 2015

Discover us online: www.hamiltoncreanpublishing.com

For my mother.

About the Author

Catriona King is a medical doctor and trained as a police Forensic Medical Examiner in London, where she worked for some years. She has worked closely with the police on many occasions. She returned to live in Belfast in 2006.

She has written since childhood and has been published in many formats: non-fiction, journalistic and fiction.

'The Sixth Estate' is the first of two new Craig Crime Novels being released in September 2015. 'The Sect' is the second.

The next Craig Crime novel, 'The Keeper', is in edits for release in early 2016.

Acknowledgements

My thanks to Northern Ireland for providing the inspiration for my novels.

My thanks also to: Andrew Angel and Maureen Vincent-Northam, my editors, Jonathan Temples for his cover design and Rebecca Emin for formatting this book.

I would like to thank all of the police officers that I have ever worked with for their professionalism, wit and compassion.

Catriona King
Belfast, September 2015

Discover the author's books at:
www.catrionakingbooks.com

To engage with the author about her books, email:
Catriona_books@yahoo.co.uk

The author can be found on Facebook and Twitter:
@CatrionaKing1

The Sixth Estate

Chapter One

Belfast. November 2014

"Would you like to say anything, Superintendent?"

Craig stared through the window, his thoughts elsewhere. It was a surprisingly small window for such an imposing room, with a tree outside so large that it shaded them cosily on the bright winter day. He could just make out its leaves, still clinging to the branches despite the season. Sycamore, or maybe not; he'd never paid attention in biology class.

The woman's insistent voice disturbed his reverie.

"It's almost eleven, Mr Craig."

He seized his chance to leave. To return next week for another silent hour.

She called after him. "You'll need to talk eventually, you know."

Perhaps, or perhaps not. Nothing could ever make him feel OK about shooting an old man, even if it had been legal. And anyway, he preferred his therapy to come from the pub.

He turned at the door and smiled; a social smile that didn't touch his dark eyes. He had more faith in his silence than he had in all her words. He was wrong.

****

The Ardlough Road, County Londonderry. Thursday, 11th December 2014. 8.30 a.m.

Bernadette Ross hadn't moved for five minutes. She'd simply stood like a pillar in the dark north-facing room, gazing, in silence. Anyone who'd ever known her would have been surprised. Racer Ross; that was her nickname, had been ever since school. Never sitting, always fidgeting, racing down the polished corridors accompanied by the fading pleas of nuns to "walk, not run".

But not today. Today only her eyes moved. They scanned the wood-lined study, rapidly at first in disbelief and then slowly, again and again, like a pendulum that had found its arc. Back and forth past the walls of books. Back and forth past the shiny antique weapons and the bureau heavy with media awards. Back and forth until her head ached and her eyes were tired, and they fixed finally on an ornately worked rug, its background once cream, now a rainbow of cherry and plum.

The wider scan had brought context: chairs turned over, the television smashed, books spine up with their pages semi-detached, as if they'd been flung, frantically, to aid escape. And the blood. So much blood. Not splashes but pints, splattered and smeared in a trail towards the back door, shining on the parquet like modern art and staining the once cream rug shades of red. Too much blood for one person, but just enough for three?

Images flashed through her mind. Pictures of afternoon tea and family dinners; formal, unsmiling celebrations. Christmas gifts exchanged, this year's already beneath the spruce tree in the hall. Three faces loomed large, older and younger, stern and less so, smiling openly and with smiles that never reached their eyes. She knew these people, she saw them every day. And now? Now? As her eyes flickered REM-like her limbs finally unfroze, long enough to do what a decent person would. Lift the telephone and call the police.

****

Stranmillis, Belfast. Saturday, 13th December. 2 p.m.

"Left a bit."

Marc Craig did as he was bid, with a malaise that said he'd been doing it for far too long.

"No, not there. Further left; over by the fireplace."

Craig obeyed again, rolling his eyes. He'd been a puppet for thirty minutes with his friend, pathologist John Winter, pulling his strings.

Suddenly John thrust out a palm, vertically, like a traffic cop. "Stop! You've gone too far. Back a bit. We're almost there."

Craig glared at the eight-foot Christmas tree in his arms, wondering how he'd got roped into an afternoon readying John and Natalie's new house for their first married noel. True, there were quantities of alcohol involved, and yes, part of him had been persuaded by the housewarming party they were throwing on Christmas Eve, and the fear that leaving the new home's décor victim to John's taste would result in the same bordello-like ambience as his lab. But larger than all of those motivations had been curiosity. John had been resolutely secretive since he'd purchased the converted chapel two months before, sneaking off on evenings and weekends to decorate it, instead of drinking with him in wine bars as he normally did. It was to be expected of course; he was married now, nesting, a newly puffed-up husband intent on hunting and gathering to protect his mate, even if the modern equivalent was buying paint in a DIY store.

Craig knew he was privileged to see the place; not even Natalie knew the full extent of her husband's efforts, through a combination of a surgical on-call Rota that would have made a Trojan balk and John swatting her away, barking "wait till it's finished, woman" in a most un-John-like way.

The detective peered through the branches of the evergreen he was grasping and admitted that he was impressed. The eighteenth-century chapel was compact and light, with a bright maple floor where worshippers had once stood, and in place of its pulpit an open fireplace that John had managed to avoid spoiling with the cliché of a faux-skin rug. The high walls were white, split by wooden beams, and a spiral staircase in one corner led to a mezzanine, holding two bedrooms in place of the old organ loft. Even the stained-glass windows had been modernised, replaced with clear, arched panels that flooded the house with light. The effect was Scandinavian and the conifer in his arms added to the feel.

John pointed triumphantly to the corner beside the

fire; a position Craig had suggested ten minutes before.

"That's it! Perfect! Prop it against the wall while I put the coffee on."

As he headed cheerfully towards the kitchen, Craig set down the tree and extracted some pine needles from his mouth. He strolled towards the windows, thinking that coffee was probably a good idea. He was driving; although, as he could see his apartment across the snow-edged Lagan, having to walk wouldn't exactly be a tragedy.

A combination of his mobile ringing and John re-entering with a tray broke his daydream, and as the drinks clattered and gurgled their way to readiness he answered the call without checking the screen. Always a mistake.

The voice that spoke was cool and familiar and Craig's stunned glance told John exactly who it was; D.I. Julia McNulty, his ex-girlfriend of thirteen months before. John took a seat and waited for the show to start, thanking God that he was out of the romantic race.

"Hello, Marc."

Craig's mouth opened and closed silently; his thoughts ricocheting between 'why is she calling?' and 'it must be work', via 'Katy will kill me if she finds out'. He dismissed the last thought instantly. If there was one thing Katy Stevens wasn't, it was bitchy.

John watched Craig's discomfort like it was a spectator sport. When he thought Craig had sucked air for long enough he waved him on to speak. The words were hardly worth saying.

"Hello, Julia."

That was it. No "How are you?" or "How's life in Limavady?" Definitely no witty repartee. John rolled his eyes and Craig scowled, turning his back. He was saved from the banality of "How's the weather?" by Julia's next words.

"I have a case I need your help with."

John watched his friend's shoulders drop in relief and knew instantly that he was back on solid ground; work, the place he ran to when real life was too much grief. The fact that Craig's life had been a challenge since he'd shot

Caleb Pitt two months before hadn't escaped his notice. He'd been drinking heavily and snapping at everyone for weeks. The pathologist leaned forward eagerly to catch what came next.

"What sort of case?"

The question seemed redundant. Craig headed up Belfast's Murder Squad so murders were what he solved. Julia knew that, so Craig was surprised by what she said next.

"A home invasion near Derry with three missing victims. Look, I don't want to say any more on the phone. Can I send you the file?"

She wasn't even sure that there'd been a murder! But he couldn't refuse her; she was an officer asking for help. He forced himself to sound keen.

"Sure. Send it through now. We can act as advisors."

Her response was immediate. "No. I need you to lead the investigation. Here, tomorrow; as early as you can."

With that the line went dead and he realised how much courage it had taken her to ring. He clicked his phone shut and turned, just in time to see John glance away, feigning interest in a wall.

"What do you think of the white? I think it opens the place up."

Craig rolled his eyes. "If you're going to talk about colour charts I'm leaving."

John took the cue eagerly. "What did Julia want?"

"You heard. It's a case."

John smiled, knowing it could be more than that, but this was poker and he wasn't showing his hand.

"Well, that's all right then. She wants your advice. You knew it might happen someday."

Craig scowled. "It's not that simple. She wants us in Derry tomorrow."

"Tomorrow! That's a bit quick."

"It's a disaster. I'm supposed to be taking Katy sailing."

John gestured at the river. "It's too cold."

"Winter sailing's great, especially if you bring mulled wine. I've been promising her for ages, for putting up with me."

Neither of them pretended that he'd been a peach recently.

John nodded. "You've been a grumpy bugger for weeks. But you can go sailing some other time. Drunk in charge of a yacht is never good."

Craig went to object but John waved him on, refusing to be diverted. "So what's the real problem?"

"You know damn well what the real problem is! I haven't seen her for a year and I'm dreading it. So is she by the sounds of it."

"Suck it up; you're a big boy. Just tell Katy why you're cancelling; she'll understand."

Craig was about to retort when his phone beeped with a message. It was the file. As he read it he frowned and John could see that his interest was piqued. Craig pulled out a pen and began making notes.

John smiled. "I knew you'd change your mind."

Craig's brow furrowed. "I'll tell Katy I have a case in Belfast."

"Don't be stupid. She watches the News; she knows there hasn't been a murder in Belfast for weeks. Just tell her the truth." John's eyes narrowed. "Unless..."

Craig glared at him. "Unless what?"

"You're afraid."

Craig's voice tightened to match his glare. "Afraid of what?"

"That you might still love her."

The shake of Craig's head was instinctive. He didn't love Julia; Katy had his heart one hundred per cent. But John was right; he *was* afraid.

"Not love. I'm afraid of hurting her."

The rest of the sentence hung in the air. *And of her hurting him.*

****

Docklands Coordinated Crime Unit, Belfast. Sunday. 8.30 a.m.

"I don't get out of my bed on a Sunday for just anyone, boss, so this had better be good."

Liam Cullen stretched out his forty inch legs as Craig poured two coffees then threw a file on the desk, nodding him to take a look.

"A case? What part of town?"

"The Derry part."

He waited for the inevitable moan. It never came. Instead, Liam surprised him by reading the cover and asking a question.

"Who invited us?"

Craig braced himself for the derision that he knew was heading his way. "Julia."

Liam had never liked Julia, either at work or socially, so his pragmatic response surprised Craig even more.

"When do we go?"

Craig's eyes widened. "That's it? No slagging about ex-girlfriends? No complaints about leaving town so close to Christmas?"

"Nope."

Realisation dawned.

"OK, which member of Danni's family are you avoiding?"

Liam's wife, Danni, came from a large Newry brood.

He gave Craig a martyred look.

"Her brother and his tribe. They're staying with us till Christmas Eve; shopping. Sorting out murders in Derry will be a rest."

Craig thought back to the time his Italian relatives had stayed when he was a kid and nodded in sympathy.

"OK. Here's what we've got." He lifted the file. "A family of three have disappeared from their home near Derry; Diana and Oliver Bwye, forty-five and sixty-one, and their twenty-year-old daughter Jane. Bwye's secretary, Bernadette Ross, arrived at the house last Thursday morning for work, to find signs of a break-in and struggle."

Liam interrupted. "How bad a struggle?"

"Bad enough to leave blood all over the floor."

"Types?"

"It's all O Positive, the most common sort. They're sourcing DNA at the moment."

"Who's running the pathology?"

"Mike Augustus."

Liam smirked; their small world was getting smaller by the day. Augustus was dating Annette McElroy, the squad's Inspector, soon to be divorced from her unfaithful husband after twenty years.

"He's covering. The usual northwest guy's off ski-ing."

Liam snorted. "Nice for some. The rest of us have nappies to buy."

"If you will keep having babies..."

Craig brought them briskly back to the case. "OK, so Ms Ross arrived at eight-thirty to find the house empty." He scanned the file, selecting the highlights. "The family are rich. Home is a thousand acre estate called Rocksbury. Oliver Bwye made millions in the newspaper world; he owned The Belfast Chronicle from 1985 until 2012. Now he mostly manages his assets and chairs committees."

Liam pictured the committees' members; the great and not so good.

"Ms Ross worked as Bwye's P.A. at the paper for six years and when he retired he took her with him-"

Liam cut in. "So she knows the wife and daughter as well?"

Craig nodded and kept reading. "Diana Bwye is well liked locally; she's involved with the church and does a lot of charity work. The daughter, Jane, sounds like a typical spoilt rich kid. Too many shoes and far too much time to get bored."

His tone said that Jane Bwye had been up to no good.

"What did her boredom lead to?"

"Minor stuff. One caution for cannabis, a few call-outs to noisy parties. There was a speeding fine last year as well. Nothing more than that."

"Yet."

Liam gazed out at the Lagan prompting Craig to ask a question.

"What are you thinking?"

The D.C.I. answered without breaking his gaze. "I'm trying to work out how many people would want to kidnap the Bwyes for their money, and how many because The Chronicle printed something to piss them off."

"We don't know it's a kidnapping yet. There's been no ransom demand."

But he was right; The Belfast Chronicle was an unscrupulous rag. Their potential suspect pool could be enormous. Liam hadn't finished.

"Any sign of bodies?"

Craig shook his head. "None. They've had search teams scouring a one mile perimeter for days, plus the local patrols keeping their eyes peeled."

Liam shook his head grimly; the chances of a happy ending were slim. "What does Gerry think?"

Gerry Shaw was the long suffering detective sergeant who'd had to deal with Julia McNulty's moods throughout the years. He'd dealt with them adeptly; it wasn't for nothing that Liam had christened him Gerry the Peacemaker when he'd trained him as a young P.C. But along with Gerry's charm went a cynical view of the world, so Craig's answer didn't surprise Liam at all.

"I spoke to him last night. He thinks they're all dead, says it would take a miracle for them not to be. But we can't go there, not until we find the bodies." Craig paused. "We don't have to work this. We could just advise the locals from here."

Liam heard the reticence in his voice and wondered what it was about. They weren't busy. They hadn't had a case since a domestic killing two weeks earlier and that had been open and shut; the husband had answered the door to them with the knife still in his hand. The next surge in murder would be at Christmas, when happy family gatherings became major bust-ups and people started killing each other over the turkey and mistletoe. They had at least a week free, so why wasn't Craig more excited about the case? Even seeing Julia wouldn't be enough to put him off such a juicy one.

He was right. The real reason Craig couldn't get excited was the same reason he'd been shouting at everyone for weeks. Caleb Pitt, the eighty-four-year-old serial killer that he'd shot and killed in October. It had been a clean shoot to save both their lives, but it had been gnawing at Craig's gut since and pretty soon it was going to eat its way through.

Craig made up his mind, silencing his uncertainty in a heavy tone.

"OK. We'll take it. Give me an hour to clear it with the Chief Constable and then we'll leave. Meanwhile, tell Gerry to widen the search to two miles in every direction, and see if Mike has put a name on the blood."

As he walked to the lift, Liam shook his head. Craig should be getting help about Pitt's shooting, not taking on another case. He'd feel bad too if he'd shot an old man, but years of death during The Troubles had hardened his heart; plus he had a lot less fire in his belly than Craig. Fire and post-traumatic stress was a combustible mix. He just hoped that he wasn't around when it finally blew.

Chapter Two

Derry City. Sunday, 14th December. 11 a.m.

Derry-stroke-Londonderry was known colloquially as 'Stroke City'. A local radio host, Gerry Anderson, had espoused the term years earlier and it had stuck. Although since the city had won the UK City of Culture award in 2013, Legenderry was used almost as frequently now. Derry or Londonderry, in theory your choice depended upon which side of the political divide you hailed from; in reality human beings were lazy so the shorter option was usually used.

Derry had been the capital of the northwest since the sixth century and was the only completely walled city in the British Isles. It was a pretty place; full of easy charm and surrounded by beautiful countryside, and as they drove swiftly through the streets on the way to its frost tinged hinterland, Craig smiled at the small metropolis' warmth, even on a winter's day.

People in Derry nodded to strangers as if they were friends, which, of course, they then became. He tried to picture the same thing happening in Belfast but it didn't scan somehow. Belfast was a cool Victorian lady, keeping her distance and scrutinising each new occupant to see if they deserved to be there. By contrast Derry had a happy urchin feel that had nothing to do with status or age.

Liam flicked through the radio channels in Craig's Audi until he hit on one playing music that he liked. The Dubliners, an Irish folk band that hailed from exactly where it said on the tin. He tapped the dashboard in time as he thought about their case.

"Going traditional, Liam?"

"I have family outside Dublin. They farm in Fingal. We used to visit as kids; climbing trees and the rest. It was great craic."

Craig pictured the rapidly growing Liam clambering to the top of a tree. He wondered at what age his height had made it an unnecessary trip.

"Andy's meeting us at the house."

Liam smiled. Andy White was a favourite of his. He hailed from Dungiven, just twenty miles down the road, and he'd been trying to get a job back there for years, transferring from Belfast to Portstewart en route.

"You requested him, didn't you?"

Craig nodded. "The more cases he does here the more likely he'll get a transfer home if one comes up. Besides, he'll cheer everybody up and this case looks like it could do with it."

As he ended his sentence he pulled over to check the GPS and then gazed around them.

"Apparently we're here."

They scanned their surroundings. They were on a narrow side road with no houses, just a low gate through a hedge on one side and the vague sense of someone's presence other than theirs.

"Where's the house?"

Liam pointed to the gate. "Must be up there. I'll nip out and take a look."

As he pushed through the gate, Craig checked the map. All it showed was a series of fields and the ruins of an old farm. A moment later Liam raced back, rubbing his hands together in the cold. He leapt in, gesturing Craig to crank up the heater and holding his blueing hands to the warm air vent.

"It would skin a fairy out there."

"Wear gloves then." Not that he ever did. "Did you see a house?"

"Nope. But there are blue lights in the distance so we're obviously in the right place."

A minute later he was proved right. A mile up the lane the track became a clearing that hosted the most unusual house that Craig had ever seen. Instead of the stone farmhouses and Georgian mansions common in the local countryside, a modern building rose in front of them, four storeys high. Its stone foundations proclaimed its origins as old, but every other surface, including the roof, was glass. Solar panels to be exact, with only the barest amount of pale wood in between to prevent their collapse. As Craig perused the structure admiringly, Liam gazed at it, confused.

"What's your problem?"

He didn't reply, just clambered out of the car and walked through the crime scene tape waving his badge. As he pressed his face against the mansion's glass wall, attempting to peer inside, Craig introduced himself to the senior uniform, smiling as he realised what was perturbing Liam so much.

"It's smart-glass. They can change the opacity."

Liam screwed up his face. "How does that work?"

Before Craig could explain, a man with a Dungiven accent did it for him.

"Science. We're wild clever up here, hey."

Liam recognised the conversational quirk of saying 'hey' at the end of almost every sentence and swung round, smiling as he was greeted by the blue-eyed, blue-shirted Andy White. Andy's blue shirt had been a constant feature since his wife had mentioned how it matched his eyes; the possible romantic benefits were too potent to ignore.

"Ach, it's the boul Andy. How's it going?"

"Far better before you got here, Cullen. Look at the state of that window; you've left fingerprints all over it!"

"You can clean it when you're doing your weekend round."

Craig let the banter run for a moment before returning to the case.

"Is Inspector McNulty here?"

Andy shook his head. "Teflon's got her chasing some burglary suspect. She asked me to fill you in."

Teflon. Non-stick. The nickname explained the behaviour and could belong to only one man on the force; Craig's erstwhile boss and opponent, the political and extremely slippery D.C.S. Terry Harrison. It was the first time Harrison had darkened their doorstep since Craig's promotion the year before and Harrison's subsequent transfer to Limavady. It would be interesting to see how he coped now that Craig was a superintendent as well.

"I suppose he's giving her hell about these disappearances?"

Andy made a face that said it all, then he rubbed his

hands eagerly.

"Now. What do you need to know?"

Craig nodded at the glass, not trusting himself to find the front door. "Can we go inside?" He gestured towards a stone building they'd passed coming up the track. "If this is the Bwyes' house what's that?"

"Staff quarters. Some people, like the cook, live in."

It figured with such a large estate. Andy led the way through what looked like a wall but turned out to be a door that retracted automatically as he approached.

Liam snorted. "I bet that was handy for the kidnappers."

"It's coded. We disabled the lock so that we could work."

He led the way through the hall into a room that occupied almost the whole ground floor. It was warm and bright, with control panels that worked everything from the heat and lighting, through to the TV and burglar alarm. Craig had never seen anything like it.

"Mrs Bwye is a real ecologist; a recycling geek. Everything in the house works on solar power."

Liam guffawed. "At least we know Friends of the Earth didn't kill them."

Craig gazed at their surroundings, frowning. The file said there'd been blood all over the floor, so where was it? Andy read his mind.

"This way. They re-modelled the old Georgian house so the only original bit is old man Bwye's study. It looks like that's where the family was taken from."

He unlocked a door into a room where none of the walls were glass and all of the furnishings were decidedly male.

"Oliver Bwye's study."

"This is where the P.A. found the blood and signs of intrusion?"

Andy nodded.

"Anything missing?"

"Not so far as she could tell."

"Was the room locked when she arrived?"

"No. But she said that wasn't unusual at eight-thirty in the morning. Bwye would normally have been in here by then and he usually only locked it when he wasn't inside."

"Usually? Find out what the exceptions were, please."

Andy nodded and as Liam skirted the room, searching for the best vantage point, Craig stared at the blood streaks on the floor. What was visible was bad enough but he knew that Luminol would reveal far more.

They perused the scene for a moment; Andy with the calm gaze that said he'd seen it earlier and Liam with a frown and paces towards the window that said he was marking out the space. Craig stood quietly, peering occasionally at the edge of the desk and bloodied rear door, where finger shaped stains showed that at least one member of the Bwye family had desperately tried to halt their egress. Finally he broke the silence.

"Where does that door lead?"

"The fields behind the house. I can open it if you like?"

Craig shook his head. "Later. I need to see the crime scene photos, and ask a C.S.I. to bring the lamp to show us the true extent of the blood."

His second request was fulfilled first and even the battle hardened Liam gasped as the lights dimmed and glowing blue stains completely covered the floor. Not just the floor; the desk, wainscoted walls and door leading to the fields were all covered with blood. Smears, splatters and thicker, heavier clots. Droplets that had fallen vertically and spray that indicated an arterial cut; at least one of their victims had been close to death when they'd left the house.

Craig pointed towards a small window and the C.S.I. obediently shone the lamp at the sill. There was no mistaking the imprints there; two hands gripping frantically in resistance as their attackers had dragged them away.

"They look like a woman's prints."

The C.S.I. nodded. "The wife or daughter; we're running them now. The ones on the back door are male, size-wise."

Craig signalled his thanks and turned on the overhead light, shrinking the visible blood back to a manageable amount. He motioned the others to join him in the main room.

"There was no blood in here?"

Andy shook his head. "None apparently. Julia thinks that whoever took them gathered everyone in the study, then they left by the back door."

"They threatened them, or injured one to make the others capitulate..."

Liam cut in. "Probably brought a weapon with them, boss. The women would have caved quickly, but unless they'd had a weapon Bwye might have fought back."

"Judging by the prints on the door, he fought anyway." Craig had a sudden thought. "Did Oliver Bwye keep a weapon?"

Andy nodded. "There's a point 22 rifle registered to him; Ruger. He cited rabbit shooting but he probably kept it for protection; they're pretty remote out here."

Craig tensed. "Where is it? If Bwye had had one he'd have tried to fire it. So either the perps took it or it's still in the study somewhere."

Andy went to shake his head, then he thought again and dashed through the automatic door to a uniformed sergeant outside. It looked to Liam like he was going to head butt the glass wall.

After a muttered exchange, Andy returned. "Nothing found in the grounds, but the gun cabinet was open when they arrived."

"Good."

Liam waited for Craig to explain; a missing rifle didn't seem good to him. Craig gestured towards a low settee and everyone sat.

"OK. We have an uber modern house, yet Oliver Bwye's study is as old fashioned as a vicarage. The downstairs is completely open, no locks anywhere, yet he has two on his doors, front and back. I don't doubt if we dig deeper we'll find a safe and other things hidden in there. Liam, get the uniforms onto that. Check with the C.S.I.s, and when they've finished tear the place apart. I want every panel of wainscot off those walls and every floorboard up. Andy, I want to know if the gun cabinet was opened with a key or jemmied, and if there was any blood or prints on it. Julia can interview Bernadette Ross––"

Andy cut in. "She's already done it."

"Then get a fresh pair of eyes. See what Annette can get from her."

Liam interrupted. "What are you thinking? And what was that 'good' about earlier?"

Craig shook his head. "I'm not sure yet. Let's just see what we find." He glanced at his watch. "I'll check in with the office then I'm off to Limavady to see Julia. Liam, you're with me. Andy, make a start and we'll be back in an hour."

As they made to leave, Andy shot them a pathetic look. Craig nodded.

"Don't worry. We'll pick up lunch on the way back."

****

Docklands. 11.30 a.m.

Nicky Morris brushed down her vintage seventies dress and scanned the open-plan squad-room, smiling happily. It was only ten days till Christmas and it was lovely and quiet; just how she liked things at this time of year. She didn't even mind that they had to work on a Sunday; they were on-call all week and once Craig had taken a case they all knew what to expect.

The P.A. strolled over to their young analyst, Davy Walsh's, desk, peering nosily at the image on his computer screen. It was a picture of the night sky, with blue, yellow and silver lights sprinkled prettily against the dense black. Just then Davy loped across the floor, carrying a plastic cup from the vending machine.

She gestured at the drink. "If you'd wanted a coffee I'd have made you one."

He smiled and edged his slim shape past her into his chair.

"I wanted hot chocolate. It's Christmas."

She made a note to buy some hot chocolate and gestured at his PC. "What's that?"

His smile became a grin and he leaned in

enthusiastically. "Cool, isn't it? It's the evolving universe taken by the Hubble Telescope Ultra Deep Field."

Before geek speak ruined what to her was just a pretty picture, Nicky searched round for something else to comment on. She found it protruding from Davy's desk drawer and pointed a finger accusingly.

"And what's *that*?"

He saw where she was pointing and tried to nudge the item out of sight, only to succeed in tearing its corner instead. The torn piece fell at her feet and she picked it up, glaring pointedly at the logo of Queen's University. Davy's old professor had been hounding him to do a PhD and it looked as if he was considering it.

She jabbed the paper with her finger. "Is this what I think it is?"

He blushed and glanced away. "W...What d...do you think it is?"

Davy's lifelong stutter had diminished during the years he'd worked on the team to only the occasional stammer on 'w' and 's', so the fact that he'd stuttered on a 'd' told Nicky that she'd really caught him out.

She drew herself up to her full five-foot-three. "I think it's an application form for a PhD." Her voice rose accusingly. "You're leaving us to go back to Queen's! Does Superintendent Craig know?"

Davy knew he was in real trouble; she never gave Craig his full title except when she was using him as a weapon. As Nicky's thoughts ranged frantically from 'how would Craig take it' to 'I'll miss you if you leave', her expression fixed in a granite mask. Davy shook his head frantically.

"I'm...they're, they're just papers...Prof Roulston just asked me to look at them...He's just..."

Nicky practically shrieked. "He's stealing you! Give me his phone number."

The noise made the more diligent figures of Annette McElroy and Sergeant Jake McLean, glance up from their work. Annette wandered across the floor.

"What's wrong?"

Nicky pointed accusingly at Davy.

"He's leaving us!"

If the words hadn't been so potentially upsetting Annette would have laughed at her melodramatic tone; Medea would have been proud. Instead, she leaned over Davy's partition and stared down at the top of his head.

"Are you, Davy?"

It was said calmly. She was just as upset as Nicky but she knew that further hysteria would result in him crawling out the door on all fours. He peered up through his hair.

"I...It's just s...something I'm thinking about. It's the PhD..."

Annette waved Nicky away to make coffee then she pulled over a chair and sat down, waiting until he was ready to speak.

"We'll miss you. Will you at least promise that you'll talk to the chief before you make up your mind?"

Davy considered for a moment. He'd been thinking about doing his PhD for a while and the urge had grown stronger in recent months. He wasn't sure if chatting to anyone would change his mind, but Craig had been good to him so he at least deserved a chance. He nodded.

"Provided you do s...something for me."

She already knew what it was. "Don't worry. I promise I'll keep Nicky off your back."

****

Craig parked at Limavady police station and flipped open his mobile. Thirty seconds later he was connected with Docklands and a miserable sounding Nicky answered hello. Her voice was so flat he thought someone had died.

"What's wrong?"

She sighed theatrically. "Nothing."

It was the signal for him to spend five minutes cajoling her into saying what was bothering her and then sympathising over whatever it was, but frankly he didn't have the time, so instead he said the words he knew would put him in the doghouse for days.

"Great. Is Annette there, please?"

Nicky said nothing, just generated an ominous silence for the moment it took Annette's warm voice to come on the line.

"Hi, Annette, can you speak?"

It was her signal to move as far away from Nicky as possible so that he could ask her what was up. She transferred the call to her desk.

"I can talk now."

"What's wrong with Nicky?"

Annette sighed; it didn't have the melodrama of Nicky's but it was worrying all the same.

"Queen's is after Davy again to do his PhD. He's thinking seriously about leaving."

Craig's heart sank. Davy was the best analyst he'd ever worked with and without him, solving their cases would be much more difficult. Not to mention that they were all fond of the lad.

"You're sure?"

"Certain. Nicky's been giving him hell about it and if we're not careful she'll drive him away."

Craig considered for a moment. PhD fees were expensive; add in the cost of losing your salary for years while you studied and he might yet have a card to play.

"OK. I'll chat to him in a minute. Meanwhile, what's happening there?"

Annette sighed again but this time it was about work. "Joanne Greer's appealing her sentence."

Joanne Greer was a nasty piece of work that they'd put away in 2013; a business woman who'd been given life for ordering the murders of three people, in partnership with a London gang boss, Alik Ershov. Ershov was dead now, hoisted by his own petard. Literally; one of his contract killers had wrung his neck for taking liberties. Greer was in Wharf House women's detention centre, serving what was laughably called hard time.

"What!"

"Apparently her solicitor has been making noises for weeks..."

"And no-one thought to tell us?"

Annette continued calmly. One of them had to be; Craig's temper was threatening to boil over.

"The Public Prosecution Service has been on. They

want us to submit a report."

"Greer hasn't a hope in hell of them granting her an appeal. She confessed, for God's sake."

"She confessed to Ershov who'd made a deal with The Met to walk free. Now she's saying it was entrapment." Annette paused, waiting for Craig to say something more, when he didn't she carried on. "Look, Greer's just chancing her arm. It'll get kicked out. Even if it isn't it'll take them months to get their case together; they won't get a court date till at least the spring. I just thought that you should know."

It was Craig's turn to sigh. Greer's appeal would be a hell of a start to 2015.

"OK, tell Jake and Carmen to get the case files and start familiarising themselves with it. Neither of them was on the team when we put Greer away. When does Ken get back from his training exercise?"

Ken Smith, or Captain Kenneth Smith of the Swords Regiment to give him his full title, was an army officer on secondment to the squad until the coming July. He'd started in a liaison role during some bomb related murders and had quickly become part of the team. They would miss him when he left, which made Craig's determination to keep Davy even more resolute.

"Friday. Just in time for the Christmas parties to start."

"He'll be doing some holiday reading then."

From Craig's run through of his troops, Annette knew that she would be handed a task next. Something occurred to her.

"Where are you and Liam? Will you be in after lunch?"

Craig said a cantankerous "No". He was regretting accepting the Bwye case now. The last thing he needed was to be off site when Joanne Greer was playing games. She was one of the slipperiest villains he'd ever put away, with the money and resources to get more slippery still.

"That's what I was calling about. We've been asked to consult on a case in Derry and I need you here."

She went to ask more but he pushed on. "Sorry, I don't have time to brief you. Ask Nicky to print out a copy of the file; it's in my saved messages. I need you here tomorrow morning if that's OK?"

Annette grinned; she loved being in the field and if that field happened to be in the countryside then so much the better. She was a Maghera girl and she missed the fresh air.

"I'll get the kids sorted and come up in the morning."

She paused, wondering whether to remind Craig about Davy or let him forget and sign off. Craig forgot nothing.

"Pass me over to Davy now, please."

Davy had been watching Annette from a distance whilst trying to avoid Nicky's martyred stare. When Annette nodded in his direction he knew his phone was about to ring. He hesitated before picking it up, dreading the conversation he was about to have. To his surprise Craig sounded cheerful, even though he cut straight to the chase.

"Morning, Davy. I hear you're thinking of leaving us?"

Davy gawped at the handset, uncertain how to reply. Craig accepted his silence as assent and took the lead.

"I want you to do your doctorate. You're bright and I've no intention of trying to stand in your way."

Davy didn't know whether to feel relieved at not having to defend himself, or hurt that Craig was prepared to let him leave so readily. He was still deciding when Craig spoke again.

"However, you know I don't want you to go so I've had an idea that might give us both our way. I need to check a few things and then perhaps we could have a chat?"

Davy's normally lightning fast brain was struggling to keep up but he could have hugged Craig for what he said next.

"Meanwhile, I'm sure you've had quite enough of Nicky's badgering, so how about you work from home this afternoon and come up to Derry tomorrow morning with Annette? Liam and I are here on a new case."

Davy just had time to stammer "Y...Yes" before Craig asked to be transferred back to Nicky. He got in the first word.

"Nicky, Joanne Greer's appealing her verdict and we

need to submit a report. I want Jake and Carmen to read all the files, but remember Jake's working flexitime."

Jake's grandfather, the man who'd raised him since he was five, had terminal cancer. The sergeant was helping his grandmother nurse him so he made up his hours as and when.

"Ken too when he gets back. Annette and Davy are joining Liam and me in Derry tomorrow, meanwhile Davy's working from home for the rest of the afternoon."

He paused, waiting for the onslaught, but all that came from Nicky was a squeak. He pushed his good luck.

"And leave Davy alone, please. I'm trying to persuade him not to leave and that won't work if you give him so much grief that you drive him away. I've got things under control, so leave the lad in peace."

With that he hung up, knowing that his few days in the doghouse had just extended to at least a week.

Chapter Three

In the time it took Craig and Liam to ascend the three flights to Julia's office, she'd been alerted to their presence and had the kettle on and a tray of biscuits set out. She was as nervous as she knew Craig had been on the phone the day before, but it was time to play the gracious hostess now.

Craig had taken the stairs two at a time but now he trailed along the narrow, windowed corridor behind Liam, his nervousness growing with each pace. He wasn't sure why; after all, the awkward greetings had been covered yesterday. Then he realised what it was; at some point Julia would ask if he was seeing anyone and he would have to tell the truth; there was no way he would deny Katy's existence. That was when things could get tense. Even if someone didn't want their ex anymore many people were still happier when said ex remained alone.

It was an atypical moment of arrogance on his part and as soon as he entered Julia's once austere office he knew that he'd been wrong. Instead of the familiar wooden floor and ancient blinds, there was a bright blue carpet, white walls and curtains, pulled back to allow the winter sunshine in. It wasn't the office of someone sad.

As Julia turned from the kettle she'd been boiling Craig's heart sank. She was dressed for a Sunday, in a pair of tight jeans and a sky-blue blouse that matched her eyes, with her red curls rambling unsubdued down her back. She looked stunning.

Liam's eyes darted from one ex to another and he saw the pallor beneath Craig's Latin tan. Fair enough, they had only broken up because of geography, not a lack of love. But what Liam saw when he looked at Julia was the exact opposite – a relaxed, confident woman. One glance at her left hand told him why. He signalled Craig frantically with his eyes but the attempt was wasted; Craig was too stressed to see anything smaller than a truck. So Liam did what any mate would do in such circumstances and what he realised he'd actually been brought along for; he ran interference. With one stride he crossed the floor; his right hand angled deliberately to shake Julia's left.

"D.I. McNulty. Nice to see you again."

As they shook, Liam turned Julia's left hand upwards so that not even Craig's panic could blind him to the large diamond ring glinting there. Craig saw it and as quickly as he realised its significance he relaxed. He'd been worried about hurting Julia's feelings but the engagement ring made it clear that there were no feelings left to hurt. He smiled genuinely for the first time since she'd phoned the day before and crossed the room to say hello, as Julia stared down, confused, at Liam's still present grip.

"Hello, Julia. How are you?"

Liam released her hand, confident that Craig had seen what he needed to see, then he sat down and scoffed the best biscuits before anyone else could. Julia smiled at Craig with the fondness that only ex-lovers share.

"I'm good, Marc. You?"

Her clear, half-English accent catapulted him back in time and he was momentarily nostalgic. He remembered their arguments and recovered rapidly.

"Fine." He gestured at her left hand. "Congratulations seem to be in order. Who's the lucky man?"

She blushed in a girlier way than he'd ever seen her do before. "His name's Matt Thomas. He's a surgeon at Peter's Hill in Enniskillen, where my brother works."

Craig smiled, relieved at his complete lack of jealousy. His smile deepened; another doctor. What was it with medics and the police?

She laughed. "He puts up with my strange little ways, which is saying something."

Craig laughed with her. "Even your smoking?"

She shrugged and smiled. "I'm down to two sneaky ones a day."

She'd had a twenty-a-day habit when they'd dated; Dr Love must have been some man to separate her from her cigs. As Liam chomped at the biscuits, he listened, smiling to himself at how Craig had managed not to mention Katy's name. He wasn't hiding her but he was gentleman enough to let McNulty have her happiness without playing tit for tat. As the chat lulled naturally, Julia waved Craig to a seat, pouring the coffees as Liam brought up the reason that they were there.

"Interesting case."

She nodded and opened a drawer, removing a buff-coloured file. "Have you been to the house yet?"

Craig noticed a framed photograph on the desk; it was of a man around his age, with blond hair and a tanned face that sported a two-day beard. The snow behind him and skis in his hand completed the image of relaxed happiness and health. Dr Thomas I presume. Julia's shy smile as she caught his gaze was endearing, embarrassed, but most of all unambiguously in love.

The moment was broken by Craig answering "we've just been there" and within a minute they were hard at work. He had a list of questions on the case, but top of it was 'who'?

"Who's your best pick for the Bwyes' disappearance?"

Julia wrinkled her forehead glumly and sat back in her chair, picking at the edge of the file.

"It depends if they're dead or just injured."

She'd got it in one. Craig joined her train of thought.

"OK. So far there's no sign that it was a burglary, so the real question is, was it a kidnap that went wrong where the Bwyes fought back, in which case they could still be alive somewhere. Or...was it always the plan to murder them? You haven't received a ransom demand yet, four days after they disappeared, which points away from kidnap, but if murder was always the intention then why bother removing the bodies? They could have just killed them and left them at the house."

Julia thought for a moment then ventured a suggestion that reminded them just how perverted criminals could be.

"Could...could they have taken them somewhere to torture them? Before..."

Craig frowned. "I sincerely hope not, but we can't rule it out. There's a third possibility I should have mentioned. Oliver Bwye could be a family annihilator who rigged the scene to make us believe that he was a victim as well. Fifty per cent of family mass murders happen from within."

Her eyes widened as he went on.

"Annihilators have four types: anomic, disappointed, self-righteous and paranoid. Anomic annihilators see their families as status symbols and if something happens to negate their worth they become disposable."

Julia shook her head. "Bwye was a model family man. Successful career, pillar of the community; his wife's charity efforts practically built the local hospice. Everyone I've questioned says there was nothing strange about the family in any way."

Craig shrugged, unconvinced, and Liam agreed. They'd seen enough of people's façades to know that often even their nearest and dearest didn't know what was on their mind, never mind the neighbours.

"You don't agree?"

Craig answered first. "No, I don't. I saw enough in a case we had in April to know that people are rarely what they seem. Five apparently upstanding people with secrets so bad that they were prepared to commit suicide rather than have them revealed. And none of their family members had a clue."

Julia topped up their coffees, nodding him on. "What's your theory then?"

Craig shook his head. "I don't have one yet, but I have a lot of questions. First of all, the study was obviously Oliver Bwye's kingdom, so how did the whole family end up in there? If they did. We still haven't confirmed whose blood was all over the floor. There's no sign of a struggle anywhere else in the house, so were the wife and daughter marched into the study at gunpoint, or did Bwye call them in?"

Liam leaned forward, gesturing at the file. "Do you have photos of the gun cabinet?"

Julia withdrew a pile of ten by tens and handed them across. He selected three and spread them out, giving an admiring whistle. Oliver Bwye's gun cabinet was antique. It must have cost a fortune, but then people with money spent it on something and there were only so many eco-friendly houses that you could build.

Craig ran a tanned finger down one photograph, taking in the cabinet's intact glass and lock.

"Did forensics find anything on it?"

Julia shook her red curls. "Not a thing; no prints except Bwye's and no blood. The lock had been opened with a key, not forced."

"Bwye's prints could have been left there at any time and the assailant probably wore gloves. The question is how did they open it? The lock's intact so that means either Bwye opened it or he gave them the key."

Liam cut in. "He might have been forced to open it."

Craig spoke slowly, thinking. "He might have...perhaps by threatening his family. I can't imagine he would have done it without duress. But his bloody fingerprints are elsewhere in the room, so why no blood on the cabinet if they had to force him?"

"Maybe they did it before he was hurt?"

Julia rifled through the photographs, selecting a head and shoulders shot of a powerfully-built man. She stared at it for a moment before handing it to Craig.

"Bwye's a big man so they'd have had to be strong or used a weapon to make him do anything."

Craig shook his head. "If they'd already had a weapon to threaten him with then why bother with the gun? Unless...they might have wanted to use it in the killings to incriminate him."

"Or to avoid a trail leading back to them?"

Both ideas made sense but something was still niggling at Craig.

Julia carried on. "Bwye was a rugby player at university; played for the old boys until 2005. He still went for a five mile run every day."

Craig glanced up sharply. "When and where?"

She looked surprised at the question. "Every morning at seven o'clock. He ran around the grounds."

"How long did it take him?"

"About fifty minutes according to Bernadette Ross. He didn't push himself; it was just to keep fit."

"OK. That means he would have arrived back at the house around seven-fifty, leaving him forty minutes to shower, have breakfast, perhaps read the papers before

Ross arrived."

She nodded. "And watch the News. Bwye showered and then went to his study to watch the eight a.m. News and check on the stock exchange. That's why he had a TV in there. Then he had breakfast at his desk and read through the papers before Ross arrived at half past."

Liam thought for a moment. "Who delivered the papers?"

Julia stared at him, startled. She hadn't asked, but instead of becoming defensive as she would have done a year before she looked sheepish.

"I didn't even think to ask. That's why we need your team on this case."

Liam tutted inwardly at the rookie mistake as Craig changed the subject. "Andy says Harrison has you working a burglary."

She grimaced. "He's annoyed with me for asking your help."

Craig bristled. It was bad enough that she'd had to deal with the pettiness of Terry Harrison for a year, now he was punishing her for trying to solve a major case!

"I'll speak to him."

He paused, waiting for her usual tirade of 'I don't need your help' and 'Just because you're a man don't think...' but nothing came. Not one objection. Instead she smiled gratefully.

"Would you? I could argue with him all day long and it wouldn't work. I've tried, but he just dismisses me because of my rank."

They all knew chauvinism had as much to do with Harrison's dismissal as status. Craig considered his next words carefully before he said them, half-wondering why he was saying them at all.

"Do you really want to work this case?"

Her eyebrows shot up in surprise. "Of course I want to work it! It's the biggest case we've had up here in years." She stared at him hard for a moment and then her face broke into a smile. "Oh, I see what you're asking. You mean do I mind working a case with you." A familiar note of sarcasm tinged her words and Craig remembered when she'd used the tone on him. "You might recall that I asked for your help, Marc. If I hadn't been completely over you do you think I would have done that? Well yes, I might have done for the sake of the case, but you certainly wouldn't be sitting here now having tea and cake!"

Strictly speaking it was coffee and biscuits but he knew what she meant. She hadn't finished.

"I'm completely over you! I'm getting married in six weeks' time."

Six weeks! It had only taken her one year to get over him and marry another man! Craig didn't know whether to be offended or pleased. A question popped into his mind. Was she on the rebound? One glance at her happiness answered the question and he gave himself a mental smack on the head for being an arrogant dick. Julia was still speaking.

"And by the way, will you please stop thinking that you have to avoid mentioning Katy Stevens' name in front of me!"

Liam stifled a grin as Craig's jaw dropped. How the hell did she know about Katy? He answered his own question. Mike Augustus. He was dating Annette and he'd obviously shared the gossip when he'd worked cases in the northwest. Craig's temper flared for a moment; he hated people discussing his private life. Then he realised Mike had actually done him a favour; he would never have found the right moment to mention Katy. In the time it took for the thoughts to flash through his mind, Julia had underlined how happy she was for him.

"She sounds like a lovely woman. I'm really happy for you; although I do think it's funny that we've both ended up with doctors. Perhaps we need the therapy." She gave a musical laugh before finishing with "Now, can we please get on with the case?"

Liam heaved a sigh of relief and turned back to the matter in hand.

"So the paper-boy may have seen something or someone else near the house that morning. The timing of Bwye's routine also means that if he'd gone for his usual run that Thursday there could only have been forty minutes between his return to the house and when

Bernadette Ross arrived for work. But Ross didn't report seeing anyone in the grounds so that means whoever took them either did it the night before or in that forty minute window between seven-forty and eight-thirty. The morning's unlikely, boss. It's too tight..."

Julia cut in. "Ross always drives up to the front of the house. They could have left by the back."

Craig nodded. "They definitely did. There was no blood in the rest of the house. OK, it's just possible they were taken that morning but the night before would be a surer bet."

He took a gulp of coffee before setting down his cup.

"Judging from the man's prints by the door, which I'm sure will match Bwye, his hands were bloody. So if he'd removed the gun he'd have had to wipe the cabinet clean of blood. I don't go with that, it's too hard to clean off every speck; Luminol would still have shown something. That cabinet was opened with a key by someone wearing gloves."

Liam decided to play devil's advocate. "Unless Bwye removed the gun before he got injured? Maybe he'd been using it to shoot rabbits the day before and left it out."

"Possible but I still don't buy it. Let's work this through. Either the intruder wore gloves and had a key to the cabinet, or they forced Bwye to open the cabinet before he got injured, perhaps by threatening him with some other weapon they'd brought." The niggle started again and he knew what it was this time. "That brings us back to if they'd brought a weapon why bother with Bwye's rifle at all, unless as Julia said they wanted to incriminate him which is a stretch. But if they didn't bring a weapon then how could they have forced a man of Bwye's size to do anything?"

He thought for a moment then his face broke into a smile. "Someone got hold of the cabinet key beforehand, accessed the rifle before the assault and used it to subdue Bwye."

Julia gawped as he pushed on.

"Where did Ms Ross say the key was kept?"

"Bwye carried it on his key ring."

"Then he would have noticed if it had been missing.

They must have copied the key sometime before that day and there must be a very short list of people who could have done that. Just Bwye's wife and daughter, staff and friends visiting the house."

Liam groaned, picturing the interviews ahead. "It's not that short."

Julia ventured another opinion. "Bwye was in the Territorial Army when he was younger so I doubt if he would be easily scared, even by a gun. Perhaps they threatened his wife and Jane to make him cooperate instead?"

Craig nodded. "They're all possibilities, but that would still have required them to have some sort of weapon, an unarmed man wouldn't have been a big enough threat. And where has the rifle gone?"

He thought for a moment. "OK, whoever herded everyone into the study it was done before any blood was spilt; there's nothing in any other room. The wife and daughter would have been terrified, but I still think one of them would have tried to make a run for it. Perhaps they caused some of the damage we found, knocking over whatever was in their way. Alternatively, if they didn't run it might mean that they knew their assailant and went along with them to play for time."

He seized the pile of photographs, flicking through them till he found some of the main living room. There were only two shots and nothing looked out of place. Suddenly he realised something; there'd been no sign of fingerprint dust in the main room when they'd arrived at the house. He shot Julia an unhappy look. "Please tell me the C.S.I.s went over the living room."

Her face fell as she realised what she'd done. "It didn't look disturbed...everything was happening in the study...I..."

Craig bit his tongue before he said something he regretted. That meant the police and C.S.I.s had been tramping through the Bwye's main living area for four days. If their assailant *had* touched anything the odds on finding a useful print now were a million to one. They had to try anyway.

"Liam, get onto the scene and get them to tape off that

room. Then get the C.S.I.s back over there."

As Liam left, Julia glanced at Craig with anxious eyes. "How badly have I screwed up?"

He shook his head. "There's no way of knowing. If Bwye's the killer and he herded his wife and daughter into the study then we won't find any but the family's prints anyway. If there was an outside assailant and one of the Bwyes tried to make a break for it through the main room it's possible that they disturbed something trying to escape and that the assailant would have had to straighten it up. They might have left a print, or else they wore gloves and didn't, but they might still have left hair or fibres." He had another thought. "Has anyone gone over that room with Bernadette Ross?"

She stared at him blankly.

"Ross knows the house, as will any of the housekeeping staff. If anything's been moved from where it's usually kept then they'll notice."

Julia nodded. She was out of her depth and everyone knew it. Craig rose and smiled reassuringly.

"Don't worry. This is what people join the Murder Squad to learn. Annette's coming up tomorrow to help and I'll ask her to involve you in everything." He gestured at the file. "May I take this? It would be useful to have the photographs."

She nodded, thanking God that she'd brought in Docklands as quickly as she had. As Craig reached the door he turned back.

"I meant to ask. Where's Harrisons' office nowadays? He and I need a few words."

****

2 p.m.

"How did they get out?"

Andy twisted round from his crouched position in front of Oliver Bwye's desk as Liam entered. He'd got a patrol car to drive him back via the chip shop while Craig was sorting out Terry Harrison. He set two vinegar stained bags on the desk and repeated the question.

"What?"

Liam tutted impatiently, gesturing at the study's oak back door.

"I said how did they exit? The blood trail leads to the back door, but Ross' statement says it was locked when she arrived that morning with the key still on the inside. How do you explain that, unless they were kidnapped by Houdini?"

Andy grinned. It was obvious. Finally he'd get to make fun of Liam, instead of it being the other way around.

"That's easy, hey. They had a copy of the key."

Liam snorted cynically. "So they managed to lock the door from the outside without pushing the key in here onto the floor?" He threw down the gauntlet. "Show me."

Andy sprang to his feet. "Fine. You stay in here." He reached for the key and opened the back door, walking outside.

Liam's "not so fast" brought him to a halt. "You have to leave the key in the lock."

"But I need it to lock the door."

"Then find one the same size to leave inside."

Andy wandered through the study in search of a stand-in. He was about to enter the living room when Liam tutted again.

"The boss put that room out of bounds till the C.S.I.s finish."

Andy rolled his eyes. "Like they're going to find anything after four days of us tramping around."

"They have before."

Just then Andy spotted a long, steel key, not unlike the one in the back door. It was so similar in fact that he put it to the test. It wasn't a match but it was good enough to play understudy. He inserted it in the lock and then went outside, carefully pulling the door closed. Liam waited for a few seconds and then bellowed through the oak.

"Get a move on. These chips are getting cold."

Andy inserted the key, shouting "done" a moment later. Liam checked the door was secured and then peered at the fake key in the lock; it hadn't moved. Andy was right. Someone had copied the key and locked the back door from the outside, leaving the original still firmly in the lock. It told him something.

"Come back in. We need to talk."

A moment later they were sitting at Bwye's desk munching, as Liam laid out his thoughts.

"How many doors are so thick that you could put a key in the outside and not move the key on the inside? Especially a key that length."

Andy smiled as if he'd been caught out. "You guessed my trick."

"I guessed that it would only work if the door was so thick that the keys didn't touch each other. Where did you do it before?"

Andy's eyes narrowed as he recalled. "Mr Rubens' office. He was Dean of Discipline at my school and his study door was as thick as he was. We used to break in and nick his canes so he couldn't punish us."

Liam guffawed loudly. "Good lad. We used to break our man's canes in two." He waved a hand towards the door. "Anyway, that was useful. Now we know that whoever took the Bwyes knew how thick that door was, which means they were familiar with the house. They also had a copy of the key. The one they left behind locks the door and so did the one they took with them."

Andy nodded. "But who could get close enough to copy the key? There've been no reported break-ins."

"What about Bernadette Ross? She was here every day. And they must have had other staff to look after the grounds; it's a big place."

Ross had discovered the crime but that was no indicator of her innocence; she could have arranged to discover it to throw them off the scent. Annette would get the truth out of her.

Andy groaned. "There are two grounds men and a gardener. With Ross and the cook that makes five. We'll have to re-interview them all."

Liam gave a slow smile. "Four. The boss is bringing Annette up tomorrow to do Ross." He glanced at the clock on the study wall and clambered to his feet. "We can puzzle it out over coffee, and I fancy a decent one in town. You're driving."

****

Craig followed Julia's directions to Harrison's office, girding himself for what he knew would be an angry encounter. D.C.S. Terry 'Teflon' Harrison was a vain, snobbish man, more interested in his rank than he'd ever been in solving a case. He'd abused every bit of power that he'd ever held; using it against his subordinates like a weapon, especially his female ones, and more than a hint of lechery tainted his encounters with them. Harrison had been his boss at Docklands until he'd been made superintendent, then Harrison had transferred to Limavady full time, where he'd obstructed Julia's transfer to Belfast, indirectly resulting in their split. He had an axe to grind with the man and he was in the mood to plant it right between his eyes.

As Craig climbed the last stairs to the seventh floor he saw a familiar face, smiling when he did. Susan Butler, Harrison's faithful P.A. A woman more sinned against than sinning; whose return to work after she was widowed had unfortunately landed her in Harrison's grasp. When they'd first met Craig had wondered if she was as controlling as her boss, but as time passed he'd seen that she was just trying to keep a grip on what she could in life because she'd already lost so much.

His smile widened as he strode towards her desk.

"Mrs Butler! It's lovely to see you again."

Susan Butler blushed, warming up her beige hair and outfit attractively.

"Superintendent Craig. Hello again."

"Marc. We've known each other too long for titles."

Her blush deepened and was joined by a smile. "What are you doing in Limavady?" As soon as she asked the question her face fell. "Is it that terrible case at Rocksbury? I knew...know, Diana Bwye. Lovely woman. Always doing things for charity. We raised funds together for Vanquish Cancer."

It backed up what he'd heard about Diana Bwye and what he already knew about Susan Butler. Something occurred to him and he leaned in, dropping his voice.

"Wouldn't you prefer to work in Belfast, Mrs Butler? It would be easier than travelling here every day from Antrim."

Her eyes filled with hope then she glanced warily at the door behind her.

"Who would I work for?"

Craig smiled. He'd heard that Geoff Hamill in Dockland's Gang Crime Unit was losing his P.A. to retirement and he said as much. Susan Butler's hopeful look changed to one of eagerness and Craig was pleased that he might be able to help her; if it screwed Teflon as well then so much the better.

"Is D.C.I. Hamill nice?"

Craig nodded at the door. "Compared to your current boss he's a prince. Shall I have a word?"

She nodded gratefully, afraid to speak in case it hexed the chance, then she turned briskly back to business and lifted her pen.

"Would you like to see D.C.S. Harrison?"

Craig straightened up. "Yes I would. And now."

She went through the mime of checking Harrison's availability and then nodded Craig on to knock at the door. It was an unheard of breach of protocol. Normally she would have made him wait five minutes till she'd checked that Harrison wanted to see him, then made him wait a while longer until he'd deemed that Craig had been intimidated enough. Terry Harrison belonged to the Reginald Perrin school of management. "One, two, three, four, make them sweat outside the door. Five, six, seven, eight, always pays to make them wait."

Craig knocked the door once and then thrust it open, pleased by the shocked expression on Harrison's sallow face. He looked the same as he had when they'd last met the year before, just after Craig had saved him from being framed in a people trafficking case and just before Harrison had screwed up his and Julia's relationship for good. He should have let him go to prison.

He'd been a lowly D.C.I. then so Harrison had had the upper hand, but now they were on a level playing field.

Harrison's eyebrows shot up in indignation and his thin mouth opened, ready with a tirade. Craig got in first.

He leaned on the desk, looming over the shorter man, and thrust his face forward until it was just inches from his foe's.

"You can forget the usual crap about how I don't have an appointment. I'm not your subordinate now."

Harrison leapt to his feet, attempting to reinstate the pecking order he felt correct. His high tenor lessened the impact of his words.

"What do you want, Craig? If you're here to defend your old girlfriend, forget it. She's working on a burglary and that's that!"

Craig drew himself up to his full height, eight inches taller than the other man. Harrison was still barking and his face had contorted into a sneer.

"We don't need your help solving the Bwye case, so you can go straight back to Docklands. I'm sure you'll have a murder in Belfast soon."

Craig snapped back. "Yes, you're making such a good job of solving it that people have been traipsing through your crime scene for days, you have three people missing, blood all over the floor and not a single, sodding clue." He reached inside his jacket for his phone. "Let's see what the C.C. has to say. He'll just love the headline 'Limavady Police run around like headless chickens!'"

Harrison's small eyes narrowed, fixing Craig's. If he thought Craig was going to blink first he was mistaken. After a minute Harrison looked away.

"What do you want, Craig?"

"I want as many men from Derry station as you can spare for the search; we're widening the perimeter. And I want D.I. McNulty back on the case. She had the wit to see that you needed help, even if you didn't."

Harrison set his jaw. "You can have Sergeant Shaw."

"McNulty, but I'll take Shaw too. They worked well with us on the Adams' case."

The Adams' case had happened two years before, when a young mother from Limavady had gone on a killing spree. Harrison fixed his gaze again. It reminded Craig of two bulls locking horns and in that analogy he was younger and fitter and bound to win. It only took Harrison seconds to blink this time and resort to the age old defence of indifference. He gestured dismissively towards the door and lifted a file, opening it to read as if he always read standing up.

"Take them both; they're bloody useless. You won't solve the case and if you want it to drag your career down, then be my guest."

He scanned a page rapidly and then flicked to another. If anyone could read that fast Craig would have been very surprised and as displays of indifference went, it sucked. As he turned to leave Harrison raised his eyes again, smiling maliciously.

"But when you fail, and you will, remember that I'll be here, cheering."

It sounded like a threat. Craig made a note to watch his back for sabotage and exited the office without a word, leaving the door wide open behind him. As he passed Susan Butler's desk he caught her hopeful glance and decided to call Geoff Hamill from the car.

****

3 p.m.

"Sorry guys. Better late than never."

Craig dumped a paper bag full of food on Oliver Bwye's desk and slumped in a chair, removing the lid of his coffee cup. Andy gawped as Liam grabbed a sausage sandwich; they'd only had lunch an hour before!

Liam patted his paunch. "Waste not, want not."

"You'll have no waist at all soon."

Liam bit off the protruding end of a sausage and laughed with his mouth full. "That's not bad."

Craig swallowed a mouthful of coffee. "I take it you've already eaten." He retrieved the bag. "We can have these later on then. What have you got for me?"

Liam waved Andy on, savouring his food.

"We worked out that whoever took the Bwyes had a copy of the back door key, hey." At Craig's quizzical look Andy demonstrated, "That makes it more likely it was someone who knew the house well. We were thinking of Ross."

Craig shrugged. "Annette will get everything there is from her tomorrow. But the key's interesting. Julia and I discussed the possibility of a copy key for the gun cabinet as well. What else have you got?"

Liam swallowed his last bite and took a slurp of tea. "There are two grounds men, a gardener and a cook. We'll have to re-interview them all."

Craig nodded. He'd been intending to anyway. "Get started on that. How are the C.S.I.s getting on next door?"

"Dusting and printing like the devil. They'll be finished tomorrow. They've another team going over this room again tonight; floors, walls, just like you asked."

"Just in time for us to get the full team together."

Liam nodded. "Aye, I hear Annette and Davy are coming up."

Craig smiled. "We've got Julia, Gerry Shaw and as many men as we need from Derry Station as well."

Liam's eyes widened. "How did you get Harrison to agree to that?"

"Brute force and threats."

"Works for me every time."

Chapter Four

Monday, 15th December. 10 a.m.

By ten o'clock the full team was assembled and Craig had two whiteboards set up in Oliver Bwye's study, now their impromptu office. They'd spent a sleepless night in a B&B and he knew they couldn't do it again and work effectively. It might be better doing the commute; justifying one hundred pounds a night each on a decent hotel was tricky when they could be down the A6 and back in three hours. As he thought of the driving he knew the distance would soon wear. The squad's budget would just have to bear the strain of a cheap hotel.

When the drinks and donuts had been distributed, Craig rapped his marker against the desk to indicate a start. He was greeted with bleary stares that matched his own from Liam and Andy, and a disturbingly bright-eyed alertness from the rest.

"I'll summarise quickly and then we'll allocate the work. At eight-thirty last Thursday morning, Bernadette Ross, Oliver Bwye's secretary of eight years, arrived for work at the house and found no-one here. She entered this room, Bwye's study, which was unlocked, and saw the place in disarray. There was furniture turned over, books out of place, the TV damaged and blood all over the floor." He waved at a pile of photos on the desk. "You can look at the photos afterwards. Actually, Davy, would you mind pinning them to that board?"

Davy nodded, excited at being out of the office and even more excited to be at the scene of a real crime, although he would rather not have had dried blood all over the place.

"There was a lot of blood in here and Mike Augustus is sorting out the DNA."

Liam stared pointedly at Annette at the mention of Augustus' name, and watched with satisfaction as a blush crept up her neck.

Craig rapped his pen on the desk. "Pay attention, Liam." He indicated the doors. "The entrance door was open but the back door was locked, seemingly from the inside. The key was still in the inside lock." He nodded at Andy. "Through Liam and Andy's efforts, which they'll demonstrate in a moment, we've established that the assailant must have had a duplicate key which they used to lock the door from the outside as they left."

Annette signalled to interrupt. "Are we ruling out Oliver Bwye, sir?"

Craig shook his head emphatically. "Definitely not. This could still have been Bwye, deliberately staged to look like someone else. Family annihilation is firmly on the table. OK, Oliver Bwye owns a rifle." He gestured at the cabinet. "It's gone but the cabinet is intact. It was unlocked using a key and there are no prints but Bwye's on the door, although we can't tell how old they are. Bwye may have removed the rifle himself, either voluntarily or under duress, we don't yet know, but there's no blood so my feeling is that our perp opened it wearing gloves. We're toying with the idea that a duplicate key may have been cut for the cabinet as well. We can't rule anything in or out yet."

Davy pinned up the photographs and Annette screwed up her face when she saw the Luminoled images of blood.

Craig nodded. "Not good, I know. No blood was found in the main reception room, but unfortunately the C.S.I.s didn't go through that room until yesterday, so we may have lost some evidence. Hopefully not."

It was Julia's turn to blush.

"The search perimeter has been extended to two miles and we've every spare hand from Derry station out there looking for clues. They'll do their thing and we need to do ours. First, everyone who was interviewed needs to be interviewed again. Annette, you and I will take Bernadette Ross this morning, she may have seen something without realising it and she was the first one in the house."

Annette interrupted. "Is she a suspect, sir?"

"Yes, but we're not telling her that. As far as she's concerned she's being interviewed as a valuable witness and we're going to treat her like one."

Davy retook his seat, trying not to walk on the blood

stains.

"Davy, have you brought everything you need?"

"Yeh. I can connect to the databases from here."

"Good. Make contact with Mike Augustus ASAP please. You and he are basically working the way you do with Des and John. You can call on them for back-up if you need to."

Dr Des Marsham was Northern Ireland's Head of Forensic Science and he worked with John Winter in state of the art pathology facilities on Belfast's Saintfield Road.

"I want you to dig deep into our victims' backgrounds, as deep as you can get. It's too easy just to assume that they were taken because they were rich. I don't want that to feature in our calculations until we've ruled out everything else." He indicated the phone. "I need a trace on this line, Davy, and on Julia's, Liam's, Andy's and my mobile phones, please, just in case we get a ransom call."

Liam had been slumped in a chair wondering whether to have another donut, but he jerked upright at Craig's words.

"Here, why are you tapping my phone? I might have a private call to make."

"Like what? Phoning the Chinese takeaway? It's only for a few days, and we'll just have to moderate our conversations. Keep them clean please; Davy's an impressionable youth." He ignored Davy's sceptical look and carried on. "Any ransom demand will come here or to the lead officers on the case––"

Andy cut in. "Do you think they might contact The Chronicle, hey? Given that Bwye owned it till two years ago."

Craig hadn't thought of it. "Good pick-up. If the Bwyes were taken by someone Bwye offended with an article, then that's exactly where they would call. Davy, we need The Belfast Chronicle's lines monitored as well. Editor-in-chief's and news desk."

Liam gave a low whistle. "You've two hopes; Bob Hope and no hope. No newspaper's going to let us tap their lines; their sources would dry up."

"Then we'll have to persuade the editor or a judge to

say yes." Craig turned to Davy. "Who's the news editor at The Chronicle these days?"

Davy's girlfriend Maggie Clarke was a reporter at the paper. The analyst's slim face fell. "You're not going to like it."

Craig knew the answer immediately. "Ray Mercer."

Ray Mercer was the worst gutter journalist that any of them had ever met and some idiot had made him news editor.

Liam gawped at him. "Mercer? Editor! Holy God."

Craig's tone was caustic. "I think God was on holiday that week. Mercer will never give us access to his line voluntarily; we might catch him out on his dirty tricks. OK, we'll have to get a warrant. Andy, you and Julia get onto that. Get legal to make the request watertight and then go to Judge Standish, he's a good man. If anyone will give us a warrant he will."

Craig waved Liam on to demonstrate the back door trick while he thought, running through a checklist in his head. Perimeter search ongoing. C.S.I.s almost finished at the house and re-interviewing potential witnesses, yes. Lining up traces for possible ransom calls, and Davy doing deep background on the Bwyes, check.

He interrupted just as Liam got to his 'voila' moment with the key, much to his chagrin.

"Davy, add Bernadette Ross and the other estate staff to the deep background checks, please. And don't forget to check out Oliver Bwye's rifle and shooting experience. Also, I want you to have a first go at forming a suspect list from people that The Chronicle hacked off."

Everyone started laughing and Craig was momentarily puzzled, until he noticed Liam's face. It was a picture of huffy annoyance.

"Could you not have waited? I'd just got to the good bit!"

Craig shrugged. "Sorry. OK, if you've finished then let's all get on with it. Davy, you can have this room as your base. Annette, you and I have to be at Derry station by eleven to see Ms Ross. Liam, sort out the other re-interviews and Gerry, stay here and supervise the searches please. You all know what you're doing."

As he went to leave the study by the back door, he turned back to where Davy was arranging his desk and dropped his voice. "I haven't forgotten what we discussed yesterday. I've an appointment to see the C.C. at two o'clock and it's top of my list."

He was out of the door before Davy had time to smile.

****

11 a.m.

Davy scanned the large study for a moment, peering into its corners and opening the drawers of the antique desk where he'd set up shop. They were all empty, victims of the savage swoop Craig had ordered that had stripped the room to its bare bones in the search for clues. Whether the search had yielded anything was yet to be determined but at least they'd put the furniture back in place.

The analyst ran his finger along a shelf of hard-backed books, selecting one; 'Moby Dick', a classic. He slipped it back and took another, then another, until finally he'd checked the titles of every book on the shelf; they were identical! Oliver Bwye had ten copies of 'Moby Dick', but why? He scrutinised the line then he played a hunch and lifted them again, one by one. He was right, one of the books felt heavier. He flipped open the cover in excitement, only to be disappointed by its normality. There was the title page and contents and then Melville's famous opening line. 'Call me Ishmael...'

So why did the book feel heavier than the rest? Davy flicked through the pages until, a third of the way through, the words ceased and a steel plate took their place. He recognised what it was immediately, a pressure lock; all he needed was the right amount of weight and it would spring open. Thirty seconds of experimenting brought success and the plate sprang back to reveal what he'd guessed it would, a half empty bottle of whisky. Bushmills; a good local make.

He placed it on the desk for forensics to check and turned back to the wall. Twenty minutes later every bookshelf had been checked and he'd found a similar story; each shelf was filled with identical volumes by different authors. Volumes of Beckett, Shaw and other luminaries piled up alongside enough whisky to keep a brewery solvent for a year.

The Generation Y-er whistled to himself. Someone had a serious drink problem and they were so keen to hide it that they'd spent a fortune on camouflage books. It was Bwye's study so it made sense that it was Bwye's secret to hide, but who was he hiding it from? His wife, possible but unlikely; Diana Bwye must have known all about her husband's proclivities. His daughter? By the sounds of it she was a wild child herself. Bernadette Ross or the other staff? Perhaps, or perhaps Bwye was simply hiding it from himself, deluding himself that he had control of the booze and not the other way round. Maybe that's why the books on each shelf were identical; Bwye had hoped that searching for the one that held the whisky would take him so long that the urge would have passed.

Whatever the reason, if Oliver Bwye had got to the stage of hiding booze he was in trouble, and alcohol and a rifle definitely wasn't a good mix. Davy made up his mind to tell Craig then he sat back down at the desk and began to work. After an hour of setting up bank, phone and criminal searches on the family and staff he yawned and reached into his bag for an energy bar, then he lifted his smartphone and made a call.

Maggie Clarke answered in three rings and he smiled. She always had her phone beside her; you never knew when someone might call with the Pulitzer Prize.

Her tone was crisp and professional. "Maggie Clarke, Belfast Chronicle."

"Hi, pet. W...What're you up to?"

Maggie smiled at the sound of her boyfriend's voice. It still made her heart leap after two years. She twirled a strand of hair round her finger and softened her tone.

"I'm just editing. What about you?"

It was on the tip of his tongue to say: "I'm in a mansion in Derry, helping with a case where three people might be dead" but it was more than his job was worth. Craig trusted him and Maggie to never cross the line. More importantly he didn't fancy going to jail for breach of confidentiality, so instead of giving into the urge to look cool he said, "the boss says he'll s...speak to the Chief Constable about my doctorate."

"That's awesome. What do you think he'll ask for?"

Davy smiled at her excitement; she was always supportive, whatever he wanted to do. If he hadn't been only twenty-seven he might have asked her to marry him. The thought stopped him in his tracks. *Only* twenty-seven; he'd thought it automatically, like he was still a child. He wasn't, even though his mother and grandmother babied him and he still lived at home.

Twenty-seven was a grown man. He could have joined the army at eighteen and if society collapsed now he'd be expected to help maintain the peace, standing alongside Craig and Liam to build houses and defend the weak. When had society become so infantilised that a twenty-seven-year-old could possibly think that he was still a kid?

And what about the second part of his thought, that he loved Maggie enough to marry her. Did he? The answer came immediately, yes, he did, but he didn't have the building blocks in place. He earned a good wage and he had savings, but if he left to do his doctorate all of that would disappear. The fees would swallow up his savings and his wages would evaporate. He knew that if he asked her to marry him she would say yes, or at least he hoped that she would. She would also say that she was earning enough to keep them both and that it didn't matter if he worked.

Davy pictured himself studying and having fun at Uni while she trudged to work every day to keep a roof over their heads. His revulsion at the image shocked him; it was followed by a blush of embarrassment at what his late father would have thought of such an arrangement. In the second since the idea had occurred to him, he'd had an epiphany. He was a fully grown man not a child, and he loved the woman on the other end of the phone. A fledgling plan formed in his head and he parked it for a private moment, then he returned to his conversation and outlined the deal he thought Craig might get for him from the C.C.

Chapter Five

Liam dandered into Derry police station as if it was his second home. It felt as if it was, partly because he'd spent thirty years in stations around Northern Ireland, but mainly because they all looked pretty much the same. Oh, some of the new ones were flashy, all right, but by and large they had a high metal fence around their exterior, a reinforced steel front door and a front desk that would have intimidated a weaker man.

He'd often thought sarcastically that the Good Friday Agreement should have stipulated comfy chairs and musak in police stations. After all, if they were going to pretend they'd forgiven every scrote who'd killed people during The Troubles and release them all from jail, then shouldn't they give them somewhere nice to visit when they re-offended? Why not go the whole hog and just give them a car and a condo when they'd got out in '98? That wouldn't have pissed off the law-abiding citizens at all.

As he bashed his fist hard on the reception's bell, Liam smiled at his own wit. The smile was wiped off his face by the man who appeared behind the glass.

"For fuck's sake leave me some bell, Whitey!"

Liam's six-feet-six height and Celtic pallor made him instantly visible, even in a force full of tall men. Years before, it had earned him the nickname 'Big Whitey' and some of the older officers still called him by the name.

Sergeant John Ellis stood behind the reception desk with his hands on his hips; a universal indicator of annoyance matched only by the combination of folded arms and ruthless squint that he adopted next. He was a man in his early fifties, almost as tall as Liam and with the same cynical world view. Ellis was a traditionalist, a man who washed his car every Sunday and wrote with a biro instead of using a PC; an unashamed Luddite despite all attempts to bring him up to date. He only had three years to go till retirement and he fully intended to resist change till he did.

Liam stared at the man he'd known since college and folded his arms to match. They gazed at each other through the glass for a moment, Liam refusing to ask permission to enter and Ellis determined that he would. An exiting constable won Liam the game. He pushed his way through the open door and strode straight past Ellis to the staff room, preparing to make himself a cup of tea. He knew it wouldn't take long for the sergeant to follow.

"Where the hell do you think you're going? Just because you're a D.C.I. now, doesn't mean you can steal our tea. Jack Harris phoned through and told me to put a lock on the biscuit tin."

Harris knew Liam too well. He was the sergeant at High Street station in Belfast where they normally held their interviews. Liam turned towards his adversary and after a ten second face-off they both grinned and the mock-enemies became the back-slapping friends that they'd been for years. Liam waved a hand around the staff room as the kettle boiled.

"What're you doing up here, John? Last I saw you, you were in East Belfast."

Ellis shrugged. "Aye well, the kids have grown and the youngest is at University; the Magee campus down the road. Brenda's folks are from Derry and she wanted to come home. Mine are all dead so I thought, why not move out West?"

He made it sound like he'd come on a wagon train.

Liam's eyebrows rose in surprise. There must be some truth in the rumour that men mellowed with age, because the John Ellis he'd trained with had been so stubborn he'd have fought with his own feet rather than give in and move house. They drank their tea for a minute, going through the niceties of 'how's the wife' and 'how're the kids?' with Ellis rudely telling Liam to use birth control or he'd be paying university fees till he was ninety-nine. Finally they got down to business.

"We've been brought in on that home invasion up near the River Faughan. I'm here to set up some interviews."

Ellis frowned. "Nasty business. I know Oliver Bwye; we're in the same golf-club."

"Where's that then?"

"Up near Drumahoe."

Liam dunked a biscuit in his tea, dropping the soggy bit into his mouth just before it fell off. He spoke through a mouthful of Rich Tea. "What's he like?"

Ellis shrugged. "OK for a rich man, I suppose. Not too impressed with himself, which makes a pleasant change." He shook his head. "Hell of a boozer though."

Liam's ears pricked up. "Oh, aye. Tell me more."

"There's not much to tell. He likes his whisky and he gets out of hand now and then. Nearly had to have a word last week."

Liam leaned forward urgently. "When last week?"

Ellis stared past him, remembering. "We were there on Wednesday night for the annual meeting; I'm on the council now." He gave a proud smile. "Got voted in unanimously."

"By the rest of the biro users, no doubt."

Ellis ignored the jibe. "We were in the bar afterwards and Bwye was there. He was the worse for wear; looked like he'd been there all afternoon. He was giving the girl on the bar stick for refusing to serve him another drink and I was just about to go across and say something when he staggered out. He could barely stand."

"Did he drive home?"

Ellis' face fell. "God, I hope not. I suppose I should have checked, but someone asked me a question just as he left and to be honest I forgot." He shook his head. "I don't think he could have done. We have lads who park the cars and it's part of their job to withhold the keys from anyone who's three sheets to the wind. I didn't see Bwye's car when we left so he must have got a taxi there and back. Do you want me to check?"

Liam thought for a moment. If Oliver Bwye had been fighting drunk the night before he'd disappeared it could be significant. He shook his head. "I'll do it. Tell me more about Bwye."

"Like what?"

"Have you ever seen him be violent? How does he treat his wife? And do you know anything about him having a gun?"

Ellis screwed up his face. "Yes to the first one, not great to the second, and yes, I do."

Liam motioned him on.

"That was the last time I had to step in; in November. Bwye played a round of golf with a local businessman, Garvan McDermott, and they got to talking politics – always a bad idea. Bwye's a staunch unionist, a minority opinion in this neck of the woods, and McDermott, mild-mannered as he is, is firmly in the United Ireland camp. Four or five drinks in, the discussion got heated and Bwye swung for McDermott. McDermott swung back and connected with Bwye's jaw. I dragged them into the car park to calm down."

"Did the fight continue there?"

Ellis gave a wry smile. "It would have done if Diana Bwye hadn't arrived in the nick of time. She'd come to take hubbie home."

Liam frowned. "I take it that's when 'not great to the second' reared its ugly head?"

Ellis nodded and sipped his tea, pausing for a moment as he chose his words. "I never actually saw him hit her... but I saw him push her once. When they were on the dance floor last Christmas. And he gave her some verbal that day in November when she picked him up." He added hastily. "If I'd seen anything more than that I'd have stepped in. But if he was doing that in public then God only knows what went on behind closed doors. You might want to check hospital and GP records to see if she reported any injuries. She never reported him to us or I'd have acted."

Liam's fists tightened. He couldn't stand men who abused someone weaker than themselves. He'd like to take them up a back alley. In fact, he'd done many a time. He forced out his next question, not really wanting to hear the answer.

"And the daughter?"

Ellis shook his head. "I don't know. Rumour has it that she's pretty screwed up, but whether that's down to abuse is anyone's guess."

"We'll check her records too. Screwed up how?"

"A minor drugs offence, driving too fast, you know the score. Like the old Specials' song says; 'Too much too young'. It's a real pity. Her mother's a lovely woman. She does a lot of charity work locally; Brenda knows her well from that."

Liam nodded. Good women and bad men, what the hell was the attraction? People should have a stamp put on their hands at birth saying Good or Bad, then stay away from anyone not like them. Natural justice and evolution would sort things out after that.

"I might want a word with your missus."

Ellis grinned. "Come round to dinner while you're here. I could do with the craic." He stared pointedly at Liam's paunch. "Although you already look like you're eating for two."

Liam guffawed through his slightly hurt feelings; he'd waved his six pack goodbye a long time before but he still had fond memories.

"Aye, that would be good. Andy White and Craig are here as well."

"Bring everyone. Brenda loves company. Any women around? She'd love a chat about what everyone's wearing in the big smoke."

"Annette McElroy. Watch it, you could end up with a coach party, and she won't thank you for that."

Ellis waved a hand dismissively. "That's settled then. When you come you can ask Brenda everything you need."

Liam glanced at his watch. "The boss will be here in a minute with Annette. They're interviewing in one of your rooms."

Ellis nodded and stood up, readying to wash his cup. "Aye, I know. They OK-ed it with the D.C.I." It was his turn to check the time. "I've sent some of my lads to the estate to help with the perimeter search. We'll get you a Rota for the other interviews now."

Liam waved him back down and lifted the teapot. "There's time enough for that. Let's finish our tea first. Now, tell me what you know about Oliver Bwye's gun..."

****

The Malone Road, Belfast.

Judge Eugene Standish was a mild-mannered man. He would have been considered easy going amongst any group, but amongst a bench of judges or an eloquence of lawyers – take your pick for the collective term for people who dressed in black and wore wigs – he was a veritable beacon of reasonableness. He didn't object to being disturbed by eager or stressed policemen at any hour of the day or night, often ambling downstairs in his dressing gown to sign warrants at three a.m. Although it would be fair to say that he preferred nine to five and that when his wife, a woman renowned for her cooking, had just put a roast dinner in front of him, was his least favourite time. But even then his ire was only shown by a raised eyebrow. Yes, Eugene Standish was definitely a mild-mannered man.

On the odd occasion when he did refuse to sign a warrant it was usually for a glaring error, such as the time an eager sergeant had requested to 'church' someone's home for drugs, or when a mister 'A Capone' instead of 'A Caplin' was to be investigated for fraud. But thankfully such occasions were rare and just gave the Judge and Mrs Standish something to chuckle about over their evening sherry. Usually he found the police punctual, respectful and accurate and he endeavoured to be the same. He'd been particularly keen to help out since his colleague, James Dawson, had been imprisoned the year before as part of a ring trafficking young women, bringing the judiciary into severe disrepute. Terrible business, made even more terrible by the fact that Standish had an eighteen-year-old daughter himself.

So it was against this background that Eugene Standish opened the door of his Victorian mansion on Belfast's Malone Road and greeted the two officers standing there. He waved Julia and Andy through the hall and into the tasteful drawing room, and offered them tea, which was declined. He scrutinised them as Julia withdrew the warrant request from her handbag. Feminism had advanced rapidly, although, as the trafficking ring demonstrated, it hadn't advanced rapidly enough. But progress had definitely been made since he'd been called to the Bar. Back then the women in justice had been very few, and those few had done their best to look like men. The curls rambling down Julia's back said that a woman's professional credibility was no longer dependent on short hair and flat shoes, and he thought it boded very well for the law.

Standish took the papers and excused himself to his study to read them, anticipating that such an approach would be a formality. So it was with shock that they heard his shout of indignation from half a hallway away. Before the echo had died down the judge appeared at the drawing room door, red-faced and waving the warrant request in his hand.

"What is this?"

His tone said he wanted an answer that wasn't silence and would brook no nonsense when it came.

Julia's eyes widened and Andy jumped to his feet, almost snapping into a salute.

"It's a warrant application, your honour." Thankfully he managed not to add 'hey'.

Standish waved the paper higher. "I can see that, man. But what on earth made you think I would sign it? It's tantamount to invasion of privacy and challenging the freedom of the press! You honestly expect me to let you tap a major newspaper's telephone lines? You must be insane!"

Andy counted to ten inwardly, willing his silence to draw the judge from his position in the doorway into the room. It worked; by the count of ten, Eugene Standish was standing in front of them, albeit still waving the papers in his hand. He glanced at Julia's startled face and realised how he must look, so he took a seat. Andy had half-expected the reaction, Craig had said that the warrant would be a stretch, but Julia was genuinely shocked. She'd visited Standish many times and she'd never seen him behave like this. Her expression and that knowledge embarrassed the judge and he waved Andy to sit, moderating his tone to the reasonableness that was his stock in trade. He tapped the papers with his left hand.

"Now then, what is all this? Please explain."

Andy waited for Julia to take the lead; it was her case and she had a reputation for being sharp, although, according to Gerry, since she'd got engaged she'd toned it down a lot. Mellowness through marriage, he wondered cynically how long that would last. Julia said nothing, just continued to stare at the judge as Andy carried on.

"You'll have heard about the missing family in Derry, your honour."

Standish hadn't so he shook his head. When Andy had finished outlining Craig's theories, Standish nodded.

"You're expecting a ransom demand and believe it will come to The Chronicle or one of you."

Andy nodded vigorously. "Aye. I mean, yes, your honour. Oliver Bwye owned The Chronicle for years. I don't know if you read it..." The judge's posture had softened so he allowed himself a 'hey'. "...hey? But it's not the most dignified of rags, and the news editor, Ray Mercer, is a hack and a half. Anyway, if the Bwyes have been kidnapped -"

Standish interjected. "By someone whom Bwye offended when he owned The Chronicle, then they might use the newspaper to communicate."

Andy nodded again and this time Julia joined in. She added eagerly.

"It's just one theory, but if they phone The Chronicle and we haven't got a trace on their lines then we might lose valuable evidence that could help us find the family."

Standish shook his grey head, not in refusal but in the certainty that The Chronicle would have high-powered lawyers who would object. He felt an appeal looming in his future but for now the inspectors had explained their reasons well enough that he could see merit in their request.

Julia and Andy watched Standish's round face wrinkle slowly into a smile, what they didn't know were all the reasons putting it there. Cameron Lawton was The Belfast Chronicle's new editor-in-chief and he and Standish had played rugby against each other at school. Lawton had hit puberty early, giving him a serious advantage in the scrum; an advantage that he'd used more than once. Schoolboy rivalries never faded, so Eugene Standish raised his pen and, with a flourish, he signed the warrant off. Time to make Lawton the loser for once, if only for a few brief hours.

****

Derry Station.

Craig stared at the pale woman across the table, then he clicked on the tape machine and nodded Annette to start. Bernadette Ross jumped at the click and then again at the recorder's loud buzz. Annette gazed at her sympathetically, as if she understood her shock, both at the sounds and at being in an interview room.

If Annette looked sympathetic it was because she really was. Her gut said that the woman in front of them had done nothing wrong and she knew that Craig's was saying the same, but on the off-chance that both their instincts were wrong and Bernadette Ross' fearful innocence masked a Machiavellian mastermind who had kidnapped the Bwyes, her warmth had to be tempered by questioning disbelief.

"Ms Ross, can you tell me how long you've worked for the Bwye family?"

Bernadette Ross glanced at the tape then at the table top, and finally back at Annette before answering in a lilting West-Bann voice.

"I don't work for the family, just for Mr Bwye. I've been his P.A. for eight years."

Craig asked a question to which he already knew the answer. "You worked for Mr Bwye at The Chronicle?"

Ross nodded. "Yes. I was his P.A. there for six years and when he sold the company in 2012 he asked me to come with him, to help manage his affairs."

Craig sat back while Annette continued. "What sort of affairs did he have to manage? After all he was retired, wasn't he?"

Ross shook her head and a proud smile tilted her lips.

"He'll never retire. Men like that never do."

Craig furrowed his brow. Interesting. She was using the present tense even though Annette's question had been in the past. It was as if Ross believed, or knew, that Oliver Bwye was still alive. The P.A. continued.

"Mr Bwye has several business interests. He's on the board of two companies and he has a portfolio of shares to handle. I'm nearly as busy now as when we worked at The Chronicle."

Annette nodded. It explained all the paperwork they'd found. "We'll need the names of the companies and details of what his roles were."

Ross lurched forward so suddenly that Annette jerked back in her seat. But her intent was far from violent if her shocked expression was any guide.

"Were! You said were! Is Mr Bwye dead? Is he dead? Have you found him?"

Ross had only just noticed that Annette was discussing Oliver Bwye in the past tense. Annette corrected her use of tense as if it had been in error.

"I apologise, Ms Ross, it was a slip of the tongue. I meant what his roles *are*. We haven't located anyone yet."

As the secretary relaxed, Annette grew even more convinced of her innocence. A sharp glance from Craig told her not to; Bernadette Ross could be playing them, it wouldn't be the first time they'd had a liar or an actor in the interview room. Annette gave Ross a moment to recover before she carried on.

"Are you working on anything special for Mr Bwye?"

Ross thought for a moment and then shook her head. "No more than usual. Just clearing the minutes of Board meetings and making arrangements for his business trip to the States in Janu ––" A sharp sob cut her short and she was silent for a moment before continuing in a firmer voice, glaring at Annette as if she dared her to disagree. "January. He's *going* to New York."

Tempted as she was to do so, Annette knew there was no point delving into Oliver Bwye's business dealings until Davy had checked everything out. It was time to get personal. She lined up her pen with the edge of the file in front of her and fixed the other woman's eyes with hers.

"When did you last see Mr Bwye?"

"Last Wednesday lunchtime at around one o'clock."

"Why not after that?"

"He was going to play a round of golf."

"Where?"

"The golf-club at Drumahoe."

"With whom?"

"With one of the golf pros I believe, although I couldn't swear to that."

Annette stared at her pen as she considered her next question. It was a Waterman, a gift from Mike. He gave her gifts all the time; he was that sort of man. She raised her eyes back to Ross' pale face, searching hard for anything she could find there. Liam had briefed them about Oliver Bwye's drinking at the golf-club that Wednesday and John Ellis' assertion that Bwye was an aggressive drunk. She wondered if the P.A.'s obvious loyalty to her boss would be strong enough to make her lie.

"How was Mr Bwye when you last saw him?"

Ross looked puzzled, as if it was a trick question. "He...he was fine. Looking forward to his golf."

Annette decided on a diversion before the main event. "And Mrs Bwye and her daughter; how had they been recently?"

Ross glanced away and Annette knew she was either embarrassed or preparing a deceit. Her tapping feet beneath the table said that whichever it was it was making her stressed. Ross kept her eyes averted as she answered in a sad voice.

"Mrs Bwye is a lovely lady."

That was it. No mention of Jane, but the omission and tone were enough; Jane Bwye caused her parents trouble and Diana Bwye had suffered because of it. Annette wondered if upsetting her mother had been enough reason for Oliver Bwye to harm his daughter. She decided a direct approach was best.

"Was Mr Bwye ever violent towards his daughter?"

Ross jerked back in her chair and her gaze skittered around the room, searching for somewhere safer to alight than Annette's face. Annette repeated the question in a stern voice.

"Look at me, Ms Ross. Was Mr Bwye ever violent to Jane?"

Her tone snapped the P.A.'s gaze back to her face and after a moment's stare Ross nodded once.

"And to his wife?"

Another nod.

"I need details, Ms Ross."

Bernadette Ross gabbled wildly. "He's very good to them, they get everything that they need... it was only when he drank. Jane's...she's difficult...she upset Diana, but then Diana would stand up for her and Mr Bwye would..."

She shook her head and Annette nodded, knowing that they would get the full details bit by bit, probably once they'd found them all dead. Right now it seemed like a betrayal too far for the faithful P.A.

Craig nodded at her to change tack.

"Last Wednesday."

Ross smiled weakly, grateful to be let off the hook. "Yes?"

"After he went to play golf, you didn't see Mr Bwye again?"

Ross shook her head sadly. "No."

"What about Mrs Bwye or Jane?"

She thought for a moment and then nodded. "I was working until six-thirty on Wednesday and Diana popped in at around five to offer me something to eat." She smiled, remembering. "She's like that. Very kind."

"Did you have something?"

"Yes. I had a sandwich with her before returning to work."

Craig had been listening silently but now he intervened. "How was she?"

Ross looked surprised. "Diana?"

"Yes."

"She looked...tired. Yes, she looked tired. And worried."

Craig pushed her for details. "Any idea what about?"

To his surprise Ross laughed. It was a weary laugh, as if there could only be one answer.

"The only thing that ever worried Diana was Jane."
"Did she confide in you?"

Ross hesitated as if wondering whether or not to keep Diana Bwye's secret, then she nodded.

"She told me that Jane was involved with a man that she knew her husband would think unsuitable."

"So Mr Bwye didn't know about him?"

Ross' eyes widened. "Absolutely not. He would have killed him. Jane was his little girl."

Even though he hit her. Had his objections been paternal protectiveness or something more?

"What was so unsuitable about Jane's boyfriend?"

Ross shook her head. "Diana didn't tell me; just that Mr Bwye would think that he was. I went back to work after that."

"She didn't mention the man's name?"

"No."

Craig needed time to think so he waved Annette to pick up the ball. She slipped back into the Q&A seamlessly.

"Did you see Mrs Bwye again?"

Ross smiled weakly. "I nodded goodbye as I left that night. She was sitting in front of the TV in the main room."

"Why do you say sitting in front of, rather than watching?"

Well spotted.

"Because it was switched off."

It was logical.

"Was she reading or doing something else?"

"No. Just sitting, staring at the floor."

Diana Bwye didn't sound like a happy woman.

"And Jane?"

"I saw her as I left. She was entering the drive as I was leaving. In her little sports car."

Annette startled. There'd been no sports car parked at the house.

"What does she drive?"

"A blue Mercedes SLK."

"We'll need the registration number."

"I know it by heart. JB1993; the year that she was

born. She's twenty-one soon."

Craig jotted it down and left the interview room. John Ellis was at the front desk, chatting to a woman through the glass. He excused himself and turned to Craig.

"John, is there a search on for Jane Bwye's car?"

Ellis looked blank.

"It's a blue SLK and it was last seen at the house the evening the family disappeared. It isn't there now. Here's the reg."

Ellis took the paper and lifted the phone, beginning the search while Craig returned to the interview room, irritated. Why the hell hadn't Julia checked the family's cars? She'd dropped the ball badly on this case, it wasn't like her; maybe the wedding was occupying her mind. By the time he'd re-joined the interview, Annette had changed topic to the Thursday morning.

"When you arrived at the house, how did you enter?"

"Through the front door into the main room. It's the only way in."

"That's not strictly true. There's a door at the back of the study."

"That's always kept locked. Only Mr Bwye has the key and only he and I have the key to the interior study door."

Annette frowned. It seemed like excessive security not to leave a spare set in the house.

"So Jane and Mrs Bwye never entered the study?"

Ross shook her head emphatically. "Never. They weren't allowed."

She hesitated for a moment and Annette knew she had something else to say. She decided against it and the moment passed. No amount of urging from Annette could bring it back.

"OK. When you entered the house that morning did you notice anything out of place in the main room?"

Ross concentrated, as if she was running her gaze mentally across every table and chair. Finally she shook her head. "Not that I saw, but then I just walked straight through to the study. But if the place had been badly disrupted, like in a fight, I would definitely have noticed."

"Was the study door open or locked?"

"Definitely open. But it was eight-thirty so that wasn't unusual. Mr Bwye always arrived before me."

"Tell me what you noticed when you entered."

"Like I told the other officer; there was blood on the floor and things were all over the place. The chairs were turned over and the television was smashed..."

Annette interrupted, checking her facts. "Why was there a TV in the study? I thought it was just where Mr Bwye worked."

Ross stared at her as if the answer was obvious. "Well yes, but Mr Bwye likes to watch the business news, to keep an eye on the stock market, and things."

And things. It sounded weak and Craig wondered what other things Oliver Bwye had watched on that screen.

"Did he go in there when he'd had a fight with his wife?"

Ross shrugged. "Probably. I wasn't there at evenings or weekends so I can't say for sure."

"Did he do anything else in there?"

Ross blushed. "That's not my business. He's a good boss."

And things. Craig speculated about what bodily fluids the C.S.I.s would find in the study other than blood while Annette drew the questioning back to the Thursday morning.

"What else did you notice in the study when you entered?"

Ross sighed. "There were books on the floor with their pages torn out."

"Torn by hand or like they'd fallen out when they'd been flung?"

Ross shook her head as if she was confused and Annette let it drop. Forensics would give them their answer.

The P.A. shuddered, remembering. "There was so much blood. It was everywhere...smeared in a trail towards the back door, like someone had dragged..."

A harsh sob cut her short and Annette waited until it subsided.

"What did you do?"

The ambiguity of the question was deliberate and the secretary glanced at her with startled eyes.

"I didn't do anything! I've never hurt anyone!"

Annette repeated her question, adding "next" for clarity. Ross' shoulders dropped in relief.

"I called 999 and waited for the police."

"You stayed in the study?"

"I couldn't move."

It seemed a normal enough response and a glance from Craig told Annette to wrap things up. While Bernadette Ross was given a fresh cup of tea, Craig and Annette retired to the staff room for one of their own. Craig spoke first.

"What do you make of her?"

Annette sipped her drink before replying. "I think she knows a lot more about Oliver Bwye's nasty habits than she's willing to say. I'd be surprised if he didn't have a mistress stashed away somewhere and he obviously drinks heavily."

Craig nodded. "Davy's checking the hospitals for reports of violence on the wife and daughter."

"It figures. A man with a type A personality retires; he was never going to find it easy to wind down."

Craig's glare said it was no excuse. "That's presupposing that the abuse has only been happening since then. My hunch is it's been going on for years. OK, what else?"

"If there have been mistresses I don't think Ross is one of them."

"Based on what?"

"Based on the fact that she's not glamourous enough. Diana Bwye's pictures show that she's beautiful, so it's likely that's where Bwye's taste in women lies."

Craig shrugged. "Maybe, maybe not. For some men a change is..." He didn't complete the saying.

She arched an eyebrow and carried on. "The daughter's obviously wayward so we need to dig further there. I'd like to know more about this unsuitable man she was dating who was worrying her mum so much, and whether her father had found out about him. Also, where's Jane's car?"

"And why the hell didn't the locals pick up on it and start the search last week?"

Craig's face said someone's head was going to roll for the omission and it might be Julia's. Annette didn't fancy sitting in on that conversation, although she was certain that Liam would want a ringside seat.

"What's your gut feeling on Ross? Guilty or not guilty?"

She considered for a moment before answering.

"Not guilty. She's a loyal retainer who sees everything and keeps her mouth shut because Bwye pays her well. But I'd like to take another run at her on the family dynamics."

Craig nodded. "Agreed. Let her go home but say that you want to see her again tomorrow, and this time she's not leaving until she tells you everything. That'll give her tonight to consider which side her bread is buttered on. Also, I want you to take her back to the house and have her check that everything's in place in the main room. We'll be doing the same with the rest of the staff." He checked his watch and jumped up. "Damn. It's nearly one o'clock. I'm going to be late for the C.C."

Annette smiled and shook her head. "No you're not. His office rang and asked if you could meet him at home in Portrush rather than going back to Belfast. It's only thirty miles so you'll be there in plenty of time."

Craig nodded but he didn't retake his seat, heading for the door instead. "Fine. You've all got plenty to get on with. Ask Davy to book everyone into a cheap hotel and let me know which one. I've things to do but I'll meet you there for dinner around six. And warn everyone I expect a full briefing afterwards."

Chapter Six

Sean Flanagan rose as Craig entered his warm, smoke-aged study, but not out of respect for Craig. He liked him but not that much, or next thing he'd be inviting him to the prom! No, Flanagan stood because his wife had shown Craig into the room and even after forty years of marriage he had that kind of respect for her. Craig could understand why. Helen Flanagan was feminine in a way that made most men long for a woman like her, and some women dismiss her as a throwback to the 1950s, before feminism had really left its mark. They would be wrong if they thought that. In fact, they couldn't have been more wrong.

Helen Flanagan hadn't been a stay at home wife, warming her husband's slippers by the fire, she'd been a teacher of such skill that she'd won the teacher of the year award twice. All while bringing up two children and dealing with a rugby playing, gun-toting cop of a husband, during decades of some of the worst civil strife the western world had ever seen.

To have managed it at all was miraculous; to have managed it without shouting at or divorcing that husband was a canonisable achievement. And yet she had. With a combination of well-placed head shaking, wise words and arched eyebrows, Helen Flanagan had ruled her home for four decades without any of her family ever feeling controlled. Forget equality, in this marriage she was most decidedly the boss. The woman deserved more than a husband who rose when she entered the room; she deserved a baton twirling parade.

As Craig and Flanagan shook hands she glanced tolerantly at the study's open window on the cold winter's day, knowing full well that a half-lit cigar was smouldering somewhere out of sight. It didn't require comment. Sean Flanagan knew it was bad for his heart and his wife knew that he knew, so she brought in a tray of coffee things and retired, leaving her burly husband in no doubt that she'd smelled the smoke without uttering a word.

The Chief Constable laughed and waved Craig to a chair, retrieving his cigar from the metal waste bin he'd purchased specially for such subterfuge.

"I'll get told off after you leave."

Craig nodded. "Looks that way."

"Does your young lady tell you off?"

Craig smiled, thinking of Katy. He suddenly realised what felt so familiar about Mrs Flanagan's approach. It certainly wasn't because she reminded him of his mother; Mirella's fieriness would have resulted in the bin being hurled out the window and it being slammed shut. No, Helen Flanagan reminded him of Katy; they had the same even tempered approach to life.

"In exactly the way you've just been chastised."

Flanagan laughed. "Hang on to her, then. It makes life easier all round." He poured the coffee before retaking his seat. "Now then, what did you need to see me about?"

Craig took a sip from his cup and set it back down. "Two things. The case is the main one. We were asked for assistance by D.I. McNulty at Limavady."

Flanagan frowned. "I was sorry to hear that you two had split up. She's a striking girl. Terry Harrison's an obstructive bugger but I couldn't go over his head on her transfer, much as I wanted to."

"It's worked out for the best. She's getting married soon, to a doctor in Enniskillen."

Flanagan scanned Craig's face and he knew that he was being assessed for signs of pain. Craig shook his head.

"I'm happy for her and I'm glad that she felt she could call us, because frankly the case hasn't been handled well so far." He brought Flanagan up to date with what they knew, adding. "People have been tramping all over the crime scene, there were insufficient men on the perimeter search, and as soon as we arrived Harrison tried to take Julia off the case."

Flanagan made a face and stared into the fireplace. The fire wasn't lit but the coal and kindling were piled so high that Craig knew a roaring blaze would burn there after he'd left. Flanagan chided Craig mildly as he stared.

"D.C.S. Harrison, please. You probably call him worse

than that outside this room, but I can't be seen to undermine anyone under my command."

Given that he'd just called Harrison an obstructive bugger it seemed the double standard was alive and well. Still, rank had its privileges and all that.

"Sorry, sir. D.C.S. Harrison put Julia on a burglary."

Flanagan glared at the kindling so hard Craig wondered if he was willing it to ignite. There was silence for a moment, filled by the soft ticking of a clock that Craig hadn't noticed and the sounds of Flanagan's Red Setter rearranging itself in its sleep. Finally the C.C. spoke again.

"Waste of resources to take an officer off a case halfway through."

"That's what I thought, so I went to see him. He reinstated her, but only after he'd made it very clear that he didn't want our help at all."

Flanagan puffed angrily on his cigar. "You're the Murder Squad for God's sake! If he had a vice raid would he try to exclude Vice?" He turned to stare at Craig with no ambiguity in his eyes. "I don't want your personal history with D.C.S. Harrison getting in the way of this case."

"It won't, sir." Craig changed tack. "Has The Belfast Chronicle been onto you yet?"

Flanagan nodded. "They've been onto the press office. Bound to happen; Bwye owned the paper for too many years to miss that gift."

Craig sighed; it hadn't been what he'd meant but he could imagine tomorrow's headlines. Flanagan knew there was something more.

"OK, what's coming my way? By the sounds of that sigh it's worse than a critical headline. Spit it out."

Craig hesitated. He'd rehearsed telling Flanagan about The Chronicle's phone tapping warrant on the trip there, but there seemed no way of saying it that improved the truth. He spat it out and waited for the roar. Instead the air was split by a loud laugh.

"The Chronicle's Board must be having a fit! Tapping their precious news desk, and the editor-in-chief's personal line. Which judge allowed that?"

Craig grinned. "Eugene Standish."

Flanagan's laughter became a warm chuckle. "I always liked that man. He has a sense of humour."

Craig took the laughter as approval and elaborated. "Bwye owned The Chronicle for almost thirty years, and under his guidance its editorials were ruthless. He criticised everyone from private individuals to political parties and there were lives he damaged badly. So, until we know different, we have to assume all of his victims are potential suspects." He paused for comment but Flanagan waved him on. "It makes sense that any ransom call will come to the house, our team, or the press. And who else but The Chronicle?"

Flanagan nodded. "Agreed. You were at The Met much of the time Oliver Bwye owned the paper but some of his headlines would have made your hair curl." He made a face. "The police didn't get off scot-free, I can tell you. Two C.C.s' careers went down in flames because of Bwye."

Craig had worked in London for fifteen years, only returning to Belfast in 2008, but he'd seen some of The Chronicle's headlines on visits home.

"We're compiling a list of possibilities. Basically anyone whose life was ruined by Bwye when he was at the paper."

"You'll be there forever on that one."

Craig shook his head. "Davy will narrow it down using his magic."

"Good analyst, that boy."

Craig hesitated for a moment then segued into his second reason for being there.

"Actually, Davy's the second thing I wanted to speak to you about."

Flanagan stubbed his cigar on the edge of the bin and threw the butt onto the fire. He had second thoughts and rearranged the kindling to hide it, before saying "What about him?"

"He's a brilliant analyst."

Flanagan retook his seat and shook his head. "If you're going to say that we need to pay him more, I agree but we can't. The analyst's pay scale is fixed and he's already at the top of it above men twice his age."

Craig gave a weak smile. Flanagan was nearer the mark than he knew.

"He's thinking of leaving."

Flanagan nodded. "It would be a pity but it figures. A brain like that could earn ten times as much in the private sector."

Craig shook his head. "Not for the money. To go back to university and do his doctorate."

He let the words hang in the air for a moment, hoping they would set Flanagan's brain running in the direction his already was. After a few seconds he added a hint.

"The fees are costly and he'll lose his salary."

The Chief Constable stared into the hearth without moving an inch. Craig could see his mind working and fought the urge to push him in the direction he wanted him to go. This must be what his wife felt like when she wanted him to do something; knowing that if she gave in to the urge to shout "just do it" Flanagan was sufficiently stubborn that he would go the opposite way. So instead, Craig planted the seed then held his silence until it took root by itself.

He sipped at his now cold coffee for what seemed like an hour until finally Sean Flanagan changed from an effigy into a man again. He rose abruptly and strode to the study door, opening it and saying three words. The first two sounded like a command; "fresh coffee". The third, "please?" was so soft and hesitant that it said they were anything but. As Helen Flanagan appeared with a fresh pot the C.C. settled back in his chair and waved Craig on to pour. When he held a cup of steaming liquid he turned to Craig with a smile.

"How's this for an idea? You don't want to lose young Mr Walsh and the force can't afford to, but we can't give him a pay rise either. So... how about we give him sufficient study leave to do his PhD over say, three or four years, plus we pay his fees? I can swing that under the training budget. That way we both get what we want and when he's Dr Walsh he can apply to be part of the forensics team; even their starting salary's higher than he's on now."

Craig pretended to be surprised. It was a pretence Mrs Flanagan must have perfected years before.

"That's a brilliant idea, sir! I'm certain he'll stay with us on those terms. And he'll probably do his PhD on some aspect of forensic IT that will be valuable to the force." He played out the scene to the end, as if it had all been Flanagan's idea. "Would you like to tell him?"

Sean Flanagan's weathered face creased in a half-embarrassed smile. "No, no. You do it. I'm just pleased to be able to help." He rose to his feet, almost demolishing a tower of books by his chair. "Now, if you don't mind I'm going to throw you out. Helen's making our afternoon snack. Keep me up to date with the case, please; I don't like surprises." He guffawed as he pulled open the door. "I imagine Eugene Standish has already given The Chronicle quite enough of those."

****

Four days earlier. Thursday, 11th December. 00.10 a.m.

The heaviness of her body had surprised him. He'd known that her husband would be heavy; fat bastard that he was, and made even heavier by the concrete overcoat he wore. But she was slim and small, yet in death she felt as if she weighed a ton. Her death was such a waste; she'd been so kind. But it was outside his control. He was simply doing what he'd been asked to do.

The man tipped the larger body over the side of the boat and felt the small vessel rise on the lake. He watched the black plastic float and swell, until the burden inside dragged first one end and then the other down through the liquid dark. He stared after it; imagining that he could make out the shape long after it had gone, then he lifted his eyes to the skyline and found his bearings from the lights on the opposite shore. It was a beautiful night; fresh and clear with a sky like cold ink. Such a pity to ruin it this way, but he had no time for contemplation; he had more work to do.

Brushing a sprinkling of rain drops from his gaunt

face he turned back to the smaller form, still identifiable as human despite its plastic packaging. He felt tears fill his eyes and smiled at his sentimentality. He'd never seen someone die until that night and it had been far harder than he'd thought; staring into her wide brown eyes as her life had seeped away. He'd wanted to open the door and shoo her free, but he'd had his instructions and once she was dead it had been too late to retreat.

He gazed sadly at the small, black shape; her death was bad enough without erasing all traces of her femininity with a concrete case. Instead, he'd left her face uncovered and weighed her slight body down with stones. He lifted her slim form to the edge and kissed her cheek once, then, reciting a prayer, he slipped her very gently over the side, forgetting that she was already beyond pain. He held her upright as her feet slid through the surface, breaking it into ripples that spread and widened as she disappeared, until he caught a final glimpse of dark curls as she descended to join her husband of twenty-five years.

A third black parcel followed swiftly to its grave and the man watched long after they'd all gone, careless of his safety. Long after the ripples had faded and the water's glass surface had reformed, until finally he turned the small craft towards shore and went home to await whatever happened next.

****

The Ardmill Hotel, Drumahoe. 8 p.m.

By eight o'clock even Liam had eaten enough to satisfy him and the whole team was sitting in the hotel bar with drinks in their hands. The only other occupant was a vacant looking barman whose task in life seemed to be drying the same glass repeatedly; that and staring at Annette's legs. Craig wandered over to order another round.

"Does it get busy here at night?"

The young man dragged his eyes from Annette's limbs to look at him, and Craig noticed that one of his eyes was brown and the other blue: heterochromia, just an interesting anomaly, but it added to the bar's almost surreal air. Late evening in a country hotel bar; it was the perfect setting for a mystery. After a long pause the man answered in a flat, tired tone.

"Nah."

Craig marvelled at what three letters could do in the wrong hands and continued.

"Then you won't get many more customers tonight?"

On a Monday evening in December, they were hardly expecting a marching band. The man continued rubbing the glass like it was Aladdin's lamp and at any moment he expected a genie to appear.

"Nah."

His intonation was deeper this time, implying a stronger negative.

"Could I see your manager for a moment, please?"

The man's eyes widened for a second then the glimmer of curiosity behind them that said he was still alive, flickered out as quickly as it had come. He set down the glass and nodded, not bothering to waste a syllable this time, then he turned on his heel and walked through a door that Craig hadn't noticed before. He returned a moment later with an older man, whose excited smile and gesticulation made the pair seem like night and day.

"Can I help you?"

Craig drew the manager to one side.

"We're here on a police case and I'd like to hire a room for our briefing."

They could have travelled the few miles to Derry Station, but everyone was tired and a lino floored room with neon lights was no substitute for a warm carpeted one with beer. Besides, they'd all had a drink, so he wasn't letting anyone drive.

The enthusiastic man's eyes ran over Craig's face and then flicked quickly across his team's. He frowned for a moment, staring up at the ceiling as if visualising every room in the small hotel. Finally he sighed. The sound held decades of frustration. It said 'we don't have briefing rooms because we're not that sort of hotel. A hotel that hosts conferences in rooms filled with bottled water, spare pens and file pads headed with our name. A hotel that carries a crest so recognisable that its name springs to people's minds as the place to be'.

Craig knew the sigh held even more than that; it was the sound of thwarted ambition and a failed career. He pictured the man at twenty, dynamic and hoping to run a large chain; preferably one with a capital 'H' or 'R' in its name. The manager's next words were said with an embarrassment that bordered on shame.

"We don't have briefing rooms. I'm sorry."

They could have retired to a bedroom but that seemed too informal even for him, so Craig thought laterally.

"Then could we hire the bar for the rest of the evening? It would mean closing it to everyone else."

The man's eager look reappeared as if he'd spied an innovation, a money spinner that he could boast to his wife about. He nodded sharply.

"Certainly. Will you need George?"

George had returned to rubbing his glass.

"No thank you. If he could leave out a few bottles of beer and wine, and show me where the coffee percolator is, that would be fine."

They agreed a price and shook hands, then George did as he was bid and left, gleefully locking the door and setting a 'do not disturb' sign outside, before he disappeared into the night to do whatever turned him on. Not much if the previous twenty minutes were any indication.

Craig returned to the group to a ripple of applause and Liam brought over the drinks as he readied to start.

"OK, I'm going to begin then we'll go around. First, logistics. We've got additional uniforms on the search and the perimeter is now two miles. The C.S.I.s have been back to the house to go over the main room and the study." He turned to Andy. "Is that almost finished?"

Andy nodded and gulped down a mouthful of beer. "They gutted the study last night and wrapped up the main room an hour ago."

"Good. OK, all we can do now is wait for the forensics to come back."

Annette rose to put on some coffee, talking as she

went. "Mike says they've had to ask Des for help; their lab is busy on another case. The C.S.I.s are sending some of the samples from the Bwyes' down to Belfast tonight."

Craig nodded. "That will speed things up." He nodded that he'd like coffee as well. "Was there a safe in the study?"

Andy nodded. "Under the floor. Nothing there except passports and some jewellery."

"Fine. We saw Bernadette Ross again today. She seemed genuine enough but I want her to take another look at the house tomorrow, to see if she can spot anything out of place in the main room. Annette's arranging that. Ross is definitely holding back information on the family dynamics. We know that Oliver Bwye ruled that house with a rod of iron and we think his wife and daughter were frightened of him. Ross admitted that Bwye had been violent to them in the past; hospital and possibly police reports should tell us about that."

Liam cut in. "Already on it."

"Good. Ross worked for Bwye when he was at The Chronicle and he poached her two years ago when he retired. Not that he has apparently; he's still on two Boards and handling all his own stocks and shares."

Craig could feel someone's eyes boring through him so he turned in his seat; Davy was staring at him intently. Craig knew he was searching his body language for some hint of what his discussion with Sean Flanagan had produced, so he glanced at the clock so briefly that only Davy saw. The message was clear; we'll talk later. He covered the exchange with a request.

"Davy, I want you to find out anything that you can on Bwye's companies, Board duties and stock portfolio."

Davy nodded. "I had a call about Jane Bwye's car around s...six o'clock. They've found it."

Craig leaned forward eagerly. "Where?"

"Burnt out just off the Fincairn Road."

Craig leapt to his feet and Davy knew he was going to search for a map. He waved him back down and produced his smart-pad, tapping one up on the screen. The group crowded round as he displayed the long road.

It ran from Drumahoe to Kilnappy and had two turn-offs near where the car had been dumped. They led variously to scrubland and open countryside and up towards the A2. Craig sighed; the arsonist could have gone in any direction.

Davy closed down the screen. "Forensics are out there now; maybe they'll find s...something."

Liam shook his head. "Fire is a forensic countermeasure. We'll be lucky if they even find the number plate."

Davy gave a small smile. "They did, in a field half a mile away."

Craig knew that his smile was for the science behind the explosion, but it irritated him all the same; they'd lost evidence because of those flames. Liam saw Craig's temper building and stepped in before it turned into words. It did that far too quickly these days.

"Why take the car at all?"

Craig frowned. "Why not? It's transport. Bernadette Ross saw Jane driving it towards the house on Wednesday evening so it's odds on that the kidnappers saw it as well."

"Exactly. They saw a small two-seater. If you're a kidnapper dragging three injured people from their house, you're going to use something large and enclosed, in case someone looks inside. You're not going to ferry them using a sports car."

Craig's eyes widened. Liam was right and he'd missed it. So why take Jane's car at all? Annette chipped in.

"Maybe they thought it was too valuable not to nick?"

"Then why burn it out?"

"Then...maybe one of them forced Jane to drive it?"

Liam was undeterred. "Why not just put her in the van with her folks?"

Craig interrupted. "That would mean there were at least two assailants."

Andy screwed up his face, confused, then he nodded as he saw what Craig meant. "Ah, I see. One to drive the van and one to drive the car, hey."

Craig nodded. "If they split up that means they were sure they had the Bwyes under control in the van." He thought for a moment then nodded Davy to take notes on his pad.

"OK. Bernadette Ross said that she saw Diana and Jane Bwye on Wednesday evening when she left at six-thirty. Oliver Bwye was still up at the golf-club. We know from Liam's conversation with John Ellis that Bwye got fighting drunk and returned home from the club in a cab." He glanced at Liam. "What time was that?"

"Nine-twenty. I checked with the taxi firm. It's a twenty-five minute ride."

"OK, good. So we know that Oliver Bwye arrived home sometime around nine-forty-five on Wednesday night, drunk and fired up after his fracas at the golf-club. How fired up is the question?"

"You mean was he fired up enough to kill his wife and child?"

Craig shrugged. Family annihilation was still a possibility but not one by which he set great store.

"I doubt it but we have to look at the likelihood. So Bwye comes in drunk, there's an argument with Diana and Jane and he assaults them both. Then he mocks up the scene to look like all three have been assaulted and disappears with the two women." He glanced at the row of faces. "Comments or suggestions anyone?"

Davy was the first to reply. "I w...was going to tell you, chief. Bwye has alcohol stashed all over his s...study."

Craig nodded him on.

"You remember the bookshelves? Well, every shelf has at least one book that's a fake, holding a half bottle of whisky. I found nine of them dotted around and there are probably more."

Liam let out a whistle and held up his beer. "Whisky beats beer any day."

Annette leaned in eagerly, adding fuel to the fire. "Ross hinted that Bwye gets up to more than business in that room. She said 'things' when we interviewed her."

Andy's eyes widened. "Women?"

Liam guffawed. "Don't sound so shocked, man. It has been known."

Annette nodded. "We need to dig further. What if there's a mistress and Bwye wanted to leave his wife but not give her any money? He could have killed Diana and Jane, faked their deaths, got rid of their bodies and then run off with the mistress. Bwye was the only one with a key to both the gun cabinet and the back door, and if the mistress helped then that could explain Jane's car being driven away and destroyed."

Liam gawped. "So he set up all these false trails to throw us off?"

Annette nodded sagely. "Bwye's a clever man. It wouldn't be beyond him."

Andy jumped in. "They could be in the south of France by now!"

Craig had let them run with the theory to hear what emerged. Now he raised a hand, before it turned into the plot of a Bond movie.

"Let's not get carried away. Annette's raised some valid points. Bwye was an angry, violent drunk, and I'm positive we'll find evidence of domestic abuse, but it's a way from there to killing his wife and child. We need to find out if there was a mistress and if Bwye had told anyone he wanted out of the marriage; see where the forensics on the house and car lead and check the background on his business dealings and phone dumps. Bernadette Ross mentioned a secret boyfriend of Jane's that Diana was worried about Bwye disapproving of; who is he? We need the interviews with the other staff members to put together a better picture of that night and we still have the searches and the possibility of a ransom call, so let's not discount all of that."

Annette was still reluctant to give up her theory of Bwye as a guilty man. Her own experience of domestic violence had resulted in a fractured hand and her husband Pete being held for trial. She had zero tolerance with violent men nowadays.

"But you're not ruling out Bwye, sir."

Craig shook his head gently, knowing what was fuelling her determination. "I'm not ruling him out or in yet, Annette. Your theory could prove to be true, but so could the daughter's partner being responsible for this. And before you ask why, I don't know yet. Maybe money. Equally this could have been a home invasion by complete strangers who wanted money and we could still get a ransom call, or maybe it's a revenge attack by someone that The Chronicle hacked off. The fact is we don't have enough evidence to rule on anything yet."

Andy raised a finger to interject. Craig smiled at his politeness; everyone else just barged right in.

"Go ahead, Andy."

"About The Chronicle. You know that Judge Standish gave us the warrant for the phone lines, hey."

Liam grinned. "God bless him."

Craig nodded. "Yes, I heard. Well done."

Andy furrowed his brow. "Aye well, don't get too excited. I've had a call from a mate at Laganside Courts. The Chronicle's already filed an appeal."

Craig sighed. Another court appearance that he didn't need. "It was inevitable. When, and who's appearing?"

"Someone called Ray Mercer's going to court. Tomorrow morning at ten o'clock."

Craig sighed again; it was drowned out by Liam's louder one.

"Is Mercer's the only name on it?"

Andy shook his head. "Cameron Lawton; the editor-in-chief. You need to know that he and Standish have history. I thought the Judge looked very pleased as he signed the warrant so I decided to dig; he and Lawton went to school together."

"Probably kicked him in the nuts during a rugby match and this is Standish's revenge."

Annette shook her head in despair. "Delicate as ever."

But Liam's crude assessment was closer than anyone knew.

Craig nodded. "Everyone in this country went to school with everyone else; it's impossible to avoid."

Annette stage whispered to Andy. "The boss went to school with Dr Winter and D.C.I. Hughes in Vice."

Andy nodded. "And my sister went to Uni with Teflon's daughter, but that's another day's tale. I just thought you should know, in case Lawton accuses Standish of bias in court."

Craig raked his thick hair, tired just picturing the scenario. "I need to be there."

Liam grinned gleefully. "Can I come too, boss? I'd love to watch Mercer get knocked back."

Craig squinted at him. "Only if you promise to keep quiet. Your mouth could lose us the case."

Liam tried to look offended but failed. Craig glanced at the clock; it was after nine and they were all tired.

"Right, that's enough briefing for tonight. Drink, eat, sleep or do whatever you normally do at night, but I want everyone at it bright and early in the morning."

He rose, motioning Davy to join him. They walked out into the cold night and descended a gravel slope onto a patch of frosty grass. When they were far enough away for no-one to eavesdrop, they sat down on a bench. Craig dispensed with any preamble.

"The Chief Constable and I had a chat about you today. He's impressed with your work."

It was hard to tell in the dark but Craig could have sworn that he saw Davy blush.

"I'm impressed as well and I don't want to lose you from the team, but neither will I stand in the way of you getting your doctorate."

Davy didn't know whether to celebrate or say nothing. He settled on the latter and let Craig carry on.

"You're already on the top of the pay scale for analysts, which in itself is a disgrace; you're worth far more than that. But it means that the force can't offer a pay rise to keep you."

Davy's heart sank, its descent only slowed by what he hoped was Craig's impending 'but'. He was right.

"But, because doing a PhD would cost you thousands in fees, and lost salary while you studied, I managed to persuade the C.C. that there might be something we could do there." He glanced at Davy, encouraged by his forward leaning stance. "So...how about you do the PhD part time over a few years and the force gives you time off to study, plus it pays your fees? That way you won't lose your salary, you don't have to find the fee money yourself and we get to keep you on the team?"

As Davy inhaled to answer, Craig added hurriedly. "When you have your doctorate you can join the forensic team, even if you decide to stay based with us, and you'll go onto their pay scale, which is much higher. What do you think?"

Davy paused mid-inhalation and did the sums; it would save him a fortune and it wouldn't prevent him moving into academia or even doing some private work in the future. In fact he could build up his academic reputation and international consulting as he worked. He didn't want to leave the squad but he needed to expand his work beyond what they did every day or he would fall asleep.

As he considered, Craig added the final touch. "I thought you might want to do your doctorate on forensic IT applications in the force and government agencies."

Davy practically squeaked his next words. "You mean MI5?" There was a spy kid in all of them.

Craig shrugged. "Six as well and I'm sure the US agencies would be interested in linking up. It depends what you propose in your research outline I suppose."

MI5, MI6, the CIA, the FBI, Davy's mind was running acronyms like Liam's ran the names of beers. Even in the dark the excitement on his face was unmistakable and he practically shouted his response.

"Yes! Definitely yes. I'll get onto my Prof and talk it through. If I could outline a proposal about the uses of forensic IT in covert and non-covert..."

Craig smiled as he disappeared into a cloud of science speak and decided that Nicky owed him at least one favour for this.

Chapter Seven

Tuesday, 17th December. 9 a.m.

"... court ... in, Nicky?"

Nicky squinted at her phone, trying to make sense of Craig's words through the static. She'd never been to the Glenshane Pass but its mobile phone reception was driving her mad. Thankfully she spoke Craig.

"Court One at ten o'clock. It's the one beside the ground floor lift."

Craig shook his head, all he could make out was 'ten' which he already knew and 'lift' which didn't make any sense at all. So he did what people did when confronted with someone they didn't understand, he shouted. This time Nicky understood. "Text" was fairly unambiguous unless you were a medieval scholar.

Five minutes later Craig knew exactly where he was going and who was likely to be there. The Chronicle was bringing the full weight of its lawyers to bear and he recognised the firm's name: Cherry and Moss. Each day cost their clients approximately two thousand pounds. Craig wondered idly whether it would be Ronald Lewiston. They'd encountered him on a recent case doing his token pro bono work and even then, knowing that he couldn't charge, he'd talked and talked. Craig sighed; if Lewiston was there they would be in court all day.

On the side of the angels were Eugene Standish, who'd decided to appear in defence of his warrant, the police lawyers and some big gun from the C.C.'s office: Assistant Chief Constable John Byrne. Craig had never heard of him but if Sean Flanagan had sent him he must be OK. Liam was huffing back in Derry; if he couldn't say exactly what he wanted to Ray Mercer, he'd decided he might as well stay in the northwest.

By nine-forty Craig had negotiated the traffic in Belfast City Centre and was driving through the back gate of Laganside Courts. A quick park-up and sprint and he'd seated himself in the bright, pine-walled court room just in time. Court One was obviously reserved for minor cases and irritations; they put the really bad boys in the mahogany rooms. He gazed around and saw Eugene Standish robed up as if he was ready to adjudicate on his own appeal. He caught Craig's eye and winked and Craig realised the robe was the equivalent of him wearing an expensive suit to a particularly difficult interview; there to underline his status and scare his opponents. Twenty-first century Woad.

They were the only ones in the courtroom until, at nine-fifty-eight, with an entrance that would have done a Hollywood blockbuster proud, The Belfast Chronicle's team appeared. Craig only recognised one of them; Ray Mercer, all weasel-faced, hook-nosed, five-feet-six of him. He strutted in with an air of self-importance that was badly undermined by the way he dressed. Beside him was an expensively clad man of around forty. It wasn't Ronald Lewiston but he had to be from Cherry and Moss, only an expense account could have afforded that suit. The brief was tall and thin, with an air of world-weariness that said he'd seen it all and thought the case was a waste of his time. The third man in the team was strongly built and regal looking and around Eugene Standish's age; Cameron Lawton, The Chronicle's editor-in-chief. Craig watched as he entered quietly behind the others and took a seat in a separate row. Everything about the man said 'ignore me, I'm not here' but Craig knew people and that very action made Cameron Lawton the one to watch.

Just then two men appeared by Eugene Standish's side. One was dressed in black and white, the force's barrister; the other was a vision of uniformed, shiny-buttoned gravitas, until he smiled, then his stern face softened into someone's dad's. He reached across the others to shake Craig's hand, speaking in a Highland burr.

"You're Craig, aren't you?"

Craig nodded.

"I've heard a lot about you. I'm A.C.C. Byrne, John. We haven't met. I'm on secondment from Scotland for two years."

Craig instantly warmed to him. "How do you like it so

far?"

"Great, it doesn't snow as much here." Byrne laughed loudly, drawing an angry glance from Mercer. Byrne gestured towards him. "One of those misery loves company types, is he?"

Craig made a face. "And the rest."

Their conversation was cut short by the clerk announcing "All rise. The court is now in session, the honourable Judge Donaghy presiding."

Both sides settled down to fight their case and an hour long skirmish ensued, with Ray Mercer yapping like a small dog and the barristers confusing everyone with legalese. Eugene Standish defended his issuing of the warrant, based on Oliver Bwye's connections with The Chronicle and the likelihood that was where any ransom call would come. They could see Donaghy was impressed by his colleague's logic, until Cameron Lawton took the stand.

Lawton took his seat in the witness box and nodded deferentially to the judge, smiling the smile of the deliberately underplayed. Craig felt himself go cold. Lawton was going to smash their case to pieces; he could feel it. In a voice so low and soft that everyone strained to hear, Cameron Lawton cited the independence of the press and civil liberties with an eloquence that would have put Bill Clinton to shame. Much to the defence team's dismay they could see the judge's opinion beginning to shift and Craig knew that when he retired to his chambers to consider there was only one verdict that Donaghy was going to return. They were going to lose their phone taps.

Just as Lawton was summing up with Thomas Jefferson's famous line "To preserve the freedom of the human mind then and freedom of the press, every spirit should be ready to devote itself to martyrdom" Donaghy's clerk appeared through a side door and approached him with a note. The judge read it then nodded at Craig and raised a hand to halt Lawton's flow.

"Gentlemen, it would seem that the defence team's case has just been made."

He beckoned Craig across and handed him the paper

while he brought the others up to date.

"A ransom call was received twenty minutes ago." He turned pointedly to Lawton. "To your direct line at The Chronicle."

At that, Donaghy banged his gavel on the bench with the words. "Case rejected." He smiled at Craig, said "good luck" and dismissed the court. Craig handed the note to John Byrne and slipped out his mobile to call Davy.

"Davy, there's been a call to the editor-in-chief's line at The Chronicle, asking for a six million ransom. Trace it if you can and tell Liam I'm heading there now to interview whoever took the call."

He turned to Eugene Standish in gratitude.

"Thanks for taking a chance on this."

Standish grinned, not because he'd been vindicated but because the development made him feel like he was at the centre of the case.

"Your job's exciting, isn't it? Let me know how it goes."

"I will." He glanced at Byrne. "I need to go."

Byrne nodded. "I'll update the C.C."

Twenty minutes later Craig was in The Belfast Chronicle's offices on St Anne's Square, calming a middle-aged secretary who was gripping her mug of tea as if it was a life belt.

Vera Patterson liked a quiet life, or a moderately quiet one at least; that was why she'd left copywriting in the news room for the more sedate world of the P.A. When Ray Mercer had been made news editor she knew that she'd definitely made the right choice; he ruled the newsroom by fear.

She'd worked for Cameron Lawton for almost two years now, mostly arranging his meetings, taking dictation and making tea. It suited her. Occasionally she got the perk of a trip to a conference abroad, but not so often that it annoyed Brian, her husband of nineteen years.

Cameron Lawton was a brilliant man and brilliant men seemed to her to fall into two camps; either thoughtful academics like Lawton, or aggressive bullies like his predecessor, Oliver Bwye. If Bwye had offered her the job of P.A. she'd definitely have said no, but thankfully he'd taken Bernie Ross to work for him and she'd taken over as Lawton's P.A. Bwye had left in 2012 so she'd been surprised when the man who'd phoned forty minutes earlier had mentioned his name.

Craig sat down beside her, watching as her violently shaking hands gradually stilled. When he was sure that she was ready to answer, he walked her through the previous hour.

"Can you tell me what you were doing when the call came in, Mrs Patterson?"

She stared at him blankly, as if she hadn't heard. He repeated the question and eventually she screwed up her face in thought.

"I was...oh yes, I was filling some envelopes."

"With what?"

Craig couldn't care less what she'd been filling the envelopes with, but the small talk was putting her at ease.

Her face lit up. "We're running a competition for the best fundraising scheme in Northern Ireland and I was sending out the entry forms."

The Chronicle's sudden philanthropy had to be Lawton's idea; it hadn't been a feature of Oliver Bwye's reign.

"And how was that going?"

"I was nearly half way through when the telephone rang. It was to Mr Lawton's line but that automatically redirects to me when he doesn't answer."

Good. She'd brought up the phone call herself. Craig let her talk.

"I picked it up and a man spoke. Actually he was whispering, so I had to ask him to speak up."

Craig interrupted in a casual voice, so as not to scare her off. "Did he sound like he had a sore throat?"

Vera shook her greying head. "No, no, he wasn't hoarse, just whispering." She pursed her lips. "I thought it was someone playing silly buggers, we get hoax calls all the time."

Craig gestured at the phone on her desk. "To this line?"

She furrowed her brow. "Well, no, to the news desk mainly, but I thought perhaps he'd come through to the wrong place. I know most of Mr Lawton's regular callers."

The words were said with a pride that Craig recognised from Nicky; the sign of a good P.A. was to know who was calling their boss before they gave their name. He nodded her on.

"He spoke up a little, but not much. And when he said what he said...well, at first I thought it was a joke."

Craig smiled encouragingly. "What exactly did he say?"

"He said 'six million for them'. Well, I'd no idea what he was talking about, had I? So I asked him, six million for what? That was when he said 'the Bwyes'." She gave him an anguished look. "I didn't like Mr Bwye, nobody did, but I wouldn't wish that on anyone."

Craig thought for a moment. How had she known that it wasn't a hoax? They'd kept the information about the Bwyes' disappearance as secret as they could. And why had she phoned the court instead of Cameron Lawton's mobile or the police? He asked the questions and she blushed.

"My friend works in legal and she told me all about the case this morning, so I checked Mr Lawton's diary." She rolled her eyes. "He's always putting in meetings and not telling me. How he expects me to keep track and not double-book him, I don't know."

It was a cry he'd heard from Nicky many times.

"I tried his mobile but it was off so I phoned the court."

It made sense. "OK, Mrs Patterson, tell me more about the call."

She shrugged apologetically. "That's really all he said. After he said 'the Bwyes' he said 'no police' and hung up."

"Nothing else? No instructions for paying the money, or a deadline?"

She looked puzzled. "Now you mention it, that was strange, wasn't it? I suppose that means he'll phone back."

They hoped.

"Was there anything about his voice? Did he have an accent, or could you perhaps tell me his age?"

"Yes."

Craig was surprised by her confident tone and by the fact that she hadn't mentioned it before.

"Which? Age or accent?"

"Both. He was young, twenties I'd say, and he had a west Belfast accent."

It was very specific and he said as much.

"Age is easy; if you answer calls all day like I do you can tell age from a voice. His was young, he might even have been in his teens but definitely not as old as thirty."

"And his accent?" It was the first Craig had heard of a difference between an east and west Belfast voice.

Vera Patterson nodded firmly. "You can tell. First of all a Belfast accent is easy to spot, wouldn't you agree?"

Craig couldn't argue with her on that and it dawned on him that if he could tell a south Belfast accent, which he could, why shouldn't someone else be able to tell east from west.

"Agreed, but what's the difference between east and west?"

"East Belfast is sharp and flat, west Belfast is sharp but much faster. Plus it goes up and down more, and some of the words are said like Irish words."

"Like?"

She'd lost him and she knew it. "Just trust me, Superintendent. I'm from west Belfast and I know a west Belfast man."

West Belfast, not west of the Bann; it was a new twist for the Derry based case. Craig shook her hand and left, apologising that she'd have to recount her story again in a statement. He was exiting The Chronicle's offices onto St Anne's Square just as Cameron Lawton entered. Lawton stopped and smiled at him.

"Good for you, Superintendent."

Craig wasn't sure which 'good for you' he was referring to; winning the case or being right in the first place. Lawton read his mind.

"You were right to tap us. I thought so all along, but the lawyers wanted me to fight it; in case it established a precedent and you decided to tap us every other week." He chuckled. "As if you've nothing better to do."

Craig gave a tight smile. "We'll need to keep the traces on."

Lawton nodded. "I understand." His expression changed to a more solemn one. "I hope you catch the bastards. Oliver Bwye isn't a nice man and he's made a lot of enemies, but still..."

"Any particular enemies spring to mind?"

"How long have you got?" Lawton's quiet voice became angry. "Bwye ruined lives, Superintendent, unnecessarily so in many cases. Newspapers might have to report the truth but we can do it responsibly and he didn't. He reported unfounded allegations, many of which turned out to be false, but by then all anyone remembered were the headlines. A three-line apology buried on page ten could never reverse the harm."

Lawton and Bwye sounded like journalistic chalk and cheese. Craig had an idea.

"Would you be prepared to make a list of Bwye's possible enemies for us?"

Lawton nodded. "If you think it would be of help."

"Definitely."

"Then I'll send it through. Now, I'd better make sure that Vera's OK."

He turned to go and then turned back, extending his hand. Craig shook it. He didn't like journalists, they'd twisted his words in ways that had harmed cases too many times, but his gut said that Cameron Lawton was that rare media bird who only ever told the truth.

Chapter Eight

The Lab. 12.30 p.m.

"To what do I owe this honour?"

As he spoke, John Winter set down the book that he was reading and moved to switch on the percolator, a sequence he'd performed a thousand times before when Craig had arrived at his lab. He was surprised when Craig shook his head.

"Not for me, John, I can't stay. I'm just here to give you a heads up that we may need your services soon."

John's eyes widened. "You've found the Bwyes?"

"No, but we've had a ransom call and we both know that kidnaps rarely end well."

The pathologist nodded glumly and flicked on the percolator anyway. Craig glanced at the clock and changed his mind about staying, taking a seat. He had ten minutes before he needed to head to Docklands; he could spend them having coffee with his friend. As they drank, he filled John in on everything, ending with the details of the ransom call.

John whistled. "Six million! They're ambitious."

Craig made a face. "Or they already know they'll never get it because the Bwyes are dead."

"Did they offer proof of life?"

Craig halted mid-sip, shocked that the idea hadn't occurred to him; he'd asked Vera Patterson about a deadline but not proof that the Bwyes were still alive. Pessimism or premonition? The caller hadn't offered anything in exchange for the money, which meant that either he thought the Bwyes' lawyers were stupid enough to cough up cash on request or...the kidnapper was as stupid as he was and offering proof of life hadn't occurred to him. Then there was the third option; that his pessimism was warranted and the Bwyes were already dead.

"No...they didn't." Craig outlined his thoughts and watched as John shook his head. "You disagree that they're dead?"

John wavered. "Possibly... Well yes, actually, I do. Once they're dead it's only a matter of time before the bodies are found, unless they've hidden them somewhere very secluded. And if you'd just killed three people would you take the risk of calling a major newspaper, with all its resources, never mind that it would get the police involved, if they weren't already? It would take balls of steel and there aren't too many men with those in Northern Ireland. Even the psychopaths here cry for their mammies."

Craig smiled at the imagery. "So...what?"

"I think they're still alive, or at least some of them are. Even the thickest thug knows you need a bargaining chip."

Craig pondered for a moment and then drained his cup. "There's one way to find out. Next time they ring we ask for proof of life."

He sprang to his feet more energised than when he'd arrived. John wondered if coffee had an extra effect on him because of his Italian genes; Latin rocket fuel.

"Thanks, John, that helped, but I meant what I said about keeping yourself available."

"Mike's already in Derry."

"I still think we'll have more than one body to P.M."

****

Craig's trip to the C.C.U. lasted just long enough to sign the letters that Nicky pushed in front of him, each obligingly marked with a pencil 'X' where she needed his name, and to talk Jake and Carmen through the boxes of paperwork that Joanne Greer's solicitors had sent through. As Jake said, there was very little appealing about her appeal.

Craig's head said that Greer had no hope of getting her sentence overturned, but he still had a gnawing doubt. Greer had been Machiavellian enough to organise three contract killings without having any funds transferred in her name. They'd only convicted her with circumstantial evidence and the assistance of a now dead man. They'd been fortunate with their judge and jury first time, but even he had to admit that a different court might not convict her again.

He left the squad-room deep in thought and began the journey back to the northwest. It was only when he was thirty miles up the road that he suddenly remembered he hadn't called Katy to say that he would be in town. Damn; they could have had lunch at least; she must be feeling nervous about him working with Julia. He turned down the CD he'd been playing and tapped his carphone. She answered quickly, in a cheerful tone.

"Hello, pet. How are you?"

Craig smiled at her voice. It was as pretty as she was and its sound always cheered him up.

"Fine. Where are you?"

Katy gazed around her, wondering how to explain that she'd played hooky to go to a beauty salon. She couldn't because that would mean saying *why* she was there and that would give away her surprise, so she lied, choosing an option that would explain the music playing in the background.

"I nipped home to collect a file and stayed for a late lunch."

She forgot that she was dealing with a man trained to spot lies. Craig heard her fib immediately and frowned, wondering what it was about. He shrugged it off just as quickly. Whatever she was lying about he would find out eventually, and there was no part of him that believed it was something bad. Katy was still talking.

"How's the case?"

"Dire. We're no closer to finding them and we've just had a ransom demand."

Her gasp reminded Craig that kidnap and ransom didn't feature in normal people's days so he softened the words with "hopefully we'll get them back." He gave her a few seconds to recover before changing the subject. "John's planning a surprise for Natalie." He added hastily, "But you can't tell her."

She laughed. "You're hopeless at keeping secrets. What is it?"

Craig pretended to be offended. "I can't tell you, it's a secret."

"Are you sulking?"

Silence.

"Marc?"

He played silent long enough to worry her, knowing exactly what her next words would be.

"I didn't mean to upset you."

Craig laughed and she spluttered.

"You pig, you were winding me up."

"It's so easy, I couldn't resist it. The secret is that John's been working like a navvy on the house and I've been helping him. You should see it, it looks great. He's going to show Natalie when we all get back from Derry; we just need to add some finishing touches for the party."

"Party! A Christmas party?"

He knew she was already visualising her outfit, almost certainly something festive and red. They chatted for a moment longer then she glanced at the clock, knowing that the hairdresser would return soon to dry her hair. It would be hard to explain the sound of a turbo-charged hairdryer when she was only supposed to be collecting a file.

"I'd better go, Marc. I've a clinic at two."

Another lie. Craig smiled knowingly; she was up to something and it obviously involved him or she would have told him straight out. Whatever it was would be fun, he knew that much. He glanced at the roundabout ahead and followed the signs for the Glenshane road.

"OK, pet. I'm almost there." He paused, wondering whether to say what was on his mind. "Katy...I..."

She didn't make him say it. "I miss you too, Marc, and I love you." Then, with a mysterious laugh, she hung up the phone.

****

The Rocksbury Estate. 4 p.m.

"OK, everyone grab a coffee, please. We're ready to start."

Craig took a seat behind Oliver Bwye's desk and glanced idly at the book shelves, wondering which of the books contained booze. He could do with a drink after the day he'd had. He made do with coffee while the others brought in chairs from the main room. Andy and Liam turned them round, to sit with their arms hanging over the backs, Annette crossed her knees primly and Davy lounged elegantly on a small chaise longue, looking as if he was in a nightclub.

"Anyone know where Julia and Gerry are?"

Annette answered. "At the station, interviewing the cook and head gardener."

Craig nodded. "Good. Who's taking the grounds men?"

Andy jerked his head at Liam. "We're doing the honours tomorrow morning, hey."

"OK. Right, I'll update you on the developments this morning first then we'll go round each of you one by one."

Liam knew from Craig's face that it wasn't good news. "Rough day in court?"

"And looking like it'll be an even rougher week." Craig sighed heavily. "OK, first The Chronicle's appeal. It was thrown out."

Andy gave a small "Yeh!" but Craig shook his head.

"We were lucky; it was definitely going to be granted. The paper's editor-in-chief, Cameron Lawton, was wiping the floor with us."

Liam gave a puzzled frown. "Why wasn't it then?"

"Because the judge got a call from The Chronicle's offices in the nick of time. A blackmail demand came through on Lawton's personal line."

Liam leaned over his chair eagerly. "What did they ask for?"

"I'll come onto that in a minute. Anyway, when the call came through it vindicated the phone taps and the judge ruled for us." He turned to Davy. "Did you record the call?"

Davy nodded and gestured at his smart-pad. "Do you w...want me to play it?"

"In a moment."

Liam cut in again, keen to move Craig along. "So you headed to The Chronicle's offices, and then what?"

"You were at the back of the queue when patience was

handed out, weren't you."

"At the front for charisma, though."

Craig had to laugh; more at the fact Liam believed it than at his joke.

"OK, I went to The Chronicle and spoke to Lawton's P.A., Vera Patterson. She took the call at ten-fifty-five. It was on divert from Lawton's direct line. Before we listen to it she had a few things to say about Oliver Bwye. So did Lawton. Bwye was more than unpopular, he was hated. Mrs Patterson said she could never have worked for him. She was a copywriter at the paper when Bwye was there and only became a P.A. when Lawton took over. He's a different kettle of fish entirely, bit of a philanthropist; they organise charity campaigns nowadays."

Liam interrupted. "In between the crap they still print. Lawton can't be that different if he gave Ray Mercer control of the news desk."

Craig shrugged. "I'm not sure that was his decision; the Board and shareholders have a big say and the crap Mercer writes sells a lot of papers. You know I'm not a fan of journalists but Lawton seems decent. He said Bwye made a lot of enemies because of the vicious way he reported, but also because he reported things that were just allegations and then, when they were proved wrong, he only issued a brief retraction buried somewhere near the back page. He ruined people's lives."

Andy raised a finger to interrupt. "Any chance Lawton can give us a list of names, hey?"

Craig nodded. "He's pulling it together now."

Liam shook his head. "If someone printed something false about me I'd shove their bloody paper down their throat."

Craig shuddered, not at Liam's threat but at the power of the press. People were so impressionable that once something was in print they believed it was true and it was almost impossible to convince them otherwise. Mud definitely stuck. He continued in a brisk tone.

"OK, the ransom call came through just before eleven and Vera Patterson answered it because Lawton's phone was on divert. She knew Lawton was in court and she knew what he was there for, not because he'd told her but because someone in The Chronicle's legal department had. Quite a few staff at the paper knew that the Bwyes were missing even before the call came in."

Liam shook his head like a hanging judge refusing a reprieve. "Someone in legal has a big mouth. It'll be all over Facebook soon."

Craig nodded. "You're right, so we need to control the message. I'm going to enlist Lawton's help with that. Before we get to that let's cover the call. First, why Cameron Lawton's direct line rather than the news desk?"

Davy glanced up from his pad. "Because they didn't want it to be common knowledge and they thought Lawton w...would deal with it more responsibly?"

Annette chipped in. "Because Lawton knows Bwye personally and so do his staff?"

Andy added. "Maybe it's symbolic, hey? That used to be Oliver Bwye's phone line."

Craig nodded. "Good points. There's also the possibility that because we're talking big money the kidnappers think Lawton can most afford to help. He holds power at the paper."

Liam shook his head. "You've just said that he doesn't like Bwye."

"I also said he's a bit of a philanthropist, and maybe he likes Diana Bwye. OK, whatever the motive was, the call came through to Lawton's personal line and Vera Patterson answered." He turned to Davy. "Did you get anything on the caller?"

"Not yet. It traced back to a call box in Waterloo Place in town. I'm pulling the traffic cams and CCTV now."

Liam shook his head. "What's with the call box? Why do the bad guys always think call boxes are safe? They watch too many old movies."

"Just as well for us that they're stupid. Let's hear it, Davy."

They listened attentively as Davy played the call and then played it a second time on Craig's prompt. When it had finished, Craig threw open the floor. Annette was the first to speak.

"He's young; late teens or early twenties. And

nervous, that's why he sounds hoarse. Plus he's whispering. He probably thought it would disguise his voice."

Andy shot her a sceptical look. "Nervous! I'd say he was bricking it, hey. Doesn't sound anywhere near tough enough to kidnap three people and leave all that blood."

He gestured at the parquet floor and all eyes followed his move. Craig glanced at Liam. He was strangely silent.

"What are you thinking?"

Liam screwed up his face as if he wasn't sure of his ground, an unusual feeling for him.

"Come on. It doesn't matter how ridiculous it sounds."

Liam shrugged. If the boss didn't mind hearing his useless speculation then he didn't mind giving it.

"He's from Belfast, west Belfast."

It was exactly what Vera Patterson had said but Craig wanted the reasons why.

"Why do you say that?"

Liam stared at him as if he was an idiot. "The accent."

Craig sighed. "Yes, but what about it and why west as opposed to anywhere else?"

Liam glanced at the others for support. "OK, is there anyone here who doesn't think that voice comes from Belfast?"

He was answered by a series of shaken heads.

"Right, so that leaves us with north, south, east or west." He turned to Annette; she had a talent for accents that only ever came out at party time. "Annette – do a south Belfast accent for us."

She gave a perfect impression of a voice from the Malone Road.

"Now east."

She changed her inflection, flattened and elongated her vowels and they could have been on the Newtownards Road. She knew west Belfast was coming next, so without urging she recited 'Mary had a little lamb' in a perfect west Belfast twang.

"I can't do north."

Davy grinned at her with new found respect. "Do east again."

Craig shook his head. "Save it for the pub. But tell me what you altered to make it sound like west Belfast."

Annette folded her hands in her lap as if she was preparing to give a master class. "I'd advise you to get a linguist to listen to the tape, sir, but I think Liam's right. It sounds like west Belfast to me. The speech is very fast and some of the intonation sounds like he's an Irish speaker."

Craig looked at the others. "Anyone disagree?"

Andy shrugged. "I haven't a clue, but he definitely doesn't come from up here."

Craig wasn't good with Belfast accents, although he could name a London one to within ten streets. He'd only lived in Belfast for ten years of his life; three when he'd been at Uni and seven since he'd returned from the big smoke.

"OK, Davy, get it to the language lab and see what they have to say. For now let's say that we have a young, frightened west Belfast lad. What else?"

Annette considered for a moment. "Shall I write the call up on the board?"

"Excellent idea."

A moment later the board bore the words; caller says 'six million for them' then Vera Patterson asks 'six million for what?' Followed by the caller's replies; 'the Bwyes' and 'no police'.

Craig squinted at the words and then turned back to the group.

"Any comments?"

Annette shrugged as if what she was about to say was obvious. "He assumed she would already know who he wanted the six million for, sir."

Craig turned to Annette. "Yes, he did. But not just her; he assumed that Cameron Lawton would know. Why?"

She answered eagerly. "Because Lawton is a newspaper man and gossip travels fast in that world?"

"Perhaps. What else?"

Andy interjected. Craig was glad he'd stopped raising a finger to ask permission. "Because he thought The Chronicle already had the story?"

Craig made a face that said he wasn't convinced.

"Why would he think that? We've kept it very quiet. It hasn't been in the press or on TV."

Andy shook his head. He had nothing to back it up but that didn't mean that he was wrong. Craig threw him a bone.

"He might have *wanted* the press to know, to get the word out there. Saying 'six million for them' would make any good journalist start to dig. It wouldn't take long for it to become a headline."

Andy nodded sagely as if that was what he'd meant all along. Craig noticed Liam and Davy exchanging meaningful looks.

"Nothing to say, you two? That's a first."

Davy answered for both of them. "W…We think they're playing with us."

It wasn't the reply Craig had expected. "In what way?"

Liam picked up the conversation. "OK, they lift a family from west of the Bann but get a west Belfast man to ring. They know it's not in the press yet, but they call a newspaper to deliver the ransom demand. They tell us they want money but don't say how to get it to them, and then they say no police, when odds on someone has already seen us milling around outside." He crossed his arms and leaned further forward over his chair. "I…we think they're winding us up to waste time.

Maybe or maybe not. The wasted time would tell. They'd spent enough time on the phone call; there was nothing more they could do on it until the linguists and CCTV searches were complete. Craig started round the group on other things. Liam went first.

"Nothing new so far. We've doubled the search perimeter, like you asked."

"What's the terrain like?"

"Mostly fields. There's a small wood to the north and a lake about half a mile northwest." He gestured towards the back door. "The C.S.I.s found car tracks leading away from the door last Thursday, but they disappeared after about a mile. They were heading due north but they could easily have changed direction after they lost them. I checked the weather; it was freezing cold Wednesday night with just the odd shower, so we were lucky they even found those."

"They were heading towards the wood?"

"Or the estate's back exit." He made a face. "Possibly towards the lake as well. Like I said."

"I'm presuming they took casts, so anything specific yet?"

Davy chipped in. "They belong to a van of s...some sort; I'm chasing possible models."

"Didn't Bwye have CCTV around the perimeter?"

Liam shook his head. "Nope. For an alleged bastard he was a very trusting man." He gestured at Davy. "The lad's pulling everything he can from the traffic cams on the main road but there aren't many round here; it's Hicksville Arizona."

Andy snorted. "Says the sophisticate from Crossgar."

Craig nodded his head tiredly. "OK. Concentrate the search around the lake tomorrow."

Liam's face fell. "You think..."

"I don't think anything yet, except that if I wanted my trail to disappear I'd use water. The ground around lakes is always a mess; it's the perfect place to transfer them to another vehicle and then churn up the mud to cover their tracks." He turned to Davy. "Davy, check out the local boat owners and anyone who uses that lake regularly. Find out if the Bwyes had exclusive rights or if it's public property."

Andy nodded. "It's definitely worth a look, hey. We'll move the men there at first light and see what we can find."

"Right. Anything else?"

Annette looked embarrassed, as if she thought she'd overstepped the mark. "I had a word with Julia about Jane's car."

Craig raised an eyebrow. Half of him was surprised and half pleased. He hadn't relished raising the topic with her but he knew that it had to be done. "And?"

"She said they'd no idea that Jane even had a car. It didn't show up on the routine checks. She was right; the only cars registered to the Bwyes were Oliver Bwye's Jaguar and Diana's Honda."

"Bernadette Ross knew the registration number."

Annette shrugged. "It's easy to remember. Perhaps it was registered in someone else's name."

Craig was puzzled. "But she saw Jane driving it towards the house that day."

"Did she, sir? She saw the car but she might have assumed that Jane was the driver. I'll ask again and get to the bottom of it." She shrugged as if the point was redundant. "Either way the car's been found."

Craig leaned on the desk. "Burnt out." He shook his head glumly. "Any useful forensics will have been destroyed."

Liam nodded sagely. "Just like the torcher planned that they would be, but that doesn't mean we can't still get something useful from Ross. Jane may not have been driving it that day and Ross could just have said that to divert us."

Craig shook his head. "Then she wouldn't have mentioned seeing it at all and drawing our attention to it. Davy, find out who the Mercedes was registered to and who bought it. There's no way that Jane had a car without her mother knowing; they were too close."

"You think her mum bought it for her?"

"And paid for the insurance. But it wasn't registered in either of their names so perhaps it's in the boyfriend's. Diana mightn't have thought he was so unsuitable after all."

Annette persisted. "What if Ross *didn't* see Jane driving? What if she just saw the car, a car that she'd seen Jane in before, and assumed that it was her behind the wheel?"

Craig considered for a moment. It raised several questions: whether Jane's boyfriend had driven the car to the house that evening, or Jane had and either or both of them were involved in the kidnap. Or did a more innocent scenario apply? Where Jane had gone to see her mother because she knew her father was at the golf-club, and she knew he wouldn't have seen her in the car. Whichever it was they would find out.

"OK, check that out and keep me up to date. Andy, any more word on the blood forensics?"

"They've matched the types. One matched to Diana

Bwye from hairs on her comb and one to Oliver Bwye from his toothbrush."

"Anything on the girl?"

"Not yet. The third DNA was canine, hey."

"A dog! Did they have one?"

"Aye, the girl had a Yorkie. No-one's seen it for days."

Craig nodded. Cut the parents and kill the dog, it would terrify the girl and keep her quiet. But why not cut her as well? Was Jane part of the plot or the kidnapper's main prize? Or perhaps she'd been killed in some other way? If the whole thing was a family annihilation, Oliver Bwye was easily smart enough to leave his blood to throw them off the track. Family annihilators normally killed the youngest first, to make the others suffer by watching, but the absence of Jane's blood didn't mean that she wasn't dead; strangulation or snapping her neck wouldn't have left any trail.

"OK, more questions to answer. What about the forensics in the main room? Annette, did Ross notice anything out of place in here?"

Andy answered first. "The main room was covered in prints. It seems Diana Bwye held some of her charity meetings here; we're eliminating the groups' members now."

Annette interjected. "Ross said she hadn't noticed anything out of place in there, so I brought her back this afternoon for another look. Forensics put everything back where it was when they arrived on Thursday morning and the only thing Ross noticed out of place was the whisky decanter. Oliver Bwye was the only whisky drinker and he always kept it on the table beside the hearth, but it was on a lamp table across the room when the police first arrived. It'd already been printed so I've put a rush on those."

Craig looked thoughtful. Was it possible that whoever had taken the Bwyes had been so confident of not being disturbed that they'd poured themselves a whisky? He prayed their killers had been that arrogant.

"Good. OK, Liam and Davy, anything new?"

They both shook their heads and Liam said what Craig already knew. "Everything is happening that can be happening and we're seeing the last of the domestic staff in the a.m. Unless we catch a break or something new happens it's just going to be hard slog."

He was right. There was nothing more they could do until tomorrow. He glanced at the clock; it was almost six o'clock.

"OK, good work all of you. There's no point you all hanging about here tonight so I suggest that everyone goes home to Belfast or wherever they want to go. We'll hold on to the rooms at the hotel."

Liam was halfway out the door when Craig thought of something and beckoned him back.

"The dog."

"What about it? I can't stand small dogs. Yappy wee things."

"What are the odds Jane wouldn't have had it micro-chipped? And GPS tagged. A dog that size on a thousand acre estate could die if they didn't trace it quickly."

Liam grinned in admiration. "Very clever. The NSPCA would be proud of you."

Craig turned towards Davy, to see him packing his bag, ready to leave.

"Davy, get onto the local vets first thing tomorrow. I want that dog found."

"W...Will do, chief."

As Liam resumed his bolt for the door Davy followed after, struggling to keep up with Liam's two man strides.

"Can I get a lift to Belfast?"

"As long as you don't moan about how fast I drive. I'll pick you up in the morning and bring you back."

Andy gathered his things for the short drive back to Portstewart which only left Annette and Craig in the room.

Annette smiled sympathetically at her boss. "Are you staying here tonight, sir?"

Craig yawned. He could do with an early night, but he'd rather spend one with Katy. Except she'd made it clear that she was on-call at the hospital.

"Looks like it. Don't hang around on my account, Annette. I'm sure you and Mike must have plans."

Annette blushed, still unused to being part of a new

couple. "The new Hobbit movie's on at the Brunswick Bowl." She paused and then added. "You're welcome to join us."

Craig laughed. "No thanks. I don't fancy playing gooseberry. You enjoy yourself; I've got plenty of work to keep me busy."

A moment later he was alone in Oliver Bwye's study, feeling sorry for himself. After a brief sulk he decided to put the evening to good use and run through the case again from the beginning. He was just retracing Bernadette Ross' initial discovery when his mobile rang and Katy's name flashed up. He answered the call eagerly.

"Hi pet, how's your on-call?"

"Cancelled."

"Did someone else take it?"

"You could say that."

He could barely hear her; the echo on the line was so bad. As he walked into the main room to improve the reception he realised that the echo wasn't coming from Belfast but from the Bwyes' glass-walled living room. Katy was standing in front of him, wearing the prettiest dress that he'd seen in a long time, saying the words as they emerged from his phone. Craig smiled and hung up.

"How did you get here?"

"Train and then taxi. I had the day off."

This was why she'd lied to him earlier.

"So you weren't at home collecting a file."

She shook her blonde curls. "I was at the hairdressers. What do you think?" She held out her hand. "Come along, we have a table booked at Browns. It's supposed to be great. Then I'm taking you back to your hotel for dessert. And I warn you, I have wicked intent on your body."

He took her hand and pulled her towards him, wrapping her in his arms and giving her a lingering kiss.

"We could always cut straight to dessert..."

She wriggled out of his arms, laughing again.

"Oh no, you don't. I'm starving, and it's not every day you get to buy me a five-star meal."

Chapter Nine

What to do, what to do. They'd deviated so far from their original path that it was hard to reverse, and yet...part of him still pictured years ahead of love and warmth, ignoring their unfortunate start. She was fearful and spoilt, but still young. They both were, but they could still have a decent life.

But it wasn't his choice alone. So much hinged on what happened next: on the police, the newspaper and the lawyers most of all. Their future was in their hands and one wrong move would crush it. He prayed that they would capitulate with the ransom and then let them live their lives in peace.

He doubted that they would; life never worked that way.

****

Wednesday. Six a.m.

Craig hadn't slept at all. Not only because Katy's visit had meant company and warmth, talking and love-making into the wee small hours. He hadn't slept even when she had; lying awake instead, imagining the fate of the Bwyes.

The caller hadn't specified when and where they wanted the ransom, meaning he couldn't picture the venue for the drop and ready his men. But it wasn't that which stole his sleep, it was a creeping uneasiness that something, even more than the obvious something, was very wrong. He couldn't put his finger on it. Each time he got close it slipped away and he jerked awake chasing it, with it far too far away to catch.

At six a.m. he gave up and slipped quietly out of bed for an early shower, closing the bathroom door and keeping the water to a trickle so as not to make a noise. Katy woke as soon as he moved and lay wondering what was troubling him so much. The case of course; some aspect of it was beyond his control. But not only that, there was something more. She could hazard a guess at what it was, but she needed to hear it from him if she was to be of any help.

She'd seen changes in him in the past few weeks; he was sharper, quicker to anger and there were fewer and shorter smiles, even for her. He'd been drinking too much as well, often alone, the signs obvious when she'd arrived at his flat. It hadn't been helped by John's enthrallment with his new marriage, meaning that their once frequent boys' nights were a thing of the past. But that wasn't the cause of the changes, and the moods and drink weren't all; there was a still, coiled aggression in him nowadays, as if he was a gun just waiting to go off.

Craig returned, washed, dressed and ready to leave, interrupting her analysis. He gazed down at her like a parent with a naughty child.

"You're supposed to be asleep."

Her smile widened to a grin. "Remind me to tell myself off."

She nodded at the kettle and as it boiled she took his hand and pulled him to sit on the bed, gazing at him with a question. He shook his head.

"I don't know what's bothering me, pet; something just feels off. Like there's a whole dimension in this case I'm missing."

It was as close to an admission that he was out of sorts as she was going to get today; personal things would have to wait. She slipped from bed and brought back two coffees, then summarised in a logical tone.

"OK, three people have disappeared and there's a lot of blood belonging to the elder Bwyes and a dog, probably the daughter's. The girl's blood isn't there, so either she went quietly or she was in on it. Now you have a ransom demand which you're assuming is for all three. That's hopeful isn't it?"

Craig wanted to say yes but he couldn't. He shook his head.

"They could be dead and the bastards would still ask for ransom."

"But they must know that you won't give it without proof of life."

Craig sipped his coffee. "Not necessarily. If the estate's lawyers want to pay it then we can't stop them. We can only advise. If they have the sense to ask for proof of life then we might stand a chance."

His dull tone told Katy the money was secondary. As she scanned Craig's face her jaw dropped.

"You think it was an inside job!"

He glanced at her admiringly, knowing that she'd read something in his face. She was right; he did think someone in the family had organised it; it was partly what had wrecked his sleep. He played devil's advocate, interested in what else she might have to say.

"What makes you say that?"

"It's written all over you. But why would Oliver Bwye arrange for himself to be kidnapped as well? Unless..."

"Yes?"

"He wanted rid of the wife and daughter but didn't want to be implicated. He wants to look like a victim too." Her eyes widened. "What if he wants to start a new life elsewhere with someone else? But he couldn't do that if he was locked up for kidnapping or murder."

It made sense, especially if, as they suspected, Bwye had a mistress, but something still wasn't ringing true. He rose to leave and her face fell.

"Did I say something wrong?"

He was surprised, then he looked at what his actions had said; not commenting on her idea and then heading for the door, anyone would think that it was their fault. He was thoughtless nowadays. He retook his seat and leaned in to kiss her.

"You've said everything right, pet. I'm sorry, but I'm just a million miles away. Go back to sleep for a while, you've a long trip back to Belfast."

Katy grinned mischievously and tucked the covers tightly round her neck. "And a whole morning's shopping to do before I go."

****

9 a.m.

Craig faced the small group and saw their bleary eyes matched his own. Liam's boomed-out words said that he'd noticed as well.

"You look like crap, boss. Bad night?"

Craig came back like lightning. "I didn't sleep. What's your excuse?"

Andy guffawed loudly. "You'll not try that one again."

Liam was undeterred. "Even on my worst day I'm prettier than you, White."

Craig let the talk continue for a moment then, when everyone had a coffee and Danish in their hands, he started to report.

"You all know about the ransom call. We have the amount but no venue and no proof of life as yet, so they'll have to call back *if* they want their money."

Even he was surprised that he'd added the caveat. Who wouldn't want their money? And yet he'd said *if*. He moved on quickly.

"We have to treat this as a real chance to get the Bwyes back safely, so I've notified the estate's lawyers to do whatever they have to do to gather the cash."

Annette cut in. She was the only one of them that didn't look like death warmed up and Craig knew she'd avoided the overheated hotel and a long drive by staying at Mike's nearby holiday home.

"Are we going to pay them, sir?"

Craig shook his head. "I hope it doesn't come to that, although we can't stop the estate if they want to." He took a sip of coffee and carried on. "Thanks to Andy and Julia we have the taps in place on the phones if they call back. OK, what else?" The question was rhetorical. "We have two of the Bwye's DNAs confirmed and the third DNA was canine, so there's a dog somewhere injured or dead that we haven't found yet."

Liam interjected. "We don't know which two of the Bwye's the blood belongs to yet, do we?"

Craig rolled his eyes. "Were you asleep yesterday? We matched it to Oliver and Diana Bwye."

"Oh. Aye well, I was probably thinking deep thoughts

when you said it."

"I don't think 'what's for dinner' counts as a deep thought." He turned to Davy. "How are we doing with the background checks?"

Davy shook his head and Craig noticed a new flash of green amongst his black hair. He didn't ask.

"It's s...slow going. So far I've found that one of the grounds men, Brendan Gordon, has a record for assault -"

Craig cut in sharply. "What sort of assault?"

"W...With a deadly weapon. He was eighteen. He was attacked in the s...street by a couple of guys and pulled a knife."

Liam spluttered into his drink. "That's self-defence, or at worst carrying a dangerous weapon! What numpty categorised it as assault?"

Davy scanned the screen for a name. "The prosecution barrister was Rory Davis. Do you know him?"

Liam rolled his eyes. "Old boy. He should have been put out to pasture years ago."

Craig interrupted. "What age is Gordon now, Davy, and who was the arresting officer?"

"He's twenty-five and it was a D.I. Terence Harrison." As he said it Davy's eyes widened. "Is that Teflon?"

Liam and Andy nodded together. "Yep."

Terry Harrison had been a creep even when he'd been an inspector. He'd landed a youngster with a serious record just for defending himself.

"Did the boy do time?"

Davy nodded. "Two years in Magilligan, out in one on licence."

Craig shook his head. If Brendan Gordon hadn't gone into prison a criminal he'd sure as hell come out as one.

"What's his record been like since?"

"Minor offences. Mostly petty theft. There was a GBH charge in 2010 just after his licence expired but he w...wasn't convicted."

Craig nodded. "Let me have the details of everything as soon as you can; I'll interview Gordon myself. Liam, I'd like you with me on that."

Liam was puzzled; two senior officers interviewing

Gordon seemed like overkill, but his was not to reason why. Craig continued.

"Right, unless none of you left here last night, which would have been above and beyond the call of duty, I'll assume we're still where we were at six p.m. yesterday. That means you all know what you've got to get on with. Yes?"

He was answered by a staggered series of nods that didn't convince him. "OK, humour me and let's go round. Annette?"

Annette smiled confidently. "I'm seeing Ross again to press her harder on the car and dog, and I was going to ask her more about Oliver Bwye's sex life, sir."

Liam's eyes widened as if he hadn't had sex for a year. Craig continued before he said something rude.

"Good. I'm particularly interested in any mistresses Bwye's had through the years, right up to the present day."

Liam gazed at him curiously. "You really think Bwye staged everything to run off with some woman?"

Craig shrugged. "It would be cheaper than a divorce. If he's found injured and the only survivor, he'll think we'll see him as a victim and be free to start a new life. He wouldn't be the first person to underestimate the police."

Liam shook his head. "I can see him killing the wife but why the daughter?"

Craig had no answer and he wouldn't have until they found the Bwyes, dead or alive. He waved Annette on.

"That's really everything, sir. I thought I'd ask Ross about the other staff as well; I don't want her to feel like a suspect when she could be of use."

"Good idea. Liam, what's your plan today?"

"To interview Gordon with you by the sounds of it. Andy'll have to supervise the search of the area round the lake."

Craig shook his head. "It'll only take us a couple of hours to see Gordon then we can pitch in on the van, lake and the rest of the interviews. Andy, can you get the statements Julia and Gerry took from the cook and head gardener and cast an eye over them, please. Anything we need to follow up we can do tomorrow."

Andy nodded; it was going to be a busy day. "I'll send them up to check on the burned out car. They might see something forensics missed, hey."

"OK. Davy, what's happening at your end?"

Davy spread his arms wide, indicating that he was covering everything. "Residual prints from the main room and in here, deep background checks on the s...staff, and I thought I'd run Cameron Lawton and Vera Patterson as well, and the victims' backgrounds of course."

Craig nodded. Davy's deep backgrounds missed nothing. He would uncover what sort of sweets they'd liked as kids. He was still speaking.

"Bank accounts, credit cards, w...withdrawals, deposits for all staff and the Bwyes. That s...should pick up anything unusual -"

Craig cut in. "What about Jane Bwye's unsuitable boyfriend? Do we have anything on him yet?"

"Nothing yet. I think your best bet is one of the s...staff knowing something, or her friends. I'm trying to find out who she mixed with, called, emailed. I should have something for you soon."

"Good."

"Other than that I'm checking the family's insurance; car and otherwise."

Craig stopped him. "You're thinking of life insurance?"

"And K&R."

Liam made a face. "What's that?"

"Kidnap and Ransom. Lots of w...wealthy people take out insurance in case they're kidnapped; to pay for ransoms, private searches, negotiators etc. It usually applies abroad but Oliver Bwye was hated here so he may have taken some out."

Craig thanked God his staff thought of the things he missed.

"Excellent. On that note, Davy, Cameron Lawton is compiling a list of people who hated Bwye, get that from him please."

Davy smiled, already two steps ahead. "He's sending

it through later. I'll run checks on the names w...when it comes in." He indicated the laptop beside Craig. "I'm running the CCTV and traffic cams around the phone box where the ransom call was made." He made a face. "I just w...wish Bwye had had some cameras rigged around his estate."

Craig thought for a moment. Why hadn't he? He had a hunch. "Davy, check if Bwye ever had cameras and, if he had, when they were removed."

Liam smiled; Craig was almost as cynical as he was. "You think Bwye planned the kidnap in advance."

"I don't think anything; I'm just asking the question." He turned back to Davy. "I know you don't discuss cases with Maggie, but has she said anything?"

Davy's girlfriend was one of the few journalists that Craig didn't dislike.

Davy smiled teasingly. "Now, you know w...we wouldn't do that, chief, but..."

Craig smiled. "Spit it out."

Davy leaned in conspiratorially. "She did mention that Diana Bwye visited The Chronicle's offices last w...week."

"Something for her husband?"

Davy shook his head vigorously. "No, that's just it! She went into Ray Mercer's office and s...spent almost an hour in there."

Liam gawped at him. "When were you going to tell us this? I drove you all the way here this morning and you never said a word!"

Davy was indignant. "S...She only told me last night and I've had better things to think about s...since then."

"Aye, and we all know what they are."

Craig waved them down. "Davy, see what more you can find out on Mrs Bwye's visit; I'd like to find out what it was about without alerting Mercer. He's an unsavoury bugger so whatever they were discussing it probably wasn't good."

Davy nodded. "OK. I'll see what Maggie can dig up."

Craig could see Liam about to start another rant about Davy not keeping him informed so he cut him off. "Everyone's got plenty to keep them busy. We'll brief again at four."

He headed for the door, not missing Liam deliberately dragging his heels.

"Liam, we've an interview to do."

Liam glared at a smiling Davy so Craig emphasised his point.

"Now!"

Chapter Ten

Derry Station. 11 a.m.

"Tell me again, Ms Ross. Exactly what did you see when you left Rocksbury last Wednesday evening?"

Bernadette Ross squinted in the interview room's neon light, trying to make eye contact with Annette. She couldn't and it was intentional. Annette was standing by the door, deliberately positioned so the light's glare hid her face. She'd been pleasant when they'd met before, perhaps too pleasant; today would be different.

Ross' voice squeaked back. "I told you. Mr Bwye had gone to the golf-club earlier and Mrs Bwye was sitting in front of a blank TV screen when I left. Then, as I went down the drive, Jane drove past me in her blue Mercedes."

Annette leaned in. "Except that you told us the car was Jane's and it isn't registered to her. In fact it's not registered to any of the Bwyes."

Ross looked genuinely surprised. She spluttered out a defence. "I didn't know that. Maybe...maybe it was hidden by Diana for tax purposes. I do know Jane doesn't have the money to buy her own car and that she kept it secret from her father. She never drove it when he was around."

"Doesn't Jane work?"

Ross shook her head. "She's supposed to be a student." The emphasis was on supposed.

"Studying what?"

Ross shrugged. "Fashion. Although as far as I can see the closest she gets to fashion is buying it."

Annette scented blood. She shifted so that Ross could see her face. "What does she use for money?"

"Mr Bwye gives her a small allowance and her mother sneaks her money when she thinks nobody's watching."

The meaningful glance that accompanied her words said there was more there if Annette dug.

"Money's a bone of contention in the family?"

Bernadette Ross smiled slowly as if she was going to

tease out her reply. A sharp look from Annette quickly changed her mind.

"The Bwyes are rich on paper, super rich even, but a lot of the money is tied up in Mr Bwye's companies and it can't be accessed unless there's a directors' vote..."

Annette interrupted. "How many directors are there?"

"Five in one company and six in the other. It takes a unanimous vote for money to be withdrawn and their agreement depends on -"

Annette interrupted, nodding. "Market forces. They won't release money if it could impair the company's chances of survival."

"Or affect the share price. So liquidating funds in a hurry is difficult, sometimes impossible."

It didn't bode well for the ransom payment.

Annette had a hunch. "What happens in the event of Mr Bwye's death?"

"The money passes to the next of kin. A lump sum is released to them; around forty per cent of the total and the rest remains in the companies. The same process applies when they die and so on." Ross' eyes widened. "You don't think..."

"I don't think anything. I'm just gathering information. Tell me more about Jane's allowance."

She thought it was time to play good cop again. She rang for coffee and took a seat, waiting till John Ellis had brought it through before restarting.

"OK, Jane's allowance."

Ross sipped her coffee, grateful that she was no longer being treated like the enemy. "Jane's twenty-one next week and that's when most of her rich friends get access to their trust funds, but Mr Bwye likes to keep his family on a short leash, so he set thirty as Jane's inheritance date."

Annette shook her head, imagining the arguments in the Bwye's house.

"He's a self-made man who grew up poor so you can understand why he doesn't want her blowing it and then coming back for more."

Annette understood. "How much of an inheritance are we talking about?"

"Ten million pounds when she's thirty."

Annette wished she could whistle, knowing that Liam would be giving a loud one about now. It made her arguments with her kids about pocket money seem tame. She settled for an "I can see why Jane wouldn't be happy."

Ross nodded but tempered it with a caveat. "Remember that there are a lot of gold-diggers out there who would marry Jane just for her money. Mr Bwye is weeding them out as well."

"I can see that. But still, it can't have made him popular at home. What did Mrs Bwye say?"

Ross smiled, thinking of Diana Bwye. "She's a gentle soul and she loves her husband despite all his faults, so she mainly tries to keep the peace..."

"And slips Jane money on the side. I see." Annette thought for a moment. "Tell me more about the car."

Bernadette Ross was insistent. "Jane is the only one who drives it."

"Even though it isn't registered to the family."

Ross shrugged. "I don't understand that. Maybe it was registered to one of the family businesses?" She thought better of the idea immediately. "No, it can't have been. Mr Bwye would never have allowed it." Something occurred to her. "Perhaps it's registered as a staff car but Jane was insured on it. Have you seen the prices for insuring anyone under twenty-five independently?"

"So Jane might have been named on a staff policy but only she drove it."

Ross nodded. "It's the only thing that makes sense. Diana could have done that, but I'm positive Mr Bwye didn't know Jane had it."

"And you're sure that you saw Jane in the car last Wednesday; it couldn't have been anyone else?"

Ross hesitated just long enough to tell Annette what had happened. She'd seen the car, a car that only Jane drove, and assumed that she was the one driving. Annette pressed harder.

"Did you actually see Jane behind the steering wheel?"

Ross' silence answered no. It wasn't the answer

Annette had wanted; it meant that they had no sightings of Jane Bwye that evening, but at least now they knew.

"OK. When did you last see Jane before then?"

"The evening before; Tuesday. She was sitting on the settee reading a magazine when I left."

"So you didn't see her at all on Wednesday?"

Annette's tone was accusing and Ross leapt to her own defence. "No, but that's not unusual. I arrive early and Jane sleeps late; she's usually out clubbing or whatever they do nowadays, the night before. I work all morning in the study with Mr Bwye, cook brings me something for lunch, then we work again until around five. Unless Jane is in the main room when I'm leaving I mightn't see her for days."

Annette sighed. It was perfectly logical and completely useless to them. "Did you at least see her car on Tuesday?"

Ross's mouth opened and shut silently then she shook her head, adding. "But that's normal too. Jane wouldn't have had the car at the house if there was any chance that her father might have seen it."

"So where was it kept the rest of the time?"

Ross spoke hesitantly as if she was afraid of giving another wrong answer. "There...there are some old out-buildings... Mr Bwye never visits them."

It was something but not much. Annette sipped at her drink and then changed tack.

"OK, the main room. You said the whisky decanter was out of place; you're sure?"

This time Ross' nod was emphatic. "Positive. Mr Bwye is the only one who drinks whisky and he's fussy about putting it back."

"So we should only find his prints."

Ross looked puzzled. "I would think so, although the cleaner comes in three times a week so you might find hers as well."

Annette prayed that the prints wouldn't match either of them; if they didn't then they might be their perp's. Time to approach the subject she least enjoyed asking about: sex. If Liam was watching now he would be rubbing his hands in glee.

She leaned in conspiratorially; to the outside world it would look like two friends exchanging a secret and that was exactly the effect she was hoping for.

"You mentioned that Mr Bwye's study was his private space and you and he had the only keys?"

Ross knew where Annette was heading and considered her response carefully. On the one hand she owed Oliver Bwye loyalty, on the other they were trying to save his life and anything that she knew might be important. She nodded and then volunteered. "He brought in women sometimes."

Annette's eyebrows shot up; she'd expected it to take longer to extract the information. They also shot up at the logistics. The house was open plan so how on earth... Ross saw her question.

"Through the back door. Only he had the key. I believe he locked the door to the main room and then let them in at the back.

Neat.

"Often?"

Ross shrugged. "Fairly often if his cash withdrawals were anything to go by."

Annette's curiosity overcame her professionalism. "How much did he pay them?"

Ross pursed her lips disapprovingly. "Far too much. The withdrawals ranged from five hundred to two thousand pounds." She wrinkled her nose in distaste. "I imagine the cost depended on what they did for him."

Two thousand! They were both in the wrong job.

"I thought it was disgusting but at least he never asked me to arrange their visits."

Annette's heart sank. That meant she wouldn't know how to contact the women. She asked the question anyway.

"Do you know who they were?"

Ross sighed and nodded. "Yes, well no, not by name, but they all came from the same place. I think he used it because it's supposed to be clean." She rolled her eyes. "It's called The Kasbah; ridiculous name. It's an escort agency in the centre of Derry."

Not quite what the founding fathers had imagined

when they'd set down roots; or maybe it was, just not their wives'.

"Was there anyone long term; a mistress?"

Ross looked indignant. "Absolutely not! Mr Bwye loved his wife."

Between hitting her and screwing escorts he had a funny way of showing it, but they didn't have time for the debate.

Annette nodded. "So you didn't see any sign that he was planning to leave her?"

Ross sat up straight, with a prim expression on her face. "None. He was a religious man. A church elder."

Annette almost laughed out loud. What sort of religion said it was OK to assault and be unfaithful to your wife? She answered her own question. Practically all of them, if their male practitioners were anything to go by. She focused back on the discussion.

"OK, we'll chase up The Kasbah." She slid a pad and pen across the table. "I need any women's names you may have overheard, and please make a separate list of Jane's friends and their known haunts." She stood up to leave and then had another thought. "Do any of Mr Bwye's business acquaintances visit the house?"

Ross was emphatic. "Never. They always conduct business at his office in town."

Annette gawped at her. "He has another office and you didn't think to mention it!"

Ross realised her mistake and back-pedalled furiously. "It isn't his office, he works from the house. It's just a room I hire if he needs to hold a meeting. A firm in town rents out the rooms by the session; morning or afternoon."

Business centres; common practice everywhere. Annette gestured tiredly at the paper.

"Write down the address."

She left the room knowing they'd just acquired several more days' elimination work.

****

Andy gazed at the muddy shore and then ruefully down

at his shoes. They were his good ones, black and shiny. But their glamour wasn't the problem; the problem was that they were brogues, with dozens of perforations punched into the leather just waiting to suck in mud. like it was what they'd spent their entire lives waiting for. Teresa would kill him when he got home.

He glanced around for a saviour: a pair of shoe covers, or an abandoned pair of wellington boots. But there was nothing, just a bunch of uniformed policemen in waders grinning at the smart-ass detective's shiny feet.

Andy never pulled rank. It was a useless ploy and people inevitably got their revenge on you in other ways, and at a time when you least expected it. But their vengeance would be nothing compared to his fiery wife's if he ruined his shoes, so he called over a young officer who looked about the same shoe size as him.

"I need your waders, hey."

The P.C. stared down at his boots and then at Andy's shoes, repeating the sequence until it had lost its comic value. Then he shook his head and folded his arms, playing to his wader-clad audience.

"Can't, sir. I'm on search detail."

Andy gestured for him to remove the boots, aware that the others had downed tools and were watching to see what came next.

"OK, I'm relieving you for the day. Now give me the waders."

The boy glanced at his feet and then at the gathered cops, weighing up the price of betrayal against a nice cup of tea in the warm. The tea won. He changed in a nearby squad car, handed Andy the waders gleefully and drove off in search of tea and a scone. Andy donned them to a chorus of "shame" and "officer class" but he didn't care. His brogues were safe and so was his dinner. The troops' revenge would come some other day.

****

"Liam, you interview Gordon and I'll say nothing unless it's essential."

Liam squinted at Craig. He'd said it like he was a

probationer who needed the interview practice. Craig caught the look and shook his head.

"It will give me a chance to watch his face for lies."

"Aye, OK. As long as that's all..."

"That's all. For goodness sake, you could interview him in your sleep; we both know that."

He took a seat in the cool interview room then realised they were both freezing and turned up the thermostat. Either John Ellis didn't use the room much or the prisoners in Derry were hardier than the ones in Belfast. A minute later Ellis appeared with a tray of biscuits and drinks.

Liam grinned. "That's very nice of you, Ellie."

Ellis made a face. "Don't call me that."

Liam gave a coy smile. "You never used to mind."

Ellis rolled his eyes. "I'm bringing Mr Gordon in now. Mind, some of those biscuits are for him." He nodded at the two-way mirror. "I'll be watching so I'll know if you eat them all."

A minute later, Brendan Gordon was seated opposite them and Craig handed him a cup of tea. He was a good looking lad; short, dark and saturnine, with the muscles and tan of a grounds man's outdoor life. He looked as if he belonged on the Amalfi coast rather than Derry, but then there was strong Mediterranean blood in Ireland's northwest. Craig wondered what Jane Bwye had thought of the boy. If he could see that Gordon was handsome what effect might he have had on a bored rich girl? Was Gordon the unsuitable boyfriend they were looking for?

Liam swallowed a biscuit and pushed the plate towards their guest.

"Have a biscuit, son. Tea's too dry otherwise." It made sense in Liam World.

Brendan Gordon shook his head and gave a defeated sigh. It came from the heart and Craig wondered how many times he'd been hauled in for interview in the past six years. Probably every time there'd been a local crime. Liam saw the young man's dejection and shook his head.

"Look, lad. I know you were badly done by when you were a kid. You were put away when you shouldn't have been. If I'd lifted you I'd just have nailed you for carrying a knife and you'd have got a suspended sentence."

Gordon suddenly became animated. "I was only carrying it 'cos they were trying to jump me into a gang and I didn't want to join."

Liam nodded in sympathy while Craig focused on something else; the neutrality of Gordon's voice. This was a boy who'd lived a hard life in Ireland's northwest, yet his lack of accent said he could have come from anywhere in the world. Liam continued.

"Magilligan must have been hard at that age."

Gordon gazed down at the table. "It's hard at any age."

"I'd say so. Well look, we're not here to blame you for anything, so just have a biscuit and relax."

Craig smiled to himself. Liam thought food was the ultimate panacea, plus, if Gordon had a biscuit he wouldn't feel so bad about having another one himself. Gordon reached hesitantly for a custard cream. His hands were lean and worn with nails bitten to the quick. Liam took a second biscuit and munched contentedly for a moment, then he returned to the business in hand.

"It's like this. We're interviewing everyone who works for the Bwyes, just to find out what they know or saw. OK?"

Gordon nodded slowly but gave Liam a suspicious look.

"I wasn't near the house when it happened. I was off work last week."

Coincidence of convenience?

"What were you doing?"

The young man looked surprised, as if what he did on his days off was no-one's business but his own. Craig saw him about to say as much then he reconsidered and shrugged.

"I was chilling at home."

"Which is where?"

Liam already knew where Gordon lived but he wanted to hear it from him.

"I have a one bedroomed flat on the estate."

"What did you do?"

"Listened to music and studied mainly. I was painting

as well. Mrs Bwye lets us decorate however we like."

Craig cut in. "What are you studying?"

Gordon stared at him like he hadn't noticed he was there. He scrutinised Craig's face untrustingly as he answered, as if he was waiting for him to take the piss.

"Landscape gardening. I want a career."

Craig nodded, but not patronisingly as the younger man had expected.

"Good for you. We'll need the name of your college."

He waved Liam on and sat back.

"Is there anyone who can verify your whereabouts?"

"Only my mum. She was in and out all week, helping me paint."

"No girlfriend?"

Craig watched as Gordon's face ran the gamut of expressions. Surprise, embarrassment, defensiveness, and something else; something that he couldn't put his finger on.

"No. Why? Is it compulsory?"

Liam guffawed. "You make it sound like a chore. Most lads your age would like a girlfriend, unless they're gay."

"I'm not gay!"

Craig's quick glare reminded Liam about Human Rights.

"Aye, well. Not that there's anything wrong with being gay, like. We have a gay sergeant."

Craig was damn sure Jake didn't want his business shared with the whole world so he cut in again.

"Do you have a partner, Mr Gordon?"

Gordon blushed and stammered "N...No."

Both detectives knew it wasn't the whole truth; Brendan Gordon mightn't have had a partner but he had a crush on someone. His red face and the way he immediately chewed his nails said that he wasn't going to give them a name. They'd have to get it some other way. Craig changed tack, opening a file that he'd brought with him.

"You were charged with GBH in 2010, Mr Gordon, but the charges were dismissed. Tell me what happened."

Gordon coloured even further and shook his head, so Liam answered for him.

"Someone who wanted to up their status by fighting an ex-con?"

Gordon nodded sadly. "Why don't they just leave me alone? I just want a quiet life."

Craig read out loud. "He had a knife but you weren't carrying, yet you managed to beat him pretty badly."

Gordon turned on him belligerently. "Was that a question?"

Craig nodded and the gardener shrugged.

"I box. He came at me so I hit him; hard."

Craig shook his head, not at the answer but at the fact Gordon had been charged with GBH when it had clearly been self-defence again. He turned the page, knowing exactly what he'd find; Terry Harrison's name again, this time as a D.C.I. He'd had it in for the boy. He'd seen cops with personal vendettas before; every crime that was committed in their area they tried to make their favourite perp fit. How many other poor sods had Harrison fitted up just to get another button on his epaulette?

He made a note to dig deeper on Harrison's past when he had the time and turned back to the case.

"What do you think of the Bwyes, Mr Gordon?"

Gordon shrugged. "Mrs Bwye's nice but the old man's a bastard." No mention of Jane.

"To you or to her?"

"To everyone. He shouts at all his staff except Bernie Ross."

"Why not at Ms Ross?"

Gordon chewed his nails again before answering with a shrug. "Probably because he can't replace her. They've worked together for years."

"What about Jane, what's she like?"

Gordon's blush deepened. They'd found his crush; Jane Bwye. He shrugged. "All right. She doesn't like her dad either."

"Oh?"

A sharp glance said the young man had realised that he'd said enough. He folded his arms. "Can I go now?"

Craig smiled to himself and signalled John Ellis to join them, then he rose to his feet.

"Sergeant Ellis here needs some information from

you. Your friends at college, your tutor, that sort of thing. I'd also like you to list anyone you've seen at the house in the past three months and the names of any of Jane's friends you might know. Then you're free to leave. Thank you for your assistance."

As they left the room they heard Gordon asking John Ellis. "Are you the gay sergeant then?"

Craig shot Liam a look that said 'Equality refresher course'.

Chapter Eleven

4.20 p.m.

By four-twenty Craig had called the group to order. Andy was rubbing his hands together attempting to get warm, so Craig nodded him to stand by the fire that Davy had lit. Davy was the only one who wasn't freezing, but then he'd been in the house all day.

"OK, first Annette with Bernadette Ross' re-interview, then Andy and Davy and then Liam will report on our meeting with Brendan Gordon." He glanced around the room then asked in an exasperated tone that no-one failed to spot. "Does anyone know where Gerry and Julia are this time?"

Davy nodded. "On their way. Harrison s...summoned them for an update."

Craig gave a deep sigh; power games. He waved Annette on, wondering what to do about Terry Harrison.

"OK, Bernadette Ross. After a bit of digging it seems the Mercedes was registered to the estate as a staff car, but Jane was the only person insured to drive it. Diana Bwye arranged it that way to stop Mr Bwye finding out. She probably didn't inform Ms Ross for the same reason. Jane is twenty-one next week and that's when most of her friends inherit, but Oliver Bwye has everything tied up in a trust until she's thirty years old, then she gets ten million. Until then he's keeping her on a very short financial leash."

Liam whistled the way Annette had wanted to earlier and just then Julia and Gerry rushed in, muttering apologies. Craig motioned them towards the fire and nodded Annette on.

"That whistle says exactly what I thought. Anyway, the delayed trust caused friction, as you might imagine, so Diana Bwye slipped her daughter cash as well as sorting out the car."

Liam cut in. "How did Jane avoid the old man seeing it?"

"She only drove it near the house when he wasn't

around. Like that Wednesday when she knew he was at the golf-club, maybe. The rest of the time she parked it in an out-building."

Davy interrupted. "My mum used to s...slip Emmie and me extra pocket money and my dad was always moaning at her. I bet it caused trouble at the Bwyes."

Annette nodded. "Although I suspect that Oliver Bwye did more than moan. By the way, did you verify domestic violence?"

Davy nodded. "Yep. Both the w...wife and daughter attended the local emergency department frequently, with s...serious cuts and bruises, and in Diana Bwye's case two different fractures of her arms. Oliver Bwye's a real charmer -"

Craig interrupted. "We'll hear more on that in a minute. Anything more, Annette?"

"Yes, sorry. Ross has given me a list of Jane's and Diana's known associates and Bwye's business colleagues. Apparently when he held business meetings he did it in town, in one of those meeting rooms you can hire."

"He never brought business colleagues to the house?"

Annette shook her head. "Never. But he did bring women. He used escorts regularly."

Liam gawped. "In his own home? What about the wife?"

"If she knew I'd be very surprised, but Bwye doesn't sound as if he'd have cared either way. He locked himself in his study and let them in the back door. Remember he was the only one with that key."

Davy glanced around the study in disgust while Liam continued gawping, open-mouthed, until Annette tipped it shut.

"Bwye used an escort agency in town; I've got the name." She reached into her bag for her notepad and flicked quickly till she found the page. "The Kasbah."

Andy laughed. "Why are none of these places ever called something normal, like Joe's Body Shop?"

Liam's bellowed laughter told him what he'd just said. Craig continued before the discussion deteriorated.

"You know this area, Andy. Have you ever heard of

the place?"

Andy nodded. "Aye. It costs a ton and it's supposed to have some gorgeous women, hey. It's wealthy business types like Bwye who go there."

"They don't want the riff-raff spoiling the goods."

Julia and Annette yelled "Liam!" in unison and Annette continued, "Those are human beings you're talking about."

Liam tried to look contrite. "You know what I mean."

Craig nodded. "Unfortunately we do. Keep going, Annette."

Annette glared at Liam as she carried on. "Bwye spent quite a bit on escorts. He regularly withdrew between five hundred and two thousand pounds cash from the bank; I'm getting more details on that. Two other things of note were that Ross just assumed that it was Jane driving the car that Wednesday; she didn't actually see her face. And even Oliver Bwye can't remove large sums of money from his companies unless the other directors agree. There are five directors in one company and six in the other and a vote has to be taken to release cash, so paying the ransom could be a problem."

Craig thought for a moment. "Who inherits?"

"Mrs Bwye, and when she dies, Jane. They get forty per cent of the total legacy in cash as a lump sum, but they would still have to get the other directors say-so to liquidate their full assets."

"Does Bwye have any insurance policies?"

Davy answered. "As w...well as the usual house and car insurance he has life insurance for twenty million on himself and Mrs Bwye."

"Not Jane?"

"No. He probably didn't think s...she would die first. He also has serious K&R insurance, like I guessed."

"Any exclusions?"

Davy smiled. Craig missed nothing.

"Not on the K&R but on his life insurance. He's excluded from any claims for death from heart disease and s...skin cancer."

Craig was surprised. How many middle-aged men would agree to that?

Davy explained. "He had a heart attack w...when he was forty, followed by a coronary by-pass op, and a malignant s...skin cancer removed when he was fifty-two. No-one would insure him for either after that."

It made sense; insurers weren't known for their charity.

"OK. Anything else?"

"Just the normal; acts of God, s...self-inflicted injury."

Craig nodded. The usual wriggle room.

"In case he decided to top himself to leave his family a fortune."

Annette snorted. "Oliver Bwye sounds far too selfish for that. Sorry, I meant to say one more thing; Bernadette Ross was adamant that no-one drank whisky except Bwye and he was practically OCD about putting the decanter back. They have a cleaner three days a week but she would have known better than to leave it sitting on a lamp table."

Craig shook his head. Had one of the first responders moved it on the Thursday morning? They'd said not, but only the prints would tell. He sighed heavily. The case seemed one step forward and two back at the moment and all they'd found so far was more people to interview.

"Thanks, Annette. Make sure you speak to the cleaner. Andy?"

Andy was staring down at his brogues, wondering if it had really been worth commandeering the waders to keep them clean. The searchers were probably planning a fate worse than death for him now. He shook himself from his gloomy thoughts to answer.

"I've set the searchers to work at the lake, but I'm not sure what we're looking for, hey. They're scouring the shore for tyre tracks, foot prints and debris, but it's a half-mile around; it'll take forever. It gets dark at four so I've told them to leave and restart tomorrow morning."

Craig gave a thin smile. "I'm not sure what they're looking for either; just keep going. Focus on the arc closest to the house and tell them to keep their eyes peeled for anything in the water."

Andy looked surprised. "You think the Bwyes are in there?"

"I was thinking more of the dog. No-one's seen it."
"Oh, OK."

Craig thanked goodness that Nicky wasn't there. One mention of a dead puppy and she'd have burst into tears. Just as he was about to ask Julia to report, Davy cut in.

"On the s...subject of the dog..."

"Davy, if you don't mind I'd like to hear from Julia and Gerry before we come to you."

Davy didn't mind at all. He'd been playing a game on his smart-pad and he was more than happy to carry on.

"What did Harrison want with you, Julia?"

Julia rolled her eyes and Gerry shook his head before answering.

"To prove that he's still in charge."

"Except that he isn't."

"Nope."

He bit into his biscuit and Julia started to report.

"Gerry and I interviewed the Bwye's cook and head gardener. Much of what they said matches what we've just heard. They both said that Bwye was violent to his wife and daughter and mentioned that he saw other women."

Liam snorted. "You make it sound like he met them at a tea-dance."

Julia squinted angrily; their old animosity wasn't buried very deep. "It's preferable to being vulgar like you."

Liam went to retort but Craig silenced him with a look.

"Carry on."

"He saw other women and overly controlled his family, so as a consequence Jane hated him."

Craig cut in. "Enough to kill him?"

Julia was surprised. She spluttered. "I s...suppose so. You really think..."

"I think Jane Bwye's was the only blood not found at the scene."

"But would she really harm her mother and her dog? Everyone says she loved her mum."

Craig conceded the point. "You're probably right; we don't even know if she was there when they were kidnapped. But..." He stared into space for a moment and everyone saw an idea forming. "...what if she found out about the kidnap afterwards and decided to capitalise on it?"

Liam gawped at him. "You mean she made the ransom demand, or got a male friend to do it?" He warmed to his theme. "Maybe the unsuitable boyfriend? God, that's brilliant, boss."

Annette shuddered. "And cold. To use your parents' disappearance for money."

Craig shook his head. "She may not have known her mother was there that night; how often was anyone but Oliver Bwye in that study? Anyway, it's just speculation and a risky strategy if she did. If she falsified a ransom demand we could end up with two, so which would be the real one? And, as Annette said, is she really callous enough to use her parents' kidnap as a way to make money?"

To his surprise Julia nodded. "Her father, I'd say yes, definitely. She hated him. Her mum...maybe she didn't know she was there, or, I suppose if her mum had already been taken then she might have thought, why not? She didn't take them but she might as well benefit. It makes sense if she was desperate to escape her father's control."

Craig wondered who'd controlled Julia enough to make her identify with such hatred. He let the group carry on speculating; free thinking often produced good ideas. After a few minutes he brought them back to earth with a bump.

"OK, we'll know our suspicions are wrong if we find Jane's body. Anything else, Julia?"

She glanced at Gerry and he shook his head. "Everything else just confirms what the rest of you have said. Bwye was a real piece of work who everyone hated, but he paid their wages on time."

Craig nodded. The rich were different.

"OK, Davy. What have you got for us?"

Davy smiled and tapped his smart-pad back to work. "Plenty. OK, the relevant negatives. Bwye never had perimeter cameras, no idea why. Maybe he had the rifle instead. The s...staff are all clean on criminal record checks, except for one of his grounds men, Brendan Gordon. No history of anything naughty anywhere else. Mrs Bwye was involved with two local charities and treasurer of one of them. I'll dig deeper but s...so far everything looks above board. Jane was a very s...spoilt girl. She may not have had her own money but she ran up her credit cards and bills at all the local s...shops, leaving her parents with no choice but to pay them off. She was s...studying fashion design but it took her three years to pass year one, so her dedication w...was definitely in question. The course mostly seemed like something to keep her dad off her back."

Craig interrupted. "Any sign of the unsuitable boyfriend? He might have gone to college with her."

Davy smiled. "There's been a s...string of unsuitable boyfriends apparently; the latest seems to be a guy called Justin O'Hare. He's twenty-three and his family are very w...wealthy so I'm not s...sure why he was unsuitable."

Gerry cut in. "The cook gave us his name as well. She said the family fell on hard times when his father made some bad deals. Said he was only after Jane for her money."

"That sounds plenty unsuitable to me, boss."

Craig squinted at Liam. He hadn't forgotten his earlier clumsy remarks. "Carry on, Davy."

"OK, O'Hare's a possibility but I'm running them all for the past two years. I'll let you know if anything pings."

"What about the list of enemies from Cameron Lawton?"

"I'm s...starting on those now, and Bwye's bank accounts -"

Annette interrupted. "You mentioned the negatives. Anything positive?"

Davy smiled at her and nodded. His hair didn't fall over his face as it usually did and Craig suddenly realised that it was in a ponytail. Another fashion trend; maybe short back and sides would become one soon.

"Two things. The dog had a GPS tag and it's moving, so that means it's probably not dead. I've got a trace on it."

Annette and Craig smiled; they were both dog lovers, although Craig's Labrador, Murphy, lived at his parents' house in Holywood. It was good exercise for his dad to walk him, even though he moaned about it, a lot.

"And the van. Des identified the treads as belonging to a Ford Transit." He tapped his screen and turned the pad round for them to see. The image of a large windowless van appeared. "It's big enough to hold three or four people in the back."

Craig thought for a moment. "OK, ask Des to check how the treads would look on mud for the likely weight it might have been carrying; factor in the weather last Wednesday night/Thursday morning. Also, check how many of those vans there are in Northern Ireland."

"Already w...working on the first and there are twenty-three of them."

"Damn! I don't suppose there's any way to narrow it down?"

"I'm cross checking the owners with names linked to the case, residents within fifty miles, employees in any of Bwye's companies and a few other things. Des did say that the treads showed a s...small slash on the left tyre."

"Meaning?"

Davy shrugged. "It probably ran over glass at some stage. It will help confirm it's the right van w...when we find it."

If they were in luck it might do more than that.

"Run the MOTs for all the vans. I want to know if any examiner noted the slash in their MOT report and advised that the tyre be changed."

Liam's eyes widened. "They're manual reports. It'll take the lad ages."

Craig fixed his gaze. "Not with you helping." He moved on before Liam could moan. "Any vans too new for MOT see if they visited any garages to have their tyres checked in the past year. It's a long shot but who knows. Anything else, Davy?"

Davy shared a look of martyrdom with Liam. He maintained the expression when he turned back to Craig.

"No s...sightings of the Bwyes at airports or ports and no activity on any of their cards. I've frozen their accounts just in case, but we'll still s...see if someone tries to use a card. Oh, and I've hacked into Jane's emails but the only people she emailed were female friends from college. That's it so far. I've a lot of checks still to run, including getting more detail on the Bwyes' GP and hospital records; it was the insurance company that told me about Oliver Bwye's heart and cancer problems. We may need w...warrants for the other records."

Craig nodded. "Let me know." He turned to Liam. "Right, mighty mouth; tell everyone about Brendan Gordon."

Liam gave Craig a faux hurt look and summarised Gordon's interview in three minutes, ending with "Oh aye, and he's studying landscape gardening."

Annette asked first. "Where? Is it the same place Jane Bwye is doing fashion?"

Liam glanced at Craig. Neither of them had made the connection. Liam flicked open his notebook.

"He told Ellis it was Stonebridge College. Is that the same place?"

Annette rolled her eyes and was tempted to say "DOH!", like her kids did when something was so obvious she should have spotted it immediately. Instead she said patiently "Yes it is, Liam. Oh, what a surprise."

He sniffed. "So what if they knew each other from college? They'd have met each other around here anyway."

"But college is a more social, equal place. If a romance was going to start it would have started there."

Liam wasn't going to be defeated. He gestured at Davy. "He's just said she was seeing that Justin O'Hare."

The bickering was giving Craig a headache so he raised a hand. "Be quiet, both of you!" His tone ensured they did as they were told. "Check out Gordon and O'Hare. Gordon blushed when we asked about Jane; let's see if O'Hare does the same. Annette, I want you and Andy to interview him."

Andy perked up at the sound of his name and asked the question that he'd been waiting to ask for five minutes.

"What was Gordon's accent like? Can we hear it?"

Craig startled; he'd forgotten to get it on tape. He shook his head. "Neutral. I don't know where he grew up but whatever his natural accent is it's been trained out of him."

Julia nodded like a sage. "I bet he was in the prison drama club. They could have ironed his accent out."

"Good point. I hadn't thought of that." He turned back to Davy. "Anything more on the ransom call?"

Davy nodded excitedly. "Sorry, I forgot. The language boys s...sent me a report. I'll read it out."

Craig smiled. Davy's stutter had always made him prefer to demonstrate things in writing and diagrams, and he avoided public speaking like the plague. So for him to volunteer to read aloud was a major step forward and a sharp glance from Craig warned Liam not to draw attention to the event. Annette nodded encouragingly while Davy found the right page.

"OK. The voice on the tape w...was, like we thought, a man in his twenties-"

Craig cut in, breaking his resolve not to interrupt. "Definitely not teens?"

Davy shook his head. "Twenties; early twenties. They were adamant."

He paused for another comment but Craig waved him on.

"The voice was in the baritone range, signalling a man likely to exhibit obvious s...secondary sexual characteristics -"

It was Julia who interrupted this time. "Like what? Secondary sexual characteristics are body hair, broken voice, musculature, etc. and most men have those. His voice has obviously broken, so how can they say more than that?"

Davy shrugged. "Apparently they can. I think they're implying that the man, w...when we find him, will look quite butch. Broad, big jaw..."

Andy cut in. "Maybe he'll have a beard and smoke a pipe, hey."

"Like Santa Claus."

Craig brought them back to the point. "Go on, Davy."

"OK. The accent is most likely from the North of

Ireland and its capital city, Belfast. Belfast accents can be narrowed to within a few streets by the s...skilled listener and this accent hails from w...west Belfast, more precisely the area around the lower Falls Road."

Craig nodded, Vera Patterson had been right. Davy saw him nod and shook his head, turning back to the paper.

"However, it is our opinion that this accent, whilst a good facsimile, may not be native to the speaker. W...We are therefore unfortunately unable to identify the s...speaker's real accent from this brief sample and request a longer sample."

There was silence while Craig thought and the others exchanged confused looks. Davy broke it.

"They always add that caveat to cover themselves. Even if the caller put on the accent at least that means he knew how to; maybe he'd lived in the Falls Road area s...sometime in the past."

Craig shook his head. "Anyone who'd watched movies about The Troubles would have been able to mimic one. Thanks for trying but it doesn't get us much further."

Annette jumped in. "I disagree, sir. It tells us that our man is definitely early twenties and not a wimp."

"True, but that doesn't rule out Brendan Gordon. He's small but he's got muscles like the Spartan 300. And twenty-five isn't far out of the age range." He sighed heavily. "I wish to hell we'd kept a recording of his voice, we'll have to go back and get one now. OK. Let's keep going. Liam, you and Davy chase the van, Annette and Andy are taking O'Hare, and get him on tape please. There are still all of Mrs Bwye's friends and Bwye's enemies to chase. Julia, you and Gerry start on Diana Bwye's charity friends. When you've finished with them go to the golf-club and see who you can find there. John Ellis witnessed Bwye's behaviour that Wednesday evening so he can give you the names from that night."

Liam interjected, looking sheepish. "We did keep a record of Gordon's voice. I knocked on the recorder just before he came in."

Craig tutted and everyone knew Liam hadn't told Gordon he was being taped. Craig decided to save the lecture; the tape could be useful this time. When he nodded Liam on he knew he'd skated past.

"I'll give the tape to the lad for comparison. Here, what about the lake? The work there's only just started."

Craig thought for a moment before admitting there was too much to do to tie Liam up with MOT checks, no matter how much he wanted to teach him a lesson. He relented grudgingly.

"OK, you take the lake tomorrow. Sorry, Davy, you'll have to do the MOT checks on your own." He glanced at the clock on Oliver Bwye's desk. It was after five. "Let's take a break for dinner. Anyone who wants to go home, do. Anyone who's staying locally tonight get ready to work."

He scanned the row of faces, searching for the most exhausted looking ones. "Julia: you, Gerry and Andy take the night off; the rest of us will keep going."

Gerry's face lit up but Julia stubbornly refused.

"I'm staying. Matt's on-call so I've a free evening. I'll take tomorrow night off, if that's OK?"

"Fine. But Gerry and Andy, go home after dinner or now if you want to, you both look wrecked." He stood up. "Right, someone find us a decent restaurant. Dinner's on me."

****

By nine p.m. Liam had walked the arc of the lake nearest the house, no mean feat in the pitch dark. Only the muddiest part of the shore was lit, by lamps jerry-rigged by the local uniforms to make sure that none of them fell in. The water would claim their lives quickly; they'd drown, become entangled in weeds or simply die from the cold.

He squinted out over the black disc. Any boats on the lake when they'd first arrived had gone now, the water off limits to any but the police. It was normally used by the locals for fun and fishing, its public rights preserved by its perimeter bordering on some council land. Liam wondered if Oliver Bwye had tried to control access to it the way that he'd controlled the rest of his kingdom, if he had then the law had thwarted him.

Liam switched off the lamps and stood in the dark, picturing what he would have done if he'd kidnapped the Bwyes. It didn't make pretty viewing. First, he would have loaded them into the van at the study door, just the way their perp seemed to have done. He stopped abruptly, realising something. There was no way one person could have lifted an injured man without help. Oliver Bwye was big; overweight would have been more accurate. If he was as injured as the blood in his study suggested then he would have been spark out. How could one man possibly have got him into the van?

He took out his notebook and jotted the question down, followed quickly by another. Disabled ramp? Then he turned back to the water and his thoughts. OK then, let's say their perp had managed to get all the Bwyes into the van. Liam stopped again; there's been no sign of Jane Bwye's blood, what did that mean? Was she an accomplice or so frightened that she'd done what she was told without needing to be hurt? Had her dog been injured to subdue her instead? Liam scribbled the questions down then gazed at the water again.

OK, so you've got them all in the van, the parents too injured to fight back and Jane scared half to death; then what? You drive away from the back door. He jotted down; 'chase the weight/tread link'. Then where? The lake? The tracks' direction outside the door had been ambiguous and they'd found nothing but mush in the mud beside the lake. The van might not have driven to the lake at all, or it might have done and gone right up to the edge. So how did they get the Bwyes into the water... or onto a boat? It brought Liam back to the idea of a ramp. He shivered violently but not because of the cold.

Just then Craig appeared at his side and they stood, not speaking, just staring at the lake, its darkness growing more oppressive with each breath. Craig broke the silence.

"They're dead."

Liam didn't move, his eyes fixed on the dark. He stared into it, through it, at the starless sky and the invisible horizon, then down, down through the still water to the tombs below. Finally he nodded.

"I know. It was the only thing they could have done once they'd left the tracks. If it had been a dry night they might have lived."

On a dry winter's night even the soil near the warm house would have been frozen and nothing would have left an impression. But the evening's showers plus the warmth had caused mud, and on wet mud tracks were unavoidable and the Bwyes' fates had been sealed.

Craig sighed; it was a defeated sound. Liam glanced at him, surprised. The boss never gave up. Craig's next words said it was just a momentary lapse.

"They probably didn't intend to kill them, at least not that fast. If they had they would just have done it in the house."

"So...they came to take them but they also came prepared to do serious harm. That's obvious from the blood."

"You mean if the perp hadn't been prepared the Bwyes would have fought back using whatever was to hand, and nothing in the house was missing or bloody. OK, so they brought a weapon, or they had Bwye's rifle."

"Yep. They intended to take them, maybe for money or maybe to kill later, but not here. That wasn't the plan."

"They must have had help to get them into the van, or it was adapted in some way, to let them be dragged or rolled in easily."

Liam smiled in the dark; it was exactly what he'd written in his book.

Craig continued. "At some point they noticed the tyres were leaving tracks."

"Before they'd gone very far. They saw the trail they'd left by the door and knew smoothing it out would mean leaving more clues. They might as well have sent up a flare. We'd have their treads and once they'd got on the main road they'd be caught on traffic cams eventually and we'd follow the trail straight to them."

Craig turned to him. "We'll do that anyway. So what are you saying? That they drove or pushed the van and everyone in it into the lake and then left alone by foot?"

Liam shook his head. "Too risky. There was always a

chance that they'd drown themselves. Once the van hit the water there'd be no predicting the whirlpool effect. Unless they were one hell of a swimmer they could have been killed."

Craig smiled. This was why, for all his bumbling clown routine, Liam was so good. Experience. Thirty years of seeing people die in every possible way, including, it seemed, drowning.

"So they dumped the bodies and drove the van away."

"You think they dumped all of them? Including whoever was still alive?"

Craig shook his head sadly and Liam knew that he was thinking of the girl. "God knows. There's only one way to find out."

He made the call and Liam turned on the lamps to guide the soon-to-arrive diving crews. Then the two detectives walked slowly back towards the house, for another hour's debate on the fate of the Bwyes and to drink whatever booze Oliver Bwye had left concealed.

Chapter Twelve

Thursday. 9 a.m.

At first Davy had just gawped at the weblink on his screen, scarcely able to believe his eyes. It was too much of a coincidence to be true; things like this only happened in the movies and even then only to Tom Cruise. He closed down the internet and returned to work, typing the names from Cameron Lawton's list into the PNC. When he'd set the searches running and poured a fresh cup of tea he re-opened the browser that he'd closed.

Strictly speaking he wasn't supposed to be checking the internet at work; there were memos about hackers in his inbox every day. Talk about paranoia. The government need to chillax. Besides, he had industrial strength firewalls in his browser, so if anything he should be worried about government viruses infecting him.

Just then an e-mail popped up. It was from Maggie and he smiled as he typed back a reply, thinking idly that now he was still going to have a salary, they should think about getting a place. Shuttling between family dinners at his mum's with his granny constantly forgetting who Maggie was and having to run through the same questions each time, and nights of passion at her flat that made him feel faintly grubby when he went home the next day to change, was starting to get old. An immediate image of his mother crying and his granny looking lost filled his mind and he knew that he couldn't move out without a papal dispensation or a ring, and marriage was still a long way away. He finished his e-mail, resigned to more family dinners, and turned back to the URL that had caught his eye.

It linked to a blog by someone making a name for themselves on Derry's local scene; the wittily named Father Fred. Wherever he was he liked to check the local blogs, it was the best way to get to know a place. Davy scanned the site, glancing at the door occasionally as if he expected the IT police to burst in. The discussion topic running was wealth and its redistribution, and the question asked was 'was it moral to rob the rich to give to the poor?' The post had started normally enough the day before, talking about the inequalities in Northern Irish society and particularly in the northwest. As he read on, he ran a trace on the IP address. It was local, in Derry City Centre to be precise.

Halfway down, the post began to discuss whether six million pounds would be enough to redress the societal imbalance and hit a power broker where it hurt. Six million; the exact amount mentioned on the ransom call! It had to be more than coincidence. The more he read the more the hairs on his neck stood up. He decided he needed a reality check so he made a call. It was answered by Nicky's husky voice.

"Belfast Murder Squad. Can I help you?"

"Hi Nicky. How're things in the big s...smoke?"

Nicky smiled. Hearing Davy's voice made her glance towards his empty desk and reinforce how much she missed him.

"Boring. We're reading Joanne Greer's case notes and trial transcripts with the lawyers, looking for ways to get her appeal thrown out. What about you?"

Davy gazed around him. "I'm in a s...study with a wall of books full of whisky. I'll send you a photo."

She adopted a maternal tone. "Just don't send me a selfie of you drinking it."

The chat continued for ten minutes until she had to go. Davy returned to his work, certain that he was back on planet earth. He checked all his searches and then returned to the blog, reading it again with more distance. There was no doubt about it; whoever Father Fred was he had to know something about the ransom demand. Six million was the exact figure he'd mentioned under the redistribution of wealth.

He was just about to call Craig when he and Liam wandered in through the back door, yawning as if they'd both been up all night. Craig's urgent grab for the percolator said that they had. He greeted Davy between yawns and took a seat.

"Morning, Davy. Anything new?"

Liam shoved a Danish pastry into his mouth and

gulped at a cup of tea, then he repeated Craig's question with a full mouth, scattering crumbs across Davy's screen. Davy brushed them away in disgust.

"Possibly. How's it going at the lake?"

He turned his screen away quickly, to avoid Liam's next spray. Thankfully it was Craig who replied.

"It's deep so it'll take a while." He gestured at the computer. "Lawton's list?"

Davy nodded. "Yes. And s...something else."

Craig raised an eyebrow, too tired to cross the room and take a look. They'd been at the lake with the divers until four a.m. and started again at eight. Four hours sleep was a new low, even for him. He motioned Davy on and watched, puzzled, as he kept glancing at the door.

"Are you expecting someone?"

Davy laughed nervously. "No...it's just..."

Liam drained his cup and headed for a refill, answering Craig's question as he did. "He's been accessing outside internet sites and he's waiting for the thought police to take him in."

Davy gawped at him. "How did you know?"

Liam shrugged. "'Cos you're always doing it. I never say anything because if you don't know how to put up a solid firewall then no-one does."

Craig watched the exchange through drooping eyes while he waited for Davy to say what he'd found. He seemed more upset that Liam had guessed his secret than anything else. Craig prompted him again.

"You said you found something?"

Davy glanced back at his screen. "W...Well...one of the things I do when I travel somewhere is to check the local blogs. They tell you about the local scene." He changed tack suddenly. "Hey, did you know blogs and things outside the mainstream media are called the fifth estate, like the independent press is called the fourth?"

Liam gestured around him. "If they're the fifth estate does that make this place the sixth?"

He was rewarded by a weak laugh. Craig motioned Davy to get back to the point.

"Well, when you're abroad the local bloggers know w...where the best clubs are and things like that."

"Does Derry count as abroad?"

Davy grinned. "That Glenshane pass is harder to cross than the Alps when it snows. Anyway, I w...was checking for a good restaurant to take Maggie to; she's coming up tonight..."

Liam interrupted before starting on his second Danish. "That place we went for dinner last night was good."

Davy glanced at Craig apologetically. "It w...was nice and thanks for dinner, chief, but it was..."

Craig finished his sentence. "For old people and you want somewhere cool."

Davy nodded. "Anyway, I came across a blog by a guy called Father Fred."

Liam guffawed. "Father Fred...like Father Ted. I get it."

"Anyway, he was holding a discussion about inequality in Northern Ireland and the redistribution of w...wealth. Like, is it moral to rob the rich to give to the poor?"

Craig lids lifted.

"Then he mentioned a figure of s...six million pounds and asked whether it would be enough to redress the balance and hit a power broker where it hurt..."

Craig was suddenly wide awake.

"I thought it was too much of a coincidence so I checked his IP address. He's somewhere in the centre of Derry."

Craig was across the room in seconds. "Show me."

Liam joined them, not quite sure what was happening but certain that it wasn't good. They stared at Davy's screen; reading for a moment as fresh comments appeared on Father Fred's debate. Craig ran his eyes over the post. 'Is six million pounds enough to redress the balance and hit a power broker where it hurts?' It was far more than a coincidence.

"Narrow that IP down and get me a real name and address."

"I'll try, but bloggers like this use routers to prevent being traced."

Craig wasn't listening to excuses.

"And check the blogs' archives for anything else relevant, before they catch on and shut it down. Ring us in the car."

He headed for the door and then realised that Liam wasn't with him. "Get a move on, Liam. We need to find who this blogger is before they shut down the site."

****

Two hours later they admitted defeat. Davy had narrowed the address to Shipquay Street and they'd been the full length of it six times, no mean feat when it was one of the longest streets in the country and they were both half asleep.

Every time they'd thought they'd had the right address and hammered on the door, they'd found some innocent housewife surfing recipes, or some teenage boy googling websites his parents would have been very unhappy about. Father Fred was obviously piggy-backing other peoples' Wi-Fi.

Craig phoned base. "Davy, if he keeps shifting routers how sure can we be that this guy is based in Derry at all?"

"Everything on the s...site is about Derry; restaurants, clubs, bars. He must be fairly young because the places he's talking about are for students and the under thirties. W...When are you coming back?"

"Have you found something else?"

"Yes, and the head of the lake search wants to talk to you as w...well."

He paused, thinking of the lead diver's face when he'd entered the study ten minutes before. His expression had said that they'd found something and that it definitely wasn't good.

Craig read the silence and knew they would be returning to at least one body. Liam saw his shoulders droop and heard the flatness in his voice.

"We'll be there in thirty minutes. Meanwhile, get the IT people to help you trace the blog. We need an accurate address." His next words were tinged with amusement. "If they give you grief about surfing the Net tell them you were checking the local blogs on my say-so."

He cut the call on Davy's sigh of relief and they returned to the car in silence. He threw Liam the keys and sat back to think. They had a blogger who knew something about their case, no, more than that, they knew about the ransom demand and the exact amount. Who else knew that but them, Cameron Lawton and Vera Patterson? He trusted his team not to leak, so that just left The Chronicle's staff. He dialled the number and Vera Patterson answered.

"Good morning. Mr Lawton's office."

"Mrs Patterson, it's Superintendent Craig. Is Mr Lawton there?"

Vera dropped the magazine she'd been flicking through and straightened up as if Craig could see her. Clergy, head teachers and police officers, they scared her stiff, had done since she was a child.

"No, Superintendent...I'm sorry. He's at a conference today."

"Ask him to call me please, it's urgent."

Vera grew even more nervous. The tone in Craig's voice wasn't just policeman stern; it was very annoyed policeman stern. She screwed up her courage to ask why.

"Is there something wrong?"

"Yes, Mrs Patterson, there is. Who else besides you and Mr Lawton knew about the ransom call?"

She froze. His implication was clear; there'd been a leak.

"I didn't say anything...I wouldn't...I'm a confidential secretary."

Craig let her babble until he was sure she was telling the truth.

"Well, unfortunately, someone did and only you and Mr Lawton knew the details of the call."

Vera's heart leapt in relief. "We weren't the only ones." It was out before she had time to consider that she was landing someone else in the shit.

Craig's tone became icy and Liam knew that someone was going to get it in the neck. "Who else knew?"

"It wasn't...they're very young...they didn't know not to..."

Craig was tired and fed up and he had no time to mess

about; his voice reflected it all.

"Who else, Mrs Patterson? You're wasting police time."

She gave a small gulp before gabbling out a reply. "Rory Cahill. He's our runner. He overheard me being interviewed by your W.P.C. and...and he told Ray Mercer, the news editor."

The way she said Mercer's name confirmed she hated him almost as much as them, but if Mercer knew about the ransom call then why wasn't it on the front page? The detective answered his own question; because it was more than Mercer's career was worth to print the contents of a police interview and he knew it, but that wouldn't stop the bastard leaking it to a blogger and then sitting back to watch as word spread. Once it was in the public forum he could print his headline with impunity.

Craig banged his fist hard against the dashboard and Liam grinned, knowing what it meant; someone was going to get a roasting and for once it wasn't him. Craig thought for a moment and then enlisted Vera Patterson's help.

"Mrs Patterson, I'd like you to arrange a meeting for us this afternoon with Mr Lawton and Mr Cahill. D.C.I. Cullen and I will be there around two o'clock."

Before she could say "I'll need to check Mr Lawton's diary" or "I've booked this afternoon off" he'd cut the call, leaving her in no doubt that the meeting wasn't a request. If Lawton and Cahill weren't there at two p.m. then the next time they met would be in a police station with very hard chairs.

****

As soon as Justin O'Hare appeared Annette smiled. He crossed the foyer of the modern office building with the energy of youth and the swagger of the arrogant. But that wasn't why she was smiling. Her lips tilted because O'Hare was the very picture of an alpha male; oozing secondary sexual characteristics like a cheap cologne. His shoulders were broader than Superman's and his jaw was as wide as it could be without him being an anatomical anomaly. She knew that when he spoke it would be in a deep voice, giving him the butch triumvirate. His age fitted their ransom caller's as well so she mentally added him to their shortlist alongside Brendan Gordon. Andy was keen to hear O'Hare's voice so he extended his hand, speaking first.

"Thanks for agreeing to see us, Mr O'Hare."

The young man looked surprised, as if he'd thought he'd had no choice. He shook Andy's hand tentatively and said "my pleasure" in the well-mannered way that he'd been raised to do. It wasn't a big enough sample to tell if his voice was deep or not, but his next words clinched the deal.

"I'm not sure what this is about. Your office just said something to do with Jane Bwye."

Bingo! He was a baritone. But it was a small victory; his accent was pure Derry, no matter how much expensive elocution teachers had tried to iron it out. Even a seasoned mimic would have had trouble disguising that lilt. Something else had caught Annette's attention; he'd referred to Jane Bwye, not Jane. It wasn't the way someone referred to a girlfriend, even a recent ex.

O'Hare led the way to a small office and they each took a seat. After the ritual of tea and introductions Andy waved Annette on. She produced a Dictaphone from her bag and with O'Hare's puzzled agreement switched it on. Another bad sign; anyone who'd made a ransom call wouldn't want their voice on tape. Andy's glance said he already thought O'Hare was a dead-end and Annette tended to agree, but they still had to go through the motions. She dispensed with any preamble.

"Mr O'Hare, you know Jane Bwye. Could you tell us in what context?"

O'Hare stared at the recorder and then back at her, before asking casually. "Is that really necessary?"

She smiled; it could just be curiosity no matter how defensive he seemed. "It will save us returning."

O'Hare smiled as if he never wanted to see them again then composed his absurdly handsome face into a blank mask. "OK. Jane and I dated for a while."

"When?"

"End of last year until this March. It was pretty much over in January but I didn't like to end it before Valentine's." He winked at Andy in an 'all boys together; you understand' way. "Girl's don't like to spend Valentine's alone."

Annette wanted to roll her eyes but he would have seen, so instead she gritted her teeth and continued. "Have you seen her since then?"

The puzzled look returned. "Around town, yes. But not as a girlfriend."

He leaned forward and she tensed. She needn't have worried; all he did was clasp his hands together on the desk.

"Look, if you don't mind me asking, what is all this about? Has something happened to Jane?"

Andy leapt in. "Why would you say that?"

O'Hare stared at him as if he was thick. "Because two cops are asking questions about her!"

Oh. Andy nodded Annette on, not answering O'Hare's query.

"When did you last see Jane Bwye in any context?"

The young executive lounged back again and stared past her through the window. His expression said that he was trying to recall.

"Last week actually."

Annette fought to keep the eagerness from her voice. "Which day?"

He glanced up at the ceiling, as if the answer was written there. "Tuesday. No, wait, it was Wednesday. Just before twelve o'clock."

"It was definitely her? You saw her face?"

"Definitely."

"Twelve o'clock midday?"

He shook his head. "At night. Midnight. She was in that sports car of hers; she loves that bloody thing more than she loves her dog."

Annette's eagerness was becoming hard to hide. If Jane had still been alive at midnight on that Wednesday, it could help them time the assaults.

"Where did you see her?"

"Shipquay Street. She was almost doing the ton. I was leaving the pub with some mates, just about to cross the road, when she came belting down the hill."

"We'll need your friends' names."

O'Hare shrugged and then narrowed his eyes. "Why? *Has* something happened to Jane? You'd better tell me or I'm not answering any more questions, and I'm definitely not giving you my mates' names."

He folded his gym-bulked arms defiantly. Andy considered for a moment and then spoke.

"We have concerns about Jane's safety and anything you can tell us would be helpful."

O'Hare's eyes widened and his arms unravelled instantly. He leaned forward again. "Sure. We weren't right for each other but she's a nice girl. I wouldn't like anything to happen to her." After a brief pause he continued. "I'll write my mates' names down, but they'll tell you the same. Jane belted past us like a bat out of hell. Her passenger must've been terrified."

Annette almost squeaked her next words. "Passenger? She had someone with her?"

O'Hare looked even more bewildered but he decided he didn't want to know what the questions were about. "There was a man in the passenger seat. I didn't see his face."

"How did you know he was a man then?"

He rolled his eyes rudely.

"Because I could see his hands and legs. It was definitely a man. He was wearing jeans, so probably young. Mind you, with Jeremy Clarkson..." A sharp glance from Annette hurried him on. "I couldn't swear to their colour." He grinned sheepishly. "We were all a bit drunk."

Andy changed tack. "Which direction was the car heading?"

O'Hare thought for a moment, trying to orientate himself outside the pub. "Towards the Guildhall."

As far away from Rocksbury as was possible. Andy checked, just to be sure.

"Was she going home?"

O'Hare's "no" was emphatic. "Nowhere close. That's

partly why I remember, well that and the fact that she nearly knocked me down."

Annette cut in. "When had you last seen her before that?"

"Months before. In June, at a friend's wedding."

"We'll need the friend's name."

"Sure."

"Did she bring a date?"

O'Hare shook his head and Annette noticed the tip of a tattoo on his neck. It was well hidden but she didn't imagine that mummy and daddy were best pleased.

"Not that I saw, but I was with someone so I didn't pay much attention. The bride and groom might know."

He glanced at the wall clock and Annette knew that it was time to leave. Justin O'Hare wasn't their perp; she'd been convinced of that the moment he'd let them get his voice on tape. But the interview had been more useful that they could have hoped for. Andy rose to leave, extending his hand again.

"Thank you, Mr O'Hare. That's been very helpful."

O'Hare gripped his hand and then said, in an anxious voice. "You will let me know if Jane's OK, won't you? She's had a hard time, what with her father..."

His voice tailed off and Annette knew that he was well aware of Oliver Bwye's violent streak.

She smiled and nodded. "Thank you for your help, Mr O'Hare. If we need to ask you anything more, where can we reach you?"

He produced a business card with a flourish that said he did it several times a day. As Annette took it she played a hunch and asked one last question.

"Mr O'Hare, I hope you won't think this impertinent, but could I ask you something related to your family?"

His eyebrows rose in surprise but he nodded her on.

"Did your father have some financial troubles, bad investments perhaps, and lose a lot of his money?"

She didn't know what sort of response she'd expected but it definitely wasn't a loud guffaw. O'Hare laughed and beckoned them to the window, waving at the streets outside.

"My father owns the building we're standing in and

the four blocks around it. He's worth millions."

Annette smiled at the young executive and mentally struck him off their list. He'd just given them more useful information. That the Bwyes' cook had lied.

****

Craig nodded at the dry-suited sergeant to lift back the cloth, fighting the urge to vomit when he saw Diana Bwye's bloated face. He knew from photographs that she'd been a pretty woman, with soft, dark curls and eyes to match; but there was none of that prettiness now. Now there was only swollen blue-white flesh, so swollen that it was hard to say where her nose ended and her lips began. Her skin was frayed, as if fish had been nibbling on it for days, and the water and weed fronds had coloured her dark curls olive green. He turned away from the gurney, waving for her to be re-covered and disguising his pity with logical questions and a brisk tone.

"Who found her?"

The sergeant thought for a moment then beckoned a young man across. He was still dressed in diving gear. The search that had started the night before wouldn't be finished for quite a while.

"McCullough, tell the Superintendent where you found the lady."

Joel McCullough was tall and thin, like a stick of liquorice, an analogy aided by his black dry-suit. Beneath his rubber hood his face was solemn; as anyone's would be when they'd just found a woman dead, although Craig suspected that it was the diver's default expression even when he felt happy about life.

He nodded at Craig. "Hello, sir." Then he turned and pointed towards the east side of the lake. "She was in the mid-depths near the shore." He indicated a wet mass of plastic at their feet. "They'd weighed her down with rocks inside this sack."

"Are the rocks still in there?"

"We didn't touch anything; forensics might still get something. Although judging by her skin I'd say she's been down there at least a week."

It fitted with disposal immediately after she'd disappeared. Craig thought for a moment before speaking again. "You gentlemen will have seen a few bodies like this in your time. Are loose rocks an efficient way of keeping them down?"

McCullough was the first to shake his head. "Useless. Too small and plastic's far too thin. The currents wear it down then the rocks fall out and up they float." He nodded at the sack. "This wouldn't have held her more than another week, even if we hadn't come looking. There's something else strange, sir. Her head was exposed. The sack was tied at her neck."

Craig stared past him into the water, picturing Diana Bwye's last moments. He shuddered, and then shuddered again at the image of her killer staring into her eyes as he disposed of her. Had making her look at him given him a sadistic thrill?

He asked another question. "So, what *would* keep someone down?"

The sergeant answered immediately. "A concrete overcoat. Encase the body completely and its weight will keep it down forever, unless it's found by accident."

McCullough nodded in agreement and Craig gazed across the lake. Oliver Bwye was in there somewhere, he was sure of that, the only question was had his daughter suffered the same fate.

****

11.30 a.m.

"Right. There have been some developments." Craig scanned the room, frowning. "Julia and Gerry missing again?"

Annette turned from adding milk to her tea. "They were interviewing Diana Bwye's charity friends and then heading to the golf-club. Maybe they didn't get the message that we were briefing early."

More likely Julia had decided to march to her own drum, like she usually did. Craig could picture her, determined to solve the case and impress him, even now that she was happy with someone else.

"OK. Bring them up to speed after the briefing, please."

When everyone was seated he began.

"A body has been found in the lake. It's Diana Bwye."

He paused for a moment to let the inevitable gasps and "No"s run through the group, then he carried on.

"She was wrapped in black plastic with rocks inside. The sack was tied at her neck, leaving her face exposed."

Liam tutted. "Useless way of keeping her down."

Annette smacked his arm. "Liam!"

"I'm only saying."

"Too much as usual."

Craig raised a hand to still the exchange. "Liam's right, however inelegantly he put it. The lead diver says it's an ineffective way of hiding a body. Covering her with concrete would have been more efficient. Which means that either our killer is an amateur or...? Anyone?"

Annette answered first. "They got sentimental because it was a woman? Could that go with leaving her face uncovered?"

"Possibly. Anything else?"

Davy chipped in. "They'd w...watched the wrong movies."

Craig shook his head. Davy's humour was becoming almost as dark as Liam's.

"Another option is that it gave them a thrill to make her watch them, but let's go with Annette's idea. Sentimental because it was just any woman or because they knew Diana Bwye personally?"

Liam nodded. Personal knowledge would go with the killer being Oliver Bwye. A family annihilator, albeit not one who wanted to be seen as such.

"If it was Bwye then he mightn't have wanted to cover her face, although if he'd hated her..." He screwed up his face. "I've seen people do terrible things to the faces of people they hated. By the way, how was she killed?"

An image of Diana Bwye's neck covered in dark bruising filled Craig's mind.

"The preliminary examination showed two bullet wounds but also marks of strangulation. We're waiting for Mike to tell us more."

"Could the marks have just been where the sack was tied?"

"Too deep."

Liam wasn't letting it go, no matter how unpleasant Craig's expression said he found the discussion.

"OK then. Manual strangulation or ligature? You know it makes a difference, boss."

Craig closed his eyes, trying to recall the bruise pattern. He re-opened them and nodded.

"Ligature, and you're right, it does make a difference. Ligature's more impersonal and it doesn't have to be done face on. If Oliver Bwye had strangled her in anger he'd have been more likely to do it face to face and by hand."

Annette thought out loud. "She must have been badly shot as well, given the blood loss at the house, but she obviously didn't die of it if they had to strangle her. That means she either got treatment for the gunshot or they strangled her soon after they left the house, probably the latter as she was dumped in the lake. If Bwye didn't do it then who did? And why? No-one's called back for the ransom."

Craig shook his head. "Let's not jump ahead. We're still speculating whether Oliver Bwye did it; the only way we'll know for sure is if: we find his body, we ask him, or forensics rules him out. Mike can help with that." He paused to top up his coffee then restarted. "Right. Diana Bwye belongs to pathology now but there are still two more people who we might find alive. Who wants to start?"

Annette raised her pen.

"Andy and I met with Justin O'Hare. He fits the physical description that would suit the ransom caller's voice, but he has a Derry accent."

"Accents can be faked."

She nodded. "True, but I doubt it this time." She held up the tape recorder. "We've got a voice sample for the linguists, Davy."

Craig cut in. "And you've already got one for Gordon." He shot Liam a chastising look. "Remember to keep

Gordon's under the net, Davy. If it matches we'll get another, official one." He motioned Annette on.

"Anyway, O'Hare was very helpful. First, whoever said his father was broke was wrong. O'Hare senior owns half of the city centre."

Davy cut in. "It w...was the cook. She told Julia."

Craig nodded. "Annette, re-interview her please. Carry on."

She swallowed a hastily drunk mouthful of tea. "O'Hare admitted to dating Jane Bwye but said that it was almost a year ago. They dated from December 2013 to March this year and it was no big love affair."

"For whom?"

"O'Hare certainly, but both of them by the sounds of it."

"Did he say who she was dating now?"

Annette shook her head. "No. The last time he saw her was at a mutual friend's wedding in June." She gestured to Andy. "We're going to follow that up, to see if Jane took a date."

She suddenly realised she'd been hogging the floor and that Andy had let her, so she nodded him to take over. Craig noticed that his ubiquitous blue shirt had been replaced today by a jumper in the same shade. Mrs White had been shopping again.

"Aye well. O' Hare was useful, right enough. He was in town with his mates last Wednesday night, rolling out of a pub around midnight, when he saw Jane drive past with a man."

Craig stopped him. "It was definitely Jane Bwye?"

Andy nodded. "And he saw the legs of a man in the passenger seat, wearing jeans, so probably young. She was driving so fast she almost creamed him, hey. He said she was doing the ton."

Craig leaned forward urgently. "Which direction?"

"Guildhall. Miles away from here."

"Did O'Hare say anything about how she looked? Scared? Desperate? As if she was being forced to cooperate?"

Andy and Annette glanced at each other, realising that they hadn't asked. Annette shook her head.

"Sorry, sir. We didn't ask. I'll phone him to check."

"Do that. Although if she was driving at 100mph in the centre of town it's fair to say she probably looked nervous, anxious or drunk. Andy, check Brendan Gordon's alibi for Wednesday night. He said he was studying, but he might have been out joyriding with Jane."

Craig thought for a moment. Bernadette Ross had seen the Mercedes entering the estate at around six-thirty that Wednesday and had assumed that the driver was Jane. Now they had a definite sighting of Jane driving the car through town around midnight that same night. Had she been at the house between six-thirty and midnight? If so, her speeding could have indicated that she was running away from their killer. But if Diana Bwye had been being attacked, would Jane really have left her in trouble? And where had the car been between midnight that Wednesday and when they'd found it burnt out? He turned to Davy.

"Davy, were there any tracks found in the mud at the back door, other than a van's?"

Davy shook his head. "No. But I've got more on the van if you w...want it."

"In a minute." Craig crossed the room and dragged the white board back with him, scribbling on it for a moment while the others topped up their drinks. A rap of his marker drew their attention.

"OK. The right hand column contains sightings of Jane Bwye's car. Davy, I need to know where it was between six-thirty and midnight on Wednesday and between then and when it was found burnt out. That means every traffic camera and CCTV in the city and surrounds needs checked."

Davy opened his mouth to object.

"Get Carmen to help you, she can do it from Belfast."

The analyst's mouth closed again. Carmen was good at IT stuff, although not as good as him of course. Craig was still talking.

"If we can track the car's movements then it might help us I.D. Jane's companion." He tapped the left hand column. "OK, Jane's blood wasn't found in the house."

He remembered something and turned to Davy again. "Has Des estimated the weight in the van from the depth of the treads?"

Davy clicked on his laptop and beckoned them over to see. "Yep. There's a bit of reverse engineering here. Giving Oliver Bwye a w...weight of 100kg, gauged from an estimate by Bernadette Ross and his life insurance form from s...six months ago-"

Craig interrupted. "He only took out the life insurance six months ago?"

Davy shook his head. "He increased it six months ago. He'd had it for years."

Craig had a vague recollection of twenty million being mentioned.

"What did he increase it to?"

Davy opened another window on his computer. "Twenty million. It was twelve million before."

It was quite a hike. Davy saw Craig's look. "That's w...what I thought at first, but all the exclusions still apply on Bwye's health, and if Bwye is dead he'll obviously get nothing. But now Mrs Bwye's dead that changes things. S...She was insured under it, so it w...was worth Bwye killing her for the insurance, or for Jane to kill them both."

Craig parked the information and nodded him on.

"OK. Mrs Bwye's weight was easier to find, she had a medical last month; she weighed 51kg. So adding their w...weights together we get 151kg, which, allowing five kilos for the dog, is Des' estimate from the depth of the treads, give or take five kilos."

Annette gasped. "Jane wasn't in the van!"

Liam snorted. "We already know that. She drove through Derry at midnight."

Andy was quick to disagree. "You're assuming the kidnapping happened before midnight, hey. They could have been taken any time before eight-thirty on the Thursday morning, when Bernie Ross arrived. Jane could have come back here after O'Hare saw her car, and still been taken."

Liam opened his mouth to argue and Craig rapped the board again, beckoning them to pay attention.

"Davy's just proved empirically that Jane wasn't in the van and we know that her blood wasn't at the scene, so for now let's say she wasn't a victim. But Andy's right, we can't rule her out of events happening after midnight; she could easily have doubled back here after O'Hare saw her in town, although her speeding in the opposite direction suggests otherwise. The question becomes, was she driving away from the house that night because she was involved in her parents' deaths, because she'd seen something and was terrified, or for some unrelated reason?"

Annette looked embarrassed. "Sorry, sir, but I have to disagree. We still have nothing to say that Jane wasn't in the van. She could have been the driver."

Davy glanced up at her words and shook his head. He'd been tapping his smart-pad in a way that Craig had often suspected meant he was playing a computer game, but half Davy's attention was already worth twice someone else's so he let him off.

"S...Sorry, I should have said. Des allowed a range of seventy to ninety kilos for the driver. That means -"

Craig cut in. "Jane was petite, no more than fifty kilos judging from her photographs, so on her own she would have been too light, and Jane plus even a tiny man would have been too heavy. Plus, the driver would have to have been a decent sized man to get Bwye and his wife into the van. Jane definitely wasn't in the van, but it was a point well made, Annette."

Davy sniffed slightly at being interrupted but Craig's miracle on his PhD had earned him at least one pass.

Liam wasn't convinced. "Correct me if I'm wrong, lad, but if old man Bwye's in the lake and he's stayed down this long, it's likely he wasn't buried with stones. What if they brought weights in the van? Did you allow for that?"

Davy thought for a moment before giving a grudging "no." Not grudging because he was wrong but because the question hadn't even occurred to him. To be second guessed was embarrassing, to be second guessed by Liam meant that he'd gloat for days. He was saved by having a new idea.

"The w...weight range Des allowed for the male driver

could still allow for twenty kilos of weights."

Liam shook his head and Davy could feel his gloating period extending to weeks.

"Not so fast, Einstein. What about if the van was equipped for disabled access?" He gestured towards the back door. "They could have just lowered a platform outside the back door and the Bwyes could have been rolled onto it. A woman could have done that. Maybe they even walked; if they were bleeding but not dead yet."

Everyone was silent for a moment, then the "ah buts" began.

"It would still have been easier for a man to roll them. Oliver Bwye was big."

"If Bwye masterminded the whole thing he could have carried his wife."

Davy shook his head. "If Bwye did it himself then w...why would he have needed an accomplice to drive the van? The weight calculations definitively say there was another man on board, but not Jane as well."

Craig let the discussion run for a moment before he raised a hand.

"Liam's made a good point. Davy, if you add hydraulic lifts, ramps and disabled alterations to the van's description, how does it affect the weight and does it narrow down the number of Ford Transits that fit?"

Davy typed in the amendment reluctantly and then gawped at the screen. It had reduced the number of vans to two! He pulled up the details.

"The modifications would only increase the van's w...weight by between twenty to thirty kilos and that's allowed for in the driver's weight range. But it cuts the possible number of vans to two. One is registered to..."

He paused until Annette prompted him eagerly.

"Who? Who is it registered to?"

Davy turned to her, astonished. "The Belfast Chronicle!"

Even Craig was shocked. "What? Are you sure?"

"Positive. The other is registered to a charity that works with disabled people."

"Diana Bwye was involved with charities."

Davy shook his head. "It's not one of hers."

Andy asked the obvious question. "What does The Chronicle need a disabled van for, hey?"

Craig shook his head. "It's not for disability. They use ramps and hydraulic lifts to load and unload bales of newspapers. When we find the van my guess is forensics will find newspaper ink all over the back."

Andy looked confused. "Are we saying The Chronicle had something to do with Oliver Bwye's kidnap?"

Craig shook his head. "We can't say anything yet, not until we find either Bwye or the van. But it narrows the search, so well done, Liam. When did you think of that?"

"Same time you did; when we were out at the lake. If the van drove to the water's edge I reckoned a ramp or hoist would make it easier to get the bodies into the water or onto a boat. A hydraulic lift would have worked as well." He steepled his fingers, trying to look wise. "I think the perp noticed they'd left the treads almost immediately, and realised it was because of the Bwyes' weight. So he killed them quickly, dumped them in the lake and then drove away, back over his own treads. That's why there were no clear tracks leading away from the lake, just mush." He gestured at the study's rear door. "The land out there and at the lake softened because of the rain that night, but it wasn't heavy enough to unfreeze the fields further away from the house, so the treads disappeared once they were on hard ground."

"There wouldn't have been a perfect overlap of the treads at the lake but it was a good enough cover in the mud. Davy, get Des busy ruling that out."

Annette was puzzled. "But they must have known they would leave treads before they came, so why not just kill the Bwyes in the house instead of loading their weight into the van?"

Liam shook his head. "They probably didn't think that it would be so muddy. Think about it; it was a freezing cold December night; even if it had rained a bit the ground should still have been as hard as rock. They reckoned without the warmth from the house making the ground at the back door unfreeze. They noticed the treads after they'd driven a minute and that's when they decided to dump the Bwyes."

"You're expecting Oliver Bwye to be in the lake as well."

It was a statement of fact.

"Aren't you? Anyway, we'll know soon enough."

Craig sipped his drink. "OK, Davy, you've more to go on now with both the van and car. Any joy on the prints in here?"

"No-one who s...shouldn't have been in the house."

Annette cut in. "What about the prints on the whisky decanter?"

"They don't match any of the s...staff and whoever it is they don't have a record. I'm still looking. The rest of the house's forensics yielded nothing."

Craig nodded. "Hopefully Diana Bwye's body will. Medical records?"

The analyst's aquiline face lit up. "Yep. I got an updated transcript from the local emergency department. Both Diana and Jane Bwye had attended hospital more often in the past two months."

"With?"

"Same as before but more frequently. It looks like Bwye's violence was getting w...worse."

"Did they report him to the police?"

"Only once. Mrs Bwye called 999 about four w...weeks ago and officers called here at the house. But when they arrived she was reluctant to make a statement so Bwye wasn't charged."

Craig frowned. Too often the abused let their abusers off the hook; it frustrated the hell out of the police. "Do you have a tape of the call?"

Davy tapped his laptop and they listened as an obviously terrified woman begged for help, saying that her husband had gone berserk and was hitting their daughter.

Craig thought for a moment. "Did they attend the emergency department that night?"

"Yes. Both Jane and her mother were treated for abrasions and bruises. Diana Bwye had a bad gash on her left arm, probably from defending Jane. It needed s...stitches."

Annette shivered; remembering the fractured hand

her ex-husband had gifted her.

"It sounds as if Bwye was escalating, sir. God knows what he did when he came home drunk from the golf-club last week."

Craig shook his head; something still didn't fit but he couldn't put his finger on it. Just then the study door opened and Julia and Gerry entered, out of breath.

"Sorry. We went to see a woman who did charity work with Mrs Bwye and got stuck behind a lorry on the pass."

Snow and ice made the steep Glenshane Pass a challenge at the best of times; add in a slow lorry and a single lane and Craig pictured them sitting there for hours. He was right.

Gerry chipped in. "Eighty minutes it took us! Eighty minutes for ten fricking miles, and when we got there she told us nothing except 'Diana Bwye bakes lovely cakes'. Remind me never to transfer up here."

They both looked frozen so Annette rushed to perk fresh coffee while Craig beckoned them over to the fire. When Julia had stopped shivering he asked a question.

"So, was it all about cakes?"

"Not entirely. She confirmed what we suspected, that Bwye beat his wife and daughter and a lot of local people knew. We didn't make it to the golf-club and I'm not sure that we will today. There's a blizzard brewing out there."

Craig walked to the window and gazed out at the whitening countryside. He loved snow, it came a close second to his love of water, but he liked it more when he could ski on it, not when he had to drive through it to Belfast. Liam's next words made him shelve his self-pity.

"Pity the poor buggers diving in that lake."

Julia turned sharply. "They're looking for bodies?"

"Aye. They've already found Diana Bwye."

Craig stilled her looming questions. "Annette will bring you up to speed later. Liam and I have got to drive to Belfast, so we need to wrap it up." He scanned the circle of faces. "Anyone got anything else they're burning to say?"

Davy nodded. "It's about Father Fred."

Gerry opened his mouth to ask something but Craig shook his head, not missing the sergeant's scowl. He wasn't repeating every piece of information for his benefit and there was no point in him making a face about it. They shouldn't have been late.

"What about him, Davy?"

"Well, it's just...one of the new comments on his blog could be from Jane Bwye."

Craig jerked to attention. "What? How do you know?"

"It came in an hour ago, in answer to the question 'Is s...six million pounds enough to redress the balance and hit a power broker where it hurts?'" He elaborated, despite Craig's reluctant to update the newbies. "That was posted yesterday; the day after the ransom call was made to Cameron Lawton's office."

Craig urged him on. "And?"

"Today's comment w...was posted from somewhere in Derry, by someone who called themselves Andromeda. In Greek mythology Andromeda was a daughter who was treated badly by her father, so I thought that it might be Jane."

Liam snorted. "A well-read blackmailer. They can run the prison library."

"Anyway, s...she answered that she'd thought it might be, but nothing could compensate for the pain they'd caused. S...So I thought...maybe, definitely, Jane Bwye?"

Craig didn't answer, just began scribbling on the board. After a moment he stepped back so everyone could read his words. Wednesday night; Kidnap. Following Tuesday; ransom call for six million. Wednesday; blog post opening the debate, almost certainly with information leaked from The Chronicle. Thursday; the battered daughter's response. He tapped the marker against the days.

"There were two days between the ransom call and this possible comment from Jane, and there have been no more ransom calls since the first. I'm going to speculate here, but unless we find Jane Bwye's body in the lake or we get another ransom call pretty damn quick, I'll think I'm right." He retook his seat. "OK, let's say that you're Jane and you come home that Wednesday evening at six-thirty, to find your mother alone just staring at a blank TV. A few hours later your father comes in drunk from the golf-club and starts a fight, just as he's done many times before. Your mother tells you to leave, trying to protect you." He scanned the circle of faces; some people were listening avidly while others looked more sceptical.

"So you go out for the evening with your unsuitable boyfriend, maybe the defiance of knowing that your father wouldn't approve of him spurs you on. Eventually you go back home, late, bringing the boyfriend with you for protection, or maybe to finally tell your father about him and hack him off. You find no sign of anyone in the main house so your boyfriend helps himself to your father's whisky -"

Annette jumped in eagerly. "And forgets to put the decanter back."

Craig nodded. "Then you notice that the study door is open, when it never is. You enter and see the blood but you don't know what to do. What do you do next?"

Julia chipped in. "Call the police."

Annette shook her head. "You run. You're young and scared and whoever's taken your parents might come back. Or, if it's your father, he may have killed your mother and you think that you're next. Jane wouldn't have known whether the blood belonged to one or both of her parents just by looking at it."

Gerry joined in. "She could have assumed that it was all her mother's and that he'd killed her. He was drunk and aggressive earlier that evening, after all."

Liam's bass drowned out the rising speculation. "Annette's right; you'd get the hell out of Dodge, but it's because you also know you'll look as guilty as hell. Your dad won't give you your inheritance for years, he beats you and everyone knows you hate him; you're suspect number one for the crime."

Craig nodded. "You're an immature young woman, probably with an equally immature boyfriend, a boyfriend who your father definitely won't like. You're the obvious suspects, especially as there are two of you. Maybe she told the boyfriend to leave and he wouldn't, but if the police had arrived to find both of them here surrounded by blood and with Jane's parents missing, they'd be suspects number one and two. So you run like hell and you keep on running. If Jane had been alone then she might have called the police because she would have looked vulnerable, but having a man with her means that together they could feasibly have attacked her parents. That's why Justin O'Hare saw the car racing through town that night. They were running away."

He could see that Andy wasn't convinced.

"OK, Andy. Tell me what you're thinking."

"Well...if you're so innocent how come you make a ransom demand a few days later?"

"You've said it yourself; a few days later, in fact almost a whole week. If Jane had planned the original kidnap then why wait all that time to make the call? And why not follow up with another call outlining how to pay?" He shook his head. "The ransom demand was an afterthought."

Annette frowned. "I agree, sir, but Andy's right. Why make a demand at all?"

Craig shrugged. "Jane can't come back to the house and she's got no money. No money until she's thirty in fact, unless she uses her credit cards and she'd know we would have a trace on those. She thinks someone has kidnapped or killed one or both of her parents, so there's an element of shock and grief there as well, especially about her mother. But she also sees money as her chance to break free of her father's control in the event that he ever comes back, so they make the ransom call. It was a stupid idea and I think they realised it soon afterwards, hence the lack of a follow up. That blog comment sounds to me like someone in pain."

Annette nodded. It was all possible.

"Perhaps the boyfriend talked some sense into her, sir. So do you think they burnt out the car to avoid a trail?"

Craig nodded. "When this is all over I think we'll find the two of them holed up somewhere, living on baked beans." His face grew solemn. "That's if I'm right and we don't find Jane at the bottom of the lake like her mum."

He stood up and buttoned his jacket. "Andy, you're in charge tonight; we'll be back later if the roads are passable. If not it'll be tomorrow morning."

Liam hoped it snowed hard. He fancied some home cooking even if it meant putting up with his brother-in-law.

"Annette, re-interview the cook and the rest of the staff with Julia, and then get to that golf-club. I want every detail you can get about Oliver Bwye's behaviour that evening. Gerry, keep an eye on what's happening at the lake then go to the mortuary and see what Mike has to say on Diana Bwye's P.M. Davy, do what you do and find out exactly where the van and Mercedes went that night. And everyone, remember to..."

He was interrupted by a discordant chorus. "Keep you up to date."

Chapter Thirteen

The man adjusted his binoculars and watched as the old black Audi pulled away from the house. He imagined its driver racing to interview this or that one, all of them innocent of the crime that the police had come to solve. He allowed himself a moment's satisfaction at a job well done, but it was short-lived, erased by the sob provoking sadness that followed. In another life none of this would have been necessary. In another life they could all have had happiness instead.

He dashed away a tear and realigned his focus to the back of the house, on the small dark door that had allowed him access and egress that night. He'd been impressed with the planning and the readiness to do what had had to be done; but he couldn't lay claim to the plan, or take credit for the confusion it now provoked. His role had simply been to do as he was bid.

The helper watched for a moment longer as men and women came and went through the door, scattering this way and that, towards the lake and elsewhere. The man driving to the lake looked tired. They all did; too many nights in a cold hotel, too many days with no respite from work. He adjusted his lens until the lead diver's face was as close as his hand; his weathered skin and pale lips testament to the elements and the freezing lake. Its use had been a last resort but a boon, and he'd been briefed to come well prepared. Now the divers had found Diana and fairly soon they would find Oliver too, but the one thing he prayed fervently for was that they would never find him.

****

Craig drove so fast that Liam spent half of the seventy-mile journey to Belfast with one hand gripping his seatbelt and the other the passenger door. The only time they slowed down was on the pass, where the snow hid too much icy danger to go above twenty mph. Liam pressed the buttons on the radio, searching for something to sooth his nerves, but the closest he got to a sedative was the crooning of a country and western song. Where was André Rieu when you needed him?

Craig was either blind to how fast he was driving or ignoring it, no doubt preparing his defence for speeding as 'urgent police business'; in which case why he didn't just stick on the blue lights and floor it Liam had no idea. On one moderately paced stretch of road, courtesy of a tractor driver that Liam could have hugged, he decided to ask what the hurry was, in his own inimitable style.

"What's biting your ass, boss?"

Craig was willing the tractor to move so hard that Liam could see the vein on his temple standing up. He answered without turning.

"What?"

Liam sighed and then tried again in English. "Why are you driving like a bat out of hell?"

"I'm not."

Craig's tone said he really believed it.

"You bloody are! You've been doing the ton since we left the estate. Look!"

Craig turned to see Liam pointing at a sign that said 'Belfast City Centre, 10 miles'. As they'd only left Rocksbury at twelve o'clock that meant he'd averaged 90 mph! Liam pressed his advantage.

"I'm surprised we haven't been nicked. We will be if you do that speed in town. Gabe Ronson runs the traffic lads and they're pretty sharp."

Inspector Gabriel Ronson, Gabe to his friends and enemies alike, had an absolute, 'right or wrong' approach to life. There were no grey areas in Ronson's universe; one mile above the speed limit was the same as fifty to him. Both meant a £100 fine and three points and he didn't care if you were rushing your pregnant wife to the hospital or for that matter if you were a cop. If you were you'd better be pursuing a perp with the driving skills of Lewis Hamilton, because any other reason for speeding and your name went in his book. Ronson had the scalps of Lords, famous actors and an ex-Chief Constable on his list; they showed his even handed approach to the law, a point Liam now laboured with glee.

"He won't let you off, you know. He nicked an A.C.C. last month."

Craig didn't show it but he was shocked at the speed that he'd been doing. He'd been so preoccupied with the case and their impending encounter with Ray Mercer that he'd completely lost track, although part of him was impressed that his twelve-year-old car could still manage it. He knew Liam was right; Gabe was a rising star, who totalled the points his team awarded speeders like he was playing a computer game with promotion as first prize.

Craig nodded. "Sorry. I hadn't realised I was going so fast."

Liam grinned. "You were pressing that accelerator like you were stomping on Mercer's head."

Craig grimaced. "Don't tempt me." He glanced at his deputy. "I'd ask you to rein me in with Mercer except you're even worse with him than I am."

Liam shook his head and gestured towards the turn-off they needed to make. "You'll be grand. If you're thinking of stepping over the line just remember he's bound to have a tape recorder running and you'll never live it down. Make him look the villain and it'll never see the light of day."

Craig took deep breaths all the way to The Chronicle's offices and by the time they arrived he was almost Zen. They climbed the four flights of stone stairs instead of taking the lift and when they reached Cameron Lawton's suite of offices, he was calmer than even Rieu could have achieved. They were surprised to see Maggie Clarke emerge through the suite's heavy glass doors.

Craig smiled. "Hello, Maggie. Nice to see you." He meant it. What had begun as a tense relationship, courtesy of his past experiences with the press, had softened over two years to being drinking buddies whenever Davy invited her along. Liam gazed down at her with a dolorous expression.

"The lad's pining for you in the frozen north."

She blushed becomingly and pushed at his arm in embarrassment. "No he isn't. You're teasing me."

Liam guffawed. "Imagine what I do to him."

She rolled her eyes and turned back to Craig. "If

you're looking for Mr Lawton, I'm afraid he's not in. He's at a conference in London today."

Craig frowned. One part of his plan awry already, but he wasn't giving up.

"Do you know a young man called Cahill?"

"Rory?"

"Yes."

She smiled as if she was fond of the boy, then her smile turned to concern. "Is he in trouble?"

Craig shook his head. He just wanted to confirm that the lad had told Mercer about the ransom call before he approached the culprit himself.

"I just need a word."

Maggie began to descend the stairs they'd climbed. "Follow me. He's in the newsroom."

Two floors down she stopped by a glass and mahogany door that looked as if it had been there for hundreds of years. It probably had; they were in the Cathedral Quarter, part of Belfast's eighteen-century linen district. As she yanked the door open, Craig was shocked by the tsunami of sound that emerged. Maggie led the way through a long, narrow room filled with people yelling, keys tapping and phones ringing off the hook.

As they walked past desks with paper piled on top, beneath them and on either side, Craig wondered how anyone worked in such a mess, but the excited young faces and a few older ones said that The Chronicle's reporters thrived on chaos.

At the end of the newsroom lay a door bearing the sign 'News Editor' and a smaller one beside it with 'Deputy' on its brass plate. Maggie opened it and suddenly they were in a fragrant oasis. When the door closed behind them there was instant peace.

Liam wandered nosily around the small room, occasionally lifting an ornament or a photograph, while Craig took a seat, marvelling at how tidy it was and how like jasmine it smelled. It reminded him of childhood summers in Italy.

"People must love coming in here, Maggie. It's like a spa."

She giggled girlishly and put on the kettle to boil, while Liam walked to her wall of windows and gazed out across the piazza of St Anne's Square.

"Great view you have."

"One of the few perks of the job."

He lifted a photograph that had pride of place on her desk, twisting it around to show Craig. It was of Davy and her, looking happier than anyone had a right to be.

"Does the lad know that you stare at him all day?"

She grabbed the photo so fast even Craig was surprised. "The lad knows."

Liam heard the kettle boil and took a seat. "Aye well, just don't expect him to do the same. I'd never let him live it down."

Craig listened to the exchange with his mind still on the case. A few sips of coffee later he decided to pick Maggie's brains.

"Have you ever heard of a blogger called Father Fred?"

She laughed and passed Liam a plate of biscuits. "Like Father Ted?" She saw Craig was serious and shook her head. "Never. What does he blog on?"

Craig was surprised. He hadn't realised that bloggers had topic areas. "What do you mean?"

"Well...for instance, the Huffington Post blogs on political issues. Another one blogs about government corruption. Then you have the vloggers, the ones who make video blogs. There are millions of them all over the world and basically, unless they libel someone, they can say whatever they want. Their host sites might censor them but the good ones can get past that."

Craig shook his head. "I had no idea. I suppose that's why they call it the fifth estate, because it's so widespread?"

Maggie shrugged. "I suppose. I know we're the fourth but I never knew what the others were."

Liam chipped in, surprising them both with his knowledge. "The first, second and third estates are clergy, nobility and the commons, the fourth is you lot, fifth is apparently blogging so I call the Bwye's estate the sixth. Get it?"

Craig was never shocked when he knew things, he just wished he would display his knowledge a bit more often. Maggie stared at Liam for a moment and then turned back to Craig.

"This Father Fred blogger. Is he local?"

Craig shook his head. "Derry. Don't worry, Davy's on top of it." He straightened up. "Now, Rory Cahill. I take it the reason you brought us in is that you want to be there when we speak to him?"

"If that's OK? You'll scare him to death otherwise. He's very young."

Craig shrugged. "It's fine, but we need to see him now."

She left the room hastily while Liam had another nosy around, looking for things to embarrass Davy with. When he heard Maggie returning he retook his seat, with an innocent expression that had never fooled anyone. The door opened and Maggie ushered in a small, thin boy not much older than sixteen. By the terrified expression on his face Craig knew that she'd briefed him, but he was still unprepared for their authority and size.

Both men rose as he entered and Liam's paunch was eye level with the boy. Cahill stared first at it and then slowly up at Liam's face, jumping back when he saw his perp-ready scowl. Maggie gripped the boy's shoulders to prevent his impending bolt and set him down firmly in a seat. She spoke in a soothing voice.

"Now, Rory, I've told you that you're not in any trouble." Not strictly true. "These officers just want to ask you a few questions."

Her words fell on deaf ears. Cahill was still staring at Liam. Craig sat and waved a hand in front of the boy's face, giving a slight smile as he turned.

"I'm Superintendent Craig, Mr Cahill. We need to ask you a few things. All right?"

The teenager nodded slowly at Craig with one eye still on his deputy.

"On Wednesday you overheard a conversation in Mr Lawton's office, didn't you?"

The boy's eyes darted frantically to Maggie and she smiled reassuringly and squeezed his hand.

"Tell them the truth, Rory."

After a moment's consideration he nodded and Craig smiled again.

"Good. Can you tell us what you overheard please?"

Another glance at Liam and Cahill suddenly decided to cooperate. "I heard Mrs Patterson telling someone that she'd had a call, asking for six million pounds ransom for someone called the Bwyes."

Craig nodded. "Mrs Patterson was speaking to a police constable, giving a statement. Did you know who the Bwyes were?"

Cahill shook his mousy head. "Not then. I asked someone and they said someone called Oliver Bwye used to own the paper."

"Who did you ask?"

"Bill Reynolds on the news desk."

Maggie rolled her eyes and signalled she would tell them more when Cahill had left.

"OK, then what did you do?"

"Bill asked me why I was asking, so I told him. I forgot all about it after that."

"You didn't tell anyone else what you'd heard?"

The boy shook his head so hard that Craig thought it would fall off. "No, no-one. I swear."

Liam frowned at him so menacingly that Cahill leapt off his chair and raced to the door. Craig blocked his path.

"It's OK, Rory. You're not in trouble, but I'd advise you not to listen at doors again. It could land you in a mess someday."

Even as he said it he knew that eavesdropping had made many reporters' careers and that Rory Cahill would do it again. He nodded the lad out and turned to see Liam stifling a laugh.

"Thank God he's gone. All that scowling was giving me a headache."

Craig retook his seat. "Vera Patterson told us that Cahill had told Mercer, so who's Bill Reynolds?"

"Mercer's bitch."

Maggie's tone said to take the words seriously. Ray Mercer probably had a coterie of snitches and gofers but

Bill Reynolds was obviously his number one.

"As soon as Rory told Reynolds he would have gone straight to Mercer. That's probably where Vera got her wires crossed." She frowned, confused. "So why didn't Mercer dig further and print the story?"

Liam answered, surprised that she'd asked. "Because even Mercer knew it was a privileged conversation between a witness and a police officer and he'd be in deep doo-doos if he did." He mock scowled at her. "You would never do that, would you, Maggie?" He answered his own question, shaking his head slowly as if he was speaking to a child. "No, of course you wouldn't. You're a good little reporter."

Craig interrupted the lecture. "I think Mercer did the next best thing to printing it; he deliberately leaked it to a blogger."

Maggie's eyes widened. "Father Fred?"

"Yep. Who then put the word out on the Net. Mercer's just waiting for enough people to ask questions in a public forum then he can investigate legitimately."

She whistled just as Liam puckered his lips. He sniffed, put out. Women whistling, it wasn't right; it went against the natural order of things. Maggie shook her head.

"My God, no matter how much I hate Mercer I have to admit that's clever."

"Clever and dangerous. He's compromising an open case." Craig stood up. "Is that his office next door?" He smiled coldly. "I want to surprise him."

Maggie walked to the door. "I have to see this."

"No. He'll blame you for helping us."

She shrugged. "He'll blame me anyway. The whole newsroom saw me bringing you in here, so I might as well enjoy myself."

Before he could object further she'd opened the door and was leading the way. As they headed next door Craig could have sworn he heard the sound level in the newsroom drop. Every reporter in the room watched as Maggie knocked on Ray Mercer's door.

"Come."

The voice sounded more authoritative than Craig

remembered, but the weasel face that greeted them looked exactly the same. Mercer stared at Maggie in surprise; it morphed into a sneer when he saw Liam and Craig.

"Well, well, the Dibbles are in town."

Craig ignored the jibe and took a seat, beckoning the others to do the same. If Mercer was flustered he covered it well, smiling coolly.

"Let me guess. You're here to collect for the policeman's ball?"

Liam quipped back. "We'll always have more balls than you."

For once Craig didn't reprimand him; he was struggling too hard not to wring Mercer's neck. His voice was as hard as steel.

"We know about Father Fred."

Mercer grinned, revealing teeth that had seen better days. "Isn't that a TV show?" When he got no response he shrugged. "Maybe not. I've no idea what you're talking about. Enlighten me."

Craig fixed his gaze. "You like to play games, don't you? Well, how about this one. I lock you up for interfering with a police investigation and you try to get out. It should take you about four days with extra time on PACE."

Craig didn't blink and Liam could see that Mercer was trying not to as well; he was frantically thinking back through the past week to see if he could cover his tracks. Craig put him out of his misery by piling on more.

"Don't waste your time trying to think up a lie. We know about Rory Cahill overhearing a privileged conversation and telling Bill Reynolds, who then told you. We know that you then leaked that information deliberately to a Derry based blogger called Father Fred, in the hope that they would whip up enough internet interest to justify you investigating and plastering the story all over The Chronicle's front page. The blogger will confirm everything I've just said."

He was confident that Father Fred would cough, if they ever found him that was. At the moment he was proving more elusive than a priest in Elizabethan

England.

A small smile twitched at Mercer's lips, piquing Craig's curiosity. It couldn't mean anything good. The smile didn't last long and Craig watched with schadenfreude as Mercer squirmed in his hard backed chair. He had no sympathy for the man. Not only had Mercer tried to engineer internet coverage that could have alerted their perp to everything they knew, but he'd been prepared to do so using the kidnap of the man who'd probably given him his first job. Oliver Bwye had owned the paper for twenty-seven years. He played the hunch.

"Bwye gave you a chance and this is how you repay him?"

Mercer jumped to his feet. "Oliver Bwye was a bastard and I didn't owe him any loyalty. He made me sweat for every penny I earned. How do you think these people get to be millionaires?"

Craig was unperturbed. He had the upper hand, although Mercer's earlier smile troubled him. What had that been about?

"You're talking about Mr Bwye in the past tense. Do you know something we don't? Perhaps you had something to do with his kidnap?"

Mercer dropped to his seat like a stone, his eyes widening in panic. "I didn't mean that...it was just a figure of speech..."

Craig let him babble for a moment then he leaned forward and fixed Mercer's wild eyes with his completely calm ones.

"When this trick comes out you're finished, Mercer. No amount of toadying to The Chronicle's Board and shareholders will keep you safe. You're a liability and big companies don't like liabilities." He watched for a moment, as Mercer's breathing accelerated and he turned pale, then he rose to his feet and beckoned the others to do the same. "Pack your stuff, because when Lawton hears about this you'll be out."

They were out of the office before Mercer had recovered and at the lift before he'd found the breath to yell after them. "You're bluffing, Craig. You can't prove anything. I'll make your life hell..."

His voice faded as they descended the two floors to the street. Craig shot Maggie an apologetic look.

"Sorry about that. Your life will be hell now."

Maggie shrugged. "But everyone's life will be better if Mr Lawton sacks him, and if Mercer did what you're saying he did then he will. Lawton's a good man."

"I'll phone him now. Will you be all right to go back to your office?"

She shook her head and gestured towards a shoulder bag that neither detective had noticed her carrying.

"I came prepared. I'm going into town shopping and then home. I'll keep my head down until I hear from you on whether Mercer's gone." She looked sad for a moment. "It's bastards like that who give journalists a bad name. I came into the press to report the truth responsibly, not to ruin people's lives." She stared at Craig meaningfully. "Oliver Bwye did some terrible things when he owned The Chronicle, he may even have made Mercer into the gutter reporter he became. Bwye's motto was 'anything for a story'; although I'm sure he never anticipated being the subject of one."

She glanced across St Anne's Square at The MAC café and smiled. "Coffee and cake first I think, and then a new pair of shoes." She waved goodbye. "Let me know what Lawton says."

As they watched her walk through the arts centre's sliding doors, Liam made a face.

"Brave girl. But what if Lawton doesn't sack the weasel? She's really put her neck on the line."

"He will." Craig threw him the car keys. "You drive us to Docklands while I make the call."

Five minutes later they were in the basement of the C.C.U. and Cameron Lawton was ranting down the line.

"That bastard Mercer will bring the whole paper down."

"Can you do anything about it?"

Lawton sounded surprised. "Of course I can. I'm the editor-in-chief. I never wanted Mercer for news editor in the first place but I was overruled by the Board."

Craig's next words were tentative. "With all due

respect, that's what I meant. Will the Board let you sack him?"

Lawton calmed down slightly.

"Oh, I see. Yes, they will. I'm in charge operationally and the moment Mercer became a problem he became disposable. I'll suspend him immediately and get the lawyers onto our liability for the leak, and the legalities of sacking him. Maggie Clarke will be interim news editor from tomorrow; she's very good." He paused for a moment and Craig knew what was coming next. "It would really assist if you could find this blogger. Help to make our case with the Board."

"We've got someone on it. We already have the word of Rory Cahill that he told Bill Reynolds what he overheard..."

Lawton cut in. "And Reynolds told Mercer? I'll have his guts for garters."

"I think you'll find that Mercer was intimidating everyone in your newsroom. Supplying him with information was probably the only way to survive working there."

He knew Lawton was nodding at the other end of the line.

"Then it's my fault for not noticing the atmosphere of fear that he'd created. I won't bollock Reynolds but I'll make him tell me the truth."

Liam was already out of the car so Craig opened the passenger door, still talking. "Thanks for taking this seriously."

The editor's tone was solemn. "If the police stepped out of line we would be the first to report it, Superintendent, but we're also on the side of helping you solve crime. You get on with finding the Bwyes and I'll sort out the mess at this end."

Craig hadn't the heart to tell him they'd already found Diana Bwye, so he cut the call and joined Liam by the lift. A minute later they were through the squad-room's doors and back on home turf. The first thing Craig noticed was how quiet it was. Nicky was watering her plants and Jake and Carmen were hunched over their desks reading, barely halfway through the tower of court files balanced against Jake's desk. Without Davy's computers whirring and Liam and Annette bickering it was as quiet as a church.

Liam soon put paid to that. He boomed across the floor like a sergeant major.

"Wake up you lazy buggers! The A-Team's back in town."

****

Rocksbury. 2 p.m.

Annette gazed at the Bwyes' cook with curiosity and the woman glared back. It was tempting to picture a stereotype when asked what a wealthy family's cook would look like, especially one where the family entertained frequently and the mistress of the house spent her time doing charity work. Female? Probably. Fifty to sixty-ish? Yes. Slightly on the overweight side, but of course; with well-padded hips and arms like a docker, bulked up from years of carving meat and carrying huge pots and pans. Rosy cheeked? Possibly, although perhaps only when in the kitchen; after all, complexion is uncontrollable and one can't select employees on whether they look rosy or not. As for temperament; bossy but affable is the order of the day if one hopes to run a pleasant, Downton Abbey type kitchen.

The woman glaring at Annette couldn't have resembled the stereotype any less if she'd set out to. Linda McCann was hard faced, lean bodied and sallow skinned, with thin lips and arms to match. The only thing that fitted was her age and probably the bossy part; any affability looked like it had fallen into the gravy many decades before. McCann looked as if she would spit in your soup as soon as stir it, and she had a chip on her shoulder big enough to drag a lesser woman to the ground.

Where Annette merely gazed at her curiously, Julia glared back at the cook. She'd lied to her when they'd met before, suggesting that Justin O'Hare's family had fallen on hard times and he was a gold-digger out for Jane's inheritance. Complete rubbish, but now they were well warned. Linda McCann had lied for a reason and they just had to find out what it was. Annette nodded Julia to begin; she'd been the one lied to so she deserved a second chance.

"You lied to us, Mrs McCann."

McCann's folded arms tightened and she squeezed out her answer in a Belfast twang. "Did not."

"Yes, you did. You told us that Justin O'Hare was a gold-digger after Jane for her money."

McCann sniffed. "Far too impressed with himself by half. She deserved better."

Annette spotted two things immediately. Linda McCann's Belfast accent and a small gleam of something she couldn't name that had flashed in her eye. She scrutinised her face closely as Julia seized on the response.

"You knew they hadn't dated for months, didn't you?"

McCann stayed silent but the gleam grew brighter, and with it Annette's certainty that she'd given them O'Hare's name deliberately, to throw them off some track. Either that or she hated the rich; perhaps that's what her chip was about.

"You also knew that Mr Bwye wouldn't disapprove of Justin, didn't you? You deliberately pointed us in the wrong direction. Why?"

McCann let her eyes roam angrily around the Bwye's main room as if she resented every brick in the wall. Annette signalled to interrupt and Julia waved her on; if she could crack McCann then she'd buy her a drink. Annette's tone was cool but understanding, like a prison psychiatrist's; not liking their interviewee very much but understanding what had made them that way.

"If you hate the Bwyes so much then why work for them, Mrs McCann?"

They knew she was a Mrs; the indentations where her rings were worn outside the kitchen said so. She wasn't cooking for the Bwyes this week but for the search team, and if Annette was right she would enjoy that much more. Making food for decent working folk, instead of for the so-called idle rich.

McCann scanned Annette's now long hair and fashionable clothes with a gaze that said 'who do you think you are?' Finally her eyes came to rest on Annette's face.

"Did I say I hated them?"

"Not in words, but it's obvious."

McCann shrugged. "Them who has money pays and them who don't works. They pay me to do a job. I don't have to like them."

"Do you dislike all of them?"

She shrugged again. "Bwye's a bastard. The wife's all right and the girl as well."

There it was again; the gleam. This time Annette recognised what it was; pride! She replayed McCann's last words, searching for the exact moment when the light had appeared. It was when she'd mentioned 'the girl'. Jane. But why would Linda McCann feel proud of someone else's child?

She met Julia's eyes and saw that she'd worked it out as well. She'd interviewed McCann first and she'd been lied to; she should do the honours. But first Annette had a hunch to check out. She rose quickly and entered the study, re-emerging a moment later with a slip of paper. As Julia read it she smiled, first at Annette and then at the cook, watching as her arms tightened again.

"Where is your son, Mrs McCann? Where is Richard?"

Davy's background checks had come up trumps. Richard McCann was twenty-two years old and the cook's only child. He was in his early twenties; perfect for their ransom caller's age. McCann's sallow skin paled and her eyes darted to Annette, as if she blamed her in particular for discovering the truth. Julia continued, her questions gaining speed and force.

How long had Richard been dating Jane? Did Mr Bwye know? Did he think Richard was unsuitable, not good enough for his daughter? Is that why Richard had kidnapped the Bwyes; to pay them back?

Annette leaned in, pouring petrol on the fire. "When we find your son he's going down for at least one murder.

The only way to help him is to make him give himself up. The longer Richard's on the run the worse it will be."

The women kept going relentlessly until they saw Linda McCann's defiance melt away and her shoulders sag, then she surprised them both by beginning to cry. Annette and Julia exchanged a glance. They sat back simultaneously and waited, hoping that when her tears subsided she would tell them where her son was. But first the cook decided to tell them something else.

"Richard and Jane love each other; always have done, since Jane was a little girl. They've known each other since she was five."

If Davy's research was right that made Richard McCann seven at the time. Linda McCann was still talking.

"I wasn't happy about it so they tried to stay away from each other, even tried to date other people..." Her face contorted into a sneer. "...like Mr Important O'Hare. But it didn't work so in July they stopped fighting it and, without my knowledge, they went and got hitched."

Julia broke her silence. "Married! You're sure?"

McCann nodded in a way that said the question was ridiculous. "Saw the certificate myself. But they had to hide it; else old man Bwye would have gone mad. He rules this house with an iron rod. Uses it on Jane and his wife."

Annette's eyes widened in realisation. Things were starting to make sense. Oliver Bwye had controlled his wife and daughter and he'd deferred Jane's inheritance to keep that control. If he'd ever discovered that Jane had defied him he would have cut her off without a penny.

"Did Mrs Bwye know?"

McCann gave a small smile, the first they'd seen from her. "Jane told her after the wedding and she helped keep it a secret. She knew they loved each other and that my Richard wasn't after Jane's money. He's doing his master's degree."

She was proud of her son, and of Jane; that was the gleam of pride Annette had seen. But none of that prevented Richard McCann being their killer.

"Where is your son now, Mrs McCann?"

The cook's lips pursed tight but Annette forged on.

"Either he kidnapped the Bwyes, or he didn't and the real kidnapper may go after him next. Do you want to risk that?"

McCann lurched forward so suddenly that Julia jumped back in her chair. "Richard didn't kidnap anyone!"

Annette played another hunch. "But he mustn't care that Jane's missing or he'd be here helping us find her. He hasn't lifted a finger to help the searchers." She snorted derisively. "Some husband."

McCann rose to the bait, practically shouting her response. "He already knows she's safe!"

Annette smiled. Jane Bwye was alive and with her husband. Richard McCann had been the man Justin O'Hare had seen that night in the Mercedes and they'd burnt out the car together. If she was right, Richard McCann's voice would also match the ransom tape. Her tone softened.

"If you're right then they did nothing wrong, but you're doing them no favours by letting them hide away. Tell us where they are and we'll bring them in safely." She paused meaningfully. "We'll find them anyway, Mrs McCann, now that we know they're alive. They're only making themselves look guilty by evading the police."

The cook vacillated for a moment. They watched as her arms folded and unfolded and her face tightened and relaxed repeatedly, like a stuttering DVD; signs of the decision she was struggling to make. Finally she set her hands flat on her knees, signalling surrender, and croaked out an address. Annette nodded.

"You've done the right thing. We'll bring them here first so that you can see them."

She grabbed a radio and called a P.C. from the ground search to watch the cook, certain that as soon as they left she would change her mind and try to warn her son.

Annette had one last question for the grudging employee. "When did you move here from Belfast?"

McCann's lips tightened again, as if she'd somehow insulted her. "I didn't say I was from there."

Annette didn't have time to play games. Her voice

grew hard. "Your accent did. When did you move to Derry? And what part of Belfast are you from?"

McCann frowned, looking for the trick in the question. Finally she shrugged.

"We moved here when I came to work for the Bwyes in ninety-nine. I'm from Divis Street."

Divis, the lower Falls Road; the linguists were good. Richard had been seven when they'd moved to Derry so both accents might have been easy for him to use. There was only one way to find out.

Five minutes later they were in an unmarked car with Andy and a constable. An hour later Jane Bwye had been retrieved from the couple's love nest off Strand Road and Richard McCann had been lifted from the university library where he was returning a book. They took them to the estate for an emotional reunion with his mother and then on to Derry Station and into custody.

As Annette called Craig to update him he stared out of his office window at the Lagan, smiling at the fact that she'd managed to find Jane Bwye and their ransom caller in less than four hours.

"What would you like us to do with them, sir?"

"Just what you're doing. Separate them and get their statements, then confirm their alibis for that night. Get a voice sample from McCann so the linguists can match it, and check if his prints match the ones on the decanter at the Bwyes'. If his voice matches I want to know what the hell they were playing at making a ransom call."

"Then what? Should we hold them?"

He squinted down at the icy river. It was a good question. Had they killed Diana Bwye? He doubted it, but he had to assume yes until it was proved otherwise. If not, then what had they actually done that was illegal: leave the scene of a crime, burn out a car and waste police time with a fake call. All minor compared to murder.

If they *were* innocent of killing Diana Bwye then someone else had done it; someone whose motive wasn't money. Until they knew what it was they had to assume that Jane was still at risk. Annette was wondering whether to repeat the question when Craig finally answered.

"Yes, hold them. They could still be our killers, but if not, Jane could be next. Tell them we want their help with our enquiries. If they say no then arrest them both on suspicion of kidnapping and murder and I'll see them first thing in the morning."

Annette was silent for a moment and he read her mind. "Take the girl to I.D. her mother's body once Mike's done what he needs to, and get her a bereavement counsellor."

"Grand. I'll keep you up to date."

Craig could feel her ending the call but he had another question to ask. "Anything more at the lake?"

"Not yet, sir. They're calling it a day soon and starting again at dawn."

"OK. Good work, Annette. I'll see you tomorrow."

Just as he set down the phone there was a soft tap on the door.

"Come."

It wasn't Nicky as he'd expected, but Carmen. He waved her to a seat but she remained in the doorway, looking uncomfortable.

"I'll only be a second. Davy called and said he could use a hand with some of the IT stuff so...I just wondered...say no, if it isn't OK...but, I just wondered if it might be worth me going to Derry with you tomorrow?"

Craig sat down, smiling to himself. He knew what her subtext was; rescue me from the Greer paperwork, please. It made sense that she was on site with Davy, and Ken was back the next day so he could help Jake with Greer, but he was reluctant to confirm it just yet.

"I'll let you know in the morning, Carmen. First I need to see how far you've all got on the appeal. Pack a bag just in case."

He waved her out and turned his chair back towards the river. The water was flowing sluggishly, slowed to a crawl by the winter cold. If it got much slower the Lagan could freeze solid like it had in 2010. He stared at it and then past it as he ran through the day's developments in his mind.

Diana Bwye was dead; shot and strangled, weighed

down with stones and dumped in the family's lake. Shooting and the use of a ligature said impersonal, yet her uncovered face and lack of defacement confirmed that someone who knew and cared about her could have caused her death. Whoever had done it hadn't hated her and nothing had been stolen from the house. So why take her at all? Had she just been in the wrong place at the wrong time, or had she recognised her husband's attacker so had to be disposed of; was that it? What if she'd been a target all along? Finding Oliver Bwye would help them with answers.

As he thought of Bwye and his wife's lack of disfiguration, the possibility of Bwye being a family annihilator faded away. An annihilator would have waited until Jane was there, killed her first to torture Diana and then killed Diana and himself; probably leaving his wife with up-close and personal injuries. They would have found all their bodies where they'd dropped; at home. Even if it was just his wife that Bwye had wanted dead, he doubted that her face would have been left unmarked.

OK then; what if Bwye had wanted to kill Diana and Jane but not himself? Craig shook his head. It still didn't make sense. He would have waited for Jane to come home and then killed them both, but it was likely they would have been killed in a more personal way - manual strangulation, or having their faces blown off with a gun.

And where *was* Bwye's Ruger? As he thought of it, Craig grabbed the phone and called Gerry, adding the gun as a priority to the divers' search. Diana Bwye had been shot twice and either her strangulation or the shots had proved fatal, Mike would let them know which. Had she been killed in the study or just wounded there to subdue her, perhaps as a scare tactic? Any assailant must already have had a weapon to force Bwye to remove his rifle from the cabinet. Unless... had Bwye grabbed for the gun when he'd seen that they were being attacked and the kidnapper had managed to overcome him, taken the gun and used it to end both the Bwye's lives? They'd find out when they'd finished at the lake.

Just then flakes of snow appeared outside the window

and Craig watched them fall, shivering as if he could feel the cold. He could, but not from the weather, what was making him freeze was the idea that Richard McCann wasn't their man. If it wasn't McCann then who and why? Who had hated Oliver Bwye enough to kill his wife and dump her body so ignominiously in a lake? He prayed that Lawton's list and Davy's searches would give them the answer soon.

Chapter Fourteen

Howard Street restaurant. 8 p.m.

Craig stared at his glass until the dense Merlot inside became translucent and he could see images in it that weren't there. When everyone had had enough of watching him commune with his alcohol John gave a quiet cough. Craig glanced up, surprised, and then suddenly remembered where he was.

John reached for the bottle to top him up. "Did it give you any answers?"

"What?"

"The wine. The way you were staring I was sure you'd invented wine reading."

Craig gave a tired smile. "As if. The only thing it told me was that I needed to drink more."

He glanced at Katy apologetically; aware that he'd barely said a word all evening. She was watching him, half concerned and half amused, always surprised by his ability to close out the world. He turned to Natalie to say sorry, but he needn't have bothered. Natalie was carving pieces off her steak with a surgeon's precision and gobbling them down efficiently one by one. She hadn't even noticed the exchange.

About to change the subject to something light-hearted, John's curiosity got the better of him; he was used to working on Craig's cases and part of him felt like he was missing out this time. He adopted a casual tone.

"So...how's Mike doing?"

Craig shrugged. "I don't know yet. He's doing the P.M. now. The forensic side has been fine."

"Hmm..."

"Is that hmm...you're worried that he'll miss something, or hmm...you're feeling left out?"

The pathologist laughed. "OK. You got me." His expression changed to eagerness. "If you think I could help with anything, I've nothing much on at the lab this week."

Natalie glanced up with a mischievous look on her

face. "Take him to Derry if you like, Marc, then at least I can get into my house and see what he's done."

John's eyes widened nervously. "On second thoughts, I've work to tidy up before the holidays. Mike will have to cope alone."

Katy turned to Natalie, surprised. "You mean you haven't been in the house yet? Who picked out the colour scheme?"

"John."

"And the carpets and furniture?"

"John."

Katy shook her head. "You're a very trusting woman."

Natalie popped the last piece of steak into her mouth, talking as she did. Craig smiled to himself; her manners bore more than a passing resemblance to Liam's at times.

"I'm hellish busy at work and John's got a better eye than me. Anyway, he knows what sort of things I like and they can always be returned if I don't."

John paled and Craig knew that's exactly what would happen in the New Year if Natalie wasn't wowed by his décor. But she would be; he'd seen the house, although it didn't seem like a good idea to mention that he had.

The meal carried on in a lighter vein, all talk of murder ended, until eventually the couples went their separate ways. As Craig and Katy walked to her car through the now lying snow, she snuggled into him and brought up the case again.

"Do you think Bwye killed his wife?"

He turned to face her, watching as a snowflake landed on her hair and another fell on her nose. He kissed them off as he mulled over her question and then kissed her on the lips as the answer formed in his mind. The words were forgotten as he lost focus on anything but her scent. Finally they broke apart and walked on in silence, until Craig picked up the question as if the kiss had been a breath.

"No."

"Who then?"

He shook his head instinctively and then suddenly stopped dead. Why was he saying he didn't know when the answer was staring him in the face? It had to be someone who hated Oliver Bwye, hopefully someone on Cameron Lawton's list. If not then the suspect pool would be endless and they might never get their man.

As they reached the car he said. "One of Bwye's enemies."

The answer satisfied both of them and they were too tired to discuss it anymore. Katy put on a favourite CD to play them from the city centre to her flat, through their love making and into a deep, deep sleep, so that they could both rise ready to start again.

****

Friday, 19th December. 11 a.m.

Craig glanced at the Audi's passenger seat, used to seeing Liam there, but today it was Carmen's red curls that greeted him instead. It wasn't a testament to Liam's chivalry, allowing the lady to sit in the front, but rather his desire to catch another hour's sleep that saw him sprawled out across the back. That was one good thing about old cars; they didn't interrupt your sprawling with fixed arm rests. Even so, Liam was struggling to get comfortable, the seat's five-feet-ten finding his six-six hard to accommodate. He boomed irritably from the back as Craig drove up the A6, well rested and eager to solve the case.

"Here, boss, when you get a new motor, could you get one with more space."

Craig answered him with his eyes fixed straight ahead. "Like a people carrier? I don't think so. You'd be asleep every time we drove anywhere, never mind what it would do to my street cred."

Liam tutted slowly. "Ah now, when you hear the patter of tiny feet you'll have no choice."

Craig refused to rise to the bait. "I'll tell you what. When John has a few kids then maybe I'll think about it."

Liam perked up and leaned on the back of Carmen's seat, tilting her forward and earning him a smack.

"God, can you picture the Doc's kids? They'd be born carrying a scalpel and wearing glasses."

Carmen joined in. "And they'd dress them in a surgical green Babygro."

An hour of chat about people's fantasy offspring began, ending just as they passed through Rocksbury's gates. As they traversed the long drive it was impossible to miss the crowd by the lake, far larger than the group they'd left there the day before.

Amongst the liveried cars and diving equipment, Craig made out a dark van, and beside it Annette. He pulled off the gravelled driveway and drove across the frozen grass, coming to rest about twenty feet from the group. Annette came to meet them.

"We've found another body, sir. By the size I'd say it was a man."

Craig glanced past her to where the slightly chubby figure of Mike Augustus was kneeling beside something black.

"Not by the face?"

Annette shook her head. "We can't see the face. The body's completely covered." She paused and Craig knew what was coming next. "Concrete wrapped in plastic. Only the shape says that it's human."

Questions churned over in his mind. He only vocalised one.

"When did they find him?"

"They started diving again at dawn and found him about ten minutes ago."

"He must weigh a ton; he'd have been right at the bottom. It was good diving to find him."

Annette nodded. "It was a miracle. They were trawling the bottom and the net caught on him; they'd never have noticed him otherwise. It's pitch black down there."

"That's what whoever did this wanted. Bwye was meant to disappear, they both were, but for some reason Diana Bwye wasn't weighted down as well."

She squinted up at him, shielding her eyes from the winter sun. "You definitely think it's Bwye?"

Craig shrugged and began to walk towards their corpse. He paused beside it, staring down at the black shape. The height matched the missing newspaper mogul's. He nodded hello to Mike and then turned back to Annette.

"Did they find the rifle?"

"Not yet."

He turned back to Augustus, marvelling at how young the pathologist always looked. He was only four years younger than he was yet he still looked like a kid. Craig gestured at the shape then rubbed his hands together in the cold. He really needed to buy some gloves.

"Show me, please, Mike."

Augustus obliged, elevating a torn edge of the black plastic. Beneath the heavy duty refuse sack lay grey-white concrete, its surface creased like the inside of the bag.

"Was the bag torn like that when it came out?"

"Yes. It caught on the winch when they lifted it." The pathologist gestured at the shape. "It looks like they put him in the bag and then filled it completely with concrete."

Craig nodded. He'd read about the technique; one of the drug cartels' more inventive methods of disposal. In Hollywood movies they only used cement shoes. Economy.

"Was he alive when they did it?"

A look of horror flitted across Augustus' face, saying the idea hadn't occurred to him. Craig wished he still had such innocence to find comfort in. Augustus nodded reluctantly.

"He could have been, but he would have to have been unconscious or he'd never have lain still for it. He's a big man."

It made sense. If the body was Oliver Bwye then he'd been attacked and rendered unconscious at his house, rolled into the van and then, when it became obvious that he had to be dumped, he'd been put in the sack and covered in concrete. Craig had more questions. He walked around the body, finding one answer at its narrower end.

"The sack was tied here, at his feet, after the concrete was poured in."

Mike stared at the bunching in the plastic. "Probably. I'll tell you for sure after the P.M."

"Will you be able to remove the concrete without

destroying the body?"

The pathologist peeled off his gloves and signalled to have the corpse moved to the mortuary van.

"I'll let you know tomorrow. I need to scan it first to see what we can do."

Craig grimaced, imagining the images they would see. A body inside concrete, inside a plastic sack. With any luck there would be a weak point in the concrete allowing it to be shattered without damaging the man inside. He wandered back to Annette to see her laughing with Liam and Carmen.

"Don't tell me. Liam's just told you a joke about mummies."

Liam gawped at him. "How did you know?"

Craig climbed into the car. "I'm psychic. If anyone wants a lift to the house, hop in."

Five minutes later they had their hands wrapped around mugs of hot coffee and Craig called the group to order. Everyone was there, raring to go.

"OK, Liam and I will start then we'll go round in order: Julia and Annette, Davy, then Gerry and Andy."

He sipped his drink and felt his hands beginning to thaw out.

"Liam."

Liam had positioned his chair to rest his legs on the desk, six inches from Davy's face. Davy's expression said that he wasn't impressed.

"Aye well. We had a bit of fun at The Chronicle's offices. Long story short it turns out that a young runner overheard the ransom discussion and told a newsman who was in Ray Mercer's pocket -"

Gerry interrupted. "Who's Ray Mercer?"

"The scrote news editor."

Annette ruled out any ambiguity. "Not a nice man. He and Liam don't see eye to eye."

Craig chipped in. "I doubt even his mother likes him." He returned to his coffee, waving Liam on.

"Aye well. Mercer wasn't allowed to write about the Bwyes' disappearance, so he deliberately leaked the info about the ransom call to Davy's mysterious blogger, Father Fred-"

It was Davy's turn to interrupt. "We have a name. I locked it down last night."

Craig leaned forward eagerly. "Good man. What is it?"

Davy's tone held admiration. "Father Fred's real name is Lauren Hayes. S...She's a school kid, only fourteen."

There was silence in the room. Annette broke it first. "Fourteen? A teenage girl managed to evade you for this long?"

It was the wrong thing to say, even worse Liam added. "A wee girl! She probably has pink bows in her hair and all. You must be scundered."

Annette smiled at Liam's idea of a teenage girl's fashion sense and pictured years of him fighting with his daughter Erin when she grew up. She might wear pink bows at four, but it would more likely be piercings and tattoos when she was fourteen.

Davy blushed to the roots of his hair. "S...She's good, I mean *really* good. She routed things through Russia and New Zealand. If she doesn't do IT at Uni I'll be really s...shocked."

Craig raised an eyebrow. "That's if MI5 doesn't recruit her first." He turned to Annette and Julia. "When we're finished here I want you to find her parents and interview her. She's not in trouble; I just need confirmation of where she sourced the ransom information. Carry on, Liam."

Liam shot Davy a final pitying look before he spoke. "Aye well, anyway, Mercer leaked the info so Father Fred could whip up interest on the internet so as, when it was out in the open, he could legitimately report on it." He smiled proudly. "Except that we caught him out."

Andy had been listening open-mouthed. "What happened then, hey?"

Liam grinned at Davy. "Lawton gave Mercer the push and Davy's woman got his job."

It was Davy's turn to be open-mouthed. "Maggie's the news editor of The Chronicle?"

Craig nodded. "As of this morning. Cameron Lawton suspended Mercer pending legal action."

The analyst puffed out his chest in pride. "She'll be brilliant."

"I'm sure she will and you can call her later to say so, but for now I'd like that blog shut down and secured. OK, thanks Liam." He turned towards Annette. "Annette and Julia, tell everyone what you got from the cook, please."

Julia seized the moment to redeem herself for Linda McCann's earlier lies.

"OK, we re-interviewed Linda McCann and it turns out that her son, Richard, was the boyfriend that Oliver Bwye would have found unsuitable. He's a master's student with no money, hardly what daddy would have thought good enough for his daughter, the heiress. Anyway, Jane was with him and they're both safe and well now in Derry station. We're interviewing them after this."

Craig interrupted. "How did Jane react when she I.D.ed her mother's body?"

Annette answered. "Really badly. She cried for hours and she wasn't faking it, sir. We'll get more from her today but I'm convinced that she had nothing to do with Mrs Bwye's death."

"OK, you can tell us more at four o'clock. Thanks, both of you. Davy, what do you have?"

Julia shook her head firmly. "I hadn't finished." Her tone reminded Craig of when they'd dated and he'd done something wrong. He waved her on.

"Richard McCann and Jane Bwye are married. They got married in July and both mothers knew."

Craig nodded, Annette had mentioned it when she'd called, but everyone else was shocked, including Liam and Carmen.

"Here, you forgot to mention that bit, boss."

"Sorry, but it's only relevant if we think they did it and we'll find that out when Annette and Julia interview them."

Liam shook his head emphatically and Andy joined in. "It's also relevant if Oliver Bwye found out somehow. He could have threatened the boy with all sorts if he'd known. That has to add Linda McCann to the list of suspects for the murders."

They were right and Craig was shocked that he'd missed the possibility. His head was elsewhere far too often these days. He conceded and parked the point for later, motioning Davy on. He was still grinning about Maggie's promotion and Craig knew that as soon as the briefing was over he'd be on the phone. Davy rearranged his face to look serious.

"OK. Apart from the blog s...stuff, I've been digging into everyone on Lawton's list and retrieving medical records. Records first. As we know, Jane and Diana Bwye attended the hospital ED regularly for bruises, cuts and broken bones. They'd been regulars there for years but it got w...worse about two months ago."

Liam cut in. "That's after Jane got married. Maybe Bwye had found out."

Craig considered for a moment before shaking his head. "If he had done then Richard McCann would have been his first port of call not Jane." He turned to Annette. "But check that out with McCann and Jane today." He nodded Davy to continue.

"Anyway, the attendances at hospital got more frequent, especially Diana's, and the s...severity of the injuries worsened. From the first of October she had four different attendances for broken ribs, the gash on her arm and black eyes."

Julia interrupted. "Didn't anyone report it to the police?"

Craig shook his head. "She refused to press charges. She probably just said she was clumsy, and without proof that Bwye had hit her, it would have been nearly impossible to proceed."

Davy carried on. "I didn't know Jane had married but I thought, w...what could have happened to make Bwye more violent two months ago? So I searched his finances, businesses, any law suits against him; I even got the name of his mistress, in case she knew anything."

Liam cut in. "When the heck did you get the mistress' name?"

Davy shrugged as if it was obvious. "While you were off chasing other s...stuff I called the escort agency. I told them that if they knew anything and w...withheld the information it would come out and they'd be liable for obstructing an investigation." As he talked he pressed print and nodded Liam to lift the warm sheet. "They called me back this morning. The lady's name is Mavis Brown. That's her address. She's not a mistress as much as s...someone that Bwye saw frequently at The Kasbah."

Craig didn't know which to laugh at first. Liam's indignation or Davy's show of cool. Instead he said. "Good work. Although strictly speaking that was more police work than analysis."

Davy shrugged again, determined not to let anything dent his good mood at Maggie's news. "W...Would you like the rest?"

Liam grabbed the print-out. "Here now, don't get cocky, son."

But Craig was interested in what he had to say.

"I couldn't find anything w...wrong in Bwye's share accounts or companies, although he wasn't as wealthy as people thought, so I went back to his GP. From w...what he wouldn't tell me I think there's something there, more than Bwye's past issues with skin cancer and his heart..." He stared at Liam pointedly. "...but I didn't want to get cocky and overstep my boundaries, so I really think that one of you should get in touch."

He pressed print again with his middle finger and the GP's name and address popped out. This time Craig couldn't stop himself from laughing, knowing that the middle finger had been purely for Liam's benefit.

"Excellent work, Davy. OK, let's see what happened to Oliver Bwye two months ago to make him even more violent. It could have been that he found out about Jane and McCann's marriage but I'd like to rule out other possibilities first."

He scanned the paper then passed it to Andy. "Andy, you and Gerry pay the GP a visit after we break. Now, what have you two got for us?"

Andy scanned the page, nodding Gerry on to report. Gerry shook his head in a way that said he was appalled by what he'd seen at the lake.

"Ach well, the divers were here last night until eight o'clock; they decided to keep going even though it was dark. They started again this morning at seven and that's when they trawled the lake bed. It's just as well they did or stone man would have been down there until the next drought."

Andy interjected. "Those divers deserve a medal; it was Baltic out there last night. Even with those dry-suits."

Craig nodded, reminding himself to say thanks. "We saw what they brought up. Mike says he'll get it scanned in a way that will avoid damaging the body."

Andy shook his head. "It's the worst thing I've ever seen, hey. What sort of bastard encases someone in concrete?"

"The sort who's read about the Mexican cartels. They do it all the time."

Liam joined the debate. "I thought concrete overcoats were the Mafia's signature."

"Usually only boots."

Davy chipped in. "I blame the film distributors. Those Cosa Nostra movies get everywhere."

"Does anyone know how fast that stuff dries?"

Craig answered. "Quick drying concrete takes less than an hour, maybe even faster in the cold. You just sprinkle water on it. I used some to fix my parents' patio last year."

Liam guffawed. "Bringing a bag of concrete with them. What next? It gives a whole new meaning to 'going equipped'."

Craig waved Gerry on. "Anything else happening at the lake?"

"Well, they're not finished yet, if that's what you mean. They'll keep going while it's light to see if they can find Bwye's gun and the dog."

Davy swallowed a mouthful of coffee so quickly that it made him cough. Through his spluttering Craig heard an apology.

"S...Sorry. I meant to say about the dog; I located it last night with the GPS. A local farmer found it w...wandering in his field and took it in; it only had a cut on one paw. He didn't know it belonged to the Bwyes'."

"At least that's someone the killer didn't get. Let Jane know, please."

Annette raised a finger tentatively, as if uncertain

whether she should already know the answer to the question she was about to ask.

"Yes?"

"Well, it's just a thought, sir, but has anyone found the boat yet?"

For a moment Craig was puzzled by the question, then he remembered. He'd asked Davy to make a list of local boat owners but had forgotten to follow it up. Liam didn't have the sense not to show that he'd forgotten as well.

"What boat?"

Annette was still hesitant. "The boat...that the killer used to take the Bwyes out onto the lake."

It still wasn't ringing Liam's bell. "The van took them to the lake."

Craig cut in before they both looked more stupid. "Annette's right and we discussed this before. The van would only have brought them to the shore; they had to have been put in a boat and taken out onto the lake to be dumped. Thanks, Annette, I'd completely forgotten about that."

"So had I until just now. But that's not the only question. How the heck did one man lift a concrete encased body onto a boat?"

Gerry grinned. "That's obvious."

Craig turned to him. "Enlighten us."

"Well, didn't we say that the van was adapted for disabled people, with a ramp so the Bwyes could be loaded into it by one person rolling them?"

"Yes."

"Well OK then. Disabled vans also have hoists, I know because we had to move an obese prisoner to court once. Forty-two stone this guy was. The only way we could lift him was with a specially adapted hoist that the health service lent us."

Annette nodded. "He could have covered Bwye's body with concrete in the van, sealed the bag and then hoisted it into the boat. The same with Diana Bwye's body. Hers would have been lighter but there were still stones with it."

"Or he may have added the stones later, when she was in the boat. He could even have done the concrete there as well."

Craig shook his head. "Unlikely. It was freezing cold. No-one would want to spend an hour on a lake waiting for concrete to dry."

Liam was annoyed that he hadn't thought of everything so he added petulantly. "OK. What about the boat then? All that weight would go right through a row boat and sink it."

Annette retorted quickly. "Then it wasn't a row boat." She turned to Craig. "I noticed some boats on the opposite shore, we should check them out."

Craig was thinking. If the killer had sailed out to the middle of the lake, dumped the bodies and returned to their van, then the boat would have been left on the Bwyes' side of the lake. He turned to Davy.

"Davy, find out if the Bwyes had a boat or anyone local had their boat stolen a few days before the disappearance. Also, if anyone noticed a boat that wouldn't normally have been on this side of the lake, on the tenth or eleventh."

Davy shook his head. "I already checked. The Bwyes didn't have a boat and no-one mentioned one when Bernadette Ross called the police." He thought for a moment. "You think the killer had always planned to dump them in the lake?"

"I think they set up every contingency. If I'm right then they stole a boat before they kidnapped the Bwyes and moored it this side of the lake, just in case they needed it. If they didn't need it someone would have noticed it and returned it to the owners with no harm done. But if they did then it was there waiting for them that Wednesday night. My guess is that after they dumped the bodies they left the boat unmoored, hoping that it would just float away."

Liam looked pensive. "So you're saying they brought the adapted van, the concrete and planted the boat, all just in case?"

"Yes."

"Then what? They left the boat but no-one noticed it on the Thursday morning when Bernadette Ross called the police?"

Craig shook his head. "Or they saw it but no-one connected it with the disappearance because the lake is a distance from the house. Maybe they just thought it had drifted and returned it to its rightful owners, or perhaps the current had carried it so far out on the lake it wasn't seen; it's a big lake. If I'm right then someone who reported their boat missing will have got it back that Thursday. We need to find them; there could be valuable clues to our killer still on board. Liam, chase that today with Davy. When you find the boat I want the C.S.I.s all over it."

The room was quiet for a moment while everyone thought. When Craig was sure there was no more to report he summed up.

"OK, Davy, keep going on everything, including the van. I want the names on Lawton's list and everything you have on them ASAP. Carmen's here to help you. Carmen, do anything Davy asks, please."

He missed her rolling her eyes.

"Annette and Julia, interview Lauren Hayes with her parents and then take Jane Bwye and lover boy. Liam, follow up on the mistress." He pushed on before Liam could make a joke. "When you've finished that I want you to focus on the boat. Gerry and Andy, tackle Bwye's GP and go back to the golf-club..."

Annette looked embarrassed; they'd failed to get there again in the snow the day before.

"...we need more details about Bwye's mood before he returned home last Wednesday night. I'll be at the mortuary or here, keeping an eye on the lake operation and working on Cameron Lawton's list. We're nine days in with no real suspects and the Chief Constable will be looking for answers soon."

As he was about to finish he remembered something. "Did Richard McCann's prints match the ones on the decanter?"

Davy nodded. "I've given his voice s...sample to the linguists as well. Just for confirmation. They ruled out O'Hare and Gordon, by the way."

"OK. Keep going, everyone. I want answers when we brief at four."

Chapter Fifteen

Lauren Hayes was a typical teenage girl. One minute resolutely defiant, folding her arms and tossing her long brown hair with its sprayed-on silver streaks, the next sobbing and glancing at her mum for reassurance that she hadn't done anything wrong. Strictly speaking she hadn't. There was no law against running a blog unless there was a law against its content: like supporting terrorism or inciting hatred, urging people to commit crime or defaming someone somehow. And, according to Davy's research, Father Fred simply expended his reverential energy in pointing people towards the best clubs and pubs in Derry. None of which, by the look of her mother's pursed lips, Lauren Hayes had ever set foot inside. But the heaviest the online discussions had ever got before was whether a member of One Direction had a girlfriend, so why the blog's sudden foray into ethical debate?

As Annette asked the question Lauren's blush gave her the answer, but blushes didn't record on tape so she started a conversation that she hoped would encourage the girl to speak.

"I see you run shop adverts on your blog."

The height of which were the local sports store and a teenage fashion outlet in town.

"Do you know the shop owners?"

Lauren's defiant arms tightened, joined by a newly sneering top lip. It moved independently in a way that would have made Elvis proud.

"I need you to speak for the tape please, Lauren."

The girl glanced at the whirring machine in the tech-pitying way that only Generation Z can; she probably had hairdryers at home that were higher spec. When no words came, her mother gave her shoulder a push, almost overbalancing the girl's unstable, arms folded torso.

"Answer the officer." The subtext was silent but everyone in the room heard it. 'Or you're in even bigger trouble when I get you home'.

Annette struggled not to smile; she'd used similar tactics on her daughter Amy through the years. Lauren spat out her reply.

"Of course I don't know them! I'm a kid."

Julia interjected. "Then why let them advertise on your blog?"

Lauren's eyes crinkled into a smile; a greedy one. All that was missing were the pound signs in her eyes.

"'Cos they pay me, stupid."

It was too much for her mother whose veiled hints at future retribution were now voiced.

"Apologise to the officer immediately, young lady, or that blog is coming straight down and you'll be grounded for three months." Anna Hayes turned to Julia, flushed with embarrassment. "I'm so sorry. She never used to be like this. I don't know..."

A glance at the tape reminded her she was being recorded and her voice faded away. Julia gave a composed smile and repeated the question. This time Lauren answered while glancing warily at her mum.

"'Cos they pay me, miss."

Annette nodded; it made sense. The girl had a blog with a huge audience and, compared to advertising in a newspaper or on TV, paying for space on a blog must be cheap as chips and reach the shops' target audiences just as well. Annette struck while the iron was hot.

"Did a man called Ray Mercer pay you?"

Lauren's top lip restarted its jive as she attempted to play it cool. Her mother's glare put paid to that and she answered sullenly.

"Yes."

Eureka!

"How much?"

Lauren glanced sideways and Annette knew she didn't want her mother knowing how much money she'd made; she might make her put it in a bank or somewhere else boring. Too late; the question had been asked and Annette knew it would be repeated at home that night, then Lauren's earnings would be wrested from her adolescent grip and locked up in a five year account.

She changed the topic. "When did Mr Mercer contact

you?"

"On Wednesday morning."

"To say what?"

"That he wanted me to run a discussion thread for him."

"Then what did he do?"

"Gave me two questions to post."

"Which were?"

The unfrocked Father Fred shrugged. "I just wrote them down. One was some blah about inequality and the second was about six million pounds. I didn't really read them."

Annette nodded. "We've seen them, and the replies." She paused, wondering how to get proof that Mercer had paid the girl without her clamming up. Julia had an idea and signalled to intervene.

"Did Mr Mercer call you on your mobile phone?"

The girl nodded.

"Did a number show up?"

Of course. If Mercer had phoned from his own mobile they had him. Annette's heart sank as Lauren shook her silvered head.

"It just said private."

Withheld, like all calls from The Chronicle would be. Damn.

But Julia wasn't defeated.

"How did you contact him?"

"He gave me an e-mail address and a mobile number, but I was only to use it in emergencies."

Result! If it was Mercer's mobile, then with Rory Cahill's and Bill Reynolds' evidence it might be enough to prove that Mercer had paid the girl to post the question on her blog. It was a small step from there to proving that he'd interfered with a police case. Annette's heart raced as Julia closed in.

"We'll need that number. Did you e-mail him?"

"Yes and he answered. He told me how to collect the money." She made a face. "He was really weird about it. I said just to send it in postal orders, but he didn't want to; he wanted to pay me in cash, so we had to arrange a drop. He left the money for me at a café he knew in town."

She said 'drop' like someone who'd watched too many thrillers and the look on her mother's face said that she thought the same. Annette saw a month of no TV heading Father Fred's way. Julia was still speaking.

"We'll need the e-mail address."

There was only a slim chance that Mercer hadn't shut down the account already, but between the e-mail provider, the calls and the drop, they would hopefully be able to nail him down. Even if Mercer hadn't used a local ATM to withdraw the cash, CCTV inside or outside the café should have captured his face. All they needed to prove was the connection.

Lauren shrugged OK, then she smiled coyly and Annette knew that she had a bargaining chip and was wondering whether to play it. A sharp squint from her mother said not even to try. The girl's next words were said in a sulky tone.

"I called him on the mobile when the money was late to arrive. He said he'd leave it there Thursday but it was yesterday instead."

Julia glanced at Annette and they nodded and rose. They had what they needed to nail Ray Mercer, unless he'd been extremely clever and they were reluctant to credit him with that.

"We'll need your mobile, Lauren. We'll get it back to you when the techs have finished."

Anna Hayes shook her head. "Don't bother. There'll be no phone for her for the next six months."

Annette gazed at her, wondering if she should say what she thought. The answer was yes but not with the noisily protesting Lauren in the room. Annette glanced at Julia and then at the girl, waiting until they'd left before she switched off the tape and retook her seat.

"I have a teenage daughter as well. Amy."

Anna Hayes sighed. "Is she as bad as mine?"

Annette laughed. "Yes, in different ways. I hope you don't mind me saying this but try not to be too hard on Lauren. She's showing signs of entrepreneurship by setting up her blog and getting paid to advertise local businesses. We've checked back and there's nothing bad on there, just local information on shows and venues. In fact, I think the tourist board should be paying her as well."

Anna Hayes was unimpressed. "She's landed us in a police station! Her father is mortified!"

Annette wasn't giving up. "She's young and naïve. The man who manipulated her into putting up those questions, questions which in themselves looked innocent, is a real player that we've had dealings with before. He used her."

She could see the angry mother softening and pressed her case.

"Perhaps you should read the blog in future so that you can spot if anything strange is posted. I wouldn't make her shut it down."

Anne Hayes smiled, relenting but not completely. "Maybe not, but she'll definitely be opening a savings account."

****

Craig stared at Cameron Lawton's list of seven names and then at the background details Davy had attached. There was no doubt that Oliver Bwye had made enemies during his years heading The Chronicle and, when he read their back stories, Craig understood why. Bwye had screwed the men into the ground, completely ignoring the effect of his articles on them and their families.

The list contained businessmen and politicians; there was even a well-known entertainer. Sure, some of them had sailed a bit close to the wind, but that wind had been whipped into a tornado by Bwye once he'd set his sights on their story, and those tornadoes had devastated their lives. They'd lost fortunes and families and more than one had committed suicide, leaving grieving wives and children; all in the name of newsprint that would fade in the next day's sun.

Craig shuddered. He hated the media of all sorts, even when they were on their side. It was too easy for them to make allegations and twist peoples' words. Now the twisting was happening online as well, merely a click away. He stayed as far away from journalists as possible and the men on the list must have wished they could have done the same. People would argue that if they were guilty of crimes and misdemeanours the public had a right to know. Some of them had been, but what of the ones who weren't? The ones whose innocent lives had been ruined by Oliver Bwye's hints and lies.

He scanned the list again; only three of the seven were still living and two of their names were circled in green, Davy's code for innocence. All three had been ruined by Bwye's coverage of their stories, and in the case of the innocent ones none of his allegations had proved true. They must really have hated Bwye; he knew that he would. He rose to make fresh coffee and then wandered over to Davy's home from home at Oliver Bwye's desk.

"This list, Davy. It says who was innocent but it doesn't say how many are free?"

Davy tapped the names circled in green. Only two were still breathing outside jail.

"OK. Concentrate on those two then. I need their movements for the past month. If they got their hair cut I want to know where."

"You think one of them..."

"I wish I did. I don't think anything except that they hated Bwye and they're walking the streets, but it's the only lead we have."

Just then the back door opened and Andy and Gerry clattered through, tramping snow onto the parquet floor. Flurries flew in to join them and Craig motioned them to shut the door fast.

"The coffee's fresh."

They weren't listening, preferring instead to huddle round the fire. After a brief thaw, Andy spoke.

"It's brewing another blizzard out there, hey. We almost didn't make it up the drive."

Craig frowned. They were briefing at four and he had a meeting with Sean Flanagan at six; the last thing they needed was bad weather making the case even more difficult.

"Are the divers still working?"

Andy nodded. "Aye, though God knows how."

Gerry shook his head. "Their dry-suits keep them warm. I sail and if you wear one you're warm even in winter."

Craig was tempted to ask about the local sailing, but he stuck to the case instead.

"What did you find out?"

Everyone took a seat at Davy's desk, much to his annoyance. Andy shook his head.

"Nothing at the golf-club that John Ellis didn't already report. Bwye was getting hammered that evening, but seems he did that pretty often. He got a taxi home."

"Remind me about the taxi."

Davy piped up. "Liam checked. They collected Bwye at nine-twenty and arrived here at nine-forty-five. The driver confirmed he was drunk; he said Bwye could barely stand and he had to w...walk him into the house."

Craig shook his head. "That doesn't sound like a man who was planning to kill someone."

Gerry cut in. "But Bwye was a violent drunk."

Craig was sceptical. "It's hard to be violent in any effective way if you're falling over. Anyway, I'm sure the body inside the concrete will be Oliver Bwye's and it would have been impossible for him to do that to himself."

Davy looked pensive.

"What are you thinking, Davy?"

He hesitated, as if what he was going to say was too far left of field to voice.

Craig urged him on. "It doesn't matter how irrational it sounds. At this point I'd be glad of anything I can get."

Davy tugged his hair from its pony tail, agitated.

"It's just...w...what if Bwye deliberately got falling down drunk that night?"

Andy interjected. "Why would he have?"

"Humour me. How often did he get that bad?"

Andy shrugged. "The barmaid said he got hammered regularly."

Davy pressed him. "To the point where he could hardly s...stand?"

"Well, no. She did say Bwye was worse than usual that

night."

"OK. What did S...Sergeant Ellis say?"

"He said Bwye was completely legless and people were disgusted."

Craig saw where Davy was heading. "Make your point."

"OK. The barmaid, the driver and S...Sergeant Ellis, who's seen a lot, said Bwye was falling down drunk. W...What if Bwye knew he was going to die that night and that's *why* he got so drunk?"

Gerry gawped at him. "Why the heck would he go home if he knew that he was going to die?"

Davy blushed as if he was being ridiculous, but what he was saying was ringing a bell inside Craig's head. He urged him on.

"Because?"

"Because...he went home because...he'd arranged his own death. And he got paralytic drunk to numb w...what he knew was coming."

Craig leaned forward. "You mean he'd paid for a hit on his family?"

Davy looked confused. "Maybe...I'm not sure yet...maybe just on himself but Mrs Bwye got caught up in it by mistake." He shook his head, signalling defeat. "I don't know. That's as far as I've got. It's just a theory."

Craig's Italian half wanted to hug him but instead he settled for a manly "well done". Andy gawped at them both as if they were mad.

"You're taking this seriously? That Bwye arranged his own death and deliberately got drunk so that he wouldn't suffer? But what about the wife? And if Bwye arranged it, then why was there so much blood from both of them? He struggled and so did the wife, hey."

Craig shook his head. "I can't answer all the questions yet, and I'm not saying it's correct, but it's useful to have another theory. OK, good, Davy. Andy, what happened with the GP?"

"Just what you'd imagine. He's not going to tell us anything without a fight. Patient confidentiality, blah blah."

Craig nodded, but its vagueness told them his mind

was elsewhere. It was; at the mortuary. He glanced at the clock and sprang to his feet.

"Andy, you're with me. Gerry, stay here and help Davy and Carmen." He realised that Carmen was nowhere to be seen. "Where is she, by the way?"

"W...Working upstairs. She needs quiet to concentrate."

"Fine."

Andy gazed meaningfully out at the snow. "Where are we going?"

"The mortuary."

"Great. Just what we need on a day like this; somewhere warm to hang out..."

****

Mavis Brown had insisted on meeting Liam at the escort agency because she had a Mr Brown at home. Liam had had high hopes for the trip but by the time he left The Kasbah and re-emerged into Derry's winter sunlight, he was a more disappointed man than the one who'd entered an hour before.

He trudged back to his car through the snow, thinking. Old man Bwye had been a frequent visitor to the agency and an equally frequent requester of Mavis' company, but Liam felt let down by both. He'd expected The Kasbah to have a reception draped in red and gold silk, not a front office like an insurance company's, with all the attendant charm. He also expected escorts to be called Leonora or Gloria, or have some other vowel-filled name; not Mavis. He'd been even more disappointed by Mavis once they'd met.

Instead of the pneumatic twenty-something he'd expected, Mavis had lived down to her name, with short brown hair and sturdy legs and an age well past her two thirds century. He pictured Diana Bwye, a pretty brunette who would have stayed pretty well into old age, and decided that Mavis must have hidden charms. Ten minutes of chat later he'd understood her attraction.

She'd hung on his every word with a look that said he was a God amongst men and every syllable he uttered was a gem. For a control freak like Oliver Bwye she must have been a dream come true. Bwye had seen her three times a week for the past year, either at the agency or, more daringly, in his study at home. Liam wondered whether he'd cared if his wife and daughter found out and then plumped for probably not. A man selfish enough to need a yes woman wouldn't waste time caring about anyone's feelings other than his own.

Three times a week didn't leave much time for a real affair and questioning of The Kasbah's staff confirmed that Bwye had often been there even when Mavis wasn't working, making do with someone else for the night. An hour of questions later and with Mavis Brown's swab in his pocket to eliminate her DNA, Liam was walking back to his car.

He stopped and gazed around him for a moment, wondering whether to have tea and a bun in a small café he'd spied, or head back to the undoubtedly freezing lake and start chasing the phantom boat. Compromise won and a takeaway accompanied him the six mile journey to the farm north of the lake. Twenty minutes later he was standing on a jetty with a young man, both of them staring down at a small speedboat.

"My parents are away, Chief Inspector. You'll have to make do with my wee brother Micky and me."

The speaker was a wiry youth of around eighteen. But around eighteen was always dodgy so Liam decided to check his name and age.

"Do you have any I.D., Mr McDermott? Only, no disrespect, but you could be some kid who'd just wandered in off the street."

It was unlikely, given that the boy had answered the door of the double-fronted farm house holding a games console and wearing no shoes. But it never did any harm to check.

Oisín McDermott produced his driving licence, reassuring Liam that he was who he'd said he was and was nineteen in two weeks.

"Grand. I just had to check. How wee is your wee brother?"

"Sixteen."

"Fine. Is he around?"

"Back at the house. You want me to call him?"

"Aye. Another pair of eyes."

Five minutes later three pairs of eyes were staring at the speedboat, anchored to the jetty by a braided mooring line. Liam rubbed his chin.

"You say it disappeared and then suddenly came back?"

Micky McDermott nodded vigorously, barely shifting the vertical mass of hair on top of his head. Hair products had moved on since the Brylcreem of Liam's youth.

"It was me who noticed it gone. Last Wednesday."

Wednesday; it fitted their timeline.

"What time did you notice?"

"When I got home from school, 'bout six. I stay late on Wednesdays for science club."

Liam nodded approvingly, picturing his son Rory building computers by the time he reached nursery. Both his children would be geniuses of course; it stood to reason with him as a dad.

"Who did you tell?"

The boy looked blank and then glanced at his brother as if he didn't want to land him in a mess. Oisín nodded him on in a way that suggested he didn't want to add lying to the police to his list of misdemeanours.

"Nobody. I...It's happened before and Dad got mad."

Oisín cut in. "I took the boat out overnight last summer without telling my dad." A light blush coloured his cheeks and Liam knew immediately that there'd been a girl involved. "He grounded me for six weeks." The lothario shrugged magnanimously. "It was fair enough. I scared them to death. Mum thought that I'd drowned."

Liam grinned. "Trying to impress a young lady by any chance?"

The blush deepened. Liam turned back to his brother.

"So you thought Oisín had taken the boat again and you didn't want to land him in it."

Micky nodded.

"OK. So you noticed the boat gone at six o'clock last Wednesday. Tell me what you did for the rest of the night, including when you raised the alarm."

The sixteen-year-old answered without hesitation. "I went in, had dinner, did my homework then watched TV before bed like I usually do. I didn't tell anyone the boat had gone."

"What time did you go to bed?"

"Ten. I had a try-out for the rugby team next morning, so I didn't want to sleep in."

Liam turned to look at the house. It was an impressive edifice with balconies on the upper floor. One of them overlooked the lake; it was too much to hope for that the room belonged to one of the boys. He was right; it was their parents' bedroom.

"Where are your rooms?"

The brothers answered together. "At the back."

"So you didn't notice any activity on the lake late that night?"

Micky shook his head.

"And you didn't see your brother so you didn't realise that he hadn't taken the boat?"

"No. He wasn't up when I went to school on Thursday, so I couldn't ask him. But I noticed the boat was still missing when I left for school at seven."

Satisfied with the boy's story, Liam turned to his dirty-stop-out elder brother.

"OK. Tell me where you were that night."

Oisín screwed up his face, trying to recall. Then he smiled, remembering. "Party at the student's union."

"What subject are you studying?"

Whatever it was they obviously didn't have morning lectures.

"Media studies."

Liam smirked. Another budding Spielberg.

"OK. Tell me about Wednesday night and Thursday morning."

The young man shrugged. "Partied at the union till three and then crashed at a mate's. I didn't get home till Thursday evening after lectures."

Before Liam could ask, he volunteered the mate's name. "Jackson Flood. He'll vouch for me."

He slipped his phone from his jeans and read out Flood's number. "I didn't even notice the boat had gone until Dad said."

Micky chipped in. "I saw it wasn't back when I came home after school on Thursday, but I still didn't want to say anything till I saw Oisín. It was Dad who mentioned it first, about eight o'clock that night."

Oisín nodded. "On Thursday evening, over dinner." He looked aggrieved. "He asked me straight out if I'd taken it!"

As if. Liam urged him on.

"So you both said that you hadn't. Then what?"

Micky cut in excitedly. "Dad got his binoculars and looked. It was floating in the middle of the lake. Dad and Oisín went out in the row boat and brought it in. It looked OK so Dad just assumed it'd got loose and floated out."

Except that it hadn't. Their killer had been clever. He'd dumped the Bwyes' bodies, sailed back to their side of the lake and deliberately left the boat unmoored, knowing that it would float back out with the current. Liam took out his phone.

"Has anyone been in the boat since then?"

Both boys shook their heads. "It's too cold."

He smiled at their solidarity and hoped that his kids would grow up as close, then he called in the C.S.I.s as Oisín McDermott got his surprised father on the phone.

****

The brick mortuary was as cold as they'd expected but at least Mike's office had working radiators. They sat on them gratefully until Craig had thawed out enough to speak.

"Diana Bwye. What did you find?"

Mike handed out hot drinks with a solemn look on his face.

"She had the ligature marks you saw around her neck, and two wounds, both gunshots. The first was to her left thigh, nasty and vascular; it explains the amount of blood we found in Bwye's study. But that wasn't her cause of death. What killed her was a second shot to the chest; straight through the heart. It's hard to be accurate on time but I'd say that they were separated by less than half an hour. Both bullets were from the same weapon, a point 22 rifle."

Andy was confused. "So what was the point of the ligature?"

Mike shrugged. "God only knows. She wasn't strangled; whoever did it didn't even break the hyoid bone. If I was being cynical I'd say they left the mark to throw us off track."

Craig returned to the gunshots. "Were the wounds caused by Bwye's weapon?"

"Probably. But until we get the gun we won't know for sure. I've sent the bullets to Des."

Craig sipped his coffee, feeling the sensation return to his hands.

"So she was dead before she entered the water."

"Definitely. There was no water in her lungs and no sign that she'd struggled to get free of the sack. There would have been plastic under her fingernails. In fact I don't think she struggled at all. We would have found skin or blood under her nails if she'd fought her attacker, but there was nothing."

Andy nodded. "If Bwye had battered her for years she might have given up fighting."

Mike's face saddened. "I've seen it happen before."

"If she knew her attacker that might've made her less likely to run as well, hey."

Craig's voice was dull. "We could speculate forever. When we find them we'll know. Anything else on her, Mike?"

"No. Just an ignominious end for a nice woman. Thank God she was dead before she hit the water; her husband's fate was even worse."

Craig glanced up from his drink. "How much worse?"

"A lot."

"You got him out of the concrete?"

The pathologist nodded. "We scanned it at the hospital first so that we didn't damage evidence, then we used ultrasound to shatter the shell at two points. Forensics are working on the pieces now but Des says it's a concrete found in every DIY store." He gave a brief smile. "Bright side. The body's intact."

Andy gave a low whistle. "This is a first for me. A concrete shell."

Craig nodded. "It's a first for all of us. You should write it up, Mike."

He knew how excited scientists got about publishing unusual cases and this one was a doozy.

"I'm already planning to." He glanced at Craig's mug. "Drink up. What I have to tell you about Mr Bwye is best done where you can see him."

Two minutes later they were staring at Oliver Bwye's blue-white flesh and shivering so hard in the freezing morgue that Craig knew they'd all be the same colour soon. He gestured at the body.

"Make this quick."

Mike obliged by inserting a probe through Bwye's right flank, marking the path of a bullet.

"OK. You can see the gunshot wound in Bwye's side. I'm sure the bullet will match the ones found in his wife. The wound is deep and the bullet nicked the liver, so there would have been considerable blood loss. I'd say that most of the blood in the study was his."

"Presumably done to disable him. He's big so they'd have needed him out of commission fast. It's lucky the shot didn't kill him; or did it?"

The pathologist shook his head emphatically. "Definitely not but I doubt that luck had anything to do with it. The wound would have been bloody painful but it wouldn't have caused his immediate death; I think they planned it that way."

Andy went to whistle again but blew out white air instead. "Someone with a knowledge of anatomy, then?"

"Or someone who could read a book and was a good shot. Either way, Bwye definitely wasn't dead when they took him from the study."

He paused and Craig knew what was coming. It was at moments like this that John would have taken off his glasses and wiped them on his coat. Mike made do with a grimace. "He wasn't dead when they covered him in concrete either."

Andy's jaw dropped. "You're kidding! He was alive?"

"Very much so, judging by the scans. They showed that the concrete was thinner in the areas over his hands and feet, as if he'd tried to push and kick it away." He swallowed hard. "There was also concrete in his lungs. He drowned in concrete."

Craig pictured the image and shook his head. "Bwye was a big man. Why didn't he fight harder?"

Mike lifted one of Oliver Bwye's arms. There was a clear ligature mark around his wrist.

"There are similar marks around his ankles. I'd say he was shot and wounded badly enough to debilitate him and possibly render him unconscious, long enough to bind him and get him into the van. Then, when your killer realised they were leaving too much of a trail they decided to dispose of the bodies in the lake. They'd come prepared with the concrete and plastic sacks."

"But not the stones."

The other men stared at Craig, confused.

"They didn't bring the stones that we found weighing down Diana Bwye; they came from the lake shore."

"You're sure?"

"I saw some identical lying there. Forensics will confirm it."

Andy nodded, seeing where Craig was heading. "So...what? They hadn't planned to kill Diana Bwye?"

"I don't think so. I think Oliver Bwye was the target. We need to check if Mrs Bwye was expected to be at home that night. If they didn't intend to kill her that might explain why they had to use the stones; they hadn't brought enough concrete for both."

Augustus shook his head sadly. "You're saying that she needn't have died. He only intended to kill Bwye, and torture him as well if his death is anything to go by."

Craig nodded. "Oliver Bwye was the primary target and the sadistic method of killing points to real hatred. This wasn't a random home invasion; this was well planned revenge."

****

Annette stared through the custody cell peephole at Jane

Bwye, while Julia did the same across the corridor at Richard McCann. They were a sorry pair. The girl's eyes were red raw with crying and her husband was sitting with his head in his hands; his shoulders slumped as if he was carrying the worries of the world. Annette turned to Julia and rolled her eyes, dropping her voice to a whisper.

"What idiot put them so close together? They'll have their story off pat."

Julia nodded. They would interview them separately but it would be a waste of time now; they were sure to have been talking to each other through the cell doors. Fifteen minutes later the two inspectors were back in the staff room comparing notes.

Annette sighed. "Jane's statement is practically identical to McCann's, even though she cried all the way through."

"About being in custody?"

Annette shook her head. "No. About her mum being dead. She's really cut up."

Julia sipped her tea and nodded. "He seems gutted as well; Diana Bwye was a popular lady. But he fits the ransom call; broad shoulders, west Belfast accent and all. He didn't even disguise his voice when he rang. Arrogant or dim?"

Annette rose to her feet, not answering. She was focusing on the next step. "What do you say we have a go at them together? We can watch how they interact. It might tell us something."

Julia gazed through the staff-room window at the increasingly heavy snow and pulled her jacket tightly around her.

"Anything that defers going out in that is fine by me. Lead on."

Five minutes' later they were in a warm, bright interview room with two bedraggled suspects and four hot drinks. Annette clicked on the tape and covered the formalities then she nodded politely for Julia to kick off. She began with Jane.

"Ms Bwye, or do you prefer Mrs McCann? Could you tell me exactly when you got married, please?"

Nice. She was establishing them as a pair.

Jane sniffed hard before answering and Annette reached into her handbag and handed a paper tissue across.

"The eighteenth of July. At Belfast City Hall."

"And how long have you known each other?"

They watched as the girl smiled at her new husband and knew that if they hadn't been there the smile would have been accompanied by a squeezed hand.

"Since we were children. From when Mrs McCann started work at Rocksbury."

Richard McCann cut in. "We used to play together." His green eyes narrowed. "But you already know all this so why are you wasting our time."

Julia's blue eyes narrowed to match. "I'm checking some facts, Mr McCann. Would you rather return to your cell? We can continue without you."

Annette smiled inwardly as McCann leaned back in his chair, subdued. Julia continued calmly, looking at her notes.

"So you've been close for years and have always done things together."

A gentle underlining that what one said implicated the other now.

She turned suddenly to Jane. "How did you get on with your mother, Mrs McCann?"

Annette winced, waiting for the tears to flow again. To her surprise Jane merely sniffed.

"I love...loved my mother. She was the best woman I knew."

McCann leapt to his wife's defence, lurching so far forward that he almost hit Annette's nose.

"They were always close. That bastard Bwye beat them both and Diana took most of it to protect Jane."

Annette scraped back her chair and stood up. "Sit back, Mr McCann, or you'll be returning to your cell."

The young man looked bewildered for a moment, gazing first at her and then at his own position. He leaned back slowly and raised his hands in peace. "Sorry, I didn't mean anything. It's just..." He gazed at his wife and finished the sentence in a weak voice. "Jane really loved her mum. So did I."

Annette signalled to take over and retook her seat. "How long had Mrs Bwye known about your relationship?"

McCann nodded. "For years. She was happy for us. But..."

"But Mr Bwye wouldn't have been if he'd found out."

He shook his head. "He'd have cut Jane off without a penny." He straightened up suddenly and Annette thought all that was missing was his chest being puffed out. "I didn't care. I don't want his stinking money, I never did."

Jane placed a hand on top of his and shook her head. "Rick's telling the truth. He never wanted my inheritance." She jutted her chin out defiantly. "But I did; it would have given us a decent life and Mum wanted us to have it. She and I had suffered enough with that bastard; he owed us both."

"You hated your father."

It was a statement not a question. She hadn't even asked how Oliver Bwye had died.

"I loathed him. He was a drunken, violent bully who ruined people's lives, including my mother's."

Annette's next question was slipped in; in a voice so soft that it caught the girl unawares. "Enough for her to kill him?"

The couple's eyes widened and then McCann did something that shocked everyone. He laughed. He kept on laughing until Jane stared at him with filling eyes that pleaded with him to stop.

"What's so funny, Mr McCann?"

"You are, with your stupid questions. Diana Bwye was the kindest, gentlest, most religious woman I've ever met, and heaven only knows why, because he didn't deserve it with his violence and his whores, she loved her husband. She would never have killed the old bastard."

Julia leaned in eagerly. "Your mother knew about the other women?"

Jane nodded sadly. "Everyone did, but Rick's right. Mum loved my father anyway. She would never have hurt him."

"What about you? You would've had to keep your marriage a secret until you'd inherited, or your father would have cut you off."

The girl's shoulders slumped. "Yes, but I didn't kill him for it." She shot them both a sharp look. "And I would never ever have harmed my mum. What was she doing there anyway?"

Annette's eyes widened and she glanced at Julia. They'd been so busy finding bodies that everyone had forgotten the most obvious question. Was Diana Bwye supposed to be at the house that night? Annette answered the question with another.

"What do you mean?"

"I mean that my mum did a lot of charity work and on Wednesday evenings she ran a committee meeting in town, for the local Vanquish Cancer branch. She never missed it. She stayed overnight with her friend Stephanie afterwards. She'd been doing it every Wednesday for years."

Diana Bwye hadn't been supposed to be in the house that night. So why had she been? Annette asked the question and immediately provoked fresh tears.

"Maybe she stayed home to tell my dad about us. She would have wanted me out of the way when she did." Jane covered her face with her hands. "Oh, God. It's my fault she'd dead. It's my fault."

"You can't know that."

But the girl's howls of anguish drowned out her words. Annette gave McCann the nod to comfort her and they left them alone for five minutes. Ten minutes more questioning when they restarted only confirmed what they already knew. Jane had arrived home at six-thirty that evening in her Mercedes, the car that Bernadette Ross had passed on the drive as she'd left for the night. But she hadn't entered the house then as they'd assumed, instead she'd stopped at her mother-in-law's apartment, to meet her husband.

They'd only gone to the main house after eleven p.m., when everyone should have been asleep. Richard had helped himself to a whisky and that was when they'd noticed the open study door, checked the room and seen the blood. They'd assumed Oliver Bwye had been kidnapped or killed and feared that they would be blamed. There'd been no sign of Diana and no reason they would have expected her to be in the house at all on a Wednesday night.

The rest was history. They'd burnt out the car in panic and made the ill-considered ransom attempt, with McCann strengthening his childhood Belfast accent to throw people off the track. Stupid yes, but no judge would convict them of anything except wasting police time or fleeing the scene of a crime. They hadn't followed through with the ransom demand and the money would come to Jane now anyway, with both her parents dead.

As the lovebirds were put back in their cages Julia wrote up their notes and Annette made a call to Craig.

"I'll ask Davy to check the details of Diana Bwye's charity meeting, sir. We need to find out why she didn't go that night."

Craig picked thoughtfully at the car dashboard as Andy turned off the Glenshane Road.

"Go and interview this Stephanie. She might have the answer. Meanwhile, what's your feeling on Romeo and Juliet?"

Annette nodded gratefully as Julia put the kettle on to boil. "Julia and I agree, sir. They might be stupid but what actual crime did they commit? OK, they panicked and left the scene and they made that stupid ransom call, but they didn't follow it up and Jane's going to inherit everything now anyway."

Craig shook his head, knowing that Annette's desire for a happy ending was getting the best of her. Julia's impending nuptials were obviously doing the same.

"That's not our decision, Annette. Put the file together and let the P.P.S. decide. You're probably right and they'll dismiss it, but it has to be their call."

Annette's sigh said that she wasn't pleased; it meant more paperwork and the McCanns being left to the vagaries of the prosecutors. Tough; romance didn't excuse bad behaviour. If it did then every newlywed would have carte blanche to commit crimes. Craig threw her a placating bouquet.

"Make a recommendation and they'll probably just get their knuckles rapped." He had a sudden thought. "I need to go. Bail them pending the P.P.S. decision." He ended the call and made another one to Davy, cutting straight to the chase. "Have you checked the Bwyes' Wills?"

Davy stared at the phone, considering asking who was calling, then he decided the joke wouldn't be worth the earache he'd get. The chief was in a grumpy mood these days.

"Diana Bwye only had a s...short one, outlining some charitable donations she'd like to make and leaving all her jewellery to her daughter."

"Did she have any money in her own right?"

"A trust from her family, the D'Arcys. I'm waiting for the details."

"OK. Presumably she'd have inherited everything on her husband's death."

"Yes. His w...will was straightforward. Everything went to Diana. Nothing to the daughter except the trust she'd get at thirty. There's something else you s...should know, chief..."

Craig cut him off. "Save it till I get there. Is Liam back yet?"

Davy shook his head then remembered it wasn't a video phone. "Not yet. He'll be here for the briefing."

"OK."

Craig ended the call without a thanks or goodbye. Andy noticed his unfamiliar abruptness and that it had been there all week long.

"Something up? You don't seem your usual cheerful self these days."

Craig glared at the side of his head. "You mean I'm not pandering to everyone's inefficiencies the way I normally do."

Andy lashed back. "I mean you're being a rude bastard, Marc, and if it was your normal personality I wouldn't bother pointing it out."

It was on the tip of Craig's tongue to pull rank then he realised how stupid he would sound. What could he say anyway? You can't tell me I'm rude because I'm your boss? Andy was right. He was being a grumpy shit but he wasn't sure why. It wasn't the case and it wasn't seeing Julia again; he hadn't felt right for months. He hadn't been sleeping and he'd been drinking way too much. He knew people thought it was the Pitt shooting, but that was crap. He was trained to deal with such things, even if Pitt had been an old man...

It was too much to think about so he shrugged and slid further down his seat. The rest of the journey was spent in silence and when the two men entered Bwye's study the tension between them was almost palpable.

Liam was lounging in a low armchair with his eyes shut and Carmen was sitting beside Davy, tapping on a laptop. Craig barked so loudly that Liam jerked awake and Carmen jumped up, alarmed.

"Wake up, all of you! What's happening at the lake?"

Liam gazed at him, confused. "What do you mean?"

"I mean have they found anything else relevant to the case; like Bwye's rifle. And where are Julia and Annette? Come to think of it, where's Gerry?"

Liam squinted at him. Craig was in a snit and intent on taking it out on them. By the looks of Andy he'd already had his share.

"Gerry's down at the lake. He'll let us know if they find anything new. The ladies who lunch are on their way back from interviewing Father Fred and the McCanns. They're making a detour to visit someone called Stephanie and they've asked if the briefing can be delayed for thirty minutes."

Craig's voice dripped with sarcasm. "Of course we can delay it. Why not? Let's just delay the whole investigation!"

With that he stormed into the main room and Liam glared at Andy.

"What did you do to him? He was OK when he left here."

Andy grabbed a chair, shaking his head. "No he wasn't, not really. He hasn't been right since this case started. Haven't you noticed?"

Liam made a face that said he was trying to recall Craig's mood. With his level of sensitivity they'd be waiting all year. Andy shook his head.

"Why am I asking you? You never notice what people are feeling."

"Here! That's not true."

Andy took out his mobile phone. "Shall I call Danni and ask her, hey?"

Liam conceded the point. "Aye, well, maybe you're right. OK, so I've noticed the boss has been a bit out of sorts the past while."

"He's a grumpy shit and he's drinking a lot more than he usually does; haven't you noticed at the hotel? Something's eating him and it's not this case."

Liam furrowed his brow. He knew what was ailing Craig but there was no point him tackling him about it; he'd just tell him to get lost. After a moment he grinned. "I know who can help. The Doc." He grabbed the phone, signalling Andy to keep an eye out for Craig. The call was answered quickly.

"John Winter, pathologist extraordinaire, at your service."

Liam smiled. If the Doc was feeling playful then he'd give him a game. He put on his best English accent.

"This is Her Majesty's Home Office here. I need to speak to a Dr John Winter."

John gawped at the handset and was about to make an excuse for his answering technique when something about the way the word Home had sounded like Hum made him change his mind.

"Very funny, Liam. What do you want?"

"What gave me away?"

"The Hum Office. That Crossgar twang is hard to hide. You wanted to ask me something. Shoot."

Liam was smarting from the crack about his accent so he handed Andy the phone.

"Hi John, it's Andy; Liam's sulking. We're ringing to ask you what's wrong with Marc. He's chewing the head off everyone and drinking like a fish every night."

John frowned. He hadn't noticed anything major amiss with Craig; perhaps they were imagining it. He was about to say so when he thought again. Craig *had* been drinking more than usual. He'd put it down to the festive season but now that he thought about it the festive season seemed to have started in October that year. He hadn't been rude to him exactly, just vague and distracted, as if he hadn't been listening half the time.

His mind ran back through the previous two months, recalling Craig verging on drunk a few times during the week. He pictured the dark shadows under his eyes that he'd put down to heavy sessions, but were there even when he knew Craig had drunk nothing the night before. He hadn't been sleeping, he'd been distracted and moody and he'd been drinking far more than he usually did. Of course...

"Are you still there, John?"

"I'm still here. Leave this with me, Andy."

Andy wasn't leaving it that easily. "Marc's being a bad-tempered shit and it's making life difficult up here."

John's tone said not to argue. "I said leave it. I'll sort it out."

Before Andy could object further he was listening to a dead line. He gawped at the hand set then turned grumpily to Liam.

"Rudeness is obviously contagious in Belfast. Whatever's eating Marc has just taken a chunk out of the Doc as well."

****

4.30 p.m.

Craig's meeting with Sean Flanagan had been moved to the next day so he'd calmed down a little about the briefing beginning late.

"Grab a drink and let's get started."

The instruction to grab a drink was redundant as everyone who'd entered the study had headed directly for the coffee. The donuts beside it as well, if their sugar coated lips were anything to go by. Craig gestured at the chairs in the middle of the room to be met by a communal shake of the head and the sound of scraping as they were dragged towards the fire.

Gerry explained for all of them. "It would skin a fairy out there, and you'll be sending us out in it again soon."

He held his hands in front of the flames giving Craig a look that would have done a Dickensian orphan proud. The performance would normally have warranted a smile, but there wasn't a glimmer of merriment in Craig's eyes.

"Let's get on with it. Liam, tell me about the brothel and the boat."

Craig topped up his coffee and ignored the cakes, taking a seat as far back from the group as he could get in the small room.

"Aye well, The Kasbah. Strictly speaking it wasn't a brothel, more an escort agency. Not the most welcoming place I've ever been; it looked like a government office. When I think of that place out near the airport..."

He was referring to a high-end brothel called Lilith's that they'd encountered on a case in 2012. It had occupied a Victorian house near Belfast's International Airport, for the convenience of travelling businessmen.

Craig shot him a warning look.

"Aye, OK then. It was clean, nothing much there except the girls and madam. Well, when I say girls, the youngest was about thirty and Bwye's particular favourite was well north of sixty."

Annette smiled approvingly; or as approvingly as a woman could when the discussion was about prostitutes. "At least he was age appropriate."

"That's about as appropriate as that place got. The waiting room was like a dentist's but behind that they had a corridor with these themed bedrooms." He turned to Craig. "You should see it, boss, they have an ice adventure room, a rodeo room..."

Craig cut him off before he reached fetish corner. "The case, please."

Liam sniffed, put out. "So the punters either go there or the women go to them."

"You spoke to Bwye's favourite?"

"Aye, Mrs Mavis Brown; he saw her three times a week. You'd think she'd have changed her name to something like Misty, wouldn't you?" Craig's frown said he was about to bollock him so Liam continued hastily. "Anyhow, I got her DNA. It's gone to the lab for elimination." He chanced a P.S. "She's nothing like Diana Bwye. Not a looker at all, but she listens to every word you say."

Gerry couldn't resist a question. "How do you know? She might just look like she's listening."

"'Cos she repeats it back to you every time."

It was Annette who couldn't resist now. "Echolalia."

Craig gave a small smile. John had told him about the medical condition so he knew what was coming next.

Liam asked the question warily, certain that the next joke would be at his expense. "What's that?"

Annette decided that a demonstration was in order. "What's that?"

"What?"

"What?"

Before it turned into a French farce Craig intervened. "Echolalia is where someone involuntarily repeats words or phrases. It can sound as if they're really interested. It's a symptom of lots of conditions, including Schizophrenia."

Liam's face fell. "So that's what Mavis has. I thought she was really into me."

"I doubt she has any condition at all. She's probably just realised it's an approach that some men like."

Craig waved him on with the report.

"Right, the boat. Now this is clever. It belongs to the family across the lake, the McDermotts. It's normally moored outside their house but one of the two sons, Micky, noticed it missing on the Wednesday around six p.m. He didn't say anything to his parents because he thought his older brother had taken it out for a joy ride. The father noticed it was missing on the Thursday evening around eight o'clock and when they checked with the binoculars it was floating in the middle of the lake. They retrieved it using their rowing boat and I've the C.S.I.s looking over it now."

Craig thought for a moment. "They saw no-one taking it?"

Liam shook his head.

"Did they know the Bwyes?"

Liam's expression said that he hadn't asked. "I'll make

the call. My guess is that everyone knows everyone around here."

"Probably, but ask. Take a trip back there this evening."

Liam knew that making the trip on a freezing cold evening was his punishment for forgetting a basic question. He shrugged; it was his own fault. Craig turned to Annette and just as he did so, Liam remembered something.

"Old man Bwye knew a Garvan McDermott. John Ellis had to break up a fight between them about politics last November."

"And you're just telling us this now? Is it the same McDermott?"

Liam thought about shrugging but the look in Craig's eyes said it wouldn't be a good idea. "I'll check."

"Do that. Before you go back there tonight."

He turned back to Annette, not missing the wary looks the group were giving him. No-one wanted to experience the sharp end of his mood next.

"Jane Bwye and McCann?"

Annette glanced at Julia and gestured her to take the lead; after all she was the local. Plus the fact that Craig was less likely to shout at an ex-girlfriend hadn't escaped her.

Julia shook her head. "Nothing that we didn't already know. She hated her father for how he treated her mother and controlled them both. She'd known McCann for years on the estate and Diana Bwye knew they'd married but agreed to keep it secret."

Craig interrupted. "What did you make of the husband?"

She smiled, spreading her freckles across her nose.

"He seems genuine. He loves her, that's for sure. He was visiting his mother that night and Jane went to her apartment after Bernadette Ross saw her drive in. They didn't come up here till after eleven o'clock. They found the study door open and saw the blood on the floor and feared the worst had happened to Oliver Bwye. They thought they would get the blame so they skedaddled."

Craig nodded. "So they burnt out the car in case

someone had seen them; to throw up a false trail."

"Yes."

"What in God's name prompted the ransom call?"

Annette shrugged. "Panic, stupidity; who knows? But they thought better of it and never called back."

Craig shook his head. "Your tone implies that no harm was done. It could have delayed the investigation for days."

She went to object then thought better of it; Craig would be in a more tolerant frame of mind once they'd closed the case. She changed tack.

"They'd no idea that Diana had been taken. She's normally never here on a Wednesday night."

Liam's ears pricked up. "Where is she then?"

"At a charity committee, then she always stayed the night with a friend called Stephanie Crewe." She glanced at Craig. "Sorry, sir, the traffic was so heavy we didn't manage to get there. We'll follow her up after the briefing."

Liam wasn't letting go. "So what stopped Diana Bwye going out that night?"

Both women shook their heads. "The only thing Jane could think of was that maybe she'd decided to tell her father about Richard. She would have wanted Jane out of the way when she did it, in case he kicked off."

Craig cut in. "You're sure that when they made the ransom call they had no idea that Mrs Bwye was missing?"

Annette shook her head. "None. Jane's devastated."

The normally sympathetic Craig wasn't impressed. "It's too convenient, Annette. She can't get her trust fund until she's thirty and if only Oliver Bwye had died the mother would have inherited everything and Jane would still have been broke. This way she inherits the earth."

Annette wasn't giving up. "But her mother would have given her the trust fund early once she'd inherited, Jane was sure of it."

"We only have her word for that."

Davy's quiet voice interrupted the increasingly heated exchange. "I might have s...something useful."

Craig's adrenaline was pumping so hard that he

barked. "What?"

Davy's dry retort stuck in his throat. Craig's expression said this wasn't the time for jokes.

"Bwye's finances. There's s...something odd."

Craig's aggression changed to eagerness and his second "what?" was more conciliatory.

"He was insured up to his ears but nearly every policy had a negation clause."

"Based on what?"

"His health."

"We already know about the heart disease and skin cancer."

Davy shook his head furiously. "No, there's more. His hospital records came through. Bwye had prostate cancer; end s...stage. I'm still gathering info but apparently he didn't have long to live."

Gerry raised a finger to interrupt. "I can tell you about that. Davy told me about his cancer earlier so I called the GP back. Once we said we knew he was more helpful. Oliver Bwye had less than six months to live."

Davy nodded eagerly and Annette had a vague thought that anyone watching would think that they were ghouls; excited about a man's terminal diagnosis. Craig wasn't excited, he was working out dates.

"When did Bwye find out?"

Davy stared at him confused.

"Bwye. When was he told he was terminal?"

Davy saw where he was heading. "His urology consultant told him in October, at an outpatient's appointment."

"Two months ago, that's what made his violence escalate."

Andy had a fleeting moment of concern; what if Craig was ill and that's why he was angry nowadays. He dismissed the idea instantly; he was just being a moody sod. Davy continued.

"There's more. Bwye had had repeated problems with his prostate through the years; benign enlargement, bouts of prostatitis, so his life insurer w...wouldn't cover him for anything related to prostate disease, as w...well as all the other exclusions. I missed it before 'cos it wasn't listed in the main exclusion section, s...sorry."

Craig nodded slowly; it wouldn't have helped them whether Davy had seen it or not. It only made sense now that they knew Bwye's diagnosis.

"So if Bwye had died of prostate cancer, skin cancer or heart disease the family would have got no insurance money at all." He gestured around the room. "But surely the estate's worth enough anyway?"

Davy shrugged. "Depends what you think enough is. Maybe Bwye's finances weren't in as good shape as he wanted. He played the s...stock market which can..."

Liam finished the sentence. "Go down as well as up."

Davy pushed his hair back from his face. "Yes. And more down than up at the moment. Most of the money Bwye had made from s...selling The Chronicle was gone."

Craig leaned in. "So what did that leave his family if he'd died of prostate cancer?"

"He would have got absolutely no insurance pay-out, unless it was for kidnap and ransom. Just Rocksbury and whatever was in his companies and s...stocks, but without the life insurance money to maintain the place..."

Craig shook his head. "OK, so Bwye knew he wasn't leaving as much as he'd planned. They still wouldn't have been poor."

Annette's voice was firm. "You're thinking like a normal person, sir. Oliver Bwye was a type A personality, bordering on egomania; he'd never have been satisfied with that. When his Will was published in the papers he'd have wanted it to say what a success he'd been. Especially if it was published in The Chronicle."

The room fell quiet as Craig thought. Had Oliver Bwye really been so desperate to leave a fortune as some sort of reflection of his ego, that he'd arranged his own kidnap to get his K&R insurance to pay out?

Annette hadn't finished. "Some treatments for prostate cancer can cause impotence. Liam, did Mavis Brown actually say that they'd had sex?"

A faint blush coloured Liam's cheeks; he wasn't used to Annette bringing up topics like that. He stumbled over his words.

"Well...no...but I assumed."

Annette persisted. "You said she wasn't the most glamourous woman, but she was motherly and a great listener. What are the odds that Bwye couldn't get an erection and only went there to talk?"

Liam's blush turned bright red. "Here, now. There's no need for that type of talk. We're not even in a bar."

She ignored him and turned to Craig. "At this stage of his disease I honestly doubt if Oliver Bwye could have had sex. Imagine the ignominy for a powerful man whose masculinity had formed the basis of his life."

Craig frowned; but it made sense. "So you're saying that he arranged a hit on himself to get the K&R. But why kill his wife as well?"

"She wasn't supposed to be there but when she was they had to kill her."

Davy nodded furiously. "That's why Bwye took out K&R insurance even though he was retired. The Chronicle had K&R on him but it lapsed when he s...sold it. He took out a new private policy eleven months ago. Maybe that's when he began having prostate symptoms."

Craig frowned. Had Oliver Bwye controlled his death like he'd controlled everything about his life, arranging his own kidnap and murder so that his family would get the K&R? It felt wrong but they had to explore the possibility. He thought for a moment then restarted in a brisk voice.

"We need to know when his cancer was first diagnosed." He turned to Annette. "Would he have felt ill enough to know he was dying eleven months ago when he took out the K&R?"

"It's possible, depends on his symptoms. He might have known that something was wrong and deliberately taken out the K&R before he went to see a doctor."

"OK, let's say he took out K&R and arranged a hit on himself that looked like a kidnapping so that his family would get the pay-out."

Julia cut in. "It means he loved his family enough to leave them well off. That's one redeeming feature."

Craig shook his head. "I'd love to say that was his reasoning but my guess is that Bwye didn't give a damn about anyone else. All he cared about was his legacy and the write-up in The Chronicle when his Will was read."

Liam nodded wisely. "So now, all we have to do is find out who he hired to kill him."

All eyes turned to him but Andy spoke first. "That's all, is it? He could have hired anyone to carry out the hit. Just open the yellow pages and stick a pin in paramilitary gangs. We'll be here all year."

A noisy debate started and Craig let it run for a moment before signalling for silence.

"This is all assumption. We've proved nothing except that Bwye had cancer and was possibly worried about being kidnapped. He could still have been genuinely abducted, or for all we know the wife was the real target of the attack and that's why they waited till she was there."

Liam raised an eyebrow and Craig smiled for the first time in hours.

"OK, maybe that's stretching it; Bwye's murder was much more sadistic than hers. But this is still all speculation. I need a lot more proof before I'm going down the contract killing road." He paused and scanned the row of faces. "Does anyone have anything else to report?"

Annette raised a finger tentatively. "We met with Father Fred and we're pretty sure that we can tie Ray Mercer to her and expose his set up."

Davy was curious about the blogger. It wasn't often that he was beaten by a kid. "What was s...she like?"

"A sulky fourteen-year-old, but if her mother doesn't ground her for the next ten years we can expect great things from her."

Craig clenched his fist. They had Ray Mercer by the balls and he was going to enjoy watching him squirm.

"Good. Annette, get onto Cameron Lawton and say we'll have proof of Mercer's bad behaviour for his lawyers very soon. It looks like Maggie's interim post just became permanent. Anything else, anyone?"

He was answered by silence. "OK. Davy, keep digging into Bwye's finances and I want to know more about Diana Bwye's trust fund and Bwye's cancer, particularly when he was first diagnosed. Andy and Gerry, go back to the escort agency and interview Mrs Brown in more depth, knowing what you now know about Bwye's cancer. Liam's feeling too shy to ask about sex. Annette and Julia, keep the pressure on forensics and I want to know more about Diana Bwye's charity work and why she wasn't at her meeting that Wednesday night. That's too much of a coincidence for me. Carmen, check whether Garvan McDermott belongs to the family across the lake and call me ASAP; Liam and I are heading over there now."

Liam shook his head firmly. "There's no way I'm getting in a boat on that night."

It took Craig a moment to realise what he meant. "I didn't mean over literally. We'll drive around." He headed for the door. "On our way we'll check if the divers have found Bwye's gun."

****

The divers had drawn another blank on the rifle and their explorations had halted for the night; the freezing water finally defeating them. Craig drove quickly and ten minutes later they were viewing the Bwye's estate from the jetty on the opposite side of the lake, accompanied by Garvan McDermott and his two sons. Mrs McDermott had sensibly remained in the warm house.

Liam stamped his feet, trying to stave off hypothermia, while Craig stood perfectly still, staring across the lake as if it held answers that only he could see. Micky McDermott broke the silence in his still-high adolescent voice.

"I watched the men checking the boat. It was really cool. Just like C.S.I."

McDermott senior smiled vaguely at his younger son and then turned to Craig with a pained expression.

"They didn't tell us what the boat was used for and before you ask, no, I don't want to know. It can't have been anything good if it attracted the police."

Craig dragged his eyes from the pitch black water, so black that only a lack of shine and prism said that it wasn't oil. He fixed Garvan McDermott with a stare that

Liam knew was assessing his innocence or guilt. Innocence won and Craig gave a smile; too small for normal times but typical of recent days. His warm voice cut through the air.

"When was the last time any of you saw the boat before it disappeared?"

McDermott stared at his two sons, nodding them on to answer. Micky obliged him first.

"Wednesday morning before school."

Oisín's deeper voice chimed in. "Tuesday night for me."

"And you, Mr McDermott, when did you last see it?"

His reply was immediate. "Tuesday after eleven p.m. I remember because I was closing the bedroom curtains before bed and Niamh had the News on."

A sense of urgency overcame Craig. "You're sure it was still there then?"

"Positive. If it hadn't been I would have gone down." He gazed pointedly at his elder son. "Just in case me laddo here was off joy riding again."

Oisín cut in indignantly. "I wasn't joy riding, I was just..."

His father raised an eyebrow knowingly. "I know exactly what you were doing out there and all I can say is I'm surprised that you didn't capsize."

The boy glanced away, embarrassed, as his younger brother grinned, eager to hear more about the ways of men and women. Craig saved Oisín's blushes. Garvan McDermott had narrowed their window for the boat's removal and now he needed him to do something else.

"That's very helpful, Mr McDermott. Now, please tell me what you know about Mr Bwye."

McDermott stared at him, confused. "Nothing. We barely speak."

Craig wasn't convinced; by the sounds of the fight at the golf-club they'd done more than talk. "Not even on boundary issues? The lake is bounded by both your lands."

He shrugged. "And the council's. The Bwyes own it; we just pay mooring and access rights."

"Is that expensive?"

"No. Mrs Bwye keeps the price down."

Craig's ears perked up. "You dealt with Mrs Bwye not her husband?"

"I didn't deal with either of them. It's my wife who sorts out the fees. She knows Mrs Bwye through a local charity."

By now Liam's face was turning blue to match his hands and, interesting though the combination of blue face and sandy hair was, Craig decided to take pity on him. He gestured him and the boys towards the house, motioning their father to wait behind. When his sons were out of earshot Craig stared hard at him in the dimming light.

"Would you like to revisit your comment about barely knowing Mr Bwye? We know you're both members of the golf-club."

McDermott had discussed the Bwyes in the present tense so he wasn't going to change that and give things away. McDermott smiled.

"Ah, so someone's been telling tales. Yes, I've played him at the club sometimes, but I don't call that knowing someone. Oliver Bwye's not a man I'll ever have in my home."

Future tense this time. Interesting. Did McDermott really not know that Bwye was dead or was it a disingenuous pretence? He needed to know more about the man.

"May I ask what you do for a living, Mr McDermott?"

Davy had described the property as a farm but apart from the exterior of the house it didn't look like any working farm he'd ever seen.

"I'm a businessman. Land development mostly; we have quite a bit in various locations across the north and Donegal."

"This was a farm originally, wasn't it?"

McDermott smiled. "You've done your research. It was a farm when we bought it but we sold most of the land and only kept the fifty acres around the house."

Neither Bwye nor McDermott had worked the countryside they lived in; making money was their game. Craig changed tack.

"Tell me about your conversations with Mr Bwye at the golf-club."

McDermott shrugged. "Politics. It's a common topic of conversation. Bwye's a staunch unionist and I fall firmly into the other camp; quite a few people around here do. I find it hard to see the logic of being in the UK when the Republic is less than ten miles away."

Craig had no intention of debating the issue; they would be there all year.

"You came to blows in November."

The businessman shrugged again. "It was nothing. Just drunken slabbering; you know the form. A few punches and it was over. Your man Ellis saw to that. I haven't seen Bwye since then. I don't like the man."

"Because?"

McDermott's fists clenched. "Because he hits his wife and I have no time for men like that. OK?"

It was OK in Craig's book, but McDermott had fought publicly with Bwye and just admitted that he didn't like him, so he warranted Davy taking a deeper look. But for now he would let him play the host. Craig changed the subject, nodding towards the brightly lit house.

"May I speak to your wife?"

"Sure. She's just cooking dinner."

As they entered the warm house the smells of home cooking filled Craig's nostrils and he noticed that Liam's blue hue had changed to red, on its way back to his usual white. McDermott disappeared into the kitchen and re-emerged with a slim, dark-haired woman whose face was a feminine version of her two sons'.

"Niamh, these gentlemen are Superintendent Craig and D.C.I. Cullen. They're here to ask some questions about the Bwyes."

Niamh McDermott stared at the policemen in turn and then quickly back at her husband. Craig expected her next words to be a question but they were chiding instead.

"For goodness sake, Garvan, they're frozen! Could you not have offered them a warm drink?"

Her mini-mes grinned, first at her and then at their dad and Craig knew that affectionate chiding was a regular event in the house. McDermott didn't seem to mind.

"Ach, no. I forgot. Sorry, gentlemen, would you like tea or coffee?" He gave them a knowing wink. "I've something stronger if you'd prefer."

Craig declined and took the coffee but he encouraged Liam to drink whatever he liked. It was after six and he was the designated driver.

As Liam sipped gratefully at a whisky, Craig followed Niamh McDermott to the kitchen for his coffee, using the opportunity to sound her out. He leaned against a worktop and watched as she basted a joint of beef before putting it in the oven.

"Do you know Diana Bwye well?"

He stuck to the present tense; in theory no-one knew that the Bwyes were dead but his team, and he preferred it to stay that way.

Niamh McDermott's muffled voice emerged from the oven. "Yes, very. We're on two committees together."

"May I ask which ones?"

She closed the oven door and sprang athletically to her feet.

"Sure. We're on the committees for Vanquish Cancer and the local children's learning fund. We've been fundraising for both of them for years."

Craig sipped his coffee and considered his next question carefully. The wrong words would tell her something was amiss with Diana Bwye, the right ones get her to open up. He needn't have worried; Niamh McDermott did all the work for him. She stood opposite, scrutinising his face in a way that said she wasn't admiring his bone structure.

"Mr Craig, my husband may be one of life's innocents but I'm not. I know something is wrong over at the Bwyes; I've seen all the activity there in the past few days."

Craig glanced at the door and she shook her head.

"You needn't worry. The boys don't notice anything unless it's wearing a football jersey or involves food, and Garvan is out of the house at seven and not back until seven at night; it's been too dark for him to see what's been going on."

She made herself a cup of tea. "I, on the other hand, am here all day and I'd have to be blind not to notice all the yellow tape and flashing lights." She stared straight into his eyes. "Diana's dead, isn't she?"

There was no point in lying. Craig set down his cup, prepared for fainting or hysterics when he answered, but half convinced that he wouldn't see either from this feisty woman.

"Yes. I'm sorry."

There was silence for a moment while a range of expressions flew across Niamh McDermott's face, then she nodded solemnly.

"God rest her soul. She deserved some peace."

Craig nodded tentatively towards a window seat and they sat down. Niamh began talking and didn't stop for breath, outlining what she knew of Diana's unhappiness and the state of the Bwye's marital less than bliss. When she'd finished, Craig topped up her drink and asked the question on both of their minds.

"Do you think Oliver Bwye would ever have killed her? Or himself?"

Niamh's snort of derision was so sharp that Craig was sure her husband would hear and come running in. He didn't, instead they heard a loud guffaw from Liam that suggested he and the McDermott males were enjoying some craic.

"Kill his wife, definitely, but kill himself, never. Oliver Bwye's a selfish pig."

"Not even if he was sick? To ensure he left his family financially secure in their home?"

Her brown eyes widened as if she thought Craig was insane.

"Well, first, Oliver Bwye was far too selfish to give up one minute of his life for anyone, and second, Rocksbury belonged to Diana; it was part of her trust fund. The only way they'd ever get thrown out would have been if she'd signed the estate into community property and Oliver had bankrupted them, and there was no way she could have done that, not even if she'd wanted to. The land and house have always passed down through the D'Arcy women; the next person to inherit it will be Jane, whether her father is alive or dead."

Craig's eyebrows shot up in surprise. Why hadn't this shown up in Davy's research? If it was true then it meant that Oliver Bwye's financial risk taking wouldn't have left his family out on the street, so why would he have needed a K&R insurance pay-out? Was it really all about his legacy? He found it hard to believe that a millionaire's obituary in The Chronicle would matter if you were dead but he parked the queries for Davy and asked another question.

"Did Jane know that she would inherit the estate?"

Niamh head shook emphatically. "Definitely not. Diana wanted to tell her but Oliver threatened violence if she did. He wanted people to think that he owned everything, and he also wanted to keep Jane in line till she came into the trust he'd set up, at thirty. It was all about control."

"And Diana told you because...?"

"Because she had to tell someone and we were close. She used to drive round here for coffee sometimes, when things got too much at home. And before you ask, yes, I knew that Oliver hit her. I asked her to take Jane and leave him many times, but she wouldn't leave Rocksbury and he would never have agreed to go."

She paused for a moment before restarting. "I can tell you one thing, Superintendent. The beatings had been getting worse recently. Diana came to committee a few weeks ago with her arm in bandages. She said that she'd fallen off a ladder, but I knew that was rubbish." Her face contorted in disgust. "The bastard slashed it." She glanced at a knife block. "If any man laid a finger on me I'd stab them."

Craig didn't doubt it.

Her shoulders slumped. "But Diana wasn't like me; she was the softest soul I'd ever met. She was very religious too, a strict Presbyterian. She believed that marriage was forever, whether your husband beat you or not. I think the charity work was her escape; the only thing that kept her going. That and her faith."

Tears filled her eyes and Craig's next words were

gentle. "It's obviously a loss for you. Would you mind if I asked one last question?"

She nodded him on.

"Are you on the committee that Mrs Bwye was supposed to attend last Wednesday evening?"

"Yes. It's the fundraising committee for Vanquish Cancer. Diana never missed it because her mother died of the disease. I was surprised when she phoned in sick but I assumed that Oliver had hit her somewhere that she couldn't cover this time."

He made a note to check with the people who'd seen Diana Bwye that day and then stood up, gazing down at her.

"I'm sorry to have upset you, Mrs McDermott, but your answers have been very helpful."

She sniffed and shook her head. "Diana's in a better place now. It's Jane that I feel sorry for, left alone with that man."

He realised that she thought Oliver Bwye was still alive and decided to confide in her. "Oliver Bwye is dead as well. Although you must keep that to yourself."

Her eyes widened in shock and then she did what Craig had guessed she would do; she smiled.

"Brilliant. I hope he died painfully." Her eyes narrowed suddenly. "And before you even think it, there's no way that Jane killed them. She's as soft as Diana was and she would never ever have harmed her mum. They were inseparable." She stared past him, distracted. "I must go and see her. She'll be lost, poor wee pet."

Craig shook his head firmly. "I'm sorry, Mrs McDermott, but that will have to wait. This has to stay between us. If it gets out that the Bwyes are dead it could impede our investigation."

She jutted her chin out defiantly then saw the sense of what he'd said and nodded once. "I won't say anything, not even to my family." She wiped her eyes with a hankie and stood up briskly, giving a mischievous smile. "But you'll have to make up some story about what we were discussing in here; my Garvan is a very jealous man."

****

Saturday. 6 a.m.

Craig's night had been spent tossing and turning, despite self-medicating heavily with beer. When he finally gave up trying to sleep and wandered downstairs, it was still only six a.m. He exited the foyer of the small hotel into its well planted gardens, and marvelled at how much snow had fallen overnight. Thank goodness they'd gathered the forensics from the lakeside before they'd lost evidence, although it looked like the divers were going to have another day from hell.

His feet crunched down the driveway to the edge of the bordering fields and he stood there gazing across the grass, hands pushed deep into his pockets for warmth and thinking restless thoughts, only some of which were about the case. He'd been there for thirty minutes; listening to the birds sing and watching them leave pronged footprints in the snow, when the still winter air was disturbed by a familiar voice.

"You should have drunk McDermott's whisky, boss. It might have helped your kip."

Craig didn't turn, staring instead at a copse of trees and marvelling at how deep in the countryside they were.

"Then I'd have a hangover like you."

Liam was close enough now for his voice to be a boom. "Hangovers are for wimps. I haven't had a decent one in years." He risked asking a question that he knew might bring no reply. "You thinking deep thoughts?"

Craig turned, shaking his head. "Not deep, just puzzled. Niamh McDermott said some interesting things. And before you ask, they can wait for the briefing." He turned to walk back to the hotel. "Is Andy up?"

"No idea. We don't sleep together, you know."

The retort that sprang to Craig's mind was too un-PC to utter, so instead they walked to the dining room for breakfast, where he continued thinking and Liam bantered noisily with the other guests.

****

8 a.m.

"This will be short and sweet. Last night Liam and I went to see the McDermotts; the family across the lake who own the boat that we believe our killer used. Mrs McDermott had some particularly interesting things to say. It seems Rocksbury belonged solely to Diana Bwye. It formed part of the D'Arcy family trust and was always passed through the female line."

Annette cut in urgently. "Jane doesn't know."

Craig raised an eyebrow. "Did you ask her?"

"No, but it was obvious." She paused, looking sheepish. "I'll go back and ask the question just the same."

"Good. Mrs McDermott was also adamant that Oliver Bwye would never have killed himself. His wife yes, but not himself."

Liam interrupted. "That doesn't stop him hiring someone to do it to him."

Craig nodded slowly. "No, it doesn't. But she said he was too selfish to give up one minute of his life for anyone, so I presume death by any hand wouldn't have been top of his list. Also, if his family didn't need money to save their home it removes a financial motive for suicide." Andy went to object but Craig pushed on. "I know what you're going to say, Andy; they might still have needed money for the estate's upkeep and Bwye leaving his family secure was only one possible motive; his ego and legacy were two more. For that reason I'm not discounting the theory that Bwye might have arranged his own death, and that his wife was just collateral damage. We'll pursue it but I'm still not convinced. His death was too bloody; a professional hit man would have made it quick and clean."

Liam muttered under his breath. "Unless one of Bwye's enemies hired him to make Bwye suffer."

Craig nodded but parked the point for later.

Annette frowned. "So what else could explain things?"

"I'm still working on that. Niamh McDermott also said that it was very unlike Diana Bwye not to attend her fundraising meeting that Wednesday night. She'd phoned to say she was sick and couldn't attend and Mrs McDermott attributed it to her suffering some injury at her husband's hand that she couldn't hide. Annette, Julia and Gerry, check that with Jane, the cook, Bernadette Ross and any of the other staff you can think of, plus ask Diana's friend Stephanie Crewe. If Diana Bwye had obvious injuries that Wednesday somebody must have seen them. We're probably talking about her face or hands, although I'm already convinced their answers will be no, given that no such injuries were seen post mortem."

Annette shook her head. "That doesn't mean she couldn't have faked a visible injury for their benefit. It's easy enough to mimic bruises with make-up."

"Why would she fake it? She'd never missed a meeting before." He carried on. "But we'll find out when we ask. If the answer's yes then the next question is, why fake it, unless she specifically wanted to stay home that evening for some reason, and that opens a whole new theory with Diana Bwye at the centre."

He turned to see Davy frowning.

"I was just starting on Diana Bwye's family trust, so I hadn't got to w...what it contained yet. But doesn't it seem s...strange that no-one else mentioned she owned the house? Especially Bernadette Ross if she knew Bwye's business."

Craig nodded as the others murmured to themselves. "It's a glaring omission as far as I'm concerned. Check everything out with the family solicitor, and the trust solicitors as well. Andy, I want you to focus on the van and the forensics on the boat please, and keep checking on the divers. I want that gun." He turned, to see Liam still muttering. "Liam, you and Davy work up the list of enemies Lawton gave us. The rest of you, I want you to go back to the family and staff members and raise the subject of the estate's ownership, obliquely, but watch their faces. I want to know who knew about the female inheritance line and who didn't. Pay particular attention to the McCanns, Bernadette Ross and Jane Bwye. If someone knew about this and could have told Jane, no matter how accidentally, we need to know." He got ready to leave. "I'm going to the lab and then on to Belfast. Nicky called last night about the Greer case so I need to check on things there, and see Cameron Lawton. I'm meeting the C.C. at headquarters this afternoon so I won't be back till five o'clock. You all know what you need to get on with."

Liam considered having a moan but cracked a joke instead.

"And if the boss can't get back up the Pass, we'll hold the briefing in the bar at six."

Chapter Sixteen

11.30 a.m.

Craig's morning had been a waste of time; he just hoped that his team was doing better. He'd been back to the Northwest Path lab to see Mike but none of his answers had changed. Dead bodies were stubborn like that. Both the Bwyes had gunshot wounds but until they found the Ruger they could have been from any of the rifles in the province. So many country men in so few miles.

He'd arrived at the lab in a grumpy mood and left the same way. The icy drive to Belfast had honed it to an anger that hadn't been helped by the sights that had greeted him when he'd entered the C.C.U. Nicky was painting her nails to the sound of John Legend and Jake was spinning round in his chair throwing paper balls into a bin. OK, it was the weekend, but they were still getting paid to work. The worst of it was that neither of them stopped when he arrived.

He hit the off button on the CD player and glared around the floor, wondering where everyone was. After a moment he realised he'd seconded everyone else but Ken to Derry, and given that the army was paying him he'd probably decided to have a weekend morning lie-in. Nicky stared at her silent CD and then at Craig's face, on countdown to the explosion that looked like it was coming next. Before it did she squeaked in indignation.

"I was listening to that...sir."

"You're supposed to be working." He swung round to face Jake. "Both of you! And when's Ken gracing us with his presence?"

Nicky rose and Craig noticed she was dressed like a latter day Stevie Nicks; this week's fashion adventure was obviously the '70s. She drew herself up to her full five-feet-three.

"What do you think we've been doing all week while you lot have been gallivanting in the wilds?" Without waiting for an answer she waved at a tower of files. "*That's* what we've been doing. Every file on the Greer case has been read, checked and categorised, ready for you to write your report for the appeal." She grabbed a document from her desk and waved it at him. "Jake's even had a go at the first draft because he knew how busy you were."

She could see a faint blush of embarrassment rising on Craig's cheeks so she emerged from behind her desk, pressing her advantage. The document became a pointer and its target this time was Jake.

"He's worked ten hours every day; reading and highlighting."

The hundreds of luminous green and red stickers protruding from the tilting tower emphasised her point.

"Ken's helped too but he's been called to the base today. And I've been making calls, lining up people you might want to re-interview after Christmas and I've...and..."

Craig could see that her ire was about to turn into something else, the glistening in her eyes warning him that he'd better eat his words very fast.

She gestured towards the corner and a large silver Christmas tree that he'd failed to notice came into focus, the pile of carefully wrapped parcels at its foot saying that while he'd been yelling at everyone in Derry, she'd been preparing a welcome home for them all.

Nicky got her second wind.

"...and now you come waltzing in here, barking because we're taking a ten minute break!" She folded her arms defiantly. "Well, sir, you can just waltz right back out again!"

She sat down with a thud as Jake stared first at her face and then at Craig's, uncertain what to say. He decided that solidarity was the answer and folded his arms as well.

Craig ran through a gamut of emotions. Anger, because that seemed to be his default setting these days with everyone, although this time it had a different target; himself. Anger also that they'd made so much progress with Greer when his murder case seemed to be going into reverse. It was irrational and petty and he knew it, but no-one had ever said that anger was highly evolved.

There was shame in the mix as well. Shame for shouting and shame for his assumption that they'd been lazy, when he'd never seen laziness from either one. Then more shame that it was almost Christmas, a time of year he loved, and yet he hadn't given a thought to presents for anyone.

For once in his life the normally rational detective didn't know what to do. Anger alone would have triggered a fiery outburst; God knows he'd had plenty of those before and Nicky usually just shrugged and made him a coffee. Add shame to the anger and it would usually have triggered an apology to the undeserving object of his ire, but this time the combination was simply too much for him and Craig could feel tears pricking at his eyes. He was about to cry like a kid! What the hell?

He ignored Nicky's widening eyes and turned swiftly on his heel, leaving the floor without another word and hammering the button on the lift until he'd reached the parking garage. He was halfway up Oxford Street before he realised where he was heading; John's lab. When he arrived his mobile was ringing and the C.C.U.'s number was flashing on the screen. He ignored it and banged open the door to John's office. The pathologist was at his desk reading a journal and he looked up, surprised. Craig was even more surprised that he was there at a weekend now that he was married, yet somehow he'd known that he would be; Natalie was on-call and John wasn't one to sit home alone.

"I didn't expect you. Need some help with the case?"

Craig didn't answer, just slumped in a chair, struggling with whether to tell his friend about his outburst or fudge the visit as something to do with work. He swallowed hard and did the latter.

"I had to come to Belfast for meetings, so I thought I'd call in and pick your brains."

John scrutinised Craig's face and made a silent diagnosis, then he poured some coffee and nodded as if he'd believed every word of what he'd said.

"Good to see you. Mike says he's hit a dead end. Two

dead, gunshots, yet no gunshot residue on either victim's hands to say that they'd fired the gun."

Craig was startled. They hadn't discussed the possibility that one of the Bwyes had pulled the trigger.

"Why did he look for GSR?"

John shrugged with the insouciance of a man who'd ceased to be startled by anything in life. "It's standard practice in shootings, no matter how unnecessary it might appear." Suddenly his eyes lit up. "Although I must say this case is an unusual one. I'm quite jealous of Mike."

Craig pushed past his excitement. "The fact there's no GSR doesn't mean that neither of them fired it. Couldn't they have worn gloves?"

John considered huffing at Craig's rudeness then remembered the conversation he'd had with Liam and smiled instead, humouring him.

"They could have and maybe whoever dumped the bodies removed them. But even if they hadn't, the concrete and water would likely have destroyed the residue anyway." He topped up his coffee. "Anyway, this is all moot. Why would Bwye wound himself and then drown himself in concrete? And he definitely couldn't have thrown himself out of the boat. Similarly I can't see Diana Bwye wrapping herself in a plastic sack, weighing herself down with stones and then shooting herself in the chest as she jumped. That's what she'd have had to do."

Craig nodded hesitantly. He knew both scenarios were impossible, but...

"But her head was exposed. The sack was sealed at the neck." He wasn't sure why he'd said it; he already knew it couldn't have made a difference. He was wrong.

John's jaw dropped. "Mike didn't tell me that! I'm going to kill him. That alters everything. She could have killed her husband then wrapped herself in the plastic bag up to the neck, filled it with stones and sealed it, then shot herself in the chest inside the bag." He thought for a moment and then shook his head. "No, that doesn't work either. At least one of her hands would still have to have been outside or the gun would have been found in the bag with her."

"The sack was frayed enough to let the stones fall out, so maybe the gun-"

John cut him off. "No, none of the holes were that big." He shook his head at his own stupidity. "And anyway, how could she have thrown herself in the lake if she was dead?"

Craig frowned, thinking. After a moment sipping his coffee he restarted. "Let's say, and this is just speculation but humour me, let's say that Oliver Bwye decided to kill himself that night for whatever reason, and he had it all planned with the help of an accomplice. Shoot to wound him in the study, leave some blood on the floor to make it look like an assault, get into the van..."

John could keep silent no longer. "Then drown him in concrete and dump him in the lake! There are easier ways to go. And what would have been the purpose of such an elaborate ruse?"

"To kill himself in a way that meant the family would get his K&R insurance."

"It's a bit drastic, to kill yourself just to leave someone else money, and why kill the wife as well?"

Craig shook his head. "Bwye was already dying and she was collateral damage. She was supposed to be out at her charity committee like she was every Wednesday night."

"Dying of what?"

Craig realised he'd omitted important information. "Sorry. Terminal prostate cancer. He had a few months at most."

John nodded slowly. "Mike didn't say. So he was killing himself rather than go through the pain and to get a quick pay out? But why K&R, why not life insurance when he died naturally. He wouldn't have had to wait long."

"His life insurance excluded prostate cancer; he'd had a history of prostate disease for years."

"So if he was abducted and murdered, K&R would have left his family secure. Nice."

Craig made a face. "Except it turns out they didn't really need the money because Diana Bwye owned Rocksbury, and Oliver Bwye definitely wasn't an altruist.

The people we've spoken to say he wouldn't have given up one second of life for anyone else. Andy thinks Bwye wanted to leave the money so that people would think he was loaded when he died."

"Kidnap and kill yourself for the K&R just to impress the world with your wealth when you're dead! Tell Andy he's talking rubbish."

"My thoughts exactly. Especially not if it meant suffocating in concrete."

John thought for a moment. "OK...so that brings us back to someone who hated Bwye enough to kill him, and the wife as an unfortunate witness. Someone who knew where he kept his rifle..."

"And knew where the gun cabinet's key was. The lock wasn't smashed."

"OK, so either someone who already knew where it was or someone that Bwye had told or given the key to."

"Deliberately told, as in someone that he'd hired to kill him? Or accidentally told because he had a big mouth? Or was it just someone who knew because they were so close to him, like his favourite escort, Mavis Brown?" Craig shook his head in frustration. "Except that a woman couldn't possibly have done all this alone; even if the van had had a hoist to get them into the boat it would have taken a strong man to tip bodies over the side of a boat into the lake."

John opened his mouth to interject then closed it again when he realised that he had nothing sensible to add. Craig had a serious puzzle on his hands and he didn't have all the pieces yet. They could spend the next ten minutes going round in circles or he could change the subject. He was tempted to say what was really on his mind, but Craig's furrowed brow said it wasn't the time for a meaningful discussion, so instead he turned the conversation to DIY.

"I've almost finished the kitchen. Everything should be ready for Christmas Eve."

Craig's mind was still on the Bwyes so he answered vaguely. "Good..." Then he realised what John had said. "What's happening on Christmas Eve?"

"Well, apart from Santa coming down the chimney,

which will be a challenge with the fire being lit, it's the house-warming party. Remember?"

Craig gave a weak smile. "I'm sure it will be great."

It was John's turn to frown. "You sound like you're not coming."

Craig nodded distractedly then stood up to leave, repeating his last words. "It will be great."

As John watched his friend leave he made up his mind. There was a conversation coming soon that had nothing to do with work and it wasn't one that either of them would enjoy.

****

Cameron Lawton's Offices. The Belfast Chronicle.

"You're certain these are the only possibilities?"

Craig gestured at the three names in front of him. One he recognised as belonging to a local councillor, Brian Ormond, who was knocking on for seventy years old. A man so small and thin that if Oliver Bwye had sat on him it would have extinguished his life. The other two names he didn't know, but 'Harold' and 'Solomon' didn't convey images of strong young men.

Cameron Lawton nodded. "I asked around and, between myself and conversations I've had, these are the only three left alive who hated Bwye enough to kill him. Your computer boy already has their details." He tapped the list. "Bwye accused Ormond of embezzlement, which was later proved false but Bwye only gave him a short apology on the back page. With Solomon Ronson he covered his son's arrest for drug dealing with unnecessary zeal; I'm talking front page colour spread."

"What about the last one, Harold Clinton?"

Lawton screwed up his face. "Nasty piece of work. He deserved everything he got. He's a paedophile, still in prison. Bwye used his case to start a fundraising campaign for a child abuse charity, one of the few decent things that he ever did."

Craig went back to his first impression. "How old are

these men? The councillor must be pushing seventy."

Lawton smiled wistfully. It was the smile of a seventy-year-old looking at a forty something and wishing that he had all those years again.

"You're right. Ormond is seventy-two, Ronson's in his sixties and Clinton's in his late seventies; he'll never leave prison, thank goodness."

Craig sighed. All seven men on the list could have families who might want to avenge them, that meant that Davy still had wider searches to do. The newsman scrutinised Craig's face.

"I hope you don't mind me saying so, Superintendent, but you look exhausted. Aren't you near solving the case yet?"

The mirror in the men's room had told Craig how tired he looked ten minutes earlier, so Lawton's words weren't a shock.

"I don't mind you saying so but unfortunately no, not yet." Craig lifted the list. "Thank you for this. If you think of anything else, please get in touch."

It was clear from Lawton's expression that he already had.

Craig leaned forward eagerly. "What is it? We need to know, no matter how insignificant it seems."

Lawton looked sad for a moment then he spoke, in a reluctant tone. "It's difficult...one doesn't like to speak ill of the dead, especially when they had such a hard life..."

Craig connected the dots. "It's something about Diana Bwye?"

Lawton's expression said yes, it also said that he wasn't sure. "Perhaps. I'm not certain... Diana was a truly lovely woman." He glanced at Craig. "You know what I mean by that?"

Craig smiled his first real smile of the day. He knew exactly what Bwye meant. Nice women, pretty women and even good women were seen every day in homes and streets. But lovely women were few and far between and their loveliness had nothing to do with their looks. His grandmother had been one, her every smile an offer of help geared towards making the recipient's life better in some way. She'd never shouted and never complained, instead carrying the burdens of the world with good grace. Everything she'd done had been tinged with kindness and he'd adored her for it. He'd never met anyone like her before or since. He stopped himself abruptly. Yes he had. Katy. Before he could ask himself what the revelation meant, Lawton continued wistfully.

"I see that you've met such a woman. They leave an impact, don't they? Diana Bwye was one. It was such a misfortune that she married Oliver."

He gazed out his office window until Craig prompted him gently. "And? You implied there was something you could tell me about her that was pertinent."

The older man shielded his eyes with his hand for a moment before he looked at Craig again.

"I think Diana was seeing another man." His tone grew defiant, as if he was daring Craig to judge. "And so what if she was? Her life with Oliver was hell, didn't she deserve some happiness?"

Infidelity clearly didn't fit with Lawton's idea of a lovely woman, except in cases of duress.

"Who is he, Mr Lawton?"

"I...I don't want to slander anyone when I'm not sure. It was just something I noticed at last year's Christmas party."

Craig's tone was firmer this time.

"His name?"

Lawton hung his head. "The Bwye's family solicitor, Joshua Kelly. I invited him to the party as he'd helped us with an article. He didn't normally attend."

"Tell me what happened to make you suspicious."

"It might be nothing..."

Craig's stare hardened.

"Joshua...he, he spilled some wine down his shirt and Diana got a damp cloth to clean it off. But instead of handing him the cloth to do it himself she wiped his shirt until the stain was gone. She, she was being kind. She always was."

"There was more than that, wasn't there?"

Lawton nodded sadly, his voice dropping. "He covered her hand with his for a moment; a very long moment and she didn't pull away." He shook his head.

"They were in the kitchen so no-one else saw but me. I might have imagined it. Perhaps she was just being kind?"

He wasn't imagining it, Craig was sure of that; but what did it mean? Diana Bwye might just have been snatching a well-deserved moment of tenderness from the brutality of her life, or there could have been more between the pair. Either way it had to be checked out. Craig slipped the list of names into his pocket and rose to leave, then he shook the editor's hand.

"You've been very helpful, Mr Lawton. We'll check everything." He smiled reassuringly. "And I won't think any less of Mrs Bwye no matter what we find."

Chapter Seventeen

Katy was in outpatients at St Mary's when her mobile rang with a withheld number. She let it cut to answerphone, too busy dictating a letter for her P.A. and wondering what to buy her mum for Christmas, to answer an unknown call. It would be some company asking her to buy something she didn't need.

Her brother always went for safe and sensible Christmas presents, getting their mum a warm cardigan or a new coat, but she was determined to bring a bit of excitement back into her life. She'd been alone for ten years since her dad had died but she was still only seventy; still lots of time to get back out in the world.

She'd just narrowed the gifts to three possibilities when her phone rang again, this time with a message; it was John requesting a call back to the lab. She rang immediately, visions of Craig lying somewhere, bruised and bleeding, and John being the designated messenger of bad news racing through her head. John was just about to say hello when she cut across him.

"What's wrong? Is Marc OK? What happened to him?"

He realised immediately how his business-like 'call me back' must have sounded and gabbled an apology.

"Marc's fine. I'm sorry; I didn't mean to scare you." Before Katy had a chance to answer, he caveated his words. "Well, he's not really fine but he's not injured. Well actually, that may not be true, strictly speaking..."

He was taken aback by her next words.

"For God's sake, John, be quiet! You're scaring me even more now." After a pause she carried on. "Just answer these questions. Is Marc hurt?"

"No." He inhaled to elaborate but she cut across him.

"Is he sick?"

"No." He knew better than to inhale this time.

"Is this about his recent drinking, moodiness, insomnia and being generally difficult?"

John heaved a sigh of relief. Answering logical questions was so much easier than free-flowing discourse.

"Yes." He paused to let her continue. When she didn't he carried on. "He's making life hard for everyone on the case. He's snappy, vague and looks like hell, well, as much like hell as Marc ever looks, and I'm worried about him."

It was Katy's turn to sigh. "So am I. I have an opinion on what's happening but I'd like to hear yours first."

"PTSD. He hasn't dealt with shooting Caleb Pitt in October. It doesn't matter that Pitt was about to kill Liam, Marc still feels like crap because he had to shoot an old man in a wheelchair, especially in the head."

"I know, but he won't talk to me about it. It's like he's ashamed, as if it was dishonourable somehow."

John nodded then remembered that she couldn't see him. "That's exactly what he thinks! For a twenty-first-century man, Marc's soul belongs in medieval times. He'd have been happier fighting a duel to the death than doing what he had to do that day."

Katy fell silent. They agreed on what was wrong and what had caused it, now they had to do something positive. She swallowed hard before speaking; she didn't want to give away Craig's secrets but she needed John's help.

"Marc's been seeing a counsellor. The force insisted on it after the shooting."

If she'd expected John to be surprised then she'd been wrong.

"I know."

Of course he did. He'd been in Craig's life far longer than she had. John was still speaking.

"I also know that he won't talk to her; all he does is stare out the bloody window for an hour once a week."

She hadn't known. Her voice broke. "He didn't tell me."

"He loves you too much. He sees it as his job to protect you."

"Even when he needs my help!"

John shook his head. She still had a way to go before she understood Craig.

"In Marc's head, needing anyone's help is weak,

especially the help of a woman he loves. He's an old fashioned bloke, Katy. He sees it as his job to protect you, not the other way round."

Katy's resolve broke and she started to sob. "But if he won't let us help him what are we going to do, John? I can't bear to see him so unhappy."

John could feel his sympathy for Craig starting to turn to anger. Guilt and remorse were all very well but not if they hurt the people you loved. His voice softened.

"Please don't cry." He attempted a joke. "If Natalie hears I've made you cry she'll beat me up."

The thought of the five feet tall Natalie making a dent on him was so ridiculous that it made her laugh.

"I'm serious! She has a mean right hook." He paused for a moment, regrouping. "OK, how's this for a suggestion? I'll take a quick trip to Derry on the pretext of Mike needing a consult, so I can really assess the Italian stallion's state, and how much longer he's likely to be up there. I'll let you know what I find. Then, when we get some time over Christmas we'll try talking to him, separately or together, I don't mind. He might ignore one of us but not both. He needs to acknowledge that there's a real problem, before his team get fed up and resign, or..."

He didn't need to finish the sentence. They both knew Craig's propensity for self-destruction far outweighed the likelihood that he would ever hurt someone else.

****

Craig's meeting with Sean Flanagan was painless; all he'd wanted was an update, not answers. Yet. The pressure would start when the Christmas headlines loomed large. Flanagan had even offered him a whisky, citing not medicinal reasons but seasonal bonhomie. It wasn't a sentiment Craig could share with two murders still to solve.

The drive back to Derry wasn't as bad as he'd feared, either. The snow had turned to slush beneath the grit from the council lorries, and a wariness of ice had kept the side roads clear of all but the fearless and there weren't too many of those.

He was left alone with his thoughts for thirty miles. He stared at the slumbering countryside, thinking of spring when the fields would be filled with plants and noise. Where would he be then; where would any of them be? He shook his head at his morbid thoughts in what had always been his favourite time of year and forced himself to focus on the case.

Had Diana Bwye been having an affair with Joshua Kelly? And if she had what could it possibly have had to do with her own or her husband's death? He corrected himself. Her affair could have had everything to do with Oliver Bwye's death, but for her to die as well seemed odd if it had. Could her lover have killed them both? But why? What possible benefit would anyone have got from her dying? He shook his head hard as if shaking it would knock the ill-fitting pieces into place, but it was no use, he needed to start the jigsaw again.

Diana Bwye and her husband were both dead. Diana shot dead and Bwye so injured that he couldn't have fought back and was drowned in concrete. The attack was well planned; a van with facilities that enabled a large man to be loaded onto it and covered in the concrete that had caused his final demise. OK, so it was planned. Craig thumped the steering wheel in irritation; it changed to surprise when he realised something else. Of course it had been planned, but not only the abduction. The boat might have been a contingency, used to dump the bodies in panic, or perhaps it wasn't, perhaps the plan had *always* been to dump the bodies in the lake. Take the Bwyes from the house to the van and then the boat, deposit them in a watery grave and drive away.

But why bother? Why not just kill them in the house and leave the bodies where they'd dropped; it would make sense, even if a stranger had killed them. Unless. Unless they hadn't wanted someone whom the Bwyes knew to see the bodies, or someone had specifically wanted the police to think it was a stranger attack.

He mulled over the first option; they hadn't wanted anyone who knew the Bwyes to see them dead. Did they have a considerate killer, concerned with Jane Bwye's or the staffs' sensitivities? Someone who knew the family or someone *in* the family? It led him back to the deaths being organised by Oliver Bwye and him worrying about his daughter's feelings.

Craig shook his head. No. By all reports Oliver Bwye was a selfish bastard who'd cared too much for himself to end even his terminal life, not the sort of man to give a damn what the discovery of his body would do to his child. That left Diana Bwye. She *would* have cared about Jane's feelings, so she definitely wouldn't want her to have found their dead bodies in the study. Had Diana organised her own death and that of her husband, then arranged for them to be disposed of in the lake? If she had then why? Craig half shook his head at the idea, but only half. Something prevented him from dismissing it completely.

He turned to the second option; someone had specifically wanted the police to think that it was a stranger attack. It led him back to the first option but with an additional strand. Richard McCann. Had Richard McCann killed his abusive father-in-law in a deliberately convoluted way so that his young wife would never find out? But why kill his mother-in-law as well? By all accounts he'd liked her. Unless Diana Bwye *had* simply been collateral damage, the unlucky wrong person in the wrong place.

Craig ran the possible scenario. Diana had cancelled going to a charity meeting that evening, a meeting that she never missed. She wasn't supposed to be in the house at all, so when Richard McCann had arrived to dispatch Oliver Bwye, he'd been taken by surprise. Or perhaps Diana had heard the noise and entered the study to find McCann shooting her husband with his own gun. McCann had been startled by the noise when she'd entered, fired at her in reflex and suddenly he'd had two injured people on his hands. And even though Bwye was a pig of a man, Diana's religious beliefs would have prevented her allowing or concealing his death, meaning that McCann would've *had* to finish them both off.

After that it was a simple matter of McCann leaving the room in disarray like a burglary, faking the bloody prints and then dumping the bodies and the gun in the lake. He'd only brought enough concrete to cover Bwye, so he'd had to improvise for Diana and use stones from the lake shore, and he hadn't covered Diana's face because he was fond of her. Jane would never know that he'd done it and they would inherit everything.

The theory worked, except that McCann had two alibis for the Wednesday evening; his mother and his wife. Craig shook his head. A mother alibi-ing her only son would never stand up in court. But would Jane really have lied to alibi a husband who had killed her mum? No, but she might have innocently given him an alibi to protect him, if McCann had told her that he was somewhere else for part of the evening.

The scenario fitted. McCann had wanted rid of Oliver Bwye for the way he'd treated Jane and to gain access to her trust before she reached thirty. With Bwye gone, Diana Bwye would never have held to the thirty clause and he and Jane would have had a comfortable life. Diana Bwye was supposed to be out of the house that night, just as she'd been every Wednesday night for years; her death was simply bad luck.

Craig nodded. OK, it fitted, so why did he still feel so uneasy? The questions came thick and fast and he answered them as they did. Why wouldn't McCann simply have knocked Diana out? Because she still might have recognised him. But surely McCann would have worn a mask, and even if she had recognised him, would Diana really have testified against him when it would have dragged her daughter down? Perhaps; she had staunch Christian beliefs that she might not have compromised, even for Jane.

The idea of Richard McCann killing his mother-in-law still stuck in Craig's throat, not from disgust but from disbelief. He shook his head at an invisible jury, imagining giving evidence on the case. If he didn't believe that Richard McCann had done it how would he ever convince twelve citizens good and true?

He made a decision and pressed dial. He needed to look into Richard McCann's eyes as he asked him the question, then he would be sure.

"Liam. Richard McCann; where is he?"

Liam held his mobile at arm's length and made a face, knowing from the background noise that Craig was driving fast. That mean he wasn't in Belfast where the average speed was less than twenty mph, he was on his way back. He waved goodbye to his relaxing evening in the pub.

"They're both at his mum's apartment. I take it you want to see him?"

"Forty minutes at the station. I'll see you there."

The line went dead and Liam muttered at his phone. "Forty minutes at the station, Liam. I'll see you there, Liam. Tote that barge and lift that bale, Liam. Sod the fact that there's a match on the box tonight."

Annette rolled her eyes at his monologue. "I take it that grumbling means the Super's on his way back and you'd been hoping that he'd stay in Belfast overnight."

Liam warmed to his theme. "I ask you. What sort of normal man doesn't take the chance for a bit of nooky? There he is, only five miles from his own bed with a warm and willing girlfriend close at hand, and what does he do?"

Annette decided to irritate him further. "He decides that solving a double murder is more important. Oh dear me, no; a man who actually does his job! Call the BBC."

He reached for something to throw at her but Davy shook his head sanctimoniously. He had ears like a bat and he'd heard everything that Craig had said.

"If you don't get McCann lifted and leave for the s...station now, the chief will get there before you." He dropped his tenor to a movie-trailer bass. "And we all know w...what'll happen then."

Annette nodded. "Especially in the mood he's been in." She drew her finger across her throat graphically, smiling as Liam grabbed his keys.

"I'm going under duress. Union rules state it's time for dinner."

As he left, Craig was thirty miles away, still pondering the case. OK, so Richard McCann was a possibility but his gut said no. He thought about the names Cameron Lawton had given him, perhaps one of them would bear fruit. Liam and Davy had been running through them, so he would ask Liam when they met. If it wasn't one of them then that still left the Bwyes' solicitor as a possibility. He of the wine soaked shirt and affectionate glance. He made another call, this time to Annette.

"Annette, has Liam finished moaning and left?"

She smiled. It was as if Craig had heard their exchange. "Yes, but he has his mobile if you need him."

"Thanks, but it was you I wanted. I need you and Davy to check out the Bwyes' family solicitor; he's called Joshua Kelly. Get Davy to do a background check so I can read it tonight and can you call Kelly's office and arrange a meeting for me tomorrow morning."

Annette raised an eyebrow. She hadn't heard Kelly's name mentioned before and she was curious.

"Is he a suspect, sir?"

Craig sighed. She was asking him what he'd been asking himself since Lawton had first mentioned the name.

"Good question. The answer is I don't know. Cameron Lawton said something that suggests Kelly and Diana Bwye might have had a thing. Although it seems unlikely. Everyone says she took her marriage vows seriously." Something occurred to him. "Get back to her friend Stephanie from the charity committee, and Niamh McDermott, the lady who lives across the lake, and see what they know about a possible affair between Diana and anyone. Then drop Kelly's name in and watch their reactions."

The lady who lives across the lake; it sounded like nineteenth-century poetry.

"Will do. Are you having dinner with us later at the hotel, sir?"

"Dinner?"

He said the word like he'd never heard it before and glanced at the dashboard clock in surprise.

"It's nearly six o'clock!"

"Yes, sir. That's why Liam was moaning."

That and the fact that the match started at eight.

"I'm sorry, I've completely lost track of the time. Have something to eat before you get on with all that. I'll see you later."

She said goodbye and smiled, knowing that Liam's stomach would be rumbling all the way through their interview. She lifted her handbag and tapped Davy on the head.

"Come with me, young man. I know a good restaurant in the centre of town." She threw him her keys. "You're driving. I have calls to make on the way."

****

By the time Craig arrived at the station it was six-thirty and Liam's mouth and stomach were groaning in unison. He was sitting in reception, eyes shut, with his forty-inch legs deliberately obstructing everyone who passed. John Ellis jerked a thumb in his direction.

"For God's sake get him out of here. He's making more noise than ten men."

Craig stared pointedly at Liam's limb barricade. "If you think I'm climbing over those you've another thought coming." As Liam stood up he added. "And I hope McCann's in the interview room."

Liam was less than amused. "Where else would he be at six-thirty in the evening? Oh yes, maybe at home having dinner like normal folk."

Craig ignored him and Ellis buzzed them through. As they pushed open the interview room door Craig watched as Richard McCann jumped at the intrusion. It always amused him when interviewees did that, as though they thought they'd be sitting alone all night.

"Mr McCann. You have no solicitor present."

McCann gazed around blankly as if Craig knew something he didn't.

"Do I need one?"

"You're being questioned under caution so it's advisable." As Craig said it he hoped fervently that McCann wouldn't think so; the delay waiting for a solicitor would make Liam grumble even more. To his relief the young husband shook his head, casting a wary glance at Liam as he did.

"Are you going to beat me up?"

Craig wasn't sure if he was joking, then he remembered McCann's west Belfast roots and wondered what had happened to his family in the bad old days.

"No, Mr McCann. We don't do that. If you're sure you wouldn't like a solicitor then we'd just like to ask you a few more questions."

On McCann's nod Liam clicked on the tape machine and ran through the formalities. Then both detectives folded their hands on the table and sat back, leaving the room in silence apart from the whirr of the tape and McCann's feet tapping nervously on the floor. The longer the silence ran the louder McCann's tapping got, until, when it had reached door-knocking level, Craig finally spoke. He stared directly into the young man's eyes.

"Did you kill your in-laws, Mr McCann?"

It was a toss-up who was more surprised. McCann at the content of the question or Liam that Craig had asked it in such a rookie way. Where was his usual circling of his opponent, winding him up to a pitch before going in for the kill? A first week probationer would have asked the question more covertly!

McCann was the first to recover, his answer drowning out the near deafening volume of his feet.

"No I didn't!"

"Did you kill one of them?"

"No!"

McCann's eyes were wide and wild, and he leaned forward so abruptly that Liam reached out a hand to halt him before he head-butted his boss. His hand said 'back off', but his brain said the way Craig had been behaving lately a head-butt might knock some sense into him.

"I didn't kill anyone. I swear it."

Craig looked unperturbed, both by McCann's answers and by Liam's obstructing arm. His voice said that he was bored, as if he was just going through the motions of the interview. Unknown to the other men in the room that was exactly what was going on.

"Where were you on the evening of Wednesday the tenth of December?"

"At my mum's flat on the estate. You already know that. I would never have hurt Diana; she was a lovely woman. She was Jane's mum, for God's sake!"

Craig waved Liam's arm away and leaned forward so that he and McCann were almost nose to nose. Liam noticed Craig's nose was completely straight; how the heck had he escaped having it broken when he'd played as much rugby as he had? His own nose looked like it had been used as the ball. Craig kept his tone conversational.

"But you wouldn't have minded killing Jane's dad, would you?"

McCann shook his head, but not vehemently.

"I didn't kill him, but I'd be lying if I said I hadn't wished him dead plenty of times. He was a bastard and there's not one person worse off for him being dead."

Craig shrugged and sat back. "That's honest of you."

McCann warmed to his theme, his naturally rapid speech speeding up even more.

"Tell me one person who's sad that he's gone. Diana yes, but not him. He was an animal. He terrorised Jane and her mum all their lives. I'm only sorry Diana didn't live to see life without him."

Either McCann was so stupid that he didn't realise openly saying you hated a man was incriminating, or he didn't care, probably because he was innocent. Craig stared into the younger man's eyes and finally his logic and instinct agreed. He rose suddenly to his feet, beckoning Liam to do the same.

"I'd like to keep you here overnight, Mr McCann, to recheck your alibi. A Detective Constable Carmen McGregor will speak to you in the morning. Do you have any objection?"

McCann shrugged. "If it helps you prove me innocent and catch Diana's killer, that's fine. Can I call Jane and ask her to tape the match? Derry's playing a special fixture."

Liam's expression turned wistful.

"Fine. We'll ask Sergeant Ellis to arrange the call."

Craig strolled towards the staff room with Liam hot on his heels. When the door had closed behind them Liam let rip.

"Is that it? Did you kill them? No. Oh well, that's all right then."

Craig gave him a wry look. "What would you have preferred? Thumb screws? He didn't do it, Liam. It's as plain as the nose on your face."

Liam touched his nose defensively. "Then why waste time bringing him back in if you already knew?"

Craig brought the ever ready kettle back to the boil.

"I wanted to look him in the eye when I asked the question. I'll be doing the same tomorrow with another man; Joshua Kelly."

"And who the hell is he?"

"I'll tell you later. Anyway. I saw what I needed to see with McCann."

Liam found two mugs and started to make the drinks. "And what did you see in his eyes, Swami? The answers to life and the universe?"

Craig laughed despite himself. "Something like that. He wasn't lying, that's what I saw."

"I thought you'd already dismissed him as a suspect."

"I needed to recheck some things before I narrowed the field down to five." He gestured at the clock before Liam could ask who the final five were. "If we hurry we can have dinner before the match." He slipped his hands inside his jacket and withdrew two tickets, handing them to his disgruntled D.C.I.

"John Ellis organised them for me. Far better to see it in person than watch the sanitised version on TV."

Liam gawped at the impossible-to-get tickets and softened towards his boss, but it hadn't escaped him that Craig still hadn't named his five suspects. He could only think of the three names on Lawton's list.

He shrugged. No doubt Craig would tell him later, after they'd found out who'd won the game.

Chapter Eighteen

Sunday. 11 a.m.

"OK, quick round up. Mike's just called, he needs me at the lab and I've Joshua Kelly to see before then. Carmen, you saw McCann this morning. Where are you with his alibi?"

Carmen glanced at Craig over a pair of black-framed spectacles that he didn't remember her wearing the day before. Liam asked first, not well disposed towards her since their hostile few months when she'd first joined the squad, and never one to let a grudge go to waste if it still had mileage. He gestured at the glasses.

"Trying to look intelligent, are we?"

Her retort was swift. "We? I'd give up if I were you...sir."

The quip scored a hit and Liam went to lash back. Craig motioned her to continue reporting, but he was irritated by her cheek to a senior officer, even if Liam had started it. He was too busy to deal with it today but her time would come.

"McCann, Carmen?"

She tried not to look smug and continued.

"I checked his alibi with two people; the head gardener and one of the grounds men. The gardener confirms seeing McCann outside his mother's apartment that evening. Apparently he was putting out the rubbish. He came out again around ten p.m. to carry something in from Jane's car. Shopping they thought. It was a grounds man who saw him that time." She turned over the page and read from the back. "I also checked Brendan Gordon's alibi. It checks out."

Craig nodded; it was as he'd thought. "Release McCann."

He turned to Annette, only to find her whispering to Julia and Gerry in a way that told him they'd been amused by Carmen's wisecrack.

"Annette. Where are you on the reactions to Diana Bwye owning the house?"

She took out her notebook hastily, chastened by his 'don't mess with me' tone of voice.

"Julia, Gerry and I split the re-interviews and the only person who didn't look shocked by the information was Bernadette Ross, although she seemed surprised by the question."

"She didn't think it was a secret?"

"Exactly. I suppose that's because she was privy to all the family's documents, so she would have seen the deeds. Everyone else thought Oliver Bwye owned everything and that was the reason he held so much power over the women in his family. In fact..." She flicked furiously through the pages, stopping first at one and then another. "In fact, Linda McCann and the head gardener both asked why Diana hadn't had him evicted, given his treatment of her and Jane."

Craig shook his head. "Marriage is a strange thing." He paused for a moment, thinking. "How did Jane take the news?"

Annette's expression changed to one of sadness. "She cried. She couldn't understand why, if her mum had owned the estate, she hadn't thrown her father out, if only to protect her. I think she felt betrayed."

Craig knew everyone was wondering how Diana Bwye could have put her husband before her child's safety and her own. Davy ventured an opinion.

"Perhaps s...she was scared of what he would do...if she asked him to leave, I mean. He was a big man."

Craig thought back to Margie Rudd, a woman on an earlier case who'd stayed with her abusive husband for years out of fear. But she'd been poor and uneducated and Diana Bwye hadn't been either. Julia spoke for the first time since she'd arrived.

"Perhaps she loved him." She glanced at her engagement ring. "Some women will put up with a lot for love."

Annette was quick to retort. She'd experienced domestic violence once and had filed for divorce right away. "And some women are stupid. It looks like Diana Bwye was one of them. She had money, her own home and a daughter to protect; there's no excuse for her staying with that animal."

"She was religious. Maybe she really believed her wedding vows."

Craig sensed a feminist battle looming and changed the subject, even though he found it interesting that Julia, a militant feminist when they'd dated, was now on the less militant side.

"OK, so the only person who's confessed to knowing that Mrs Bwye owned Rocksbury is Bernadette Ross. How sure are you all that they weren't faking their surprise?"

Gerry and Julia answered in unison. "Very." Annette's nod backed them up.

Davy cut in. "The W...Wills were straightforward, like I said before. When Oliver Bwye died everything passed to his wife and when she died, everything went to Jane."

Liam chipped in. "Unless the wife had died before him, then he'd have owned the house while he still lived."

Davy shook his head. "Nope. The house would have reverted to the trust and then onto the next female relative in line, in this case Jane. Bwye couldn't have got his hands on it no matter how hard he'd tried, although Jane would've had a job to evict him."

Craig thought for a moment. "OK. So the only people who stood to benefit financially from killing Diana Bwye were Oliver Bwye, who would have got her life insurance, but as he was going to die in a few months it would have been of little use. And Jane and Richard McCann and we've ruled them both out. So..."

The whole group stared at him, wondering what pearls of wisdom he was about to cast forth. There'd been no robbery and the only people who'd stood to benefit from the Bwyes' deaths had either been killed or proved innocent. That left a killer who'd wanted the Bwyes, or more likely Oliver Bwye, dead for some other motive.

Davy couldn't contain his curiosity. "So w...what, chief? What possible motive is left for their deaths?"

Craig deferred revealing his thoughts for a while longer.

"You have a list of three people. Councillor Brian Ormond, Harold Clinton and Solomon Ronson. They're the only three men alive that Cameron Lawton feels hated Bwye enough to kill him." He sipped his cooling coffee and shot Davy a begging look. As he topped it up Craig carried on. "Bwye accused Ormond of embezzlement, which was later proved false but Bwye only printed a brief retraction on the back page. Bwye covered Solomon Ronson's son's arrest for drug dealing with a front page colour spread."

Gerry whistled. "That was a bit unnecessary."

Liam nodded energetically. "It certainly was. The family are very respectable. Orthodox Jews. It ruined their reputation and the father's business. He was a pharmacist."

Craig nodded. Everyone would have assumed the pharmacist was supplying drugs to his dealer son. He continued.

"Harold Clinton was the only one of the three that Lawton thought deserved everything he got from Bwye. He's a convicted paedophile. Still inside, Liam?"

"Doing fifteen in Maghaberry."

"That rules him out in the killings unless he took out a contract, which any of families of the men on Lawton's longlist could have done. As an aside, apparently Bwye used Clinton's case to start a fundraising campaign for a child abuse charity. One of the few decent things he ever did, according to Lawton."

Annette snorted derisively. "A children's fundraiser who beats the hell out of his own kid."

Craig nodded. "Bwye was a bastard. It's hard not to be glad that he's dead."

The shock that filled the room was palpable. Not at the words, God knows every one of them had hated Oliver Bwye from early in the case, but at the fact that Craig had said them. No matter what he felt he was always professional. It was an uncharacteristic lapse.

Craig carried on as if he'd said nothing.

"OK, Clinton's locked up and the others are elderly. Ormond is seventy-two and Ronson's in his sixties. It doesn't rule them out but it makes killing Bwye more of a risk."

Julia shook her head. "Not if you have a gun."

Liam spoke before Craig could. "It's not their age that rules them out, it's other things. Davy's been checking them out so I'll let him tell you."

Davy tapped the smart-pad on his knee and the screen's glow highlighted the tiredness on his young face. Annette dreaded to think what the rest of them looked like.

"OK, Brian Ormond, s...seventy-two, currently in St Mary's Hospital having post-surgery radiotherapy for squamous cell s... skin cancer. He's been in since early November. S...Solomon Ronson and his family have been visiting relatives in Israel since June. I've checked passports and airports and they haven't been back here during that time."

Craig shook his head. "It doesn't rule out extended families or a contract." He turned to Liam. "You and Gerry get your ears to the ground and see what the Derry snouts can find. If it was a professional contract there can't be that many round here who could have done it efficiently. John Ellis can help you with local knowledge. Annette, you and Julia check into the men's extended families. They-"

Just then the back door burst open and Andy stormed in. Craig hadn't even noticed that he wasn't there. He stood by the doorway triumphantly.

"They've found it! The divers have found the Ruger."

Liam dampened his excitement. "Well, unless you fancy diving in after them, shut that bloody door. You're letting the heat out."

Andy kicked the door shut with his heel and grabbed a seat, continuing in an enthusiastic tone.

"It was near where they found Mrs Bwye, weighed down in the same way."

Craig interrupted. "In a plastic bag, weighted with stones?"

"Yes; identical. They're hoping the plastic might have protected any prints."

Liam and Craig shook their heads in unison and Liam spoke first.

"No way. There were no prints on the boat except the McDermotts'. Whoever dumped it and the rifle wore gloves."

Craig gave Andy an apologetic look. "He's probably right, but it's a good find anyway." He scanned the group. "Anything more on the van; anyone?"

Davy nodded. "A motorway patrol found a burnt out carcass that might be a match."

Craig sat forward enthusiastically. "Cameras? If it was dumped on a motorway there must be footage."

Liam warmed to the theme. "And he must have had a car parked nearby as getaway. Try the local A roads and do a ten-mile sweep for CCTV. We might catch a break."

Annette sounded a note of caution. "He only said it *might* be a match, sir."

"It'll match, Annette. There are only two adapted vans of that type in Northern Ireland. What are the odds of finding one burnt out so close?"

She wasn't persuaded. "And how many in the whole of Ireland? How many on the ferries to mainland UK and Europe this week, not to mention the ones already replated and sprayed by now? They'd have to be a real amateur to burn the van out so close by."

Craig's face fell. Liam wasn't as quiet in his disappointment.

"Ach, why did you have to say that?"

Craig shook his head. "Because she's right, Liam. We'll check, but the chances of it being our van are slim, unless our man was a complete novice."

Liam wasn't done. "So what does that leave us with? An expert stranger attack, or revenge by the families of the men on Lawton's list."

Annette scrutinised Craig's face, reading something there. "Or the Super's so..."

Craig smiled; Annette was on the ball. Liam looked confused. "The Super's so? What does that mean?"

Craig stood up, signalling that the briefing was closed. "It means you all know what you've got to get on with and we'll meet again at five." He turned to Andy. "OK, show me that gun."

****

The rifle looked just like any Ruger, except for the slime and weed that had somehow entwined itself around it, despite its plastic overcoat. The mysteries of open water. The plastic was in a separate evidence bag and Craig scrutinised both as they lay side by side in the divers' van.

What would the gun tell them? That it was Oliver Bwye's, probably, and that it had fired the bullets they'd found. That it had been dumped at the bottom of the lake at the same time as the bodies? Again, probably; forensics would prove that much using samples of water and silt. Craig prayed fervently for prints, but without them what other information did the rifle's discovery yield? It said what they already knew, that there was a third person in the boat. There was no way Diana Bwye had survived her fatal wounding long enough to wrap the gun and dispose of it neatly in the lake, and Oliver Bwye definitely couldn't have dumped it; concrete tended to inhibit athleticism.

So what did that leave? A third person, yes, perhaps even a fourth. Craig dismissed the idea as soon as it appeared; the McDermott's boat was small and Bwye's sarcophagus would have made it cramped; two more people was all that it could have held. Diana Bwye and who else? And was that person their killer, as most juries in the land would believe, or merely a helping hand after the event? Someone who'd assisted the Bwyes in ending their lives because that's what they'd wanted to do, or someone who'd aided one of them in arranging both of their deaths?

He shook his head at the thought; not because it was wrong but because it was something that had to remain just a thought until he was certain of his facts. And there was only one way he knew how to get there; by relentlessly working the case.

****

Miller Street, Derry.

Craig knocked on the modern office door, not expecting

the woman who answered. The building was refurbished and bright, like so many others in Derry; a testament to the work done to move the city from its troubled past to the beacon of prosperity it had become. Derry was resolutely forward looking in a way that even the country's capital hadn't achieved.

But the woman at the door wasn't modern in any way. Her hair was pinned in a bun at the nape of her neck, with occasional grey hairs peppering its native black. Her clothes were simple; a navy A-line dress from a catalogue, with flat lace-up shoes that matched. Only her face said that she wasn't old; its absence of lines saying that she was probably younger than him. Yet she'd decided to present herself like a grandmother; Craig didn't have the time to ask why, just whether her boss was in. Joshua Kelly, solicitor at law; the man that he'd come to see.

The woman smiled at the question and the smile lit up her face, shedding the years and making her look as young as she actually was. She waved Craig to a seat and lifted her coat before knocking on an inner door.

"Mr Kelly, I'm for lunch now. There's a Superintendent Craig here for you. He's your one o'clock."

An innocent enough introduction in a solicitor's office where the police were probably frequent visitors; inquiring about clients or seeking confirmation of court dates. But that wasn't Craig's purpose today. The secretary nodded goodbye as she passed, leaving him to stare at the inner door she'd left ajar. No man's voice had said "Thank you" when she'd spoken and he'd seen no movement behind the door; nothing to say that the room's occupant had heard. The two men waited on either side of the wood, until finally Craig heard a sigh and his name was called.

"Superintendent Craig, please come in."

The man behind the door resembled his secretary in only one way; he looked much older than his years. Joshua Kelly, Josh to his friends, was barely forty yet he looked a decade more than that. Unlike his P.A his aging wasn't a façade; it persisted despite his modern glasses and resolutely cool suit. Craig looked again and saw that he'd been wrong. Kelly didn't look old; he looked exhausted, as if he was carrying all of his clients' worries, plus his own.

Craig took a seat and scanned the solicitor's lean face. Everything about Kelly was dark: black hair, black suit, tanned skin; everything about him but his eyes. They were pale grey, so grey that Craig wondered if they were lenses, until he glanced behind him and saw a photograph of an older man with an identical pair.

The lawyer gazed at Craig for a moment then his gaze dropped to his desk; steel and glass, loaded with tired beige files and well-thumbed books.

"How may I help you, Mr Craig?"

He asked as if the answer was inevitable and Craig knew that conversational preamble had no place here. He played his cue.

"How long were you and Diana Bwye lovers?"

Kelly gasped so loudly that Craig was uncomfortably surprised. Had he got it completely wrong? The gasp faded and the solicitor shook his head, in a way that said Craig had *almost* been right.

"In our heads, forever, but in reality we never even kissed. Diana was a good woman; she would never have broken her wedding vows."

Craig wasn't giving up. "But she loved you."

The solicitor gave a weak smile. "She said so, but it obviously wasn't enough for her to leave Oliver, no matter how bad he was."

Honesty was working so far, so Craig decided to go the whole hog. Whatever Kelly said wouldn't stand up in court, but he could interview him officially later; for now he really needed to know the truth.

"Did you kill Oliver Bwye?"

Instead of the indignation of an innocent, the dark solicitor gave a tired shake of his head. "No, but I wished him dead a million times."

If wishing someone dead worked there would be very few people left in the world.

"And Diana?"

The question provoked a very different response.

Kelly leapt from his seat and stepped forward, looming over Craig. Craig was unperturbed. Years behind a desk would have made Kelly soft and he'd long ago prepared himself for pain; it was a requirement of the job. The sad thing was the idea didn't bother him nowadays; he would almost have welcomed a blow. At least then he'd be feeling something.

Kelly yelled in his face.

"I would never have harmed Diana, I loved her!"

"Enough to do whatever she asked?"

The younger man's grey eyes locked on Craig's dark blue so intently it was as if he was staring straight through him; seeing something else, something in the past. Without another word he fell back into his chair. Craig repeated his question, but he knew that he'd lost the man; Kelly's thoughts were elsewhere. He'd have to abandon his questioning unless he arrested him and he had no grounds for that except a wine stain, Kelly's admitted love for Diana Bwye and half a hunch. He left the office in silence, chilled by the sound of wracking sobs before he reached the outer door.

****

Liam banged the desk phone down so hard that it bounced and sprang back on its cable to whack him in the face.

"Ow!"

He banged it down again, more firmly this time. Annette glanced up from the page she was reading at the red mark on his cheek.

"Who was that on the phone?"

Liam rubbed his face, making the mark worse. "Nicky." He searched for a mirror until Annette relented and gave him the one from her handbag. He squinted at the mark and made a face as she tutted sympathetically.

"That's going to bruise."

"Sodding phone."

A lecture about his rough handling was pointless so she turned back to what had provoked his bad mood.

"What did she have to say?"

Liam looked blank.

"Nicky. Why did she call?"

He slumped in a chair beside her. "To make the boss an even bigger pain in the ass. Greer's appeal's been given the go ahead. They've decided not to wait for our report."

Annette sprang to her feet, knocking her papers onto the floor. "What! But that case was solid! What grounds are they citing?"

"The fact that the money went through the Russian's accounts, not hers. They're saying they can't link her directly to employing the hit-men and it was just the Russian's word against hers. She's saying she just said what he told her to say and he's dead now, so..."

Panic filled her eyes. "You can't tell the chief till this case is over."

Liam gawped at her. "I'm not telling him at all! If Nicky's got bad news she can bloody well tell him herself. He won't yell at her half as much as he'll yell at me."

Annette's face set determinedly. "No-one's telling him anything until we're back in Belfast." She grabbed the phone and waved it dangerously close to Liam's face, making him rear back. "Just you leave Madam Nicky to me."

****

Craig was preoccupied when he arrived at the Northwest labs. Joshua Kelly had loved Diana Bwye and his reaction had said that he definitely hadn't killed her. That only left Kelly with two possible roles; mourner or accomplice after the fact. The former was more likely, based on his lack of reason for wanting her dead. As Craig entered the long corridor to pathology he stopped abruptly in his tracks. Damn! He'd forgotten to ask Kelly about the estate's female inheritance line. He'd have to call him on the way back to the house.

He carried on walking till he reached a glass door and opened it without knocking. He'd expected to see Mike when he entered, but a leaner, more familiar face also smiled hello.

"John! What are you doing here?"

John's smile creased his angular face like origami. "I take it you're pleased to see me."

"Yes. But..."

"Mike asked for a consult, and I can see why. It's a tricky case."

Craig grabbed a chair and sat down. "Not that tricky. Bwye was shot and disabled first, then loaded into the van, drowned in concrete and dumped into the lake. Mrs Bwye was shot and killed, possibly by Bwye but more likely by someone else, either their killer or..."

John raised an eyebrow. "That tone says you're not convinced, and you're right to be sceptical." He gestured at Augustus. "We've found something that doesn't fit. Let's go to the dissection room."

Craig talked as they walked. "The divers found the gun."

"Good. Where?"

Mike's higher voice answered. "In the lake, near where they found the bodies. It was in a black plastic sack weighed down with stones."

John nodded. "OK. Now you can match the bullets, the stones and with any luck the perforations will show that the plastic sack came from the same roll as the Bwyes'. It's doubtful we'll find any prints on the gun. Forensics hasn't found any but the Bwyes' prints on anything so far."

"The survivor's from Lawton's list drew a blank. We're looking at their families now."

John made a face. "I don't think so."

Before Craig could ask why not they'd arrived at the room and Mike was removing the sheet from Oliver Bwye's jowly face. Craig stared down at him for a moment.

"What are we looking for?"

Mike shook his head. "You can't see it so I actually don't know why I uncovered his face."

John smiled. "Showmanship. I do it all the time."

Mike put the sheet back and turned towards the wall, flicking on an X-Ray screen. Images of a head and torso came into focus.

"OK, again, what are we looking for?"

Mike tapped the screen with his finger. "That's Oliver Bwye's head." He drew his finger down. "And this is his throat and oesophageal tract."

"Which they filled with concrete."

"Yes." He pointed to another film that showed Bwye's throat. "This is an MRI scan of the concrete in his throat. Can you see the markings?"

Craig peered at it for a moment before admitting defeat. "It just looks like solid material."

"It is, but I had a hunch so I asked the materials lab in Belfast to take a closer look."

John interrupted. "That's why I drove up. Des was going to email the report..."

"But you fancied a road trip? In this weather!"

John had a ready prepared excuse that sounded better than 'I'm here to check you're not making everyone's life hell, or worse, about to endanger your own life'.

"Natalie's hounding me to show her the house. I thought getting off side for a while would give me a few more days." He smiled. "Not that I don't trust her but I've hidden all the keys."

Craig perked up. "So you're staying here tonight?"

John shook his head, feeling instantly guilty. "Sorry, no. I'm heading back in an hour, but Natalie won't know that. She'll think I'm away for days. I can nip back and finish the house in time for the party without her ever knowing that I'm there."

Craig hid his disappointment behind a joke. "You're a dead man if she finds out that you lied."

"I'm in the right job then."

Mike's patience was wearing thin.

"If you two have quite finished...?" He tapped the screen's magnification, enlarging the concrete. "What you're looking at here are micro fissures in the concrete. They formed as it dried."

Craig was genuinely puzzled. "So?"

"So it tells us how quickly it set. It was quick-setting concrete, but even so the concrete in his throat dried first."

"But didn't that happen because it was poured into his

throat first, to suffocate him?"

"Yes. Logic says that the area that's filled first should set first, but not as quickly as it actually did."

John cut in. "You're going to like this, Marc, trust me."

Mike's eyes grew wild. "He will if you ever let me get it out! The materials lab confirmed that the fissures in Bwye's throat don't match the ones in the rest of the concrete."

It was Craig's turn to interrupt and Mike raised his eyes to heaven. "But isn't that to be expected, given that the throat is internal and warm and the rest of the concrete probably set in the back of a cold van?"

Mike's eyes lit up and he decided not to tell Craig off. "Yes, yes, you're right, but that wasn't the only thing that made the difference. Body heat alone wouldn't account for it. The fissures in Bwye's throat suggest that he was also in a warm external environment when the concrete there dried."

Craig's eyes widened. "It was poured down his throat while he was still in the house! Bwye was already dead when they put him in the van."

"That's what we think. Bwye was shot in the study to incapacitate him or maybe even to render him unconscious, and then finished off by having the concrete poured down his throat where he lay. Then he was put in the van already dead, covered in concrete to weigh him down and taken to the lake to be dumped."

He turned back to the bodies excitedly and lifted the sheet from Diana Bwye's face.

"Mrs Bwye died instantly from her second gunshot wound, to the chest, then she was put in a plastic sack and weighed down with stones. So I thought, why not cover her with concrete as well?"

Craig was still thinking so John answered. "No time, not enough concrete, or the killer didn't hate her as much as he did her husband?"

Mike shook his head and John frowned. Mike had only told him about the concrete fissures in the husband's throat so why were they re-examining Diana Bwye?

"No. Well, yes and no. The concrete would have dried in the van in the same time it took Bwye's to dry, so I don't think time was a factor. I agree the killer didn't hate her as much, but that's irrelevant either way."

"You're being annoying, Mike."

Craig cut in. "No, I think he's onto something." He waved Augustus on.

"OK, let's say that the killer's main target was Oliver Bwye. He needed to disable him quickly because he was a big man, so he killed him in the way I said. But he didn't expect Diana Bwye to be there; Annette says she normally went to a committee meeting that night."

Craig smiled. It was the first time he'd mentioned Annette, even though they'd been seeing each other for months. Augustus saw his smile and blushed.

"OK, so if Diana Bwye wasn't supposed to be there, she became an unexpected problem to be dealt with. Perhaps she screamed, so they shot her to shut her up and accidentally killed her, or perhaps they'd already decided to kill any witnesses before they arrived..."

John interjected. "Which means that they weren't masked."

"OK, yes, let's say that they weren't masked. OK, so they disable and kill Bwye and then Diana appears. They shoot her in the leg to shut her up and put her in the van, but either they don't have enough concrete to cover her..."

Craig was getting confused. "Not even enough to suffocate her?"

Augustus smiled. "Exactly! That's my point. They could have suffocated her easily by pouring concrete down her throat, just by using a little less concrete on Bwye's torso. So why *not* kill her that way? Why risk a second shot that might have been heard by the staff?"

"Because they knew her and liked her?"

"How about instead of like we put love? How about this is someone who cared so much about her that they couldn't bear to watch her suffocate, or to erase her identity by covering her face?"

John snorted rudely. "What, so they shot her through the chest? Very romantic."

Craig waved his scepticism down; Mike's theory fitted with where his thoughts were heading. But he still needed one question answered. He nodded at Diana Bwye's body.

"She definitely died from the second shot through her chest, not strangulation from the ligature. Yes?"

Augustus nodded. "Yes. The ligature mark was left for distraction. The gun barrel was actually held against her chest. There were scorch marks on her blouse and skin."

Craig walked to the head of the trolley and gazed down at the dead woman. After a full minute's silence John had to ask.

"What are you thinking, Marc?"

Craig shook his head, working furiously through possible scenarios. He wasn't certain enough of anything yet to confide it, but he needed to ask a question.

"Mike, is there any way that she could have shot herself?"

The two doctors stared at him, stunned, then they scrutinised the body frantically. John drew back the sheet to reveal Diana Bwye's scorched and bruised chest and examined her arms and hands, while Mike examined her gunshots; then they covered their victim and both took a step back. Mike spoke first.

"Her arms are certainly long enough..."

Craig urged him on. "She could have propped the rifle against a wall and reached the trigger. It would have left the same wounds but..."

John shook his head. "There was no GSR on her hands."

Craig pressed his case. "Gloves, or could the water have washed it away? She was submerged in that lake for days and she wasn't encased like her husband."

Mike shook his head in disbelief. "I suppose...it's possible, but why would she have killed herself? Surely with Bwye dead she would have had even more reason to live?"

Craig shook his head. "Motive's a different thing; I haven't got there yet. I just need to know if it could have played out that way."

John led the way back to the office and they resumed

the conversation.

"So you're saying that she killed her husband and then killed herself?"

Craig shrugged. "I'm not saying anything yet. We still have suspects to rule out. I just needed to know if it was physically possible and you've said that it is."

Mike shook his head, still not sold on Craig's idea. He favoured a professional hit.

"Forensics found some blood on the boat, but still nowhere near enough, although I suppose the van..."

John followed through on Craig's suicide scenario. "It still doesn't negate the need for a third person, even if they just helped by dumping the bodies in the lake. Diana couldn't have dumped her husband by herself."

Craig nodded. "The third person could have been purely a disposal man. Someone who loved her, which by the sounds of it was a pretty large group; she was a popular lady. Their job was to arrange a cover-up to protect the people left behind. Maybe that's what the ligature mark around her neck was about, although if so, that was overkill."

John nodded. "An amateur. Chucking in evidence to try and throw you off the track."

"Not that amateur. It's worked for ten days."

Mike looked stunned. "So you're saying that this was a murder suicide by Mrs Bwye, with an elaborate cover-up to protect her daughter? If it was then it's succeeded. There's no way that we can tell Jane definitively that her mother was responsible for this mess."

Craig shrugged. "It's all just speculation at the moment. They could still both have been murdered and the reason the killer didn't cover Diana's face was because he ran out of materials or time, or he had some last minute remorse because she wasn't the originally intended victim. And we still have the possibility that Bwye organised a hit on himself for the K&R money, although it sounds a bit altruistic for him, from what I've heard."

John shook his head sadly. "This third person must have cared a lot for her to risk prison."

Mike stared wistfully into space. "I would do it for

Annette."

Craig smiled. "Good to know. I'll make sure to tell her that you'd be happy to kill her when I get back."

Augustus blushed deep red. "I didn't...ach, you know what I meant. The whole thing's quite romantic. Almost Shakespearean."

"Except in Shakespeare's version the lover would have topped himself as well."

Craig's eyes suddenly widened and he pulled out his phone. It seemed like an age until it was answered and, when it was, Joshua Kelly's quiet voice came on the line. The detective hung up without speaking and slumped back, relieved. John squinted at him curiously.

"I take it Romeo and Juliet isn't today's show?"

Craig shook his head. "Just another hunch that could be nothing. Like I said, we still have suspects to rule out."

John muttered something to himself and Mike asked him to repeat it.

"I said; just remember that Romeo doesn't die until the end of the play."

Chapter Nineteen

A call to Joshua Kelly on the way back to Rocksbury confirmed the estate's female inheritance line and the fact that Jane had never been told. There were a few more gaps to fill in then they would have as complete a picture of the crime as Craig believed they ever would.

The briefing started slowly, punctuated by more yawns than a university lecture. Davy was the liveliest one in the room. In fact, he looked positively excited so Craig waved him on to start.

"I've more info on Ray Mercer and the van."

His words were drowned out by a particularly loud yawn from Liam. As he tried to continue they were obscured again by two size thirteen feet banging onto the desk. Craig rolled his eyes.

"What did you say, Davy?"

"I s...said that no forensic evidence s...survived from the van but there was enough left of the doorpost to find the VIN number. It was registered to The Chronicle. It w...was adapted with a hydraulic lift and hoist, for deliveries and w...waste paper disposal."

Andy glanced up from his hot drink. "Didn't someone say that Diana Bwye went to see Mercer recently? What if she went to ask for the loan of the van?"

Davy answered him. "I've been trying to find out w...why she saw him, but no-one at the paper seems to know."

Craig sipped his coffee for a moment before commenting. When he did it was in an exhausted voice, more because of what he had to say than his physical tiredness.

"Mercer knows why she visited him, but how the hell do we get him to tell us? I can't see him cooperating now that we've cost him his job."

Liam sniffed. "He wouldn't have cooperated anyway. He's a belligerent sod. Anyway, why bother with him when odds are his lackey Bill Reynolds will know?"

Craig sat up straight. "Liam, you're a genius." He continued as Liam acknowledged the truism with a smug smile. "Annette, call Jake and tell him to get Bill Reynolds into High Street. Cuffs, cell, the works; put the fear of God into him. Obstructing a police investigation or something like that. When he's stewed for a while, he'll tell us why Mrs Bwye saw Mercer." He turned back to Davy. "Davy, ask Maggie to see if Rory Cahill knows anything as well. He keeps his ear to the ground." He relaxed back in his chair. "By the way, did the tyres match?"

"Slash and all. It's definitely the van that was here that night. W...We're dealing with a novice, burning it out so close to the crime scene."

Or someone paid to act like one. Craig shook his head; more pieces that didn't fit. Annette thought of something.

"Was anyone seen on CCTV, near the van or getting into a car?"

"Plenty of images of someone near the van wearing jeans and a hoody, but they kept their face turned away from the cameras the w...whole time. The most we can s...say is that it was a man, around six feet tall and slim build."

Liam went to ask a question.

"Before you ask, yes, they had a car w...waiting about a mile overland but they'd taped over the number plate and the cameras lost them once they hit the back roads. All we've got is a Ford of some description."

Julia summed up the situation in six words.

"Ford car and average man; ubiquitous."

Craig nodded. She was right and his guess was that their averageness had been a deliberate choice. Whoever had ended the Bwyes' lives, or aided them to do it themselves, was being protected by their ordinariness. The description fitted Joshua Kelly, but it also fitted half the men in the room. He changed the subject.

"You said you had something on Mercer?"

Davy grinned. He'd never met Ray Mercer but he disliked him on Maggie's behalf. "We've got him on a street camera entering the drop s...site. The guy behind the café counter seemed to know him, so it should be easy to check."

Finally some good news. "Excellent work, Davy. Carmen, contact the café and follow up on that." He paused, running through the outstanding issues in his head. "What about the names on Lawton's list? Anyone in their families stand out?"

A shake of Davy's head answered him. "S...Sorry, chief. I dug into the relatives of all seven, living and dead; kids, cousins, in-laws, but there's no-one jumping out. And without a print or DNA to go on..."

"You could be there all year."

Craig was mulling over whether to tell them his theory about murder suicide when the desk phone rang. It was Des. He got straight to the point.

"There was a print on the gun that wasn't Oliver Bwye's."

"Des, you're a genius."

"Well yes, I am actually. It was hell to find. On the side of the magazine. They must have left it when they loaded it."

"Name?"

"I'm running it against every print we have. You'll have your answer in about an hour."

Craig was pretty sure whose it would be; Diana Bwye's. It was the only scenario that made sense. OK, it could have been the avenging relative of someone whom Bwye had wronged, but how could they have got access to copy the keys to the gun cabinet and the rear study door? And surely they would have worn a mask and gloves, so why the need to kill Diana Bwye when she could simply have been left tied up?

Bwye couldn't have killed himself, and anyone he'd hired wouldn't have killed his wife unless they'd been contracted to; contract killers only did what they were paid for, no more. The young lovers definitely hadn't done it, he was convinced of that, and he couldn't picture Joshua Kelly shooting the woman he loved.

He decided to outline his murder suicide theory to the group, but instead of the gasps of disbelief he'd expected he was merely greeted with blank looks. Annette and Julia asked the question together, the one he still didn't have the answer to.

"But why?"

Annette continued. "Oliver Bwye would have been dead in months anyway so why would Diana have sacrificed herself?"

Craig countered with another question. "Did she know that he was dying? Do we have any records of her attending GP or hospital appointments with him, or of her being told?"

"I..."

"It's something we need an answer to. Annette, get onto Bwye's consultant now. Andy, you get back to the GP. And someone ask Jane if she or her mother knew he was terminal."

While they made the calls, Julia asked the question again.

"Why? Even if she didn't know he was dying, why kill him now, all of a sudden?"

"His violence had been escalating in the past two months; perhaps she was afraid that he would harm Jane."

"So why kill herself?"

Craig thought for a moment. He was just about to share what he'd learned about Diana Bwye's attitude to marriage, when Liam interjected thoughtfully.

"Has anyone noticed anything about this house? I mean apart from the weird windows out the front."

Everyone looked puzzled, then Gerry ventured a design viewpoint. "She liked neutral colours?"

Liam raised an eyebrow. "I didn't mean the décor, although thanks for that. I meant the religious stuff. There's a bible or framed religious tract in every room and their bedroom was like a monk's cell."

It coincided with what Kelly had said so Craig nodded him on.

"You're a bunch of heathens, and I mean that in a completely non-sectarian way before anyone gets on their green or orange high horse, and most of you probably wouldn't know a bible if one bit you. But I'm telling you that someone in this house was seriously religious and I'm guessing that it wasn't old man Bwye or the girl."

"What's your point, Liam?"

"My point is if Diana Bwye was that religious she would have felt as guilty as hell about everything. About marrying a man who was unfaithful and went to escorts, a man who hurt people during his career, not to mention that he hit her kid."

Julia chipped in. "And her."

Liam shook his head. "That wouldn't have mattered to her as much as him hitting Jane. If I'm right we're talking serious self-sacrifice here and people like that offer their suffering up to God. But when Bwye hurt *other* people, she would have blamed herself for his actions one hundred per cent."

Julia was confused. "Not blamed him?"

"Well, yes, in a way, but even then she would have seen his deeds as evidence of *her* failure to help him be a better man. Religion 101; take the blame for everything. Trust me; I grew up around people like that, Catholic and Protestant. Northern Ireland's falling down with them, and if Diana Bwye was that religious she might have seen her failing marriage and his violence as her fault, and maybe she just couldn't stand it when she saw him getting worse." He sniffed and folded his hands on his paunch like a priest. "Here endeth the sermon."

Craig glanced round the group. Carmen and Gerry were both nodding.

"You agree?"

They answered in unison. "Yes."

Gerry continued. "I've met people like that. They take on the worries of the world."

"OK. So why not ask Bwye to leave?"

Gerry shook his head. "She would never have divorced him. Till death do us part."

"Separation?"

"Nearly as bad. You're damned."

Carmen shrugged. "Or maybe she asked him to leave and he wouldn't. Maybe he threatened to take her through the courts and go for the estate."

Liam nodded. "Good point. You've another source of guilt right there; Jane would have lost her inheritance."

Just then Annette finished her call. "Bwye never

brought his wife to his hospital appointments and the consultant says he forbade them to inform her or Jane."

A moment later Andy came back with the same answer.

Diana Bwye hadn't known that her husband was dying and that Jane's torment had an expiry date. All she'd seen was an increasingly violent man who was making her daughter's life hell.

Craig decided to play devil's advocate. "OK, why couldn't she have killed Bwye and continued living? She could have done good works as penance."

Liam tutted slowly. "You're missing the point, boss. She felt guilty about *everything*. She could never have lived with the guilt of murdering him, and she wouldn't have believed that she deserved to live. If she killed Bwye she had to kill herself as well."

It was a brand of religion that Craig knew nothing about. He was from a mixed marriage and was agnostic himself, but even his devout Italian family didn't practice their religion in such a punitive way; their version of Catholicism included more festivals than guilt. But Diana Bwye was strictly observant and if Liam was right it fitted with what Joshua Kelly had said.

He thought for a moment. They had to wait for Des to call back with the print confirmation and for Jake to interview Bill Reynolds so there was only one more thing he could think to do. He picked up the phone and called the solicitor again.

"Mr Kelly, do you hold any documents belonging to Diana Bwye?"

Joshua Kelly stared nervously at the phone, uncertain how to answer. He'd felt interrogated when Craig had been there earlier and he felt the same way now. He summoned all his law school training and endeavoured to keep his voice calm.

"I hold her Will, but I've already disclosed its contents to your analyst."

Craig paused deliberately, to make the solicitor anxious. He wanted to see what more came out. When he sensed Kelly wondering if he'd cut the call he spoke again, watched by his curious team.

"I didn't mean her Will, Mr Kelly. What else did she give you to hold?"

It was a bluff and Craig knew it, but it was a bluff he was prepared to lay money on. There was a silence at both ends like some aural staring contest, until finally Kelly blinked first and sighed.

"She gave me a sealed envelope two weeks ago, with instructions never to open it unless I was forced to."

"Consider this being forced. I'll be there in thirty minutes."

****

Thirty minutes later Craig and Liam were seated at Joshua Kelly's desk, staring at an envelope sealed with red wax. Liam gestured at the image embossed on it.

"What's the seal?"

"The D'Arcy family crest. They were aristocracy in their day. They owned half the land from here to Donegal."

Craig turned the envelope over in his hands. Everything about it said quality, from the weight of the paper to the elegant black script on the front; 'Diana D'Arcy'. She'd returned to her heritage in death. He had a good idea what the letter would say but a good idea never stood up in law, so he signalled the solicitor to open it, listening to the crack of the wax and the silky sound of the paper unfolding. Kelly read in silence for a moment as Craig stared intently at his face. As the lawyer paled and his eyes filled with tears Craig got one part of his answer; this man had played no part in either of the Bwyes' deaths.

He nodded him to read aloud and they listened as Diana D'Arcy Bwye apologised to the world. She outlined how violent her husband had been ever since they'd married, and how he'd grown much worse in recent months. Her fear was that he would someday kill Jane, a fear that had increased since she'd married Richard McCann. The strain of keeping their marriage secret was beginning to tell on her, and she believed that someday soon her husband would find out and then both Jane's and Richard's lives would be at risk. There was no sign that she knew Oliver Bwye would die soon.

Her next words were telling.

"I don't mind what Oliver does to me, I made my marriage vows before God, but for a child who deserved safety and love Jane was owed a better life. It was my duty to ensure that she had one and I failed."

She continued that Bwye was threatening to contest the female inheritance line and sell off the estate. His threats were probably just to torment her, just as he'd done all of their married life, but she would have had no way of knowing that.

As Kelly read on tears spilled down his cheeks, becoming so heavy that he could barely speak. Craig took the letter and continued reading. It was a sad story of love and disappointment and when he reached the final paragraph everything fell into place.

"I have made a plan that I know will damn my soul, but I pray that God will forgive me some day. I've made copies of the keys to Oliver's gun cabinet and rear study door. I intend to shoot him with his rifle and then kill myself. There's a man who has agreed to help me, someone whom you will never find. His only task is to take us in a van to the lake and dispose of us both there. Oliver is evil so he must suffer when he dies and I've found a way to ensure that."

Liam murmured "the concrete" as Craig read on.

"Then I will kill myself. This man's job is only to put us in the water and dispose of the gun and van. I borrowed the van from The Belfast Chronicle; it seemed fitting somehow. I ask two things of the police. Do not pursue this man; he is nothing, just a friend who has suffered a great deal in his life and agreed to help someone else in pain. He didn't kill either of us. His hands are clean. The second thing I ask is that you allow Jane to believe that we were killed by a stranger. I beg you not to destroy my daughter's love for me by telling her the truth."

Kelly had recovered enough to read so Craig paused at the final sentence and handed the letter back. "Finally, Joshua, you are a kind man and you deserve to find happiness. We were not to be. Perhaps in a different life. Love, Diana D'Arcy."

Kelly set the page on the desk and dropped his head into his hands. The detectives waited for a moment, then Craig lifted the letter and envelope and slid them into an evidence bag. They left the office without a word, leaving a lonely man to mourn the woman he had loved.

****

Sunday. Midnight.

It was their final night in Derry so John Ellis had finally got his dinner guests. Five to be precise, once everyone who'd had a nearby home to go to had gone, leaving just the core Docklands team. Dinner was excellent, but at almost midnight, when all the craic had been had and Brenda Ellis was beginning to wilt, it was finally time to leave. Liam suggested they go in search of more drink, but in the wee small hours the only place still serving was a club. So that was how they found themselves now in a dimly lit nightclub in Derry, complete with throbbing music and matching lights.

Liam took a swig of beer and shook his head at the taste; he hated bottled beer but not many nightclubs sold draught.

"Aye well, that's all the 'i's dotted and 't's crossed. Reynolds confirmed Diana Bwye asked to borrow the van for a charity gift run, and Des has confirmed her prints on the gun."

He said it like it was the end of the story but Craig was left feeling discontent. He'd updated Sean Flanagan a few hours earlier and signalled his desire to pursue the man who'd disposed of the Bwyes. Normally Flanagan would have been gung-ho, but swathing cuts through the force's budget meant that justice wasn't the only mistress he had to serve, and Mistress Stormont held on to her money like every other good-time girl.

"Sorry, Marc. Unless something obvious appears I want you to let this go. It could take months of man hours and we mightn't even get a sniff. Even if we did what would we charge him with? Accessory after the fact maybe, but with no forensics even that would be a stretch. All we have is a letter from a self-confessed dead killer to say that he helped at all." Craig had heard him shaking his head. "I'll speak to the P.P.S. and let them decide, but my guess is their answer will be 'not in the public interest to pursue.' Don't worry; you'll have plenty to do after Christmas now that they've granted the Greer appeal."

That was how he'd found out about Greer. It was probably just as well that none of his team had told him; he would very likely have exploded, like he had when he'd got round to bollocking Carmen for her cheekiness to Liam.

So here they were, drinking bottled beer in a nightclub in a last hurrah before they went home. Suddenly Liam nudged him; he'd spotted two dark-eyed beauties approaching across the dancefloor. "Incoming at three o'clock. I'll take the one on the left."

Craig shook his head and drank even more. The last he remembered was Liam being dragged round the floor by a short girl with the strength of ten men, and Davy deep in conversation with her friend. Carmen and Annette rolled their eyes, especially when Liam's love interest told him he was a "fine big man." Just what he didn't need; an ego boost. Their cynicism changed to amusement as he fought off her good-night kiss and legged it out of the club. The photos would appear in people's inboxes before the Christmas break.

Chapter Twenty

Belfast. Christmas Eve. 9 p.m.

The tree was spectacular but what John had done with the rest of the living room impressed his guests even more. Not only was the house a masterpiece of Nordic décor but he'd continued the theme with decorations from different Scandinavian countries. With glass icicles from Denmark and handmade decorations from Norway, the place looked like a snow palace, and when John turned out the lights and switched on the tree even the cynical Carmen gave an excited gasp.

Two hours and several bowls of punch later, the crowd of police, medical and lab party goers had thinned to a core group of ten, the rest hurrying home to fill stockings for little ones or open their presents in peace. Craig had been mellow all evening, aided and abetted by John topping up his glass as he'd sat beside Katy on a small chaise longue. She gazed at the tree like a little girl and Craig smiled and ran his fingers through her curls, wondering whether to give her present now or wait till they got back to her place.

None of them had noticed the front door opening, left trustingly on the latch as people came and went, and no-one had noticed the unwelcome spectre at the feast. John and Natalie were in the kitchen, giggling at the mess that would wait until after Christmas to be cleaned up. Ken was attempting to arm wrestle Mike in one corner, egged on by Liam and Jake. Only Annette, chatting quietly to Danni and the voluntary designated driver for them all, had felt a breeze as the door was flung open, and only she wasn't blinded by the mulled wine, enough to see a camera flash.

She turned to see where it had come from, just as the scrawny figure of Ray Mercer entered the main room. Without anyone touching the music the sounds of Sinatra seemed to fade and Annette knew that she had to reach the reporter before any of the men did. She raced across the floor, slipping awkwardly in her high-heeled shoes, but she wasn't quick enough to stop Craig seeing the reporter and in two strides he was by her side. She stood between the two men, feeling Craig straining at the leash and watching as Mercer's face contorted into a sneer.

Her eyes said 'leave now, for pity's sake', but Mercer had come to say something and no amount of pleading was going to shut his mouth before one of the men's fists did.

"Well, well, it's party time at the zoo. So this is how cops and doctors play. It'll make a lovely article, especially now I've got a photo."

Annette could feel Craig's temper building and she willed him to say nothing. It was a forlorn hope, but his voice was cooler than she could have hoped for and for a moment she thought that things might still be OK.

"Why are you here, Mercer? Don't you have a hole to crawl into?"

The journalist's eyes narrowed. "I'm here because you are, Craig, just like I intend to be everywhere you go in future. You cost me my job, so I'm freelance now. That'll give me plenty of time to make yours and your family's lives hell."

John and Natalie heard something was wrong and emerged from the kitchen, just as Mercer added.

"Friends and girlfriends too. I'm going to dig up every dirty little secret that you're desperate to hide and plaster it all over the press." He stared at Katy and Natalie in turn. "Every malpractice suit, every bad decision." His eyes swivelled towards Jake and Ken. "Every one night stand that you don't want anyone to know about."

Liam stepped forward and Mercer grinned maliciously. "I'm particularly going to take my time with you, Cullen. I'm going to dig back through all your years on the force and find something to bury you with."

The only thing holding Craig back was that he was in someone else's home. John saw there was still a chance to stop things and his voice echoed across the room.

"Get out, Mercer. You're a sad little man who can't be happy unless you're making someone else miserable."

Mercer replied by closing the distance between them

as John moved Natalie quickly out of the way. He brought his face close to John's and whispered something in his ear. No-one else heard it, but Craig saw his friend blanch and in seconds he'd crossed the room, his fist curled to strike. Katy dashed after him and just as Craig's arm rose she shouted out his name.

"Marc! No!"

Mercer hadn't moved and wasn't defending himself and suddenly Craig saw the blindingly obvious. This was what he'd wanted. Not for John or Liam or Jake to lose it, but him. Mercer wanted him to hit him so he could get him thrown off the force. He knew he had a temper and he also knew he was more likely to use it in defence of someone else.

As Craig's fist fell the momentum was so strong that he couldn't halt its progress; the only thing that he could do was turn away. Perhaps he didn't really want to stop. He was so angry that it had to be satisfied somehow. All his months of guilt and pain had to find somewhere to go.

For a moment he was deaf to everything except the ringing in his ears, and the only things he could see were Mercer's sneer and Katy's shocked blue eyes. Then the blood reddening his sleeve and spraying across John's maple floor and the glittering shards of glass at his feet made things feel surreal. Detached. Nothing to do with him.

He felt nothing as the blood spread and no pain as his knees hit the floor. Nothing except a sudden peace that made the Christmas tree lights fade away.

Chapter Twenty-One

2nd January 2015

Craig gazed at his bandaged right arm as if it didn't belong to him. It almost hadn't; severed arteries were hard to fix and torn tendons a challenge to mend. But the surgeons had managed, just. Five hours in theatre, with Natalie gowned and masked, watching the plastic surgeon like a hawk. That's what he'd been told anyway; he had no memory of events after Mercer had threatened John.

He'd lost a lot of blood and it had been a stupid thing to do. And yet...

The woman's voice broke through his thoughts.

"You're smiling, Superintendent."

Yes he was. He knew why, and he knew that to say why would land him on a psychiatric hold, and make Katy and his mother cry again. So instead he turned away from the Sycamore tree and buried his dark thoughts, preparing to cooperate.

Punching the glass had been a stupid thing to do and yet... In that moment he'd felt a freedom that he'd never felt before. Free of guilt for the first time in months, free of the murderers they locked away, free of the problems the whole world faced.

It was indulgence and it was selfish and he would have to wait till it was his time to go to feel it again, that or make the people that he loved cry. He stole a last glance into the abyss before it closed for another few years then he smiled again and answered the woman's unvoiced question.

"I think that I'm ready to talk."

THE END

Core Characters in the Craig Crime Novels

Superintendent Marc (Marco) Craig: Craig is a sophisticated, single, forty-four-year-old. Born in Northern Ireland, he is of Northern Irish/Italian extraction, from a mixed religious background but agnostic. An ex-grammar schoolboy and Queen's University Law graduate, he went to London to join The Met (The Metropolitan Police) at 22, rising in rank through its High Potential Development Training Scheme. He returned to Belfast in 2008 after fifteen years away.

He is a driven, compassionate, workaholic, with an unfortunate temper that he struggles to control and a tendency to respond to situations with his fists, something that almost resulted in him going to prison when he was in his teens. He loves the sea, sails when he has the time and is generally very sporty. He plays the piano, loves music and sport. He lives alone in a modern apartment block in Stranmillis, near the university area of Belfast.

His parents, his extrovert mother Mirella (an Italian pianist) and his quiet father Tom (an ex-university lecturer in Physics) live in Holywood town, six miles away. His rebellious ten years younger sister, Lucia, works as the manager of a local charity and also lives in Belfast.

Craig is now a Superintendent heading up Belfast's Murder Squad, based in the thirteen storey Co-ordinated Crime Unit (C.C.U.) in Pilot Street, in the Sailortown area of Belfast's Docklands. He loves the sea, sails when he has the time and is generally very sporty. He loves music by Snow Patrol and follows Manchester United and

Northern Ireland's football team, and Ulster Rugby.

D.C.I. Liam Cullen: Craig's Detective Chief Inspector. Liam is a forty-nine-year-old former RUC officer from Crossgar in Northern Ireland, who transferred into the PSNI in 2001 following the Patton Reforms. He has lived and worked in Northern Ireland all his life and has spent thirty years in the police force, twenty of them policing Belfast, including during The Troubles.

He is married to the forty-year-old, long suffering Danielle (Danni), a part-time nursery nurse, and they have a four-year-old daughter Erin and a two-year-old son called Rory. Liam is unsophisticated, indiscreet and hopelessly non-PC, but he's a hard worker with a great knowledge of the streets and has a sense of humour that makes everyone, even the Chief Constable, laugh at times.

D.I. Annette McElroy: Annette is Craig's Detective Inspector who has lived and worked in Northern Ireland all her life. She is a forty-seven-year-old ex-nurse who, after her nursing degree, worked as a nurse for thirteen years and then, after a career break, retrained and has now been in the police for an equal length of time. She's in the process of divorcing her husband Pete, a P.E teacher at a state secondary school, because of his infidelity and violence. They have two children, a boy and a girl (Jordan and Amy), both teenagers. Annette is kind and conscientious with an especially good eye for detail. She also has very good people skills but is a bit of goody-two-shoes. Since her marriage broke down, she's acquired a newly glamorous image and is seeing Mike Augustus, a pathologist who works with Dr John Winter.

Nicky Morris: Nicky Morris is Craig's thirty-nine-year-old personal assistant. She used to be PA to Detective Chief Superintendent (D.C.S.) Terry *'Teflon'* Harrison. Nicky is a glamorous Belfast mum, married to Gary, who owns a small garage, and is the mother of a teenage son, Jonny. She comes from a solidly working class area in East Belfast, just ten minutes' drive from Docklands.

She is bossy, motherly and street-wise and manages to organise a reluctantly-organised Craig very effectively. She has a very eclectic fashion sense, and there is an ongoing innocent office flirtation between her and Liam.

Davy Walsh: The Murder Squad's twenty-seven-year-old computer analyst. A brilliant but shy EMO, Davy's confidence has grown during his time on the team, making his lifelong stutter on 's' and 'w' diminish, unless he's under stress.

His father is deceased and Davy lives at home in Belfast with his mother and grandmother. He has an older sister, Emmie, who studied English at university. His girlfriend of two years, Maggie Clarke, is a journalist at The Belfast Chronicle.

Dr John Winter: John is the forty-four-year-old Director of Pathology for Northern Ireland, one of the youngest ever appointed. He's brilliant, eccentric, gentlemanly and really likes the ladies, but he met his match in Natalie Winter, a surgeon at St Mary's Trust, and has now been happily married for seven months.

He was Craig's best friend at school and university and remained in Northern Ireland to build his medical career. He is now internationally respected in his field. John persuaded Craig that the newly peaceful Northern Ireland was a good place to return to and assists Craig's team with cases whenever he can. He is obsessed with crime in general and US police shows in particular.

D.C.S. Terry (Teflon) Harrison: Craig's old boss. The fifty-six-year-old Detective Chief Superintendent is based at the Headquarters building in Limavady in the northwest Irish countryside. He lives in a converted farm house at Toomebridge with his homemaker wife Mandy and their thirty-year-old daughter Sian, a marketing consultant. He has also had a trail of mistresses, often younger than his daughter.

Harrison is tolerable as a boss as long as everything's going well, but he is acutely politically aware and a bit of a snob, and very quick to pass on any blame to his subordinates (hence the Teflon nickname). He sees Craig as a rival and resents his friendship with John Winter, who wields a great deal of power in Northern Ireland.

Key Background Locations

The majority of locations referenced in the book are real, with some exceptions.

Northern Ireland (real): Set in the northeast of the island of Ireland, Northern Ireland was created in 1921 by an act of British parliament. It forms part of the United Kingdom of Great Britain and Northern Ireland and shares a border to the south and west with the Republic of Ireland. The Northern Ireland Assembly holds responsibility for a range of devolved policy matters. It was established by the Northern Ireland Act 1998 as part of the Good Friday Agreement.

Belfast (real): Belfast is the capital and largest city of Northern Ireland, set on the flood plain of the River Lagan. The seventeenth largest city in the United

Kingdom and the second largest in Ireland, it is the seat of the Northern Ireland Assembly.

The Dockland's Co-ordinated Crime Unit (The C.C.U. - fictitious): The modern thirteen storey headquarters building is situated in Pilot Street in Sailortown, a section of Belfast between the M1 and M2 undergoing massive investment and re-development. The C.C.U. hosts the police murder, gang crimes, vice and drug squad offices, amongst others.

Sailortown (real): An historic area of Belfast on the River Lagan that was a thriving area between the 16th - 20th centuries. Many large businesses grew in the area, ships docked for loading and unloading and their crews from far flung places such as China and Russia mixed with a local Belfast population of ship's captains, chandlers, seamen and their families.

Sailortown was a lively area where churches and bars fought for the souls and attendance of the residents and where many languages were spoken each day. The basement of the Rotterdam Bar, at the bottom of Clarendon Dock, acted as the overnight lock-up to prisoners being deported to the Antipodes on boats the next morning, and the stocks which held the prisoners could still be seen until the 1990s.

During the years of World War Two the area was the most bombed area of the UK outside Central London, as the Germans tried to destroy Belfast's ship building capacity. Sadly the area fell into disrepair in the 1970s/1980s when the motorway extension led to compulsory purchases of many homes and businesses, and decimated the Sailortown community. The rebuilding of the community has now begun, with new families moving into starter homes and professionals into expensive dockside flats.

The Pathology Labs (fictitious): The labs, set on Belfast's Saintfield Road as part of a large Science Park, are where Dr John Winter, Northern Ireland's Head of Pathology, and his co-worker, Dr Des Marsham, Head of Forensic Science, carry out the post-mortem and forensic examinations that help Craig's team solve their cases.

St Mary's Healthcare Trust (fictitious): St Mary's is one of the largest hospital trusts in the UK. It is spread over hospital sites across Belfast, including the main Royal St Mary's Hospital site and the Maternity, Paediatric and Endocrine (M.P.E.) unit, a stand-alone site on Belfast's Lisburn Road, in the University sector of the city.

Printed in Great Britain
by Amazon